For my later father Owen

THE DEVIL KNEW NOT

The devil knew not what he did, when he made man politic

William Shakespeare, Timon of Athens, Act 3, Scene 3, Line 29

Nationalism is an infantile disease. It is the measles of mankind.

Albert Einstein, letter in 1921

Nothing that I can do will change the structure of the universe.
But maybe, by raising my voice, I can help the greatest of all
causes – goodwill among men and peace on earth.
Albert Einstein

Bill Newton Dunn

ALLENDALE PUBLISHING

ISBN 0-9528277-1-9

First published in 2000 by Allendale Publishing, 27 Sterndale Road, London W14 0HT

Dust Jacket by Nick Newton Dunn

Printed by Antony Rowe Ltd, Chippenham, Wiltshire

All the characters portrayed in *The Devil Knew Not* are fictional and entirely imaginary, and no resemblance to any person living or dead is intended by the author. The lack of democracy in the Council of Ministers is true.

Bill Newton Dunn is married with two grown-up children. He is MEP for the East Midlands region of Britain, and previously was MEP for Lincolnshire from 1979 until 1994. As well as several political pamphlets, his previous books are :

Greater In Europe, 1986, a criticism of UK politics in Europe

Big Wing, 1992, the biography of Air Chief Marshal Sir Trafford Leigh-Mallory

The Man who was John Bull, 1996, the biography of the improviser Theodore Hook

Perched on the edge of a trestle-table Owen Mann's situation was precarious in three ways. He was sweating on a hot June night in a crowded town-hall north of London. He was attempting to keep a close eye on a million votes being counted around him. And Eva's grey-blue eyes were bewitching him...

* * *

The previous autumn. Friday 1st November. 04.00 in Athens

Anyone seeing the man would have known he was nervous. But nobody did : the night was cloudy and had been chosen because there was a new moon over Europe. He was dressed in shabby dark clothes and was holding a brown paper package gingerly with both hands. He looked around, to the left and right, high and low, to check what he had already checked, that no video-cameras were recording what he was about to do.

The sound of noisy revellers in a car approached. He froze in a shadow until it had passed the end of his street. When the silence was total again, he tiptoed toward the wooden pole of a broken street light. He bent down carefully and placed the package at its base. He removed his hands and relief flooded into him. He backed carefully away and, after twenty metres, turned and skipped into a brisk walk.

The timing-device in the package was set to trigger just before dawn. The man had been told that it was important to get the timing right but not the reason why. Nobody was to be hurt except unlucky passing animals.

Around the same time in nineteen other cities across Europe similar small bombs were set to explode. There were variations in timing which were probably caused by different national attitudes to punctuality. In Unter Den Linden in Berlin the bomb was precisely on time. The second last explosion, a day late, was the bomb in a narrow side-street off Plaza Mayor in Madrid ; it was late possibly because the Spanish word *mañana* implies putting something off until tomorrow.

Last of all was the bomb in the central bus station in Dublin - a delay perhaps explained by the legendary exchange between a Spaniard and an Irishman : "Paddy, do you Irish have a word like mañana ?" "No, Pedro, we have nothing that expresses the same degree of urgency."

One bomb did not explode at all, in Brick Lane which is a centre for Asian immigrants in the east end of London.

No claims for responsibility were received by the press anywhere. No pattern in the bombing was discerned. All the explosions were small and the locations were diverse - outside a hotel in a Swiss ski resort, under a bridge of the Seine in Paris, in a Moscow street near Gorky Park, in a churchyard in Szczecin, and outside a burger bar in the winding pedestrian-only Stroget street in Copenhagen.

Little material damage was caused. The smallness of the explosions meant that only local newspapers reported the incidents. Europe's national media were distracted by the crash of a commercial airliner at London's Heathrow airport in which five passengers were killed including an obscure Euro-politician.

Only an alert clerk, whose job was to collate statistics at The Hague in the Netherlands, noticed the overall pattern of the twenty bombs. At a routine daily meeting she reported it under the heading of minor incidents.

In a central European city, however, in an unassuming three-story building near a gorge, the bombing was judged to have been an outstanding success. Not perfect, but a considerable step forward compared to any coordination that had been attempted previously. Instructions, sent out by encrypted e-mail, had been followed efficiently - how to construct devices from easily obtainable materials including weed-killer, sugar and a cheap watch, how to select locations but avoid prominent places, and orders to report back promptly.

As the reports came back in, full details were recorded in a computer, entry to which was protected by a password known only to one man. That man was confident that, in precisely six months, the next bombings would be much bigger. Blood would be spilled but that was a necessary part of his plan.

* * *

Thursday 18th December. Midnight. North of London

Owen Mann was awed by the challenge that lay ahead of him.

He was standing in cold darkness outside a town hall fifty miles north of London. Inside the gaunt Victorian building behind him the counting of a quarter of a million votes had just finished. After a recount against three rivals, he had been declared the winner in Britain's last ever by-election to the European Parliament. Aged thirty-two he was now the most junior of eighty-seven Euro-MPs who serve the British public in Brussels and Strasbourg.

Two months ago he had not envisaged going into politics. He had been working in a small goldsmith business. It had a promising future because his business partner, Stan Hijena, was a technical genius although a difficult human being to work with. He had patented a new manufacturing process which had great commercial possibilities. The process created cheap but perfect copies of gold treasures in museums which their shops could sell profitably.

Longterm prospects for the business were excellent, but times were currently hard. But suddenly his personal burden had grown infinitely heavier when his older brother Fred had been killed in the plane-crash at Heathrow at the beginning of November when he was returning from Brussels. Fred had been a popular and influential Euro-MP, a member of the Radical party which was in government at Westminster.

Shortly after Fred's funeral a man called Jack Terrier had telephoned Owen. Jack Terrier was a no-nonsense county councillor, aged sixty, who chaired the local Radical party.

Owen had ridden his motorbike to a pub to meet Terrier. The politician had explained that Fred's parliamentary seat was now vacant. The local party needed a new candidate who could win the seat in the face of unfavourable opinion polls. Fred's widow, with two small daughters, was unwilling to step in. Terrier suggested that Owen had the best chance of holding the seat for the Radicals, frankly because he was local and because of the popularity of the Mann surname.

Owen's reaction to the offer had been negative. He was not political and the goldsmithing needed him, particularly now they were on the verge of a sales breakthrough. He felt angry with Fred, illogically he realised, that he was being forced into a situation which he did not want. As usual, his older brother was pushing him about.

Terrier had not given up easily. He pointed out that the seat was unlikely to be won because the opinion polls were unfavourable : but the publicity in the campaign would be valuable for the goldsmithing. And what if I should win, Owen had asked. Then, replied Terrier, you will have answered the highest of callings, the opportunity to shape the future. Politics was a seat at the top table.

To himself Owen admitted that he had occasionally thought about following his brother into politics. The long hours in goldsmithing, the continuing lack of much money, and the absence of a social life had made him wonder about an alternative.

To be the Radical candidate just this once was tempting. It offered him a break from the hard grind of commerce and from his maddening business partner. Owen had accepted Terrier's proposal reluctantly but with a secret inner excitement.

He had broken the news to his two business partners, Stan Hijena and his wife Rose. Neither seemed worried by Owen's news that he would take a month off as his annual holiday.

During December Owen had fought an exhausting election campaign across the large Euro-constituency. Jack Terrier was his campaign chairman. It was physically tiring but the heavy effort of telephone canvassing and nonstop talking to people was also taxing mentally. It had been like climbing Mont Blanc without prior training in mountaineering. His opponents had taunted him, saying that he was merely an inadequate clone of his brother.

Now, outside the town hall, his elation at winning was diluted by the prospect of being the holder of the job for the shortest ever period. In only six months the next full-scale elections to the European Parliament would take place across Britain and Europe. He would have to fight all over again for his seat.

A car pulled up, driven by Jack Terrier. Owen climbed into the comfortable passenger seat.

"Not too tired for the celebration ?" asked Jack.

"No, but I'm booked on the first plane in the morning to Brussels to take my seat."

Owen settled back in the luxurious car.

"Jack, give me some advice. What must I do to survive beyond the next six months, and get myself re-elected next summer ? My rivals have been exposed to the public for over four years since the last full election. I'm way behind them."

"It will be tough. You will have to find a way to get yourself known by the public. Make a big splash. And there's less time than you imagine. It's not six months, but three."

"Only three months ?" asked Owen with dismay.

"The electoral system is changing from first-past-the-post to proportional representation. Next June, instead of individual Euro-constituencies, each political party will offer the public a list of several candidates covering a bigger region. Our region will be called North of London, and it will elect six MEPs. On the current opinion polls we Radicals can expect only the top two from our list of six candidates to be elected as MEPs.

"We shall select our six candidates in March. The position which you achieve on the list will be crucial. If you are not in the top two, then you have little hope of being re-elected in June. It's as tough and as soon as that, I'm afraid."

Tonight Owen had clambered to the summit of his mountain. He had expected to enjoy a celebration and a rest. But already there was a new peak beyond this one and it looked steeper and harder to climb.

*   *   *

Seventeen days later. Sunday 4th January 13.00 Westminster

A discreet lunch party was underway in a private house in Lord North Street

The short elegant street contained just twelve small terraced houses although its front doors carried numbers scattered between 3 and 19. The facades were decorated by black wrought-iron railings and flower-filled stone window-boxes. For those in the world of British politics, its location was highly convenient so most of its addresses were owned by wealthy political figures. Half a mile in one direction lay the Houses of the Commons and the Lords ; even nearer in the other direction lay Smith Square, home to a great political party and the fine deconsecrated church of St. John's where there were frequent concerts and a popular restaurant in its cellar.

Outside the discreet facade of one of the houses several black cars with chauffeurs were waiting quietly. Inside, the walls of the dining-room were panelled with smoky oil-paintings of ancestors. Above the circular polished dining table hung an exquisite crystal chandelier.

It was a Sunday so there was no risk of the Commons division-bell forcing the two MPs who were present to rush off to vote. The only activity in the Commons that day was the routine sweeping for electronic bugs by the security services.

The lunch could not have been held at any of the three restaurants in the division-bell area which are popular with MPs - the Vitello d'Oro in Church House, L'Amico in Horseferry Road where Neil Kinnock lunched Gorbachev in 1984, or Shepherds in Marsham Street. Even using a private room in a restaurant would have run the risk of sharp journalistic eyes spotting well-known faces going in or out and speculating why they were together.

A journalist should have recognised nine of the ten faces round the lunch table. Two were chairmen of multinational businesses. Four were Euro-sceptics in Britain's opposition Progressive party, two being MPs and two Lords, one of whom had once been Prime Minister for a year. The host and two other guests were media giants, one the proprietor of a mass-circulation tabloid newspaper, another owning a chain of radio and television stations, and the third was the editor of a prestigious London evening broadsheet.

The only person whom a journalist would not have recognised was a forty-year old Portuguese named Enrique Sãta. Like the other men present he wore a bespoke Savile Row pinstripe suit. His skin was faintly olive, his eyes dark, and his jet-black hair was receding and oiled.

The wife and daughter of the host served delicately grilled fresh salmon with a bearnise sauce made piquant with red pepper berries. It was accompanied by a mixed salad and a chilled white Hugel wine from Alsace. A salad of exotic fruits followed. Next, in the sequence favoured by the British, came a selection of cheeses including a pungent Munster from Germany and a mouth-tingling Roquefort from France.

After strong coffee and cigars had been served they withdrew. The host tapped a silver spoon softly on the table and smiled at his guests: "My friends, thank you all for coming. I hope you are sufficiently fed and watered ?"

Hearing a general murmur of approval he continued : "Down to business. All of us round this table agree about the threat which is posed by the European Union against the independence and sovereignty of Britain."

Someone rapped the table in approval.

"I have invited you here to discuss how we can defeat its onward march. We love our country and want to preserve its unique identity. The EU, as I shall call it for short, hasn't yet given itself the name of the United States of Europe, but that is the direction in which it is rapidly heading. Its Treaty of Amsterdam in 1997 and the Euro currency in 1999 reinforced the trend. Each of us here has different reasons for fearing the EU but our individual differences only strengthen our overall case."

He sipped his mineral water. "Now, who would like to start the discussion ? Sir Patrick Crogall ?"

Crogall was a self-made billionaire who owned the majority of shares in a publicly-quoted multinational. British-born and still with his first wife, he was nobody's friend but respected by everybody for his awesome ruthlessness. When he opened his mouth the others shivered at the sight of his famously large teeth.

"I believe I can speak for international commerce" he began. "The power of a nation state to control international trade has gone for ever. Sorry, House of Commons !" His teeth smiled at the two MPs but not his ice-blue eyes. "Real power now lies in multinational board-rooms, not in national parliaments."

The MP sitting furthest away from him challenged him in an Essex-estuary accent : "What is the role of the mother of parliaments ?"

Crogall wasted only a moment in chewing him up and spitting him out. "Your role is to persuade us multinationals to build our factories here in Britain and not somewhere else. Backbenchers are irrelevant. The idea that your parliament is still sovereign is a mirage."

The MP's face showed surprise and distaste.

"I shall give you an example" Crogall continued inexorably like the Mountain bearing down on Mohamet. "The House of Commons was powerless to ban tobacco advertising on the cars of worldwide Formula One motor racing. It took the EU to do it but even then the industry won a nine-year delay. Now the tobacco industry plans to keep its cigarette brand-names alive by advertising alternative 'legal' goods carrying the same names. For example, a well-known cigarette will also become the name of fashionable travel-bags which can still be advertised."

As an afterthought he added "Do you need another example ?" The MP was studying his plate and shook his head.

Nobody challenged Crogall. Smiling respectfully at the ex-Prime Minister, he continued : "Capitalism has defeated Socialism. We are entering an age of unrivalled prosperity. I profoundly agree with our host about stopping the EU. It represents a growing threat to international business. In a few years, the EU may have swallowed twenty-five countries, and that Tower of Babel, the European Parliament, will legislate against business far more effectively than any national parliament."

He paused, wondering whether he might have spoken too strongly but nobody demurred. "I don't require you to agree with everything I say. But, like you all, I oppose the onward march of the EU."

The other industrialist nodded vigorous agreement. Next round the table to speak was the second MP, the Euro-sceptical James Edge-Smith. He was small and aggressive with ginger hair that flopped over his forehead like a monk's tonsure. Commentators believed his attitudes were shaped by the death of his father in the Second World War.

"Same conclusion but opposite analysis" he began. "The nation state is losing its powers so they must be restored. The United Kingdom of Great Britain and Northern Ireland is a natural entity which created the greatest empire the world has ever seen. We survived invasion by foreigners for nearly a thousand years while no other continental European country has been continuously democratic for even the last one hundred. The House of Commons is the mother of parliaments and must never be subservient to bureaucrats in Brussels. Some Euro-fanatics in Brussels talk about electing a President of Europe. What would that do to our Queen ? The EU has to be stopped and right now." He thumped the table, making the glasses rattle.

Next to speak was one of the Lords whose white hair, grey eyebrows and black moustache had made him widely recognised by the public.

"I don't want to become an identikit European. I don't want Brussels to lay down laws to standardise everything. A free-trade market in Europe is a good thing. But the downside is foreigners invading our beautiful land, particularly non-Europeans. They gain access to the EU via frontiers which are less well policed than our own. Lax frontier-controls in Europe means easy access into Britain for drugs, criminals and illegal immigrants."

The newspaper proprietor joined in, the Geordie twang in his voice loud and clear. "Allow me to speak for the media. The race is on to build worldwide media networks. There is a growing danger that Brussels will pass laws which restrict our activities inside the EU which is one of the richest and most stable markets in the world. If my network is not allowed to grow, the world's media markets will be dominated by Asians and Americans. That is why I too oppose any more power for the EU."

He was supported by the editor who was round and bald. He spoke with an English public-school accent : "I see Britain as a beautiful, if decaying, stately home which is in desperate need of love and repair. The EU is building council houses across our ancestral lawns. We should be preserving and restoring our heritage, not letting it be changed beyond recognition. Later this year the national and European elections will be a good opportunity to change things."

The proprietor interrupted. "I'm thinking of sending someone to Brussels to dig up some dirt. Is there anyone you could send too ?"

The editor thought for a moment. "I could send McKirk. He'd do it well."

The anti-EU consensus round the table was obvious. The host glanced at the ex-Prime Minister. His silent nod of acquiescence was enough. The discussion had reached its conclusion.

"Thankyou everybody. We're agreed on our goal. No more power for the EU. I suggest we each step up our efforts in our own fields. One final point. Not all of you have spoken to my friend here, Mr. Enrique Sãta. He is very much one of us. Enrique is a discreet financier who has a remarkable network of influential connections across the continent. Our battle cannot be fought in Britain alone. We need money and that is where he comes in."

The quiet Portuguese lowered his head in a polite bow to the company present. He had absorbed everything that had been said and was thinking to himself : "These guys are just playing. They know nothing, and need to know nothing, of my plans."

The host continued : "Enrique runs a financial foundation in Antigua which is out-of-reach from Europe's tax authorities. I propose that he builds up a fund which can be used to advance our cause. If industrialists provide the finance, if politicians make Euro-sceptical speeches, if editors provide Euro-sceptical publicity, if we link our efforts with like-minded people across the continent, we shall become an irresistible force. We stand every chance of winning our historic mission of defeating the EU federalists and preserving an independent Britain."

Around the table everyone concurred with silent nods or a quiet "Here Here". Not a word would be breathed to others about their plan. Britain and the other great European nations would be saved. Capitalism would flourish in the new millennium. Sãta would be the group's fund-holder. They would reconvene in two months over another Sunday lunch.

* * *

Six days later Saturday 10th January 08.00 North of London

An alarm-clock woke Owen Mann. Outside his duvet, the air felt cold.

He slid out of bed and walked the few steps to the bathroom. Plugging in the electric razor, he glanced in the mirror. It showed a six feet tall bachelor with brown eyes, curly dark-brown hair and a swarthy skin which his father said derived from their Welsh celtic ancestry. Not married but with a current girlfriend, after several others had slipped from his grasp.

His swarthiness did not bother him but had inhibited his schooldays when he had been teased about it. The teasing had given him an insight into the feelings of the underdog and a desire to help others in difficulty. It had also given him a drive to out-perform the fools whom he had despised at school.

Returning to the bedroom he dressed in a cream shirt, pale blue tie, and a slightly creased dark blue suit. He went downstairs to the little kitchen to make his usual breakfast of toast and coffee.

It was to be an important day in an important year. He had stepped onto the first rung of the political ladder by winning the election and now was learning his trade as the newest MEP. He hoped that his talents might be recognised but knew that nobody helped you climb the greasy pole : success in politics came, not from waiting for ability to be recognised by a benign all-seeing father-figure, but by seizing opportunities before others grabbed them first.

The worry that nagged him was whether he had a longterm future in politics. Not because he lacked political skills but because in the coming June election he would either be re-elected and thus climb the second rung, or be defeated and fall off the ladder altogether. His by-election victory had been narrow and the fight to hold his seat would be desperate.

He thought ahead to his morning task, the fortnightly surgery for constituents which he had taken over from his brother. He glanced at the clock on the kitchen wall, put on an overcoat and left the house. It was a cold but sunny January morning so he decided to walk the fifteen minutes to his party's local office where the surgery was held.

The office was on the first floor above a shop in a side-street off the town's High Street. He climbed the worn-carpeted stairs and greeted a cheerful plump woman in her fifties with floppy brown hair who was typing at a word processor.

"Good morning, Rosemary. How are you today ?"

"Fine thanks, Owen."

"Many people coming this morning ?"

"The usual mixed bag. Some oddballs, others with genuine problems. Eight people at half-hourly intervals."

Rosemary Jones was the political agent who ran his constituency. She handed Owen the sheet of paper on which she had typed the names.

"Like a coffee ?" he asked.

He switched on the kettle. Waiting for it to boil, he sat at the empty desk of his secretary, Lynda Black, who did not work on Saturdays.

Knowing he would be there this morning, she had left a pile of incoming letters for him to read. Efficiently she had attached a yellow sticker to each with a suggestion of how he might reply to it. If he agreed, she would draft the reply for him to sign later.

The first appointees arrived punctually at nine. They were Mrs. Morfil, aged around forty and very overweight, and her teenage daughter.

The mother heaved herself onto one of the two simple wooden chairs opposite the desk. Rosemary sat in a corner with a notepad. Owen liked her to be present. She wrote notes but her real role was as a witness in case anybody should afterwards make an accusation of improper conduct against their MEP. It had happened to others.

"How can I help ?" Owen asked Mrs. Morfil.

"Mr. Mann, this is my daughter Deirdre. At Christmas she was in France travelling back from a school holiday and she bought a second-class rail ticket. She joined the train but the second-class seats were full. A kind inspector suggested that she sit in one of the empty first-class compartments. Later a different inspector imposed an on-the-spot fine on her for being in a first-class compartment with a second-class ticket. He didn't understand Deidre's French and because she didn't pay straightaway the fine was doubled. Afterwards, because the doubled fine wasn't paid within fifteen days, a French court redoubled it. It's so unfair."

She handed Owen a document received from the court in France. Owen smiled at Deidre to try to reassure her and replied : "I sympathise. It's hard arguing with officials, especially not in your own language."

"Can you do anything to help ?" asked the mother.

"The inspector was probably within the rules but I'll fight it for you. I'll start by writing to the French Ambassador in London on my official European Parliament notepaper. Hopefully he will intervene on your behalf. I'll let you know as soon as I receive his reply."

After the Morfils had left, Rosemary commented : "It sounds as if, for once, you might get some help for them. So often these problems can't be put right. Or constituents fail to tell the full story. They paint their case in rosy colours but leave out the weak points."

"Unfortunately" replied Owen, "helping them makes little difference to whether or not I win the election in five months. There are too few surgery cases to have any influence over millions of voters."

There were several minutes before the next appointee was due. Owen reflected ruefully how very marginal his seat was. His narrow victory had been due to his brother's reputation and because the low turnout of voters in a by-election had favoured him. With the high turnout of voters at a full-scale election he would have lost. And now the procedures were changing and he would have to fight for a high place on his party's list of candidates.

His new electoral region would contain four million voters, fifty times the size of a Commons constituency. It would be impossible to be known personally by more than a minuscule percentage of the public. Worse, his party, the governing *Radicals*, were slipping behind the opposition *Progressives* in the current opinion polls.

His embryo political career might end soon after it had started. Like the question which had been put mockingly in the hearing of Jimmy Carter, the American President when he was campaigning, unsuccessfully, for re-election : "Gentlemen, do I detect that rare creature, a One-Term President ?" Owen feared he would become a political footnote as the shortest-serving MEP, and would have to resume his business career alongside the Hijenas.

His father would be relieved if this happened. His parents had not been wealthy and had sacrificed much for his brother and himself. His father had been a dreamer who had invested his own ambitions in his children. Their mother had been dominant in the home, their father obeying her without question. Only the two boys had dared to challenge her. Questioning her orders had led them to challenge assumptions in the world outside, to a belief that things needed to change, and so toward politics. When Owen told his father that he too was going to abandon business in order to enter politics, the old man had asked with unconcealed disappointment "Why not stick to a *real* job instead of a soapbox ?"

Fred had joined the Radical party. Owen remembered him consulting Jack Terrier, then a local councillor, about how to become an MP or an MEP.

"No qualifications of any kind are necessary" had been the

surprising reply. "Join the party of your choice, and help other people fight their elections. If you enjoy it, get your name on the party's list of possible candidates. Then get the local activists to pick you as their candidate. Nothing to it !"

Fred had chosen to become a candidate for the European Parliament, rather than for the House of Commons. The power of the Commons seemed to both brothers to be seeping away, downwards through devolution and upwards to Brussels. The European Parliament was becoming increasingly important, so joining it - not for the money since MPs and MEPs receive identical salaries - would be the way to make a real difference in future.

Owen had become concerned at the way in which the European Union was developing. It appeared to be swallowing Britain into a kind of United States of Europe superstate where everybody would be forced to be the same. He agreed that there should be common rules of behaviour in Europe so that the carnage of two World Wars could never be repeated. But Britain, British interests and the British way-of-life, should be defended better than they were. Decisions about British life should be made in Britain and not in Brussels.

Once elected Owen had found being an MEP a fascinating job despite the lack of public recognition. Running a surgery was enjoyable and worthwhile. And the European Parliament had more power than he had realised : its responsibilities had grown each time the national governments had made new treaties, through the Single Act in the mid-1980s, the Maastricht Treaty in 1991, and the Amsterdam Treaty in 1997. Now the European Parliament shared equal powers with national ministers in most policy areas and, without the British public realising, it was getting near to having the same responsibilities as the House of Representatives in Washington DC.

Owen knew that his political fate was mostly beyond his own control, and would be determined by outside events. Nevertheless, if he could show enough of his constituents that he made a difference to their lives, that he was not mere lobby-fodder, if he could make a splash as Jack Terrier had said, it might nudge the public towards re-electing him.

The door bell rang downstairs. The next visitor, an elderly widow, had arrived. Owen went down to assist her up the stairs.

By one o'clock the flow of constituents had finished. Owen packed his papers into his briefcase, and reflected how very appropriate the word 'surgery' was. No blood was spilled and there were no surgical operations, but plenty of listening to the problems of unhappy people and trying to help them.

He had learned to listen patiently. A few days after he was elected, his home telephone had rung just as he was leaving the house. The caller started to describe a difficulty about obtaining a passport. By chance Owen had dealt with a similar query the previous day, so the right contact and number were in his head. He had interrupted the caller : "Excuse me but I need to leave straightaway for an appointment. Please write down this number and the person who answers should be able to solve your problem. If not, come straight back to me."

In the evening Owen returned home to find the telephone ringing. It was the same caller but now very angry. Owen sat in his rocking-chair and listened to a long tirade against himself. Eventually he asked whether the man had telephoned the number given to him in the morning. The man said he had not and restarted his harangue. Owen persuaded him to try the number next day. As the caller rang off, Owen reflected that the unhappy man had not wanted his advice so much as a sympathetic shoulder on which to cry. His mistake in the morning had been to be too abrupt.

As Rosemary locked up the office she asked : "What are you going to do now ? Get a good rest, I hope."

"I'm off to watch the town's team playing football and this evening I'm having supper with Nina."

After watching his local football team lose, yet again, Owen showered and changed his sweater for a smart sports jacket. He pulled on his black leather jacket and trousers, squeezed his head inside his motorcycle helmet, and rode fifteen miles to a village. At the far end of its main street he parked outside a detached timbered cottage. He pressed the bell and heard its familiar chime.

The door was opened immediately by a dark-haired woman in her late twenties. She was wearing a scarlet knee-length body-hugging dress. During the week her hair was up but now it was flowing onto her shoulders and Owen was glad to see it. She gestured him inside, smiling warmly. With the door shut they embraced and kissed passionately.

"Owen darling."

"Hi, Nina my love."

"How was Brussels last week ?"

"I'll tell you about it. There's a decision which I need to discuss with you. But something important first."

He held out the bottle of good white wine which he had brought.

"You know where the corkscrew is."

They had been seeing each other for nearly half a year. For a short period she had wavered over somebody else and had put Owen 'in the freezer', as she described it when she apologised to him afterwards. Previously she had lived with a boyfriend for several years. Owen knew nothing about the man except for one comic incident which she had recounted.

Her lover had grumbled that, when he returned from his day's work, he no longer found her sitting naked on the stairs waiting to pounce on him as she had when they first lived together. The following evening she had waited exactly as he had desired. She heard his footsteps approach the front-door and as the key turned in the lock, she heard him say 'Nina will be glad to see you, Tom' : he had brought a colleague home for a drink without any warning. In a fraction of a second she had managed to scuttle upstairs to dress herself.

Owen had met her at a dinner party, each accompanied by someone else but they had sparked immediately. Next day Owen had telephoned her at her bank. In the evening they had met in a City pub. Afterwards Nina had a train to catch, so they had taken a taxi together to the station. They had arrived with seconds before her train was due to leave, and ran to the platform together arriving as the guard blew his whistle.

Nina stared at Owen hesitantly as the train started to move. She leaned forward, and gave him a lingering kiss on the lips. The train left the platform. After a glance over her shoulder Nina turned back to Owen and laughed : "I had to decide 'shall I kiss him or shall I catch the train ?'" From that moment he had loved her. It had meant another hour's wait for her but she had insisted that he must not linger with her.

Since his by-election success, however, Owen sensed that Nina had become restless at his repeated four or five-day absences each week on the continent. Their relationship had reached a plateau and was no longer growing deeper. She was not politically active but that was not the problem. He wondered whether she was actually of a different political persuasion ; her convent education, her bijou cottage and her career in a City merchant-bank did not fit comfortably with his more radical view of the world. She had expressed no interest in visiting him at the parliament.

They sipped the wine while Nina finished cooking supper. Owen wondered whether she was using a recipe from the early edition of Mrs Beeton's cook-book which he had given her for her birthday.

"What's the decision on which you need my advice ?" she asked, smiling at him.

"Do you remember, before Christmas, I hoped to obtain an important responsibility from the parliament's Environment committee ?"

"It was something to do with an anti-pollution law for all of Europe. You wanted it because it might help your chances of re-election."

"Unfortunately I missed out."

"So what do you need to discuss ?"

"Another report is available instead."

"What is it about ?"

Owen stood close to Nina as she prodded boiling potatoes with a fork. He explained what had happened.

Early last Tuesday morning, he said, he had ridden through the rain to Heathrow. A violent thunderstorm was blowing over central London with an east wind that drove it towards the airport.

Having parked his motorbike, he wove through Terminal One like an animal along a beaten track, buying two newspapers on the way. The route he was travelling, to Brussels, was always busy. Brussels was a double capital, not only of Belgium but also the headquarters of the European Union. Flights carried an endless two-way stream of businessmen, politicians and lobbyists.

On the plane he settled into his pre-selected seat, in the aisle at the front of economy class. He settled down and opened the broadsheet *Daily Gazette*.

Three items held his attention. Yesterday tensions had surfaced in the House of Commons. In a debate one of the government's backbenchers had asked : "Was it not time to consider strengthening Britain's border controls ?" This was controversial because the EU's goal was for all its member states to abolish their border controls with eachother. But a General Election in Britain was due within a year and the Radical backbencher wanted his leader to curry popularity with the public by taking British policy in a populist anti-foreigner direction.

The second item was in the Gazette's foreign news section. Owen read with emotion a vivid description of a horrific atrocity in Algeria. In a desert village the throats of a hundred women and children had been cut.

Extremism, he reflected, was an eternal danger. The Nazi extermination camps at Auschwitz and Dachau were little different from the machine-gunning of tourists in Egypt or throat-cutting of villagers in Algeria. We were all human beings together : no man was an island. Wherever democracy lost control, extremism stepped in. Who had said that 'the price of liberty was eternal vigilance' ? Owen had looked it up once, expecting it to be Winston Churchill but found it was John Philpot Curran speaking in 1790 in support of the right to elect a Mayor of Dublin.

The third item which caught his eye was a short editorial on the centre page. Headlined 'A WASTE OF TIME AND MONEY' it was a blanket denunciation of Britain's MEPs.

> Britain's eighty-seven Euro-MPs are non-entities. Who can name even one ? What has any of them ever done for Britain ? None has even achieved Andy Warhol's dictum - that everybody would be famous for fifteen minutes. Our MEPs are a waste of tax-payers' precious money.

On the opposite page was a feature article which enlarged on the criticism. It was written by a senior reporter, named Murdo McKirk.

Owen read it through indignantly. It was a populist and inaccurate diatribe. He was one of those eighty-seven under attack. Since being elected, he had worked hard. The article seemed to be wrong in every way, except one. It was true that he was unknown to the public and, worse, to nearly all of his own constituents.

The plane taxied out to the runway amid the driving rain. It waited in a queue for several minutes, then accelerated along the concrete and lifted through the low clouds. Heavy gusts shook it but Owen relaxed into his seat, confident that the pilot wanted to survive as much as he did.

Having finished the newspaper he opened his briefcase and took out a treacle toffee and a document with a mauve cover.

Treacle toffees were delicious but frustratingly hard to find. The only place which seemed to stock them was an Asian newsagent near his home.

If Sherlock Holmes had seen the mauve document, he would have announced that Owen was an English-speaker who was involved in EU affairs. Documents in the other ten official EU languages were printed on other colours ; yellow for German, orange for Dutch, light-blue for French, and so on.

The document was a proposal for a new EU environmental law for reducing pollution in the atmosphere. As all EU proposals must be, it had been drafted by the European Commission in Brussels. To the public it would have been baffling and dull but it absorbed Owen because he hoped the parliament's Environment Committee might appoint him to be its rapporteur for the proposal.

Nina interrupted : "What is a *rapporteur* ?"

"The committee appoints one of its members to draft a report for them about a proposed law. The member they choose is their rapporteur."

"It sounds French."

"It is. Rapporteurs are part of long French parliamentary tradition – as is so much in the EU."

"Why ?"

"Because we British have dragged our feet behind almost every European initiative since 1945. We have proposed almost nothing positive ourselves. So the parliament is modelled on a French system."

"What happens to a rapporteur's report ?"

"It is debated and amended by the committee. Finally he leads the debate on it by the whole parliament. And he receives most of the publicity."

Owen kissed the back of Nina's neck and carried the two plates of food to her dining-table. As they ate he continued his story.

He had hoped that a pre-committee caucus with the other MEPs of all nationalities in his political group who were also members of the Environment Committee would agree to his appointment that afternoon. Then his group's coordinator on the committee, a German named Schnecke, would announce Owen's name to the full committee as their choice for the rapporteurship. The committee should approve it automatically.

On the plane an empty seat separated Owen from a fellow passenger, a fat middle-aged man in a crumpled suit with a tie whose colours looked as if they included bacon and egg. He had thinning grey hair which was badly brushed and stuck upwards in tufts. He wore grey metal-rimmed spectacles.

The man turned and caught Owen's eye : "I can't help noticing your mauve-covered document. Might I ask whether you're the new Euro-MP ?"

He held out his hand : "My name is Murdo McKirk. I'm with the Daily Gazette."

It was the reporter who had penned the offending article. Owen was instantly revulsed but concealed it, and shook McKirk's hand : "I'm Owen Mann. I'm on my way to meetings of two parliament committees, on Environment and on Civil Liberties."

A stewardess offered them tea or coffee. McKirk asked : "Any doughnuts ?" and was visibly disappointed by her negative reply.

Owen cleared his throat and said : "I've a bone to pick with you."

McKirk, surprised for a moment, countered : "My feature in today's paper ?"

"How can you write such inaccurate nonsense ?"

"Steady on" countered McKirk. "That's your opinion so we hold different views. What I wrote is what our readers think. Surely we can agree that you're not well-known. I didn't recognise you, even though I'm sitting beside you - and you didn't know me."

"A complaint to your editor might make you write more favourably next time."

"I doubt it. He penned the editorial which is opposite my feature. You ought to see this as an opportunity to prove us wrong. Give us something to praise you and we will."

Owen wondered if he had been over-critical of somebody who was potentially a powerful ally. He thought of reminding McKirk of Stanley Baldwin's rebuke to Northcliffe and Beaverbrook in the 1930 Westminster by-election, that they were 'exercising the prerogative of the harlot through the ages, power without responsibility', but he backed off.

"Why not come along and watch my Environment committee this afternoon ?"

"Thanks, but I've got several appointments" said the reporter. "But I may drop in at the bar in the parliament tomorrow evening. Will you be there ?"

"Could be. What's your purpose in visiting Brussels, may I ask ?"

"My editor wants a series of articles about corruption in Brussels. I'm sure you have some good ideas on that ?" McKirk grinned encouragingly.

"There are many allegations in circulation. But getting solid evidence is difficult, and I haven't searched for it."

"My editor believes" said the journalist, "and I agree with him, that politics in Britain are basically honest. There are always cases of sleaze to uncover in local government. But the boys and girls at Westminster are mostly beyond it since the Downey and Nolan enquiries in 1997. In Brussels where there's Latin blood, different traditions apply. We think there's deep-rooted corruption in the EU, if only we can dig up the evidence. That's my mission."

"Will you only report sleaze or also the good work done by the European Parliament ?"

"Not the good work. Without conflict it's not interesting for our readers."

"No conflict ? The parliament is full of conflict."

"You don't make the conflict clear to us," McKirk countered.

"The difficulty is that the political parties are multi-national. Your readers can't identify with any particular party because British MEPs, like all nationalities, are in a minority. Just as at a football match, if you don't have your own team to root for, the interest is absent."

There was crackle on the plane's intercom and a male voice spoke. "This is the Captain. I have a technical problem. We are two minutes' flying time nearer to Ostend than to Brussels so I am are going to land at Ostend." He spoke calmly and gave no other details.

Owen and Murdo looked at each other, both startled that a period of two minutes was enough to force a change of destination. A stewardess walked methodically down the aisle, checking that seat-belts were fastened.

The plane descended at what seemed to be normal speed but it was impossible to judge. The passengers sat silently, hoping or praying. Recent events raced through Owen's mind : his brother's fate ; and Christmas just spent with his elderly parents, wondering if that visit to them might be the last time he would see them together, although not in the way he now feared.

The plane continued its descent. There was no message from the Captain.

Green fields appeared and they were beneath the clouds. Suddenly the plane's wheels made contact with the runway and the brakes pulled the plane safely to a halt.

The intercom crackled and the Captain spoke again : "Welcome to Ostend - instead of Brussels, I'm afraid. My problem was that the instruments showed the plane's tail was vibrating too much. I hope you agree that my decision to stop at Ostend was better than to fly on hopefully to Brussels. You will be asked to disembark here, and the plane will be taken out of service to be thoroughly checked. I apologise for the delay that this will undoubtedly cause to you."

Spontaneous applause from the passengers showed that they

supported his decision.

Mobile steps arrived outside the plane. The passengers disembarked and were led across the tarmac. Inside the small terminal building the news was discouraging. No other plane was available to fly them on to Brussels. Instead a bus had been arranged which they could board as soon as their baggage had been retrieved from the plane's hold.

Owen and Murdo sat together on the bus and continued their conversation. Murdo admitted that he was not going to become an editor. And he was too late to move across into television journalism which was increasingly for young reporters. In his private life he was divorced, having been married to a fellow journalist but their careers and ambitions had driven them apart and there had been no children. Why did he write ? As usual, Shakespeare had said it first. Othello, describing his wooing of Desdemona, had said : 'A man writes to be loved, such is the process.' Now, although he still hoped to achieve a few more scoops, really he was looking towards retirement and would like to find a good woman with whom to settle down.

An hour later the bus delivered them to Zaventem airport, ten miles outside the city of Brussels. The journalist and the MEP took separate taxis. Owen checked his watch ; it was one forty-five. The Brussels rush-hour had not started so Owen hoped that he might still arrive for the tail-end of his political group's caucus before the committee started.

The British Radical MEPs were members of the international Socialist group in the parliament, just as the British Progressives had joined the international centre-right group called the European Peoples' Party. Being part of a larger group was the best way to gain allies and therefore leverage, as well as resources and staff paid from the parliament's budget. The British Radicals were well positioned because the Socialists were the largest political group in the parliament although not with an overall majority.

The purpose of the caucus before the Environment committee started was for its Socialist MEPs to agree their plans. One matter to be settled was who would be rapporteurs for new topics which were coming onto the committee's agenda and for which the Socialists had taken responsibility.

The taxi took twenty minutes to carry Owen to the European Parliament and was delayed in a queue near the entrance. Waiting to get out, Owen squinted up at the parliament which, at the time of its construction in the 1990s, had been the biggest construction project in Europe. It resembled a huge ocean liner built of silver and glass except that its sides undulated. He saw the spectacular Spaak building, nicknamed 'Caprice Des Dieux' because its elliptical shape resembled a popular local cheese. It was topped by an arch which echoed the arch above the door to the old Quartier Leopold railway station immediately to the west.

Owen regretted that Europe's new parliamentary buildings were less memorable than, say, the Capitol in Washington DC with its famous steps and dome, or the neo-Gothic Houses of Parliament in London. He believed the architects had missed a chance to create a memorable building for Europe's taxpayers to visualise as their guardian against secretive EU bureaucrats and ministers.

The parliament's entrance-hall was full of arriving people - staff, MEPs, and visitors - a few having disembarked from trains which stopped right outside. Owen feared that the elevators would stop at every floor so. To save precious seconds and carrying his suitcase, he rode up the self-starting escalators and ran along a corridor to the meeting-room where his colleagues held their caucus.

But the room was empty. Puzzlingly the clock on the wall showed an hour later than his wrist-watch. He remembered the one hour time difference between London and Brussels. Moving his watch forward an hour was normally a routine task but on the plane today he had forgotten it. The caucus had finished so the Environment Committee would already be in session.

Catching his breath, he walked as fast as he could along the corridor to the committee room. He pushed the door open quietly, placed his suitcase in a corner, and signed the members' attendance list on a desk near the door.

He glanced round the room. It was the committee room with the unattractive pale mauve carpeting. Seated to his left was the committee's chairman, a senior Radical MEP known affectionately as 'Saint Ken' because he had chaired that committee for most of the parliament's life, and had probably wielded more influence over environmental policy than anyone else in Europe.

The chairman was flanked on his own right by several of the committee's permanent staff and on his left by two MEPs who were his vice-chairmen. Ordinary members of the committee faced the chairman from a series of crescent-shaped continuous wooden desks with individual dark green modern chairs. Each place had a bottle of still water and a glass. As the chairman saw them, the politically-left members sat to his left, the politically-right to his right. There were about two hundred seats in all plus another thirty at the back for the public. Around the walls were smoky-dark windows : behind each was a booth of interpreters, one for each EU official language.

Owen took his seat among his party colleagues and shook hands with his neighbours. Frequent hand-shaking was not a British habit, but was something he had learned to do. Continentals expected to shake hands on first meeting each day and again on parting, and not to do so could be taken as a deliberate slight. He was getting to know some of his continental colleagues. He would never know them well but was confident already that some could be trusted, and others not. Each was an individual with different hopes and fears, an overall cross-section of the European menagerie. Each one's personal political agenda was like an iceberg, mostly hidden from view. But deep in the hearts of most of the six hundred and twenty-six MEPs lay the challenge of how to get themselves re-elected next time.

The coordinator for his Group in the committee was the amiable but lethargic German, Hans Schnecke. Seeing Owen arrive, he scribbled a note, folded it methodically and passed it along the row of members. It was in English :

> Owen. Good News and Bad News. You did not attend the caucus. There was a big argument. I am so sorry. In the end I had to give the rapporteurship to your party colleague, Tom Ostler. That is the Bad News. The Good News is that I will save another rapporteurship next time for you. Hans.

Bitterly disappointed, Owen recognised that he had broken the first rule of politics - to 'Be There'. So much for his hope of winning favourable publicity back home.

Should he fight the decision ? He had no right to the appointment, so his best tactic was to accept the inevitable. If he did so gracefully, he could call on Hans Schnecke for a favour in the future. He caught the eye of the German, shrugged his shoulders and grinned in silent acceptance.

But he was furious with the despicable Tom Ostler. A member of his own Radical party from the same region of England had stolen his rapporteurship. Ostler was not in the room but papers lying on his desk showed he had been present earlier and had left already.

Owen despised Ostler for his arrogance and egocentricity. When Ostler had participated in an audience with the Pope in Rome, before Owen had been elected, he had issued a press release to his local papers with the headline 'Pope meets Ostler', instead of the other way round. Owen wondered what Ostler's early upbringing had been like and whether his father or mother had ignored him as a child.

Ostler's most notorious moment had been at Strasbourg's starred restaurant, 'The Crocodile'. He had dined there one evening with the Radicals' press officer, a decent man named Charles Browning. After their meal they had shared a whole bottle of the house's oldest Napoleon brandy. Their bill amounted to several hundred pounds. Ostler announced that he had not brought any money and Browning must pay and use his allowance from the Socialist Group for liaison with the press. Being an employee, Browning had no choice but to pay but had taken his revenge the following day. Ostler's behaviour was splashed across the front of a British tabloid newspaper coupled with quotations from a recent speech he had made criticising wastefulness in Brussels.

Owen's failure to *Be There* reminded him of a story of power politics in the first days of the elected parliament. In July 1979 three leading Liberal MEPs - from Germany, France and Luxembourg - were competing for two key jobs. The prizes were the Presidency of the first elected parliament and the leadership of the Liberal Group. The Luxembourger believed he had made a private deal with the German but discovered, too late, that it had not stuck. He stormed along to the German to demand an explanation. The latter, rubbing his hands together, had dismissed him with the words "Business is business." The Luxembourger had riposted that 'This shows it is only possible to make a Gentleman's Agreement with a gentleman' and had had to be content with becoming the next President of the Commission.

Schnecke passed a second note along the line to Owen :

I got your note about making a collection of after-dinner stories from different nationalities. It's a good idea and would make a good book. I have tried to think of something in German for you. How about this one ? Hans

Owen had read several volumes of comic after-dinner stories published by MPs at Westminster. He had decided to try to compile a similar volume from Brussels. He had sent out a circular letter to MEPs of all fifteen nationalities, inviting for a story from each. This was the first reply.[1]

Nina's eyes had filled with tears.

"What's wrong ?" he asked, touching her hand. "Are you sad that I didn't get that rapporteurship ?

"No. I've just eaten a mouthful of horseradish that was hidden in a lettuce leaf. Go on."

The committee had been listening to a statement by the Commissioner responsible for EU Environmental matters. He was now answering questions from MEPs.

"Finally, the question about EU laws concerning straight bananas and cucumbers. Those stories are untrue. There never has been any EU law concerning the straightness of either. There are only voluntary marketing standards, not laws, arranged by the fruit and vegetable industry itself. The industry requires bananas or cucumbers to be packed by similar curvature so that their boxes can be labelled without having to be unpacked. That is all. There have also been misunderstandings about other foods - such as suggestions of banning British sausages and British chocolate - which are equally false. The Commission does not wish to ban any of these foods, but the opposite. It wishes to create a level playing-field across the EU, to give maximum choice to the public, to allow all of these foods to be sold everywhere provided they are safe."

Owen was sorry to have missed the opportunity to pose a question. But he doubted whether there had been such a memorable exchange as had taken place in the 1970s when Sir Nicholas Soames had been one of the two British Commissioners.

Soames had appeared before a parliamentary committee one afternoon carrying a glass of brandy and smoking a large cigar. A French MEP, clearly a connoisseur of Debussy's musical composition 'L'apres-midi d'un faune', was heard to whisper in admiration : "Regardez ! L'apres-midi d'un Soame !"

The Commissioner finished his answers and left the room. The chairman introduced the next topic.

Around half-past six the committee ceased its work for the day. Long ago the parliament had agreed that the interpreters would be guaranteed fixed working hours and were not required to continue indefinitely while members luxuriated in the sounds of their own voices.

Owen left the committee room with his suitcase and headed in the direction of the hemicycle.

"What's a *hemicycle* ?" interrupted Nina.

"It's the main debating chamber. It's called that because it is nearly circular in shape."

Owen approached a long curved wall of pale wood in which were 626 small pigeon-holes, arranged in national blocks : each door was labelled with the name of an MEP.

Opening his pigeon-hole Owen found the usual accumulation of EU papers plus several letters and Christmas cards. Before Christmas he had signed and mailed four thousand parliament cards to people in his constituency, using his brother's mailing-list : after all, all had votes as did all their families. Most of the cards in the pigeon-hole, however, proved to be from people to whom he had not sent cards.

He also found a fax message from his fellow Radical MEP, Bill Patel. Patel was the only other British Radical member of Owen's second parliamentary committee, Civil Liberties. Patel's message was that he was unable to attend their committee tomorrow morning because he was having a medical checkup.

Owen carried the stack of papers and his suitcase across the wide walkway away from the hemicycle and headed for his office on the twelfth floor of the G building. One of the toughest aspects of being a new MEP had been the sheer overload of information reaching him. It arrived by fax, e-mail, letter, voice-mail, mobile and desk telephones, and documents in two pigeonholes.

From the office he telephoned his usual hotel, a small family-run establishment which had been recommended in a guidebook for its comfort and friendly atmosphere. It was situated in the city centre near to Belgium's tomb of the Unknown Soldier.

The receptionist answered his enquiry with news that the hotel was full. Owen asked if the patron, Mr. Katvis, was available. There was a short pause. Owen pictured his fine set of whiskers.

"Katvis here. How can I help ?" asked the proprietor.

"This is Owen Mann, from the parliament. When I last stayed with you before Christmas, I stupidly forgot to make a reservation for tonight and tomorrow."

"Mijnheer Mann. For you, a good client, zere is no problem. I will find something. Come when you are ready. Byebye."

Later, Owen descended to the parliament's ground-floor and asked for a car and chauffeur. The cheerful driver proved to be one of the only two British chauffeurs. He had previously been a bomb-disposal officer. Always talkative he gave Owen his views on British politics during the short journey to the hotel.

Katvis was as good as his word. Having checked in, Owen walked to a local bistro which usually provided a good supper. His route took him through the Place des Martyres, a stunning eighteenth-century square, untouched by modernity, with cobbles and a central fountain. The buildings were shuttered and decaying because of a long-running dispute between the city authorities and property developers. Brussels had been poor at preserving its old buildings and Owen hoped the square's ancient splendour would not be destroyed. But it was for the city not the EU to decide.

Next morning his alarm-clock woke him from a dream that he was sliding slowly towards a precipice and would topple off in two months. He spent the whole day in the Civil Liberties committee because of the absence of Bill Patel, despite the numbing tedium of some of the debates.

The committee finished at half past six. As he was leaving, a young man in a suit and tie approached him.

"Mr. Mann. I hope I do not delay you ?" he said and politely offered his hand. "My name is Pietro Gatto. I am a member of the secretariat of this committee. You have heard about your colleague Mr. Patel ?"

"What about him ?"

"This afternoon he sent a message to our committee chairman, Mr. Chomik. He has gone into hospital and will not be able to perform his parliamentary duties for several weeks. It makes a problem for us."

"I'm sorry to hear that. Why ?"

"Before Christmas Mr. Patel was nominated for a rapporteurship. It was to investigate the current state of Fascism in Europe. Because he is ill, the opportunity of the rapporteurship falls to you instead. You are the only other member from your party on this committee so you have the first refusal. That is if you are willing to accept the responsibility ?"

"Fascism in Europe ? Why is that being investigated ?"

"Because the committee fears it is growing and wishes to assess what should be done about it."

Owen could not see how taking on Patel's rapporteurship would help his own electoral prospects. Anti-pollution would have been interesting to his local press, but fascism would not strike the same chord with its readers.

Not wishing to appear uncooperative, he searched for an excuse. "My diary is pretty full. I'm in no position to take on Mr. Patel's commitments."

"The Chairman understands this. But he noticed how you sat through the committee all day and was impressed by your keenness. He is willing to fit in with your diary."

A manipulative bureaucrat, thought Owen. His objection having been brushed aside, he thought again. He had lost the chance of the environmental rapporteurship, and there was no prospect of another in the near future. With the election only five months away, this might be his only opportunity. Hobson's Choice, this or nothing.

"In that case, I might be interested, Mr. Gatto. Tell me what's involved ?"

"Excellent. The Chairman would be delighted," said Gatto. "To start there are short visits which I had planned for Mr. Patel to several European countries to meet local experts. The first are to Norway and Sweden the week after next. Next month in February there will be a Public Hearing of witnesses invited from all over Europe. Then your report has to be written and finalised by the committee so it can be debated in May before the elections in June. Might these arrangements be convenient for you, Mr. Mann ?"

Owen opened his pocket diary and flinched. Unlike the weekly cycle of work at Westminster, the work-cycle of the European Parliament was monthly. The parliament's committees met in two consecutive weeks. In the third week the political groups met separately to prepare their future work. The fourth week was in Strasbourg for a plenary session of the whole parliament where full-scale debates and important votes were held.

Going to Oslo would oblige him to miss a socialist Group meeting in Brussels. That did not matter so much as the week's skiing holiday which he had booked long ago and would now have to be cancelled. The following week's constituency appointments would have to be rearranged which might inconvenience his potential supporters, a bad move to make. But it was his last opportunity of a rapporteurship.

"May I give you my decision after the weekend ?"

"Certamente" said Gatto. "However the timetable is short and there is a lot of work to be done. If the report is not finished and debated before the elections in June, it will lapse and the work would have to be started all over again in the autumn."

"Explain the timetable to me, Mr. Gatto."

"Today is the middle of January. We would go to Norway and Sweden in two weeks' time. You may think of other people whom you would like to interview. A meeting with a member of your own British government might be valuable. The Public Hearing is in mid-February. All your interviews should be completed soon after the Hearing so that your report can be drafted, translated, printed and distributed, and be ready for discussion by the committee by early-March. If members like it enough, the committee will vote on amendments to your draft by the end of March. Finally, it should be debated by the full parliament at one of the last two plenary sessions in Strasbourg, in either April or May."

"It sounds a tight schedule."

"Very tight" confirmed Gatto. "But I am available to help you, if you wish. I can make the flight bookings and accompany you on the visits to take notes. Travel and hotel expenses are paid from the usual parliamentary allowances."

Owen promised to give Gatto his decision on Monday, yes or no to the rapporteurship.

He looked at Nina. "That's my dilemma, Nina. Investigating fascism won't win me votes in the election in June. But it's my last chance of a rapporteurship and of leaving a mark in the sands of time. And if the media become interested it might help. What do you think ?"

Nina saw it straightforwardly. "I can't see what you have to lose - except time otherwise spent back here knocking on endless doors asking uninterested people for their votes." Owen knew she hated the prospect of having to accompany him campaigning. "I think you should grab it" she said.

"It'll involve a lot of work if I'm to finish it on time. And that won't help 'us'" replied Owen.

Nina made an unhappy face and went into the kitchen. While she made decaffeinated coffee Owen reached for his jacket which was hanging on the back of his chair. From a side pocket he extracted a small square box about the size of an apple. Moments later Nina returned with two mugs of coffee, sat down on the sofa and patted the seat beside her. Owen sat down and put the box into her hand.

She opened it carefully and took out a bundle of tissue-paper. Unwrapping it she found an antique silver bracelet and gasped. She put it onto her left wrist while Owen explained that it was Victorian and he had found it in an antique shop. She took his face in her hands and kissed him passionately. He put his arms round her neck and drew her towards him. Her tongue pushed into his mouth, acting as an invitation. He gently unbuttoned her dress and found, to his delight, she was wearing nothing over her warm sumptuous breasts. The coffee grew cold.

Afterwards they lay together, wrapped in a large duvet. He again kissed her beautiful face and the end of her nose. She muttered that it was not a good nose because it was slightly bent. Owen reassured her that nobody would ever notice unless she pointed it out first. She snuggled closer and replied : "I'll never tell you to go away."

After a pause she asked : "Where'll you be next week, darling ?"

"I'll be in Brussels from Tuesday to Friday." Owen knew that his reply would disappoint her. He added, trying to repair the damage : "See you at the weekend ?"

She qualified her reply : "Probably, although it's just possible that I may have a business trip for the bank."

Owen had learned that travelling by both of them made it hard to deepen a relationship. It had been so simple when it was merely mutual lust. He remembered a conversation he had heard between a young cousin and one of his friends, both aged twenty. They were discussing a girl, extolling her long fair hair, and her generous "melons" as they called them. After a while he had intervened : "But what's she like ? Is she funny or intelligent or what ?" The cousin was astonished : "Weren't you listening ? We've just told you. She's blonde with big boobs."

Would it be easier, he wondered, to remain single, to be like the divorced government minister who some years previously had hugely impressed the media by admitting to simultaneous mistresses ? Was building relationships particularly hard for MEPs because they travelled endlessly from place to place ? In the Westminster hothouse, where there were more divorces for serving MPs prorata than for MEPs, relationships were easier to make and unmake.

Owen fought off sleep while Nina soliloquised her own worries. Guiltily he muttered "yes", or "really ?", or "amazing !" to prove that he was following her. Once he was aware of her waiting for his comment, proving that he had nodded off.

He awoke around dawn. Nina lay beside him, still asleep but looking stunning. Trying not to disturb her, he slipped out of bed. She heard him and kissed him as he left.

He needed to return home because that morning he had an appointment with Jack Terrier for a pre-lunch drink in a local pub. Jack was "chair" of his constituency party as left-of-centre politicians prefer to be called. Owen was uncomfortable about calling his friend a piece of furniture, but used the left's required term because it was not a battle worth fighting. A Chair, and an Agent, were two of the most important regular contacts that a member of parliament had. The Chair was influential in deciding a member's chances of getting re-selected and in getting the activists out to help at an election.

Owen briefed Jack on events coming up in the parliament in Brussels and Strasbourg. He asked for Jack's opinion about taking on the rapporteurship about fascism. Jack's advice was the same as Nina's : "Go for it, Owen."

* * *

On Monday morning Owen telephoned Pietro Gatto and accepted the appointment as rapporteur. He cancelled his week's skiing, promising himself he would go next year, either safely re-elected or free to ski for as long as he wished.

He invested the remainder of the day in vote-hunting in his constituency. He toured a factory of a multinational, United Technologies, and tried hard to show an interest in the high-technology devices which they manufactured. He spoke at a lunch of a Probus Club for retired businessmen and afterwards gave the prizes at a girls' school. In his short speech to the girls he told the anecdote of the male television soap star. Facing the problem of saying something original to each prize-winner as they queued to receive their awards from him, he said to one girl : 'What are you thinking of doing when you leave school ?' She had given him a sly look and replied : 'Well, I was thinking of going straight home, but...'

His duties over, he changed clothes and dressed in a thick jumper and a bright-coloured scarf. He rode to the northernmost end of the London Underground network and left the bike at the station. As his train approached the inner city it filled up with boisterous men in colourful outfits singing and shouting. Owen shared their excitement because, as well as supporting his lowly local soccer team, he was an avid supporter of a top London team in England's Premier Division. This evening's game was a European Champions match in which his club were to play a top German team.

Leaving the station he merged with the large cheerful crowd, mainly men, who were heading towards different entrances into the stadium. Police on horses and a rigorous ban on alcohol appeared to ensure good order. The high expectations of the crowd had been whipped up by xenophobic headlines in tabloid newspapers : 'Achtung, surrender !', 'Watch out, Krauts !', and 'Blitz Fritz !'

He passed through the turnstile and showed his season ticket which guaranteed him the same seat for all his team's home matches. It was not in the Directors Box, as was demanded by self-important politicians. He preferred the anonymity of the crowd and enjoying its repartee.

The teams emerged from a tunnel and ran onto the pitch. The crowd's cheering rose to a frenzy. Loud loudspeakers played the home team's anthem. At the south-east corner of the ground, in a separate enclosure were a small number of German supporters, waving red, gold, and black scarves.

The shouts of the home supporters near Owen usually were good-natured, and occasionally witty. Early in the game the home team's fullback executed a meticulous tackle and cleared the ball upfield. An ecstatic fan shouted to him : "Great tackle, Nigel ! If I had a daughter I'd want her to marry you."

The home team scored first and the crowd went delirious. They started a chant to mock the Germans : "Are you San Marino in disguise ?" A single voice called out "You were shit even when you were good."

But the Germans were a skilful team and fought back. Their black centre-forward was outstanding and equalised for them just before the half-time interval. He had an unusual hair-style so a section of the crowd, not far from Owen, started to target him with abuse. Each time he touched the ball, they chanted : "He's got a pineapple on his head." When he was knocked to the ground, they sang: "There's a pineapple on the ground."

It did not appear to affect the quality of the attacker's play, but Owen became increasingly angry. He turned to look at the back of the stand. Would the police, standing there in their prominent orange jackets, intervene to stop the chanting ? To Owen's astonishment they did not move.

After half-time, the Germans scored two more goals, which effectively ended the home team's hopes of victory. The crowd fell into a dismayed silence. A lone voice shouted : "At least we won the war." A snigger ran round the stadium.

The match finished three-one. After the game was over, Owen filed out of the ground with the other supporters. He was disgusted at the racist attitudes of a small minority of the supporters. Having time to spare, he made his way slowly round two sides of the stadium against the tide of fans heading for the station. He hoped he might be able to see the German team departing in their bus and have an opportunity to apologise to them for the abuse.

At the team entrance to the stadium there was a seething throng. He heard shouts of "Scum" and "Schweinhunds". He pushed slowly through the crush to try to see what was happening. A wedge of people to his right heaved and almost rocked him off his feet. As he recovered his balance the jostling increased. He saw several burly young men with cropped haircuts leading the anti-German abuse.

Next to them was a girl in a thick dark-green coat who looked terrified. She was pushed against a wall and was in danger of being crushed. Owen wriggled towards her as she shouted for assistance: "Hilfe, Hilfe." One of the skinheads, realising that she was German, palmed her in the face. She doubled up as another punched her in the stomach. Reaching her Owen shoved one aggressor away. He was punched in the face to an illogical shout of "Jew lover" and then several times on his chest and stomach. A fierce kick on his shin from a metal-tipped boot sent him to the ground.

A police whistle sounded. Several policemen grabbed the skinheads. As Owen climbed onto his feet he saw the three short-haired men being frog-marched towards a police van.

The crowd dispersed rapidly. A search revealed knives carried by each of the three thugs. With order restored, a policeman asked both the frightened girl and Owen for their names and addresses as witnesses. The German girl who was shaken but uninjured said she had become separated from her companions. A policeman walked her to a police-car to drive her to her destination.

Owen limped back to the Underground station, deeply ashamed about the bad publicity which had been created both for his team and for Britain.

* * *

His bruises next morning did not prevent him from making the journey to Brussels. Both his parliamentary committees were to meet in the afternoon, on Environment and Civil Liberties.

His suitcase was light because he now kept a spare razor and clothes in both of his offices, in Brussels and Strasbourg. A desktop computer was provided in both but he had to pack papers and diskettes which might be required for the days ahead.

At Heathrow airport he left his bike in the short-term park beside Terminal One. Short-term parking was free to him provided he did not remain longer than five days. At the end of a tiring week it was blissful to climb almost from the plane straight onto his machine. It was a concession given to British MEPs and to members of the Westminster parliament by British Airports Authority who said they wanted to make legislators aware of the difference between who ran the airlines and who ran the airports.

Reaching his office in Brussels with time to spare he decided to table a Motion for a Resolution. Like an Early Day Motion in the House of Commons, it enabled an MEP to draw attention to a particular issue to which other members could add their signatures if they wished. His motion would deplore racial incitement and violence. In due course it would be forwarded to an appropriate parliamentary committee. Most committees took no action with these motions but might incorporate the points into a relevant report if one was being written at the time.

Owen did not hope that any action would be taken as a result of his Motion. A European committee could issue words but could not take action against hooligans in a corner of London. But it would allow him to send a press release to his local media to show he was trying to get matters improved.

He typed his draft motion on the word processor in his office, pressed the last key and the screen went blank. He remembered that it was not the machine's fault as he once thought. The text was lost because he had forgotten to save it. He retyped the Motion, better this time, printed a copy and walked to the Tabling Office where a French-speaking woman accepted it.

He decided to spend his afternoon in the Civil Liberties committee because Bill Patel would not be present. He took his seat as the gavel was rapped by the chairman, Josef Chomik. He was a north-German of Polish origin who, in earlier times, might have been called a Prussian. In his mid-sixties, rigid, stout and whiskered, he seemed to be at risk from a heart-attack whenever he became too excited.

The man beside Chomik whispered something to him. It was Bruno Wielblad who headed the staff of the committee. He was also a German and spoke four other languages, and had a legendary capacity for drinking.

Nodding agreement, Chomik spoke : "The first matter on our agenda concerns the appointment of new rapporteurs. What have the coordinators of the political groups to recommend to us ?"

First to speak was the coordinator for the largest political group, the Socialists. Mrs. Bridget O'Leumadair was a graceful grey-haired woman in her fifties with a charming Irish brogue.

"Chair, the coordinators of the different groups met last week. As usual we made bids for the available reports." Owen had learned that the bidding involved notional bank-balances of points awarded to each group pro-rata to its numerical strength.

She read out the reports on which she had spent the Socialists' points and the name of a rapporteur for each. One purchase concerned the committee's wish for a study into the state of Fascism in Europe. She announced that the rapporteur would be Owen Mann.

An angry noise erupted. Chomik stared at the left side of the committee room.

"Is there an objection ?" he asked with a look of surprise. "I expect none on routine matters such as the appointment of rapporteurs. They are settled in advance between the Group coordinators."

Giorgios Xamilopardis, a tall thin Greek member with a black beard, spoke fiercely into his microphone. Owen wondered what his objection would be. He knew the Greek to be warm-hearted but notorious for an inability to contain his tongue : continuing an argument endlessly, and using several words where one would suffice, was his speciality. Among other members he was known affectionately as 'Catastropho-pardis' because of his ability to reduce any situation to chaos. Owen put on his headphones as a female interpreter did her best to convert the torrent of Greek into English.

"Chair. When the parliament wrote a report on this subject some years ago, its author was British. It is wrong that the same nationality should have this important responsibility twice in succession."

Noises of support came from other members. The Greek's tirade visibly irritated Chomik and he banged his gavel.

"My dear colleague. I fail to share your opinion. You know the rules as well as anybody here. All nationalities are equal and we do not discriminate between them. The coordinators have already agreed which political group will undertake each report. The Socialists wish to appoint Mr. Mann for this one. That is all."

He sipped a glass of water and, with the visible satisfaction of a card-player playing an ace, added : "You yourself might have obtained the report if you had been present at the meeting of coordinators last week." Somebody laughed.

"But you were absent. All I can offer as consolation is that the minutes of today's meeting will record that you expressed your view forcibly. I am sure that, as an experienced parliamentarian, you do not wish to force this matter to a vote ? To do so would risk upsetting the delicate balance between the political groups which we have all worked hard to achieve."

The bearded Greek started to rant again. Chomik ignored him, and gave the floor to another member who had caught his eye from the right side of the room.

It was a Frenchman, Guy Gafosse. He wanted to disqualify Owen with a different argument. He complained that a Briton should not have been given this rapporteurship : "Mr. Mann is Euro-sceptical like all the British. They drag their heels over European integration. This report will be a part of our great European happening. It is history and can not be avoided. Either Britain can choose to be isolated in which case she is finished, or she can take part wholeheartedly and make the necessary sacrifices."

Stung by the Frenchman's arrogance Owen interrupted with a question of his own : "If Britain has to make sacrifices, what sacrifices has France made ?"

The Frenchman riposted : "The greatest. We allowed Britain to join the European family."

Chomik banged his gavel and gave the floor to another member on the right of the room. It was an Italian member of the far-right group. Mr. Moffetta was famous for his bouffant hair in black-and-white stripes.

"Mr. Chairman, we from the European Right object violently to this proposal. This report about so-called fascism is intended to create a witch-hunt against my fellow parliamentarians all over

Europe. We object, not only to the rapporteur but to the whole proposal and will do everything possible to prevent it. Last time this parliament held a similar enquiry, my group leader, Mr. Rocher, went to the European Court of Justice to try to stop it. I warn you that we shall do whatever is necessary again to stop this wasteful and destructive proceeding. It is a disgraceful misuse of taxes paid by hardworking citizens."

Chomik remained impassive. He was an old hand who had no intention of being deterred. "What you said will be noted in the Minutes as is your democratic right. However, I believe that a large majority of this committee wishes to proceed with the proposed rapporteur." The noise of desk-tapping by members showed he had their support. "Now" continued the Chairman, "we shall move swiftly to the next item on the agenda. We have lost too much time."

Owen relaxed in his chair. He had obtained a rapporteurship, although not the one he wanted. To his surprise his instinct was one of pleasure. It might not help his re-election prospects but, if he did the job well, he could leave something behind. He mentally rolled up his sleeves and wondered what he might discover about fascism in present-day Europe.

After the committee finished for the day, he walked to the long bar around the corner from the hemicycle in the Spaak building. The bar had modern furnishings and two television screens which listed what parliamentary meetings were scheduled. When there was a debate in the hemicycle, one screen listed the next three speakers to be called.

Owen bought a half-litre of beer. He walked toward the windows past little tables with bright red, blue, yellow or green cushioned chairs, and chose a square black-leather armchair.

Shortly afterwards Murdo McKirk appeared. Owen waved and he came over.

"What will you have, Murdo ?"

"A cold beer, please, and a doughnut."

Owen returned to the bar, bought the beer and an almond croissant, and carried them to McKirk by the window.

"No doughnuts in Brussels. How are you finding things so far ?"

"There's much more going on than I imagined," replied the hack. "I've a lot of sorting out to do."

He made a start on his beer. "And you, Owen ? Any achievements for me to publicise ?" he asked with a grin.

"Afraid not." Owen described his failure to obtain the anti-pollution rapporteurship in the Environment committee and his success with fascism in Civil Liberties.

McKirk shook his head : "We can't use that. Fascism isn't news in Britain. Now if you were to take the contrary view, that pollution or fascism should be increased, that would be news. But not the sort you want."

Owen pointed out people in the bar whom he knew. He introduced McKirk to a Dutch MEP named Petrus Van Der Muis. The Dutchman was a small lively figure with white hair. He seemed to open every conversation in English with 'How's life ?'

"How's life, Owen ? By the way, I have a Dutch story for your book." Owen accepted the piece of paper which he offered.[2]

Most of the nearby chairs had filled up. Lord Butcher, a Progressive MEP, stopped by and joined the banter. "Owen you were very lucky. That report should have come to my Group."

"Certainly not," said Van Der Muis, very irritated. "You British Progressives are 'Euro-sceptical'. You want no more power to go to Brussels. Being so negative you should be rapporteurs on nothing."

Butcher wore a wig and when he became agitated it tended to slip, as it did now. "We certainly should be rapporteurs. We are elected MEPs and being opposed to a federal Europe is the view of many people" he snapped.

"Really ?" countered the Dutchman calmly. "Your English dictionary says 'federal' means 'decentralised'. Isn't a decentralised Europe what you want ? Your party at Westminster misuses the word 'federal' deliberately. They pretend that it means 'centralising' in Brussels. The truth is that 'federal' means the opposite : it means that decisions should be made away from Brussels and as close as possible to the people affected by them."

"Britain should be an independent nation. We were mis-led in the referendum in 1975" countered Butcher.

"Fantasy" sighed Van Der Muis. "I've had this discussion before with Brits." He fished into his wallet and pulled out a yellowed newscutting. "When you held a referendum about Europe in 1975, your *Daily Telegraph* newspaper wrote an editorial - see, it's dated 5th June 1975 - which said that it was

> increasingly convinced...that Western Europe's integration is mandatory for its survival and prosperity...political unity is Europe's only key...

"Notice" emphasised the Dutchman, "that it used the words 'integration' and 'political' in a favourable way. You suffer from a bad memory. The British were not deceived at all in 1975."

"Things have changed since then" riposted Butcher.

"Nonsense. You are as perfidious as your Albion ancestors. Since 1975 you have shared a lot of powers with us. Your government signed the Single Act in 1985 which brought in majority voting, then the Maastricht Treaty in 1990 which took us further into 'ever closer union'. You British want a Single Market, so there must be EU-wide laws and a supreme European Court to enforce penalties against offenders. Face the facts : you British are already in a semi-federal arrangement. In the past you helped to create successful federations, such as the USA, Australia, and Germany. Why are you against one in Europe ?"

"Individual states such as Virginia in the United States, or Bavaria in Germany, have no say in Foreign Affairs or Defence. We Progressives want to have our say in world affairs so we need a different model for Europe."

"You had better make up your minds" said the Dutchman. "Either you continue along the 'ever closer union' road with us, or you quit the EU and have no say in future European decisions. If you leave the EU, you'll have no influence but you'll still be affected by our decisions. Why not face reality and accept that the future is political and is not only about free trade ?"

Butcher muttered something inaudible. Van Der Muis pressed his view : "I have quotes about this by your former leader who told the Commons," he reopened his notebook and quoted again :

> "I believe with a number of honourable members who spoke yesterday, that the paramount case for being in is the

> *political* case for peace and security."

"Political, your leader said," the Dutchman emphasised, "not just trade. Fifteen years later in a letter to your Foreign Secretary when he resigned from the cabinet the same word was used again. Your leader wrote to him" he read, quoting again :

> We want Britain to play a leading part in Europe and to be part of the future *political*, economic and monetary development of the European Community.

The Dutchman looked triumphantly at Butcher : "You notice that she repeated that word 'political' again, fifteen years later ? You British weren't mis-led in 1975. It was always political. You just can't face reality."

"We shall try to renegotiate the Treaty of Rome" replied Butcher.

"You will fail. You would need unanimity among all countries to do it and nobody will agree with you."

"We shall call a referendum about whether the U.K. should remain in the EU."

"The British public will vote to stay in, unless you allow the populists to take over " countered Van Der Muis.

"The British people have a demos, a sense of common purpose. There is no EU demos, no sense of common interest among the different peoples of Europe, which makes them accept government from eachother's hands" replied Butcher, adjusting his toupee.

"Apart from the fact that *demos* was an early socialist word which meant 'the common people', immigrants into Britain do not share your concept of demos. The future belongs to multiracial societies. Furthermore power has shifted beyond the nation state and the British are separating into Welsh, Scottish and Irish. Your party, Lord Butcher, is proceeding up a blind alley. It will result in catastrophe for you at the polls."

Butcher shrugged and walked away.

An attractive woman walked past on her way to the bar. Owen noticed McKirk's head turn as his eyes followed her. She had dark shoulder-length hair. Her one-piece sleeveless dress showed a trim figure.

Moments later she passed again carrying a glass of white wine. She stopped and spoke : "Mr. Mann. I hope you don't mind me saying this. I was interpreting for the Civil Liberties committee this afternoon. I thought you handled the attack on yourself in a most gentlemanly fashion. I'm sure you did yourself good."

McKirk listened, showing a strong interest. Owen introduced them : "Have the two of you met ? Natasha Farfalla, one of the English-booth interpreters. Murdo McKirk, a news-hound from London who has come over here to muck-rake, I'm afraid."

McKirk offered her a business card and enquired politely : "Are you Italian ?"

"I'm Welsh, but my husband is from Milan" she replied.

"When you've got a spare moment, I'd be glad to have a chat with you."

"I'd be delighted" she responded, her dark eyes smiling. "But you must understand that we interpreters know nothing. The speeches made by the members pass into our ears and out of our mouths without us remembering what they say. Not that they aren't exceedingly interesting of course," she added with a grin to the listening MEPs.

She wetted her lips with the wine : "Mr. Mann, you missed a comic moment when you were out of the committee. A Frenchman, Mr. Loutré, who comes from Normandy, was complaining about some impossible problem. He claimed it could only be solved if everybody acquired the wisdom of his fellow Normans. My colleague in the English-booth, without thinking, interpreted this as 'This can only be solved if we have Norman Wisdom'. The Brits in the committee laughed noisily but Mr. Loutré did not see the joke. Humour doesn't interpret easily into other languages."

Tom Ostler, another Radical who was listening, interjected ;

"But sometimes there are comic misunderstandings. Such as the time in the Agriculture committee, when 'frozen semen' was put into French as 'matelots congelés', which means frozen sailors."

"And when an English mention of 'shooting rapids' was understood by the German interpreter as 'shooting rabbits' and led to a weird discussion about hunting" added Natasha.

McKirk's eyes shone but his brain struggled to conjure the words for an unpractised question. He stuttered : "I saw a poster advertising a production of *HMS Pinafore* by the Gilbert & Sullivan society in Brussels. Are you a fan by any chance ?" he asked.

"Yes, but I'm away for the next couple of weeks" replied Natasha, giving him a smile. "I am free-lance. Sometimes I work for the other EU institutions, such as the Commission or the Council of Ministers, sometimes at business conferences and even at film festivals."

"Film festivals ?"

"I worked at a French festival last May. Working with a male colleague he and I interpreted soundtracks into English for the cinema audiences. We did the same film twice, in the afternoon and evening, so I understood the plot better the second time round."

McKirk was curious and asked : "You do the female voices, and he does the male ones ?"

"No, we each do twenty minutes alone then have a break. When you're 'on', you do all the voices, male and female. It's not difficult. What I found more alarming was doing a press conference afterwards with the stars. I was worried that I wouldn't recognise some who were famous."

"Did you have time to enjoy the films ?"

Her face became melancholy. "Those that I saw left me with the impression that there is great sadness in Europe. The films dealt with unfulfilled dreams, lost loves, children up against the horrors of exclusion, violence, the Nazi past and other depressing themes. No, I didn't enjoy them. Will you excuse me ?"

She took her glass of wine and went to join a group of interpreters. Murdo gazed after her as she walked away.

Minutes later their beer glasses were empty.

"Stay in touch, Owen" said Murdo as he got up to leave. "One day we might even work on the same side."

Owen returned to his office. The light on his answerphone was flashing. The message was not from Nina as he hoped but from the only daily newspaper in his Euro-constituency. They asked him to ring their news-desk as soon as possible.

Local papers were always short of news. Getting into the national media was much harder. He telephoned the news editor, Joe Robinson.

"Thanks for ringing back. Tell me what happened at the football match in London. One of my reporters picked up that you were a witness to a riot. The police inspector gave us a glowing account of your help."

Owen described the anti-German chanting by the thugs. The local publicity would be valuable, he thought, and some consolation for his bruises.

* * *

That same afternoon Enrique Sãta, the financier, was working in an unassuming building which he owned in a city a thousand miles east of Portugal, the land of his birth. A century ago the building had been a prosperous family home. Now, there was no brass plate outside the front door, but it served as his European headquarters.

His office, his inner sanctum, was a panelled room with an enormous map of Europe covering the whole of one wall. Pins and flags were stuck on it in various places. From the windows he had a magnificent view of a deep gorge. The desk at which he was sitting was heavy, polished and antique. He was holding separate meetings with each of his three principal assistants in order to review their work.

The first assistant was a stocky male, aged around forty-five. He was Ukrainian born of Hungarian parents and his name was Istvan Diszno. He had grown up under Communism and claimed to have been a highly-trained member of the USSR's elite *spetsnaz* assault force. Sãta was relieved that he had finished listening to Diszno because of the man's habit of chewing raw garlic. He was the least bright of the three but exceptionally loyal, and valuable for short-term projects such as 'hits'.

Seated now at the other side of Sãta's desk was Rado Zaplasiti. He was aged thirty, skinny with light-brown curly hair, and wore metal-rimmed spectacles. An intellectual who spoke several west European languages fluently, his native tongue was Serbo-Croat. He had grown up under communism. Having witnessed the chaos of the Balkans, he believed profoundly that society required firm discipline.

Zaplasiti was finishing his report : "I've finished analysing the techniques which our colleagues in France, Norway, Austria, and to a lesser extent in Italy, have used successfully to win votes in elections. Last week I started teaching these methods to our friends in other countries. The first place is Denmark where, until now, they have concentrated on violence and fighting each other."

Sãta leaned forward, keenly interested, and asked : "Rado, it may be easy for them to make a short-term impact in elections. But, until now, nationalist parties haven't had enough activists to make them capable of using the democratic process to build longterm success. What are the lessons from successful nationalist campaigns that you are teaching ?"

"Longterm success comes from finding people with ability, and teaching them how to set up local party branches. It's about recruiting young people by opening centres for unemployed youths, and holding music gigs to recruit youngsters and raise money. It's about showing them how to distribute leaflets, how to listen to what people want and promise to give it to them. It's about denouncing the established political parties as discredited and corrupt, and using slogans like 'Only our party represents the ordinary man against the elite in the capital' and 'We create work while the government creates paperwork.'"

"Sounds good. This summer in June there will be European elections in all fifteen EU states. Can you complete the training before then ?"

"Providing you agree, President, after Denmark I think Sweden looks full of promise, then the three Benelux countries, and after that the Iberian peninsula. Maybe a month each to get them going."

"First class, Rado. Your work is going to bring our movement enormous longterm gains. Is your budget sufficient ? There's more if you need it."

"Thank you, President." Zaplasiti left the room.

Five minutes later, on the hour, his third assistant knocked and entered. Monika Pasarea was aged around thirty and of Romanian origin. She had high cheek-bones, full lips, and dark-blond tressed hair which fell below her shoulders. She was wearing a pin-stripe suit and spectacles.

Sãta waved her to the empty chair. "Monika, before we get to your fund-raising, there's a small extra project I want to give you. The European Parliament, that unknown and expensive body of nobodies, has started a report on what they call," he glanced at a sheet of mauve paper lying on his desk, 'The Situation of Fascism in Europe'."

He puffed his cigar. "The parliament wrote a similar report in 1990 which came to almost nothing because national governments took no action. I'm sure this new report will prove equally flaccid. But, since our movement is more advanced than it was then and our future is very ambitious, we must keep an eye on what they are doing. Monika," Sãta smiled across the desk at her, "in addition to fund-raising, I want a regular update from you on what is happening. If the parliament's investigation looks like becoming a problem for us, we can take appropriate measures."

"Certainly, Mr. Sãta" she replied.

"One unbreakable rule, Monika. If it becomes necessary for you to meet the parliament's rapporteur, to assess him, only meet him once in order to protect your cover."

She nodded agreement : "I understand."

"Now, let's go through the fund-raising programme..."

After their discussion had finished, Sãta strolled to the window to finish his cigar. He reflected on how far he had come. Born to wealthy parents in Portugal, he had been educated at an elite school in Connecticut followed by a year at INSEAD, Europe's outstanding business school at Fontainebleau. He was convinced that the chaotic fluid world of the twenty-first century would need a disciplined elite to run it. Too much democracy would be detrimental to discipline and high standards.

After gaining his MBA degree at Fontainebleau, he had started a business trading with Portugal's ex-colonies in Africa. This took him to Angola with its three-sided civil war. He had joined the anti-communist forces led by Jonas Savimbi. Initially the weakest of the three factions, it was later backed by the West. Joining as a raw recruit, Sãta gained a reputation as an able tactician but also as a ruthless killer. He had risen to become Savimbi's youngest colonel.

He recalled with a smile the story of God Almighty looking down on the leaders of the three Angolan armies, and offering them one wish each. Roberto, leader of the Western-backed FNLA said he wished the ground to open up and to swallow Neto, the leader of the Soviet-backed MPLA. Neto, for his part, wished for a bolt of lightning to descend from Heaven which would destroy Roberto. Savimbi, leader of UNITA, declared humbly that he had no wish - except that the wishes of the other two should be granted.

Seeing the conflict as war without end, Sãta had quit Angola and used his contacts to trade in arms with ex-Nazis in Paraguay and other South American countries. He had built a considerable fortune and had married a beautiful Mexican heiress. She and their two young boys now lived in Port Jefferson, an enchanting village on Long Island south-east of Manhattan but conveniently near to Kennedy airport.

Politics, the ultimate calling, had always fascinated Sãta. But, until recently, he had found no spare time for it. Now, with his considerable personal resources, he had taken to it with gusto.

His great insight, he considered, was that the right-wing parties all over Europe were unsuccessful because each pursued its own short-sighted introverted goals. Few had won much public support. Yet extreme parties with different political goals had proved that success could be won - like the Basque Independence party in northern Spain, and Sinn Fein in Ireland.

He had been an observer at a summit of right-wing nationalist parties in France. It had been chaotic, noisy and disjointed. The discussion had been about a forthcoming visit by an American, who had subsequently been imprisoned in Germany for disseminating Nazi propaganda. They had debated how to organise a football riot in Oslo where the England football team were soon to play but their plan had been prevented by the police who had received inside information. They had planned the annual march in August to commemorate the suicide of Hitler's deputy Rudolf Hess, which the Danes were to host that year in Roskilde. But it had descended into chaos after the police, media and anti-fascists were tipped off in advance.

Right-wing parties in Europe with few exceptions had not gained ground in recent years. Sãta's hunch was that their failure to attract public support had been because of infighting among themselves. There had been no coordination among them across borders. This he had decided to change.

He had recruited three able assistants and paid them handsomely : Istvan Diszno for short-term projects : Rado Zaplasiti to train the parties in electoral techniques ; Monika Pasarea for fund-raising. One by one, the separate national ring-wing parties were being persuaded to regard each other as allies not foreign enemies. Each party had accepted a programme to train its activists about how to succeed in democratic elections. With his central coordinating role, Sãta assisted the smaller right-wing parties with finance raised from business including his latest contacts recently made in London.

To raise money Monika deployed the argument with international businessmen that globalisation had allowed them to escape from the control of national parliaments. If they did not wish a strong EU to develop which would shackle their activities instead, they should contribute to the Sãta Foundation. Their contributions would help the work of weakening the EU, in ways that could not be traced back to them.

Sãta's personal dream was to build a European-wide political party of the far-right. After all, the European federalists had inserted a clause into the Maastricht treaty calling for the creation of pan-European political parties. He was only doing what his enemies wished.

In the approaching European elections, he intended to create a united front out of different nationalist parties. He would stand as a candidate himself, as head of his party's list in Portugal. With proportional representation, he hoped his front would win a large number of MEP seats from several countries ; if not an overall majority, then enough to hold the balance of power in the European Parliament. The beauty of it was that the public imagined that the parliament was still powerless : they had not understood the powers which had been conferred on it by the Treaties of Amsterdam and of Maastricht. The parliament was now very powerful, and almost an equal partner with the Council of Ministers.

If his nationalist front won enough seats, he could block any further progress by the EU and maybe even start to reverse what had been achieved so far.

He dared not dream of where success might carry him ultimately.

* * *

Owen awoke in his hotel. He remembered it was Thursday and he was in Brussels. He strolled to the parliament, bought a *cappuccino* and a *pain au chocolat*, and carried them upstairs to his office. A cappuccino was his favourite version of coffee because of the chocolate powder scattered over the frothy milk. It was the nearest he could get to toffee in coffee.

A fax was waiting, sent by Lynda Black from the constituency office. It contained a news-cutting from the local paper. The three thugs at Monday evening's football match had appeared before magistrates, and been sent to prison for three months. The report included Owen's photograph and praised him as 'a Good Samaritan'.

During their court appearance the thugs had denied that any of them had written the fascist pamphlets which had been scattered on the ground outside the football stadium. The words were too long. "My mate could not have done it," said one. "He left me a note the other day which asked me to feed his pet. Even I could see that his spelling was bad. I could understand how he made a mistake with 'please' because it has six letters. But he even got 'dog' wrong."

The newspaper commented that, as travel became easier with open borders in the EU, so the phenomenon of football hooliganism was likely to spread. It called for improvements to the joint strategy adopted by all EU governments - for exchanging information on known trouble-makers, and for networks of liaison officers. It understood the politicians' dilemma which lay in balancing the need for good public order against respect for individual freedom.

Owen returned to the committee-room for the final session of Civil Liberties. Waiting for it to start, Guy Gafosse sidled up.

"Monsieur Mann. As an apology for my attack on you, may I offer a French story for your book ?" Owen listened to Gafosse and shook his hand.[3]

Chairman Chomik opened the morning's proceedings. Immediately 'Catastropho-pardis' interrupted with a point of order.

"What's your problem, my friend from the Peleponese ?" asked Chomik.

"Chair. Mr. Mann has disqualified himself from being our

rapporteur about fascism."

"Pray why ?"

"Yesterday he tabled a Motion for a Resolution concerning fascist behaviour of football hooligans in London. Under the parliament's rules, the tabler of a resolution may not also be the rapporteur on the same subject."

Xamilopardis's face was triumphant. But Chomik trumped him.

"Technically, my dear colleague, you are right. But, as chairman, I consider Mr. Mann's Motion to be an indication of his strong interest in the subject. He is the only member of his party on the committee who is available to take the report. Any other choice would upset the delicate balance between the political groups. I hereby *rule*", he emphasised the word by repeating it, "*rule* in favour of Mr. Mann continuing to be the rapporteur."

Xamilopardis did not give up. "Chair, I protest."

"My friend, protest if you wish. You are a Communist, so I admire your anti-fascist views. But if you employ pedantic delaying tactics any longer, you will kill the chances of the report being completed before the election - and you will prove to have been a good friend of the fascists."

Xamilopardis fell silent. Chomik gave him a split second to speak, then moved on with the committee's business.

Owen's appointment as a rapporteur was in the bag. He leaned back, feeling both pleasure and apprehension.

* * *

He returned to his office where a telephone message and two faxes awaited him.

The message was from Nina. She said that, after all, she would be away this weekend on a business trip, so was sorry not to be able to see him. She sent him 'lots of love'.

He felt gloomy but his heart rose as he read the first fax. It came from Bill Patel, his absent colleague on the committee :

> Glad to hear you are taking on the fascism report. Let me know if I can help. Meanwhile here's my story, true I'm told, for your collection.[4]

Owen's mood fell again as he read the other fax. It was short, typewritten and lacked any signature. It said simply :

WE KNOW WHO YOU ARE

Beneath the five words was a curious sketch of the British flag with a swastika at its centre.

Owen was dumbfounded. Was it a threat ? Should he take it seriously ? Was it significant that the sender had taken the trouble to discover the exact number of his fax machine - although a telephone-call to the parliament's switchboard would discover it ?

He sat and thought for some moments, then telephoned one of the Quaestors in order to get professional advice. The Quaestors are five MEPs who are elected by the other members for thirty-month periods. Their role, like shop-stewards in a factory, is to look after members' interests within the parliament.

One of the five Quaestors was British, Arthur Angler, who was a British Radical like Owen. He was famous for his ability to solve the most difficult of crosswords, although whether that was his main qualification for the job was unclear.

On the telephone Owen explained the threat which had materialised from his fax machine.

"I suggest you report it to the head of security in the parliament. His name is Kikker" explained Angler.

Kikker answered his telephone immediately but sounded unimpressed by Owen's question because he was suffering from a bad cold.

"From where was the fax sent ?" he croaked.

Owen looked at the top of the fax to find the header which would identify its origin. There was none.

"Have you interrogated your machine ?" Kikker continued stoically.

"What does that mean ? Can it speak ?" Owen asked jokingly.

Kikker croaked a patient sigh. "By pressing a particular button, your machine will print out the numbers of all your recent incoming and outgoing faxes. Then, knowing the sender's fax number, you could ask somebody in the country of origin to identify the sender for you."

Technology was easy, thought Owen, when it was explained in simple terms. He interrogated his machine and the printout gave the source as a number which started with 0044207, which he knew signified central London.

Not wishing to alarm Rosemary or Lynda in the constituency, he faxed the European Parliament's Information Office at 2, Queen Anne's Gate in central London. He asked if they could identify the number of the sender.

Next he telephoned Hijena at their goldsmith workshop. With a one-third share of the business to protect, he suggested that his most useful role would be to look out on his travels for potential new customers.

Hijena replied that they were managing very well without him. He muttered sceptically that he'd already tried selling to the continent once before and nothing had come of it - but, by all means, Owen could keep a look out and let him know of any opportunities.

With no answer yet about the source of the fax, Owen took a lift downstairs to the kiosk situated just inside the main entrance of the Spaak building. As the lift stopped at each floor it emptied and filled. Owen regretted that he knew so few people because many of the faces belonged to beautiful and beautifully-dressed women who obviously worked in the parliament. His difficulty lay in deciding which language to use to start a conversation, and whether they belonged to a political group which was compatible with his own. The result, so far, was that he had never got started.

The best-dressed women were the Italian and Spanish, probably because they were wealthier or had obtained their jobs through personal connections. By contrast the north-European route to winning jobs as assistants was puritanical, through ability more than glamour.

He had hoped to buy two London newspapers to read over lunch but found there were none because there was a one-day general strike in Belgium. He decided he must learn how to locate each day's newspapers on the Internet and how to print them out, free of charge.

After a newspaperless salad in the ground-floor canteen, he strolled to Pietro Gatto's office. They needed to work out which countries to visit in their research into fascism, and a list of questions to ask.

They agreed to start the research with the most relevant right-wing personality of them all who also happened to be the nearest geographically. The leader of the National Front in France, Jean-Joel Rocher, was a French MEP although not an MP in Paris. If the Frenchman was willing, it should be possible to make an appointment to meet him on the European Parliament's premises. Owen picked up the telephone and rang Rocher's office.

Correlate's secretary promised him a reply as soon as she could. The next day a note appeared in Owen's pigeonhole offering an appointment in three weeks when the parliament would be in Strasbourg.

Next Owen telephoned the London office of the Home Secretary, Sir David Bronwen. Put through to his 'special advisor' by the name of Toby Beaver, Owen asked for an appointment to discuss the fascist situation in Britain. He was allocated thirty minutes in ten days' time.

Back in England, his weekend without Nina was drab. Saturday morning was spent at a 'New Year Fayre', organised by party volunteers to raise money. He watched his local football team on a grim January afternoon with less than a hundred spectators present. The home side scored a rare goal although they did not win the match. In the evening he attended a fund-raising Buffet Supper organised by another party branch. On Sunday he rode sixty miles southwest to have lunch with his parents. They were delighted to see him and as supportive as ever. But they were visibly getting older and their horizons were shrinking. His mother enquired discreetly about Nina. She failed, as always, to conceal her disappointment that there was no sign of her becoming either a mother-in-law or a grandmother.

* * *

On Monday morning Owen returned to Brussels because the Civil Liberties committee, which he now found interesting, would meet in the afternoon. It would hold a first debate about his investigation the next morning.

From his office in the evening he telephoned Nina.

"How was your business trip ? Dull ?"

"Hello, darling. I was in Lisbon. I'm sorry but it couldn't be avoided." She paused : "Darling, I'm actually waiting for a call about it now. Can I ring you back ?"

"Of course. I'm going out to get something to eat. I'm staying at my usual hotel. Don't worry how late you ring."

When Owen reached the hotel Katvis said there was no message for him. He fell asleep over his book around one in the morning but Nina had not rung.

In the committee next morning, Chomik introduced the fascism investigation by announcing that it was going to be important. He invited Owen to open the committee's debate. Owen did so, using notes provided by Pietro Gatto.

"The parliament has held two previous investigations on this subject - in the 1980s and again in the early 1990s. Today we want to see how things have changed. I propose that we look at fascism in each of the fifteen member states of the EU, and also in the six states who are negotiating to join the EU as new members - Cyprus, the Czech Republic, Estonia, Hungary, Poland, and Slovenia."

Others members followed, giving their ideas. Several had previously been government ministers in national parliaments, some with direct experience of dealing with fascists. A socialist Swede, Lars Anka, said he would like to have a private word with Owen afterwards.

Owen had been warned by Gatto that two members of the committee, both from the far-right, might make noisy objections to the whole project. However only one of the two was present, and although he took notes he did not speak. He appeared to have recognised that he could not prevent the report going ahead, so it was wiser to avoid creating unnecessary ill-will and keep his powder dry.

A diversion from the subject was introduced by Lord Butcher, the British Progressive. Breaking his normal silence he spoke calmly so that his hairpiece stayed in position.

"Chairman. As you know I'm also a member of the House of Lords in London so I have a dual mandate. I would remind members that the EP's Rules of Procedure allow MPs from national parliaments to attend and speak at our committees, but of course not to vote. Few have yet done so - and none at all have come from Britain. Nor, I regret to tell you, has the House of Commons made any reciprocal arrangement for British MEPs to contribute their expertise to discussions at Westminster."

Chairman Chomik ignored the digression and made an announcement : "Dear colleagues. This is such an important topic that we shall hold a two-day Public Hearing in Brussels in mid-February. Witnesses will be invited from all corners of Europe. They will bring us evidence about the state of fascism in their part of our continent. Please suggest names of suitable witnesses whom we can invite, and give the names to the secretariat. We shall maintain a balance among invitees, between left and right, and between the different nationalities."

The discussion ended after an hour and Chomik moved to the next item on the agenda. Owen was left with a feeling of anxiety : so much to be done, little time to do it all, and some just wasted by irrelevant speeches.

Lars Anka caught his eye. Anka was a tall blonde Scandinavian who walked with a curious waddling gait. They left the committee room together. In the corridor outside, Lars said :

"Two things, Owen. If you decide to visit Sweden during your research, I can help you. I hate the Nazis, but through an unfortunate family connection which I did not like to mention in the committee, I could arrange for you to meet one of them in my country. When you hear his views at first hand, you won't like what he says, but it might be valuable for when you come to write your report."

"Lars, that's great. I'm off to Stockholm next week. Pietro Gatto will let you know where we're staying."

"The second thing is that, just as you English tell stories against the Irish, we Swedes joke about our neighbours the Norwegians. I have one for you."

Lars told his brief story[5] and looked at Owen quizzically. "Is that too horrible to be included ?" Owen shook his head ambiguously because he already had one anti-Norwegian story from an American friend.[6]

Back in his office Owen found that an e-mail had arrived from the parliament's office in London. They had identified the source of the anonymous fax as a main post-office where fax facilities were available to the public.

He read the threatening fax again. Had it come from a post office as a way of evading detection or did the sender not possess a fax machine of his own ? The five words gave no sign that the sender knew about his appointment as rapporteur. He seemed simply to be an aggressive Londoner who had taken the trouble to discover his personal number.

A shiver ran down his spine. He felt safe in his office, in a parliament dedicated to democracy, in a building protected by security guards. But outside he would be less safe and he must mention it to his local police.

Seeking reassurance and wishing he had a treacle toffee, he telephoned Nina's cottage. She had asked him never to phone her at the bank. Her answerphone was switched on : 'Sorry to miss you. Leave a message and I'll call you back straightaway. Beep coming.'

He asked what was she doing at the coming weekend.

The following afternoon, Thursday, he attended his parliamentary delegation which was preparing to receive a delegation from the Knesset, then took the train back to London. There had been no reply from Nina.

* * *

It was Saturday morning and surgery time again. Owen's first caller was an old man in his eighties. Having shown him carefully to a chair, Rosemary gave him a cup of tea with two sugars and Owen asked how he could help. The old man replied apprehensively :

"I married very young in 1941. For most of the war I was in the army. While I was away a stray bomb hit the town and my lovely young wife was killed. When I came home nobody could tell me where she was buried. Many of the bomb's victims were placed in a common grave just outside the town. I didn't pursue it and never married again. Now, before I go myself, I want to know..."

His voice gave way as he wiped tears from his eyes. Owen understood ; he wanted to discover where his young wife lay, to be able to lie beside her for eternity. The old soldier went on :

"The Town Hall says they don't have a list of the people who were interred there. My local councillor said that was the answer so he couldn't help me. I asked Sir Harry, our local MP, but he wasn't interested. So I'm appealing to you for justice. Europe is my last hope."

Owen felt full of sympathy. The old man could not be expected to know the niceties of who was responsible for which policy. He explained, carefully, that the problem, although a very important one, had nothing to do with Europe. There was nobody in Brussels who could provide a list of names buried in the grave. Nor could anybody in Brussels force the town hall into action.

"I'll write to Sir Harry at the Commons and plead with him to take up your case" Owen promised.

After the surgery was finished, he bought a bouquet of flowers and rode his Suzuki to Nina's village. If she was there he would knock on her door. But her garage was empty and no lights were burning in her cottage. He rode on, and surprised his parents by joining them for supper in front of their television.

Next morning, Sunday, he met Jack Terrier in the pub. They took their pints to a corner where Jack listened to Owen's plans about the rapporteurship. Unexpectedly, since he had earlier advised in favour, Jack was critical.

"Writing a report about fascism is a .waste of your precious time, Owen, with the election so near. England is a green and pleasant land and there's none of that stuff here. What the other countries do is their own business. You must concentrate on being selected. You know that it's going to be hard. Selections and elections are won or lost before the campaign starts, by good spade work and careful preparation. For the life of me I can't see how this report will help you to achieve that."

Returning home, Owen reflected on the duality of political life : party activists saw priorities as straightforward and black-or-white ; but in parliament, where nobody gets all of their own way, life was about juggling options and making compromises. No wonder politicians earned the reputation of being two-faced. As the Labour MP Jimmy Maxton had said many years ago, 'If you can't ride two horses at the same time, you shouldn't be in the bloody circus.'

He left an affectionate but impatient message on Nina's answerphone, asking for a call back, and set off for a long walk by himself in the countryside. When he returned there was a reply from Nina who had milked her machine.

"Sorry darling. It's my fault. I'm visiting my grandmother in Glasgow. She's not at all well. And I've had to bring work from the office ; you know how hard it is with my pea-brain. Ring me in a week and we'll have a talk. Must rush now. Lots of love."

At least she had rung. But something jarred. He had noticed that people who wished to deceive tended to pile excuse upon excuse, giving more than one reason in an anxiety to convince. Those who had only the truth to tell usually gave a simple explanation of what had happened to them.

Nina's two excuses had been her sick grandmother and volume of work. If she was with her grandmother surely she could have found a moment to telephone him ? And why had she said it was her fault?

Despite her attractiveness, she suffered from low self-esteem : more than once, he had asked her not to call herself 'pea-brain'. He suspected that one way she countered her low-esteem was passion. But sex was fleeting and, to regain the feeling, it had to be sought again and again. Did she subconsciously feel that his endless travelling was him abandoning her ? Was she taking out 'insurance'? Or was there somebody else ? Again ?

*   *   *

On Monday Owen took the Underground to Saint James's Park station. He crossed Petty France to a huge concrete fortress-like building opposite which houses the Home Office.

Pushing through the swing-doors, a sign warned him that 'The Current State of Alert in this Building is Black'. A receptionist asked for his name and checked it against her list. He was directed through two security checks and asked to wait.

He sat on the edge of an uncomfortable chair and mused about the curiosity that, in Britain, a Secretary of State ranks higher than a Minister, whereas on the continent a Minister outranks a Secretary of State. He decided, exactly as Shakespeare had written of roses, that ministers probably smelled the same whatever they were called.

After ten minutes a young man in a dark suit appeared, holding out his hand in greeting.

"Hello, I'm Toby Beaver. I'm the Home Secretary's Special Advisor. I work in his Private Office and assist him with party political matters, whereas official government business is managed by his team of civil servants."

Owen had heard something of Beaver. He was known as a clever speech-writer and researcher. All senior ministers had personal assistants like him : their salaries were paid by the party and not by the government. If they were loyal to their masters, and shone in their work, a political fast-track lay ahead of them.

Beaver led the way to an elevator which carried them up several floors. He steered Owen through a dark polished door, past several secretaries sitting at desks, and through another door into a large office. The near end of the room was furnished with a sofa and comfortable chairs : at the far end was a large desk, behind which was sitting Her Majesty's Secretary of State for Home Affairs, the Right Honourable Sir David Bronwen MP PC.

Owen had been looking forward to his first meeting with this legend in the Radical party. Sir David Bronwen had served in parliament for over thirty years. Entering the room Owen saw a man in his mid-sixties who appeared older. He had thinning white-yellow hair, yellow fingers, and was chain-smoking strong Benson & Hedges cigarettes. Last year he had recovered from a mild heart-attack and had announced that this was his final parliament. He would not be standing for election again.

Contrary to the stereotype of soft-hearted left-wing Radical ministers, Bronwen had built a reputation for toughness. He had built more prisons, and forced judges to pass longer sentences than his Progressive predecessor in office. Commentators thought he should have joined the Progressives not the Radicals. But he had not come from a privileged family background and was rumoured to have lost even his small life savings when some consortia in the Lloyds insurance market in London let down their investors in the 1980s and 1990s.

"Secretary of State, this is Owen Mann MEP" announced Beaver.

"Take a pew," said Bronwen smiling from behind his desk and waving Owen towards the sofa. The MEP did as he was asked and was surprised to find how far down he sank. Bronwen came over and settled on one of the armchairs beside the sofa : this gave him a strategic height advantage over his visitor. Beaver sat discreetly nearby with a notepad.

"I've got only a few minutes, I'm afraid" the legend apologised and pulled at his cigarette. No smoke was exhaled and Owen wondered what had happened to it. Bronwen continued : "You might wonder why I need to meet you at all, since MEPs have no jurisdiction over Home Office affairs. Matters such as policing and internal security are the responsibility of national governments, not of Brussels. To be brutal, I can't see why you're bothering to research and write this report. It seems to me a waste of time when you ought to be concentrating on your own re-election."

He stared severely at Owen for a moment. "But since you are doing it, it's important for us to compare notes. You and I may be the only Brits batting on this : you in the European Parliament, and I if it should happen to get as far as the Council of Ministers. We must sing the same song. A General Election is due soon, either before or after your own European election campaign. It's essential that there are no differences in public between Radical MEPs and Radical MPs."

"Now," he coughed, relenting with a smile like a break between dark clouds, "I accept that your report is going ahead, so tell me about it, and put your questions."

Owen drew a deep breath and plunged in. He did not expect Bronwen to reveal much that was new or interesting, but it was worth trying.

"Home Secretary, I'll start by asking how much fascism there is in Britain ?"

The reply was curt. "There is no fascism here except on a tiny fringe."

"But in the last General Election" Owen countered, "the British National Party put up more than fifty candidates. That qualified them for a free television broadcast which they used to link Black and Asian immigrants with crime. The Post Office distributed two million of their election leaflets free of charge. Surely all that free publicity must have had a significant influence on the public ?"

"Theoretically. But note how few votes they received. Only three of their fifty candidates saved their deposits i.e. obtained over five per cent of the votes cast in their constituency. Not a single one of them came remotely near to being elected. I assure you that the security services - who answer to me as you know - are on top of what is going on. I cannot tell you more than that. We operate on a 'need-to-know' basis and, I'm sorry Owen, you don't need to know." To soften the blow Bronwen added : "Backbench MPs in the Commons aren't told either."

The MEP tried again. "Why is the British National Party permitted to conduct a hate campaign against Muslims ?"

"Because our Race Relations Act protects ethnic but not religious groups."

"You can't agree with that surely ?"

Bronwen shrugged. The MEP continued : "British fascist organisers are low calibre and their branches are no more than drinking clubs for overweight middle-aged men who feel important by belonging to a gang. But their very existence suggests that we do have some determined British fascists. In particular there is a white group called *Combat 18*. The two digits in its name, one and eight, are said to symbolise Adolf Hitler's initials which are, of course, the first and eighth letters of the alphabet."

Bronwen's answer was crisp. "We know all about them. What are you getting at ?"

"They are said to have been behind the riot which caused a football match in Dublin to be cancelled between Ireland and England. And also a match in Rome, England against Italy, when there was open fighting on the terraces. Were the authorities in full control there ?"

Bronwen swatted the point aside. "If you look at what's happened to its leaders since those regrettable incidents, you'll see that we have them in a firm grip."

Gatto's briefing notes had given Owen a different story. During the 1980s, the British security services had monitored the activities of the Ulster loyalist paramilitaries in Northern Ireland but, curiously, not what they did in mainland Britain. Loyalist killer squads had started cooperating with fascists in England, running guns and selling drugs. To infiltrate the loyalists in Britain, the government's own secret services had invented Combat 18 as a front organisation. They had recruited known Nazis with booklets and phonecalls using their code-names taken from computers stolen from their offices.

Up and running, Combat 18 had forged links with the Ulster Loyalists and in this way loyalist activity in mainland Britain had been monitored. At the same time, a British MEP in the European

Parliament had joined the far-right MEP group, to his colleagues' astonishment because he was an able and likeable democrat.

Combat 18 had taken on a life of its own. It had expanded, beating up anti-Nazis in east London, fire-bombing left-wing bookshops, dealing in drugs, and drawing up hit lists of potential victims. The government decided that Combat 18 had gone too far, and tried to pull the plug on it, but had failed.

To test Gatto's story Owen asked Bronwen : "Was Combat 18 a honey-trap set up by the British secret service ?" He intended to follow up with a question about why the secret service had been allowed to spend tax-payers' money on publishing violent racist bile, but feared that would over-antagonise Bronwen. He ended his question with : "If Combat 18 was really run by your ministry, that would confirm that there are few genuine fascists in Britain."

"Your suggestion is both nonsense and offensive."

Astonished, Owen brought out his evidence. "It wasn't nonsense according to one active fascist who said recently, and I quote :

> 'Two years ago things looked really good. We had control of the vast majority of Britain's Nazi and fascist right, we ran the music scene, we were in close contact with our comrades in the Ulster paramilitaries and money was pouring in. We had three sections operating, C18, the NSA, and Blood & Honour. Our international links were strong with the top continental Nazis. Now we are in a shambolic state and our international links are with the nobodies.'

Bronwen shrugged. "Where did you find that ?"

"In *Searchlight*, a monthly magazine which monitors fascism in Britain."

Bronwen shrugged again. Owen tried a new angle of attack : "Why do you still maintain controls on EU citizens at British borders ?"

Bronwen scratched his head. "The reason is 'because we still can.' We live on an island so it's easier for us to defend our natural frontiers than it is for people who live on the continent and have land borders. When the EU expands to take in new countries, we doubt that their eastern border controls will be good enough to block millions of Asians wanting to come in and share our prosperity. And, if we drop controls, we will have to introduce identity cards and that might not be popular."

"But it means that we cannot have high-speed EuroStar trains running from anywhere but London."

"Why not ?"

"Because, Home Secretary, passport and customs controls would have to be constructed at each railway station where people boarded the trains."

"That is a price we pay for keeping Britain's borders safe."

"But Britain is riddled with drugs so our conventional border controls are not effective. Eighty per cent of heroin imports are brought in by Turkish gangs in London, and the market in crack cocaine is dominated by Caribbean-based groups."

Bronwen's answer was deadbat : "Our border controls prevent even more drugs from getting in."

"Surely, using customs officers to make random searches at frontiers is an inefficient use of resources. Successful busts against serious smuggling are invariably the result of shared intelligence with other police forces. Isn't the real problem that Customs & Excise is afraid of job losses ?" Owen threw in one of his few trump cards, "And at least one senior official in the Customs service is an active member of the BNP ?"

"My expert advisers tell me otherwise."

From the corner of his eye Owen saw Toby Beaver incline his wristwatch towards Bronwen, indicating that Owen's time was up. Owen followed up his question ; "Isn't keeping our border controls really about controlling immigration into Britain ?"

Bronwen nodded, showing irritation for the first time. "Race relations in Britain are excellent and our border controls are essential for maintaining them. I don't want to see the National Front here winning fifteen per cent of the vote, as they have in France. The National Front in Britain had its peak membership in the 1970s when it had seventeen thousand members following Enoch Powell's speech in 1968 about 'rivers foaming with blood'."

"Was that when the opposition leader made a statement about the

British being 'really rather afraid that this country might be swamped by people with a different culture' ?"

"That was later, in a 'World In Action' television interview on 27th January 1978. That leader went on to say : 'People are going to react and be rather hostile to those coming in.'

"Astonishing."

"Owen, the point to grasp is that today we have no fascist MPs in Britain."

"That is because our first-past-the-post voting system for Westminster doesn't allow small parties a look-in, British fascists and communists have to infiltrate the large parties instead."

The cabinet minister ignored the offensive implication, that fascists or communists might have wormed into the Radical or Progressive parties. He leaned towards Owen :

"I've little time left, and I'd like to ask you one question. What else are you doing in your investigation ?"

Owen wondered whether he should give a full answer. Bronwen had given away nothing. Any information which he gave to Bronwen might be used to rubbish him in a newspaper as an example of wastefulness by MEPs. He agreed with attacking waste but preferred that his own work was not the target. But Bronwen and he were members of the same party, so it would be discourteous to withhold the information.

"I've appointments with several MEPs, including Rocher, the leader of France's National Front. And I'm off to Norway and Sweden next week."

Bronwen stood up and held out his hand to indicate the interview was over.

"Good luck ! Toby will go through any other details with you outside." Bronwen walked back to his desk at the far end of the room.

On the way to the elevator, Owen asked Beaver whether he could return later if he had further questions.

Beaver replied cheerfully : "Of course, but I'm uncertain what else, if anything, Sir David wants me to reveal."

As he left the building, Owen thought to himself : 'Nothing learned there, except that there is more potential for fascism in Britain than I thought - if the fascists ever get themselves organised and if our voting system changes. Hopefully I'll find out more in Oslo the day after tomorrow.'

* * *

He still had two hours in hand before his train was due to leave Waterloo international station for Brussels. At a newsagent in Petty France he asked for treacle toffees, unsuccessfully. He strolled in the sunshine towards Parliament Square. He passed Westminster Abbey, crossed Saint Margaret Street and stopped at Saint Stephen's entrance, the public's entry into the House of Commons.

He slipped his MEP pass-on-a-chain around his neck. Issued by the police it bore his photograph and allowed him to bypass the security checks and to walk straight through to the Central Lobby. Its usefulness stopped there because it did not allow him to buy a cup of tea in a Commons cafeteria or an alcoholic drink for an MP, or to use the library, or even to park his motorbike.

But bypassing the queue of waiting tourists was something good. For their first ten years Britain's MEPs had been denied even this tiny privilege. While MPs' unpaid American research students had been given free access, tourists and MEPs had been searched by the police for concealed weapons and bombs.

To try to improve access, Radical MEPs had asked Radical MPs about arranging easier access along the lines of American students. They had been assured that it was desirable but a constitutional point to which all-party agreement was necessary, and unfortunately the Progressive party was blocking it. Progressive MEPs asked their MPs and were told that it was the Radicals who were the problem. The truth was never known. A decade later a pass for MEPs, but only into the Central Lobby, was provided.

Owen reached the high-domed circular Central Lobby with its watchful policemen, waiting visitors, and exits to the four points of the compass. He filled in a form to see an MP and left it with a policeman at a desk, then turned sharp left through a narrow arch and climbed some ancient winding stone stairs. Reaching the Strangers Gallery, he was greeted silently but cheerfully by a senior usher named Milburn who lived in his Euro-constituency. He squeezed onto one of the narrow benches to listen to whatever debate was in progress in the Commons chamber.

Down below, only a dozen MPs were present on the green leather benches. The press gallery was empty. There was a short ceremony when a new MP, winner of a by-election, swore an oath of loyalty to the monarch. Owen believed, as an MEP who did not have to swear anything, that it should have been loyalty to his constituents.

A debate began which concerned a new European Regulation which had arrived from Brussels. Owen tried to listen to the speeches but his thoughts wandered. Into his mind came an analogy of a cage at the zoo where each inhabitant knew its place relative to the others. Those who wanted to cause trouble sat at the front closest to their enemies. Those who wanted to show loyalty to their leaders sat behind them. Those uncertain of their views sat at the back.

Owen studied the wording of the motion under debate : 'The House *took note* of the regulation from Brussels'. The words *took note*, as opposed to *approved* or *enacted*, meant that MPs had no power to change any aspect of the new European law. MPs could only take note and rubber-stamp it into British law, while British ministers surreptitiously 'gold-plated' it by adding extra regulations of their own., often making industry less competitive.

MPs had surrendered the power to reject or amend a European law as long ago as 1973 when the United Kingdom had joined the EU. MPs had voted to give total power to ministers to go to Brussels and make a legally binding commitment on behalf of Britain. The commitment was irrevocable without any right of amendment afterwards by Commons backbenchers. If MPs disliked what their minister had done they could force him to resign, but they could not reject the legally-binding agreement which he had made.

The only value of the debate which Owen was watching was theatre, a play to convince the public that MPs were still in control of Brussels laws as well as what happened inside Britain. Typical of the British love of continuing old ceremonies, thought Owen, when some powers had evaporated.

Suddenly Owen sat up with a spark of interest. In the chamber below the next MP called to speak was Sir Harry Pedreven. He was a senior Progressive backbencher who represented a corner of Owen's Euro-constituency. They had met once and briefly. Pedreven was about sixty and seriously overweight. He considered he should have held government office but had never done so.

But he was a skilful speaker. He said that the debate was futile and therefore the full sovereignty of the Commons must be clawed back from Brussels.

Owen agreed with him that no more powers should be transferred to Brussels without powerful reasons why. But it was absurd to ask for powers to be clawed back from the EU : that would break up the level-playing-field of the Single Market from which the British benefited, as major exporters.

Pedreven finished with a complaint about continentals ignoring EU laws. He asked fiercely why the Commission in Brussels did so little about it but omitted to mention 'gold-plating' by the Commons.

Owen wished that Pedreven had mentioned that MPs and MEPs ought to be working together, as allies not as rivals, to control their respective executives. In this he believed the Commons compared badly with most continental parliaments. Access for MEPs to the Commons was made difficult and the Progressive party's 'bonding' sessions for all its MPs included only three token MEPs.

By contrast, in Copenhagen, the Market Committee of the Folketing, made up of Danish backbench MPs, set limits beyond which a Danish minister in Brussels could not commit Denmark. In the Bundestag in Berlin, German MEPs were provided with offices, alongside German MPs. In the Greek parliament there was a joint-committee of MPs and MEPs to debate Greece's interests.

The Dutch parliament's upper house obliged Dutch ministers to consult it at least a fortnight in advance before agreeing to any new EU laws. When Owen had visited its debating chamber he had enjoyed the chamber's decoration. It was painted to appear like the inside of a castle. Near the ceiling the ambassadors of the world looked in over the battlements. Only one was trying to climb in : he was from London.

After the knight of the shire had finished his speech, Owen left the gallery. It was four o'clock, time for a drink with Adam Drake, a friendly Radical MP, whom he had asked to meet.

He returned carefully down the winding stairs to the Central Lobby and sat on a bench to wait. Moments later Adam Drake arrived from the direction of the chamber carrying a file of papers..

"Let's get a drink in the Strangers Bar" said Adam. "It's too cold to go outside on the Terrace." Owen was disappointed because sitting on the terrace beside the river Thames provided one of the most attractive views in the world.

Drake bought two beers and they settled into armchairs. A letter dropped out of the folder. The MP showed it to Owen : "I've been having an acrimonious correspondence with a difficult constituent. His latest letter says that if I am not polite to him he will not write to me any more."

Owen laughed and mentioned the debate to which he had been listening. "Why," he asked, "do MPs like Pedreven insist that the traditional powers of the Commons are sacrosanct when the world outside is changing so rapidly ?"

"It may be partly the mountaineer George Mallory's immortal reply about why he climbed Mount Everest, 'Because it's there'. This place once controlled the world's greatest empire and its powerful sense of history grips all MPs. They struggle to get here and hate to discover it's only the centre of an offshore island and that powers are slipping away."

Adam sipped his beer : "And partly it's caution and inertia, sticking to the way we've always done things. For example, last autumn, I was abroad with a delegation in China, but I was forced by our Whips to fly back to vote on the Dog Registration bill. We won with a majority of forty-three. I returned to China but it was difficult to explain why to the Chinese."

"Being in the Commons now is like driving a beautiful car at night without lights. It's fun but we have no idea what is going on outside."

"While the world outside is changing rapidly."

"Our problem is that we prefers to manage changes gradually" the MP continued. "The most successful policies are those pushed through slowly without causing noticeable pain to the public. Like Huxley's experiment with a frog."

"With a Frenchman ?"

"No, with a cold-blooded amphibian."

"Are you sure you don't mean a Frenchman ?" joked Owen.

"I mean something you find in a pond. Huxley wanted to measure the highest water temperature which a frog would endure. He put it into a saucer of water, raised the temperature by half a degree each day, and waited for it to jump out. Eventually the frog was cooked *alive.*"

"Why ?"

"Probably because it could never be bothered to jump out."

"The UK is exceptionally slow to recognise change" nodded Owen. "I believe we could have had the powerful European Central Bank in the City of London instead of in Frankfurt where it is. But there was no sign that our rulers at the time wanted it, and apparently they chose to host a lesser European bank, either out of scepticism that the Euro currency would fail, or fear that it would succeed and drag us in."

"We got the BERD ?"

"Yes, the Bank for Economic Reconstruction and Development in Eastern Europe."

"You believe that we threw the Central Bank away ?" asked Adam.

"What EU institution did Britain get instead ? Just the EU agency in Canary Wharf which monitors the safety of new pharmaceuticals."

"That one choice does not say much for your overall argument that Britain is lethargic in recognising change."

"There are many other examples" sighed Owen. "Our past leaders resisted joining the Common Market in 1956 and even the first European-wide soccer competitions in the 1950s. Earlier still they resisted rearmament against Hitler in the 1930s. Back in 1583, the mathematician John Dee tried to persuade the English government to change from the Julian to the Gregorian calendar, but the idea was resisted until a hundred and seventy years after the rest of Europe. And we British celebrate William Caxton for setting up his first printing-press in Westminster. Yet, when he started, printing-presses were already working in seventy cities in eight continental countries, led by Gutenberg who had started in Mainz forty years before."

Owen drained his glass. "Adam, our problem goes even deeper. The continentals have noticed that, despite always dragging our feet, we

British always join everything eventually. So they go ahead without us, write the rules to suit themselves, leaving us to join afterwards and complain that we don't like it. We give ourselves the worst of all worlds. Pathetic, isn't it ?"

"It's a different world out there in the EU," agreed Adam. "Here in the Commons the government with its majority expects to get its way and win everything. MPs here have not yet learned how to play the compromise game, which you must in international politics where everyone is a minority player."

"I shan't forget a remark made to me here by one nationalist MP" reflected Owen. He said 'I'm against your MEP parliament, Owen. But if I had a son, I'd advise him to go there and not to the Commons. The European Parliament is tomorrow's parliament.'"

As Owen stood up, he asked whether Adam could get him a ticket to watch Prime Minister's Questions on a Wednesday sometime during the spring when he was in London.

"No problem. Just ring my secretary" was the helpful reply.

Walking back through Central Lobby, Owen saw Murdo McKirk deep in conversation with a Progressive backbencher. McKirk, with his sensitive political antennae, spotted Owen and called out :

"Owen ! I'll be in Strasbourg in a couple of weeks' time. Shall we have a drink together ?"

Owen headed outside to fresh air and Waterloo station.

* * *

In her office in Sãta's building beside the gorge, Monika Pasarea checked her electronic mail, as she did several times per day. Several new messages had appeared, including one which mentioned Stockholm and a date. She wrote a note in her desk diary, deleted the e-mail, and picked up the telephone.

* * *

Next morning, Tuesday, Owen joined the Socialist Group meeting in Brussels. Its working-groups were scrutinising each report which would be debated at next week's plenary session in Strasbourg.

Owen sat at the back and took no active part. Instead he planned the interviews that lay ahead.

In the afternoon he and Pietro Gatto flew to Norway's capital Oslo.

They arrived in darkness and snow. A taxi took them to a hotel in the city centre in Radhusplassen where Pietro had booked rooms. Next morning Owen looked out of his room's window, and saw the edge of a fjord and the unusual view at the heart of a capital city of sailing boats, ferries, and oil-rigs under construction.

After breakfast two Norwegian journalists arrived at the hotel to meet them. Removing thick coats and snowboots they introduced themselves as Ingrid Reindyr and Jens Snomann. The four settled in the hotel's coffee-shop around a corner table with a jug of strong coffee and a plate of sweet Norwegian biscuits.

Jens, who had a pale face and white hair, opened the discussion. "A hearty welcome to Norway. Please explain to us the purpose of your visit. We would like to help you the most possible."

Owen explained the research, then asked : "Could you start by telling us how much fascism there is in Norway ?"

Ingrid rubbed her nose, frozen by the extreme cold outside, and replied : "You remember that Norway has held two referendums about whether to join the EU ?"

Owen nodded. "Both times, in 1972 and in 1994, you Norwegians voted 'No' by a narrow majority. Why ?"

"One reason was our imagined fear of Brussels getting its hands on our oil and our fish. But another reason was the Norwegian dislike of foreigners. In this country the immigrants are mainly from Pakistan and Vietnam, and our people fear them."

"Again, why ?" asked Owen.

"Because" answered Jens, "second and third-generation immigrants have failed to merge into our Norwegian way-of-life. Our right-wing politicians take advantage of these negative feelings by whipping up hatred against the immigrants. So, yes, we certainly have fascists in Norway."

"Do the right-wing cause much trouble ?"

"Our authorities are very firm with them. The best-known example was a year ago when there was a big Nazi gathering here in Oslo. The police surrounded their building, forced all the Nazis to come outside, and spread-eagled them face-down on the pavement, stretched out neatly side-by-side. It caused a lot of laughter with the public and was a great humiliation to the fascists."

"Did that deter them ?"

"Unfortunately not. Their gangs now attack immigrant schools, armed with steel chains and canisters of tear-gas. They daub the school buildings with racist slogans."

Ingrid chipped in. "There are several separate far-right parties and they hate eachother. One runs a mail-order empire and is one of the world's biggest distributors of Nazi rock CDs."

"Another is the awful White Electoral Alliance party," added Jens.

"How are they awful ?" interrupted Pietro.

"They call for sterilisation of immigrants and of Third World children who have been adopted by Norwegians. Their revolting slogan is 'Repatriate and Sterilise !'"

Owen felt deeply disgusted but asked calmly : "Do fascists stand as candidates in your elections ?"

"Yes and successfully," replied Ingrid. "In our General Election five years ago the right-wing Fatherland party campaigned for tighter curbs against immigration and refugees. It took one in eight of all votes and won 22 seats out of 165 in the Storting, our parliament. They held the balance of power. In our recent election a French racist came here and was interviewed on television the night before we voted. He expressed warm feelings for the leading far-right party. Next day it won 15% of the votes, won 25 seats, and became the second largest in parliament. Right-wing feelings are growing in Norway. But they weaken their power by fighting among themselves."

Jens and Ingrid stayed to talk until midday. They photographed Owen and Pietro for their newspaper and returned to their office.

"If we can help you some more, just let us know !" said Ingrid Reindyr with a warm smile, her nose now glowing red.

Owen and Pietro wrote up their notes over lunch in the hotel. They concluded that Norway's fascists were extremely unpleasant, that they were making headway in elections but, due to their own divisions, they were less effective than they might be.

There was spare time before the evening flight to Stockholm. Pietro chose to visit a museum of Edvard Munch's paintings where he hoped to see the famous 'Scream'. Owen preferred the Viking Ship Museum where he gazed in awe at a restored black longboat. If today's fascists were as fierce as the raiding warriors of a thousand years ago, he hoped never to encounter them.

They met up at Oslo airport for the flight to Sweden. As a travelling companion Owen found Pietro to be excellent company. Pietro described his home in south-west Austria at a town called Klagenfurt not far from the Italian border. Famous for its statue of a green dragon in the marketplace, Klagenfurt lay at the foot of Austria's highest mountain, the Gross Glockner, and beside a beautiful inland lake called the Würtersee. His parents and unmarried twin sister still lived there.

His education had been in the classics and he enjoyed music. He told what Owen thought was a rather good musical joke[7] and which he made a mental note to add to his book.

Their plane landed punctually at Stockholm's Arlanda airport, amid pine forests forty kilometres outside the city. Because they were re-entering the EU, Owen showed his blue MEP laissez-passer to the airport official instead of his red British passport.

"An honour to meet you, sir" said the border guard, slightly bowing his head. It made a stark contrast with the time Owen had returned to Dover from Calais before Christmas. The British official, possibly seeing a laissez-passer for the first time, had asked aggressively : "What is this, and how long do you intend to remain in Britain ?" Owen had explained his job and added that passports might one day be unnecessary inside the EU, to which the grumpy official had replied : "I hope I'll be retired by then."

They changed money into Swedish crowns. Pietro commented on how much easier it would be if Sweden joined the Euro - instead of having to pay commission to a bank and worry about exchange rate fluctuations. Hopefully Sweden and the UK would join one day, he said.

Over dinner in the city-centre Pietro briefed Owen about the Swedish Nazi situation.

Next morning although it was cold they left their hotel on foot. With their destination nearby, they walked briskly through the snow and soon reached a solid modern block. Inside, a receptionist directed them downstairs to the basement office of *EXPO* magazine.

Two women welcomed them warmly. The elder, Agneta Kanin, had prominent buck-teeth : the other, Carlotta Glop, was an enthusiastic youngster with chin-hugging blond hair. They settled their two visitors into comfortable chairs in Agneta's snug office and Carlotta fetched mugs of strong coffee.

Agneta explained to Owen that EXPO magazine monitored the activities of fascists in Sweden. She outlined the latest position. "Nazis in Sweden are among the best organised in Europe. They have about three thousand skinhead followers and are big producers of hate music. Last year they staged seventy rock concerts and marketed thirty new CDs. You can even buy skinhead dolls in our shops."

The strength of the right-wing surprised Owen. "Why are Swedish Nazis more successful here than in other Scandinavian countries ?"

"It's due to the embarrassing part of Sweden's recent history," replied Agneta. "During the Second World War, unlike Norway and Denmark, Sweden was neutral. Our Nazis have never experienced the feeling of defeat."

Carlotta added "Also Sweden has a liberal attitude towards immigrants and refugees and this creates hatred in some quarters."

Pietro had briefed Owen that EXPO magazine had become famous two years ago. Owen asked for details.

Agneta instinctively lowered her voice : "Our magazine campaigns against the far right - just as Searchlight does in Britain. Our Nazis failed to defeat us, so they tried a despicable new tactic."

She folded her arms defensively. "The fascists chose a small newsagent shop. They smashed its windows and warned the owner not to stock our magazine. They repeated their attacks against other small shops. In this way they set out to destroy our sales, a typical example of Nazi censorship."

Owen's mind began to wander while Pietro took notes. Fascists were merging into a nightmarish crowd in his head.

"Why didn't they attack your own offices here ?" Pietro took over the questioning.

"Because we are in a basement without windows, as you can see."

"Did they give up ?"

"No, they escalated. They daubed café windows with slogans such as 'No support for EXPO'. They sent masked hit-squads on night attacks against the youth headquarters of the main political parties. Boneheads visited news-stands and told them, if they continued to stock EXPO, they would be vandalised, not once but again and again. And they hit at our printers."

Carlotta picked up the story. "So we went public. A national daily newspaper, actually the highest-selling one in Sweden, printed our story and a wonderful thing happened. Our circulation leapt from our usual three thousand a month to an incredible three-quarters of a million. Now it's fallen back to a more realistic level."

"And the Nazis have quietened down ?"

"Not at all" said Agneta. "But they fight among themselves. You're here at an interesting time. Each year Swedish Nazis parade through the streets of Stockholm. They claim to be commemorating our eighteenth century warrior king, Karl the Twelfth."

Carlotta broke in. "If you saw the parade you'd realise that some of them are not too bright, like the leader of the Sweden Party."

Seeing the visitors did not recognise the reference she explained : "Last year he tried to light a cigarette in a hamburger restaurant using the fifty-thousand volt stun gun which he carried."

"And ?"

"He was arrested for carrying an illegal weapon."

The four left the office together and walked to a cobbled medieval street in Gamla Stan, the oldest part of the city, where they lunched. Owen had not been to Stockholm before, and was very attracted by its many old buildings, bridges, and stretches of water.

After an excellent meal and more talk the visitors thanked their hosts and returned to the hotel to collect their suitcases. There was a message for Owen which asked him to telephone a man called Anders Groda on a local number.

Owen used his mobile phone from the hotel lobby. A woman's voice answered against a background of heavy music. She understood English and called out for Groda.

After a pause, a suspicious male voice said : “Groda. Who’s this ?”

“Owen Mann from the European Parliament.”

“Herr Mann ? Good. I’m Anders Groda. Your colleague in the parliament Mr. Anka asked me to call you. He said you might like to hear about my political ideas.”

“I’d be very interested. Is it possible to meet you today ?”

“You could come to the bar where I am right now”

Owen promised they would be there in an hour. Pietro said he would not stay long. He had to leave for the airport to be back at the parliament for his other duties ; he tried to be conscientious, he said.

Owen felt that it was not worth his returning to Brussels for the tail-end of an uninteresting Group Meeting. Not knowing Sweden, he decided he would stay for an extra day on his own.

They drafted a press release together which Gatto would send to the Brussels press crops including McKirk, and to Owen’s local papers.

They took a taxi from the hotel. Its driver was a cheerful woman who practised her English on them. As they neared the bar, she fell silent. She pulled up outside and, after being paid, gave them a look of scorn.

The entrance to the bar was down a scruffy flight of stairs and into a cellar. It was dimly lit. In one corner they saw six burly young men with cropped hair talking noisily round a table which was stocked with empty beer bottles. In another corner a man and a woman were sitting in silence.

The man stared at Owen’s suit and scowled. He stood up, and came towards them. Aged about thirty, he was wearing black jeans and a leather jacket ; his hair was fair and cropped, and his eyes protruded slightly.

“Mr Mann ? I’m Anders Groda. Come and sit here.”

He led them back to his corner table and introduced the woman. “This is my girl friend, Monika Pasarea. She’s not with our party so probably won’t say much.” The woman was wearing a white tee-shirt and blue jeans, and her burnished dark blonde hair was tied up in a tight bun. Her face was mouse-like with high cheekbones and full lips.

They all shook hands. As he sat down Owen felt conspicuous in his suit and loosened his tie. A stocky waitress appeared beside the table and took their orders - three beers and a fizzy orangeade for the girl.

Owen invited Anders Groda to explain how he had become involved with his political movement.

"Maybe you won't like it or maybe you will" the Swede replied with a hopeful smile. "As a teenager I got into a few fights. I went to football matches where I made some friends. We had a good time showing other supporters we were the boss. My friends introduced me to their rock music which is really great. We went on marches together, like the Hess march in Denmark where I met people from other countries including some from your British 'Combat 18'. Maybe you know them ?"

Owen shook his head. "The marchers were fascists ?"

Groda's face showed strong irritation. "We are not fascists. Our enemies give us that bad label."

"What are you ?"

"We are nationalists."

His girlfriend Monika had not spoken. She was examining her finger-nails and appeared to be bored. Owen glanced at her. She yawned, stretching her arms back over her head. Owen noticed her small breasts which protruded against her tee-shirt.

He turned to Groda. "Did your movement place the bombs which stopped the Olympic Games from coming to Sweden ?"

"No, my group is not violent. There are other, despicable, organisations in Sweden with whom we do not work. The Aryan Brotherhood is a Nazi prisoners group. The National Socialist Front are Combat 18's errand boys. Nordland is a music publishing operation. Maybe you should speak to them."

"Tell us what your party's policies are."

Groda expanded on his movement's highly offensive views on immigrants, gypsies, and homosexuals. He described their 'Race Soul' concept, that the Swedish nation is bound together by blood and soil. He thought that the Russians were Europe's natural allies because they were more racially pure than the Americans.

Encouraged by their attentiveness Groda described the strategy of 'leaderless resistance' which was being adopted by a rival group, the White Aryan Resistance :

"'Leaderless resistance' was devised by the Klu Klux Klan in America. Cells of freedom-fighters, usually very small or even one-person, operate independently. Nobody gives them orders or advice."

Pietro nodded, unsuccessfully concealing his distaste : "The concept was developed by Josef Goebbels in Germany near the end of World War Two. He called it his 'Werewolf' resistance operation. His goal was to continue killing the enemy after the war had been lost. Leaderless werewolves were to deliver Nazi revenge by assassination."

Owen had heard enough. He was disgusted but remembered where he was sitting. "Don't you realise where this leads to ?" he asked Groda angrily. "Back to the 1930s."

Groda shrugged and did not answer. Gatto stared at his watch and excused himself. He must leave immediately for the airport to catch his plane, he said.

Groda decided that he too had spent long enough with the visitors. They had listened but had not been converted to his thinking.

"I also have to leave" he said. "Monika, are you ready ?"

To Groda's obvious surprise, Monika replied "Anders, I have nothing else to do till later."

She looked straight at Owen. "Mr. Mann, would you like to have one more drink ? I could tell you what to see in Sweden rather than discuss politics."

Something interested Owen. Having no other appointment he accepted her offer. Gatto departed in a taxi, Groda on foot.

The bar had filled up while they talked. The heavy beating music had been replaced by the melodic strains of an accordion. Owen tucked his notebook into his briefcase, took off his tie, and allowed his glass to be refilled.

"Work is over for the day" Monika suggested. "Will you have time for sightseeing in Stockholm ?"

He nodded. Despite the surroundings Monika was very pleasant to talk with. She suggested places which he ought to visit. She asked about him and about his investigation. Warming to her interest, Owen described his plans and the Public Hearing which would be held in Brussels in the middle of February.

Monika was a good listener. Owen sensed a rapport grow between them although he was keeping up his guard.

He asked about her. "What do you do ? Are you a student ?"

"No" she laughed. "I help to raise money for a private financial foundation. It makes me travel quite a lot."

Owen interrupted. "That phrase rings a bell. Sometimes I get tired of explaining to people what a Euro-MP does. Once at a party I replied defensively to somebody 'I travel a lot' and it worked like a charm. They thought I was a salesman and lost interest immediately." Monika laughed.

"If you don't mind, I prefer not to talk about my work either" she said.

"I won't ask" said Owen. "Monika, your English is so good but I can't identify your accent. You're not Swedish, are you ?"

She laughed. "Thanks for the compliment. I'm from what you would call Middle Europe. My mother was born in the Hungarian part of Romania but I grew up in America."

"Pasarea is a Romanian name ?"

"Can you guess what it means ?" she giggled.

"Beauty ?"

"You're very flattering. But no free compliments, please." She paused. "It means 'Bird'." She flapped her elbows as if she was dancing to the Birdie Song.

The bar was full now and people had started to sing. Neighbours at a long table invited Owen and Monika to link arms with them. Soon they were all standing on tables, swaying to the music and boisterously stamping their feet to the beat. To Owen's right was the stocky waitress, on his left the much softer Monika. She squeezed his arm. Despite her warmth and charm he felt increasingly uncomfortable.

His tension was caused, not by Monika, but by the heady feeling of camaraderie. Was this how it had felt in the beer-cellars of Austria and Germany before the Second World War ?

Having drunk more than several beers, he decided it was time to leave and said so to Monika. She did not press him to stay but signalled to the barman for a taxi. Owen offered to take her wherever she needed to go. However she replied, pulling on leather coat and gloves, that she would prefer to walk, not having far to go to meet Anders Groda.

"Thanks so much for the talk," he said, looking into her eyes. He liked her enormously but, as the girlfriend of an active fascist, she represented danger. "If there's anything more you can tell me for my research, will you let me know ?" he asked. He pulled a business card from his pocket and handed it to her.

She held his gaze and replied "Of course." She took his card but did not offer one of her own.

He tried once more. "Monika, I should be very glad if we meet again. If your travels bring you to Brussels or to England, will you let me know ? Is there an address or telephone number where I can reach you ?"

She ignored the question. Her eyes were warm but her voice cool. "It's been nice meeting you, Owen. Sleep well and goodbye."

Owen leaned forward and pecked her on the cheek. To his delight she responded lightly. The taxi took him back to his hotel. That night he slept soundly.

Next morning, as he sobered up, he felt silly : he had sung in a Nazi bar : he had failed to get a phone number from Monika : and his head was muzzy. But in the shower he started to sing.

The morning was fine but cold. After breakfast he followed Monika's advice and joined a guided boat-tour around Stockholm's harbour. He learned why the city is known as the Venice of the North with its archipelago and thousands of islands. The Vasa museum awed him ; a magnificent preservation of a fully-laden war-ship which had capsized in the harbour on its maiden-voyage in 1628 and had been raised intact in the 1960s.

For a late lunch he stopped in a café and enjoyed a smorgasbord sandwich of pickled and smoked fish. Continuing his walk he came to a park which seemed to be popular with the locals. Suddenly, a hundred or more men, marching four abreast and wearing uniforms, stomped into the park. Their flag identified them as the NSF, the National Socialist Front who, Owen remembered, were the allies of Combat-18. Most were young males and several carried swastika flags. They were led by a drummer.

People whom Owen had imagined to be mere passers-by started to throw bottles and stones, and to shout abuse. Four policemen arrived quickly and separated the groups but only after one of the uniformed men had kicked a woman bystander.

The Nazis marched out of the park. A jeering crowd of about fifty followed, mainly young anti-racists. Owen followed out of curiosity. The Nazis stopped at the Central railway station where one of them made a speech for fifteen minutes. Watching without understanding Owen asked his neighbour in the crowd what was being said. The man, pleased to show off a knowledge of English, gave a summary.

He said that the speaker was promising 'war against international monopoly capitalism and the Jewish world order of finance magnates'. His supporters were chanting 'Down with capitalism' and 'Smash democracy'.

Extra police had arrived but were watching from a distance. When the speaker finished, the senior policeman issued a warning that the meeting was illegal and asked them to leave.

The Nazis marched off in formation, now escorted by the police. They paraded through the Old Town and across the bridge into south Stockholm at which point Owen gave up his pursuit. He had not seen either Groda or Monika among the marchers.

He returned to his hotel, collected his suitcase and walked to the railway station. He took the high-speed X2000 train which carried him in four hours to the port of Malmo in southern Sweden. He slept in a hotel by the station.

Next morning he caught a hydrofoil ferry to Denmark because the new road bridge was not open. Forty-five minutes later he disembarked at Copenhagen.

It was another fine day for tourism. He visited the Carlsberg Glyptotek collection where he fell for Rodin's sculpture 'The Kiss'. In the Danish National Museum, he wandered into a room full of Viking tombstones. With Danish efficiency, cards had been pinned on the walls giving an English interpretation of each epitaph. One inscription in particular impressed him : '*Gunnulf lies here. Few are born as good as him any more.*' Like his report on fascism today, people a thousand years ago had been worrying about the future.

In the Tivoli Gardens he sat with a beer beneath a tree. He thought about Nina and Monika. Why was he unable to settle with the right woman ? If he loved Nina, why was he attracted to Monika, whom he had only just met ? They had enjoyed each other's company, but she spelled danger, and anyway had not wished to pursue the acquaintance.

He thought of a remark by the English language's greatest improviser and wit, Theodore Hook. "I once knew a lovely girl, all kindness, all gentleness, all goodness. From her I parted in the midst of gaiety, and in a crowd of idlers who were participating in it. We shook hands, and I left her. I never saw her again. Had I known that I then beheld her *for the last time*, my heart would have burst."

It was unlikely that he would meet Monika again, he realised.

After an early Saturday night in a comfortable small hotel he decided to pursue a suggestion which Gatto had made. He crossed on a ferry into north Germany, hired a car and drove fast along the autobahn eastwards towards Weimar.

Although he made good progress he was frequently overtaken. The high speed and aggression of the large Mercedes and BMWs astonished him. It felt to Owen like time for Germany to set a speed limit on its motorways. But he doubted that they ever would do so because they were the manufacturers of Europe's luxury cars. He did not want to see an identical speed-limit throughout the EU. Different maxima should continue to be set by the each member state. But a German limit of some kind would be welcome.

Approaching the city of Weimar he came to a small town called Buchenwald. He stopped outside the town and left his car in a car-park set among dense trees beside what appeared to be an old hunting lodge.

He walked through an archway and joined a visitors group with an English-speaking guide. They walked through an archway which appeared to be an old hunting lodge. It was actually the entrance to one of Hitler's concentration camps, open to the public to visit, and to leave.

The guide suggested they consider visiting the camp museum which contained lampshades made of human skin and shrunken skulls which had sat on officer's desks.

He followed the group across a large open square where thousands of Poles had been forced to live in tents through a bitter winter and most had died of starvation or cold. They came to a wooden hut where Polish officers had been taken one-at-a-time for a medical checkup ; each officer had stood to be measured with his back against a vertical ruler fixed to a wall. There was a small hole near the top of the ruler, through which each officer was shot through the back of the head. The body was moved immediately into a connecting hut where it was burned in gas ovens while the next officer arrived.

Owen felt profoundly upset. He trudged slowly back through the arch and found his car. It was deep winter but no doubt, when spring arrived, the birds in the trees would sing again, even here.

He drove west. By evening he reached the motorway south of Frankfurt and stopped at a roadside motel to sleep but found it was full. Driving on anxiously in the dark, he speculated what to do without a bed for the night. At the next motel he secured the last available room.

Trying to sleep, he looked forward to arriving in Strasbourg next morning. It was a pleasant city but an absurd waste to have to go there. It was ridiculous that the European Parliament was forced to divide its work between three different cities. Luxembourg hosted half the parliament's staff, mainly document-translators ; Brussels hosted committee meetings ; Strasbourg hosted twelve plenary sessions per year. The arrangement had not been made by MEPs who yearned to work in a single centre. It had been an absurd deal struck between countries acting selfishly and secretly in the Council of Ministers.

He had explained to Nina how it had happened. "In the 1960s, there was a small part-time European Parliament made up of a few national MPs. They debated with each other for a few days each month. Temporary facilities were offered by three cities. Later when the elected parliament acquired considerable size and power, no country would surrender its rights. At a summit of EU leaders the British proposed that the three-site arrangement be perpetuated and that Strasbourg be made the official seat of the parliament. It was extraordinary, coming from a party which prided itself on efficiency. Europe's taxpayers were condemned to waste at least fifty million pounds per year, moving staff and equipment to and fro, week after week.

Why had the British suggested it ? The meeting was in secret so nobody knew for sure. It was said to have been an inducement to the French to sign up to the Uruguay Round, the agreement to liberalise world trade. The French, very likely, would have signed anyway but this way they got Strasbourg written into the Amsterdam Treaty.

Some MEPs preferred to be in Strasbourg because it symbolised Franco-German reconciliation and because it gave the parliament a distinct identity separate from the bureaucrats of Brussels. But most MEPs were not taking the myopia of the national leaders lying down. Certainly the parliament had its offices in Luxembourg ; the names of its staff were visible on each office door. In practice however, many of them lived and worked in Brussels, and even drew extra allowances for technically having to live abroad... Owen fell asleep.

*　　*　　*

On Friday afternoon, while Owen was on the train to Malmo, his secretary Lynda Black drove to his home. She admired the snowdrops in his small front garden which were starting to bloom. She let herself into the house with the key which he had given her.

She gathered up the fifty letters which lay on the mat, three days of mail since Owen had left for Brussels. She sorted them into two heaps : white envelopes and brown packets. The white ones would be letters from individual constituents and they would receive priority from her.

The brown envelopes would be circulars and magazines, sent by commercial organisations who wanted to influence Owen's views.

Lynda put rubber bands round each heap and carefully locked up the house. She returned to her own home where she made a cup of tea then settled down to open the white envelopes. She subdivided the individual letters into two types. The larger pile was those to whom she could draft answers herself, needing only to ask Owen for a signature. The smaller pile was letters which Owen ought to see before she drafted a reply, and which she would discuss with him when he telephoned her from Strasbourg on Monday.

She smiled as she remembered the weak joke which he made when they first set up a filing system : "Let's label the separate files - constituency letters, Brussels letters, German letters, and, um, Letters from France." She had been amused to learn that the French returned the compliment, calling them *capots anglais*.

Next Lynda turned to the brown envelopes. One contained a video cassette, a method used by lobbyists to get their message across.

What message was being peddled this time, she wondered. She slid the cassette into her video-recorder and pressed the Start button. It was the last thing she remembered doing. There was a blinding flash and a violent explosion.

As the police inspector explained afterwards, a bomb had been concealed inside the cassette. It had been set to explode when played in a VCR, and had contained enough explosive to destroy the room and to kill the person watching it.

An ambulance rushed her barely alive to hospital. She had lost her left arm and, if she lived, would require extensive surgery to her face and upper torso. But she died three hours later.

The inspector told the press that in the recent past similar letter-bombs had been posted from Denmark to well-known people in Britain who were in mixed-race marriages. It was too soon to state from where this bomb had been posted.

*   *   *

In the building by the gorge, Sãta was reviewing the work of his three assistants. They were seated round his desk. He was puffing a cigar. "Monika, anything to tell us about the European Parliament's investigation ?"

Monika pushed her tresses over one shoulder and opened a thin folder. "Routine so far, president. The rapporteur - he's the MEP who leads the research - is an Englishman, politically on the moderate left. So far, he's visited Norway, Sweden, and a minister in his own country."

"Any action needed from us ?"

The other two assistants listened intently. Their futures were bound together.

"None yet. Last week I travelled to Stockholm to observe the rapporteur and I met him."

Sãta stiffened. "You met him ? Whom did he think you were ?"

"He wasn't aware of who I am" answered Monika. "A local nationalist called Anders Groda did the political talk."

Sãta puffed out smoke. "And your assessment of the rapporteur ?"

"He's conscientious and he's assisted by a bright Austrian staffer."

"Any vulnerability that we might be able to exploit ?"

"So far as influencing the content of his report, I believe neither of them would be amenable to a bribe."

She paused then added. "But we obtained this." She opened the folder and pushed a photograph across the desk to Sãta.

Sãta glanced at it then stared with fascination. It showed Owen standing on a table, arms linked with Monika and another woman, and a swastika flag behind them on the wall. He returned the photo to Monika who replaced it carefully in the folder.

"Excellent ! Continue the monitoring."

"President" she continued. "An important event is coming. There's to be a Public Hearing about nationalism in Brussels with witnesses coming from all over Europe. Each witness will describe the nationalist situation in their own country."

"When ?"

"Ten days from now, on the ninth and tenth of February."

"Somebody must be there" snapped Sãta. "Monika, you can't do it. I'll go myself."

* * *

Owen drove across the bridge over the river Rhine, over which the Germans had marched into France three times since 1870. Now there were no controls and he did not stop.

Minutes later he was in the centre of the city of Strasbourg. He drove to his usual hotel, the Nouvel, which despite its name was old. It was said to have been the Gestapo's headquarters during the Second World War. No German MEP stayed there.

He returned the hired car to the local depot and strolled along the river bank. He admired the hardiness of the swans and passed an open field where, stunningly, fifteen storks were grazing. After half an hour he reached the parliament at the eastern edge of the city. He entered the archway of the Tower block which contained the offices of the members. He crossed the black-and-white chequerboard courtyard which reminded him of a mediaeval Italian town square.

Inside the atmosphere was bustling as the first members and staff arrived to wake up the building which had been cocooned for a month since the December session. His office was on the tenth floor of the Tower : not large but with air-conditioning, a day-bed, a shower, a desk, and a pleasant view over the river with the Cathedral spire in the distance.

On his desk lay a folded note, marked 'Extremely Urgent'. It read : 'Please ring your local police in the UK, Beatrice.' Beatrice was an Italian staff member who worked for the Socialist Group.

The police told him about Lynda. They said they had been trying to contact him for two days and had been extremely concerned because nobody had known where he was. Could he come to see them as early as possible, to help their enquiries and to receive security advice ? The inquest would be opened tomorrow at midday.

Owen was devastated and agreed to return to England. "There's only one flight to London this evening. Would first thing tomorrow morning do ?" he asked.

"Where would you stay tonight, sir ? It'd be better if you didn't return to your home until we've talked to you."

"I'll find a hotel."

"Thankyou sir. See you in the morning."

Owen telephoned the office of the Group's Chief Whip and explained why he would have to miss votes on Tuesday and possibly Wednesday too. Returning home was unavoidable but it was a wrench because plenary weeks were busy. As well as debates, votes, and question-time, he had appointments with lobbyists and with visitors. And, because most members were present, it was the best time for consulting parliamentary colleagues.

The evening flight to London was almost empty. At the start of the plenary week, most passengers travelled the other way. At the airport he had no motorbike, because he had taken the train to Brussels last week. He took the train into London and found a small hotel where he slept uneasily.

Next morning he presented himself at the local police station. He could give them no clue of who might wish to kill him. The inspector had done his research and asked about the incident at the football match although he confirmed the thugs were in prison.

Owen explained it was no surprise that the sender had known his home address. It was available in the parliament's *Grey List* where all MEPs' addresses were published.

He mentioned the threat faxed to him in Brussels. The inspector took details and promised to follow it up. A policeman would be posted outside Owen's home until further notice. His telephone calls and incoming letters would be monitored.

In the constituency office the media were besieging Rosemary. Owen promised to speak to all of them after the inquest. He booked a return flight to Strasbourg for Wednesday morning.

The inquest was grim. Owen answered the coroner's questions and it was adjourned it soon afterwards. When Owen left he was biting back tears. At the office he dealt with the many media enquiries and arranged for security devices to be installed both in his house and at the office.

He telephoned Jack Terrier who was incandescent with anger : "This is your fault, Owen. If you hadn't wasted your time on this idiotic report, Lynda would still be alive. You must give it up immediately."

Owen replied that he did not think it was not that simple : rather than give in to terrorism and make her death meaningless, he preferred to fight on.

Next morning, still emotional and angry, he flew back to Strasbourg. After lunch, he went to Rocher's office to keep their appointment.

The Frenchman had spacious offices which parliament assigns to the leaders of political groups. The outer door stood open.

Owen knocked and entered. Inside, a young man with short hair and a bleached-blonde receptionist stared at him. She spoke his name.

“Monsieur Mann ? J-J expects you.”

She spoke a few words into an internal telephone, listened, then scratched her left ear.

“I am so sorry. J-J apologises that he is occupied and cannot see you. He hopes maybe to see you later in the week.” She added that J-J did not feel able, right now, to fix a new appointment.

* * *

The current president of the parliament was a bouncy Italian named Michelangelo Canguro. His ambition, while in office, was to improve cooperation with national MPs. He had written to the presidents of all fifteen national parliaments in the European Union. He invited them to send MPs to Strasbourg for a joint-sitting with MEPs. He called the gathering an ‘Assises’. One Assise had been held previously, in Rome in November 1990.

The dates were the Wednesday to Friday of this particular week in Strasbourg.

His invitations had been accepted everywhere. From the British parliament the Speaker and Lord Chancellor replied with names of MPs and Lords who would attend. Among the Progressives would be Euro-sceptics James Edge-Smith and Sir Harry Pedreven, and among the Radicals the Euro-phile Adam Drake.

Most of the Westminster contingent flew to Strasbourg on Tuesday and dined together at the three-star Crocodile restaurant. Only Sir Harry Pedreven was unable to come until the next day.

Next morning free buses collected all the MPs from their hotels. They were briefed in the parliament about what to expect. The Westminster contingent was horrified to hear that they would have to sit in the hemicycle in political groups and not as a national block. Told that a final motion, on which the whole Assises would vote on Friday, would be drafted through all-party all-nationality negotiations, most of the British refused to be involved. Edge-Smith pointed out that all-party negotiation was not how it was done in the mother of parliaments. A real resolution, he insisted, was tabled by the government and opposed by the opposition.

On Wednesday morning the opening session in the hemicycle was ceremonial. The presidents or Speakers of all sixteen parliaments welcomed the gathering and eloquently expressed their hopes for improved cooperation. Edge-Smith allowed himself a loud derisory laugh at the Italian's absurdly federalist speech.

At midday Pedreven arrived with his wife who, despite his Euro-sceptical views, turned out to be a charming Dutch lady. Directed politely by an usher to sit in the hemicycle among the centre-right group, he refused and sat alone at the back among the independents who were of several nationalities.

Owen sat in the hemicycle and listened to the speeches. He was fascinated to hear the different national approaches to the longterm European goal of an 'ever closer union'. The French goal was to prevent the Germans from ever again occupying their territory. Germany feared its own nature and wanted to exert its future influence economically. Austria needed to keep pace with Germany whose language it shared. Spain had re-entered the real world after a hundred and fifty years of dictatorships and civil-wars, and wanted to recover its traditional influence. Portugal wanted to stay close to Spain, but not to be part of it. The three small Benelux countries - Belgium, Netherlands and Luxembourg - wanted influence over France and Germany, which they could only obtain through a share in EU decision-making. Italy yearned for strong government which it had lacked since the fall of ancient Rome. Greece wanted protection from Turkey. Ireland wanted to escape dependence on England. In Scandinavia the Danes needed to keep pace with the U.K., their largest trading partner, while Finland needed to escape the Russian bear-hug, and Sweden wished to preserve its Scandinavian links and also have influence inside the world's greatest trading bloc.

By Thursday morning all-party negotiations about the wording of the final resolution were completed. It was discussed in separate meetings by each of the political groups. Edge-Smith denounced the resolution as "disgracefully undemocratic" because it was a compromise of too many different political views.

Throughout the day MEPs and MPs made their speeches. Adam

Drake expressed support for 'ever closer union' but urged that enthusiastic Euro-philes did not run ahead of public opinion.

Edge-Smith smoothed his ginger tonsure and denounced 'ever closer union' as "monstrous". Continentals listened to him with incredulity. Owen's neighbour in the hemicycle, Pierre Hirondelle, asked : "Surely, if you had proportional voting in Britain, he would be in a separate Nationalist party, not a Progressive ?" Owen nodded vigorously.

It was unusual for Hirondelle to be present. He normally slept during the day and was active in the evenings, usually in the company of a different woman each time. He relieved the tedium by giving Owen a French story for his book.[8]

The debate ground on. By Thursday evening, the sceptical British from Westminster had realised that the compromise motion was going to pass by a large majority because it had been negotiated between all the political groups. Damage limitation was urgent, so they quickly drafted amendments to it. But having left it so late they found themselves without allies and therefore had no chance of success.

On the Friday morning each and every amendment was put to the vote. The British contingent was bewildered, not having looked at the other amendments before voting. They had assumed that, as in the Commons, only a few would be selected for a vote, and they would be whipped into obedience and be told how to vote.

In the final vote on the overall amended resolution, the Westminster contingent split three different ways : Drake and others in favour, Edge-Smith and others against, and a few who wished to vote in favour but abstained out of fear of their party back home. Pedreven had already left for the weekend in Paris.

Owen, meanwhile, was wondering how to fill the gap left by Rocher's failure to give him an interview. On Thursday afternoon he spotted Rocher sitting in the hemicycle. The Frenchman was present to give support to speakers from his far-right group but his demeanour, arms folded eyes closed, showed boredom.

Seizing the opportunity, Owen walked round the chamber, and introduced himself. He asked courteously whether he might have a few words. Looking surprised Rocher shrugged and nodded agreement. He patted the empty chair beside him.

Aged fifty Jean-Joel Rocher was very tall and very thin. He was wearing a suit, tie, and gold-rimmed spectacles. His hair was cropped and grey. His eyes were small and close together. When he was silent his tongue flicked in and out, moistening his lips.

The language of the interview was French. Nothing else could be expected from a politician whose slogan was 'Les Francais D'Abord', meaning 'the French people first'.

"Please pose your questions. I must leave in a few minutes." said the French fascist leader.

"May I ask your attitude to my report ?" Owen asked.

"It will be severely biased. Therefore I ignore it."

Owen had expected a difficult start and his face must have betrayed disappointment. Rocher continued:

"Allow me to explain. My party represents neither the extreme right nor the far right. We represent the *national* right. We are vilified as being fascist, racist and anti-Semitic, yet we are none of these. We are *nationalists.*" He emphasised the word. "Vilification of us is the strategy of the corrupt establishment parties, of the professional anti-racism lobby, and of the dangerous Masonic sect. They wish to undermine the only party which offers France a glorious future. Your committee is full of corrupt politicians out to destroy my party."

Owen replied on the offensive : "If your party is not anti-semitic, how do you explain your slanders on French Jews and the attacks by your supporters on Jewish cemeteries ? Many people remember you referring to a French government minister who was Jewish, by using a French pun which linked his name to Hitler's gas-ovens."

Rocher shrugged. "I explained this to this parliament's Committee on Immunities. After I spoke those words the French authorities tried to cancel my parliamentary immunity in order to prosecute me, despite my right to freedom of speech. Is it a crime in Britain to criticise a government minister ? No ? It is in France. My joke was a misunderstanding. My party is small and I do not have speech-writers. I make up my speeches as I go along. Sometimes, I admit, my jokes are not the best."

Gatto's briefing notes had told how the committee had refused to waive Rocher's parliamentary immunity from prosecution, on grounds which were incomprehensible to British MEPs. Their reason was *fumus persecutionis*, which meant that any MEP must continue to be protected by parliamentary immunity, however disagreeable their views, if there was any suggestion, or smoke, of political persecution.

Reading the notes, Owen had wondered whether British MEPs enjoyed immunity from arrest. Gatto's briefing mentioned one curious case when a British MEP had not paid his 'Poll Tax'. The British government had prosecuted ordinary tax-defaulters but not the MEP. Possibly they feared losing an appeal in the European Court, thereby conferring an immunity on British MEPs which MPs at Westminster did not enjoy except in their debating chamber.

"And the charge of racism levelled against you, Mr. Rocher ? At your party's summer university you made a speech about 'inequality of the races'."

Rocher's answer was polished. "At the last Olympic Games black athletes performed better than whites."

The interview was interrupted by applause in the hemicycle after a speech by Betty Borboleta, a black communist originally from Libya but now an Italian MEP. Rocher's hands remained firmly clasped on his desk.

"How do you explain the success of your party in France ?" Owen asked.

Gatto's notes said that Rocher had first entered the political stage at the end of the 1950s as a young activist in Pierre Poujade's populist movement. For a time Poujadism had been successful among shop-keepers in France. It was more populist than fascist but provided a good grounding.

"Initially it was slow and difficult," replied the Frenchman. "Traditionally in France the working class supports the Communists and the shop-keepers support the Gaullists. Through years of meticulous door-to-door political work, we have won them over. Areas of southern France are receptive to us because of the concentration of retired *pieds noirs*. You understand the expression? They are the former French colonists from north Africa who regard France's withdrawal from Algeria as treachery.

"Now my party achieves a growing, share of the popular vote in

France. In the recent regional elections we gained nearly one sixth of all the votes in France. In four big cities the mayors are active members of our Front National. They are doing excellent work, down to renaming the streets with suitable nationalist names., and removing unsuitable books from public libraries."

"Problems continue to mount in France" he continued. "Unemployment is high especially among youngsters. My party has a full range of policies, from unemployment to the environment. We oppose the EU's Maastricht treaty. Our priorities place pensioners before immigrants and those without papers."

"Who are 'Those without papers' ?"

"Immigrants who cannot, at present, be deported because they came from French colonial territories or because their children were born in France. My party is committed to a policy of zero immigration, repatriation of illegal immigrants, and an end to social benefits for non-French citizens."

His mobile telephone rang. Rocher interrupted his monologue to answer it. He listened for a moment then continued his reply. "We have opened centres to help young people who are without work. In Paris our party has its own retail shop. We help the homeless through our soup kitchen which was founded by a Lutheran priest at Gare St.Lazare in Paris. We have started a trade union branch, and a branch for policemen.

"You must understand the decadence of the establishment in France. *Change*," he gave the word special emphasis, "is essential. We shall abolish the Fifth Republic founded by De Gaulle. We shall create the Sixth Republic which will defend French national identity and become the standard-bearer for nationalist movements throughout the world.

"French interests must always come first. The ideas of the European Union might be attractive in theory to some people. But the abolition of frontiers, the single currency, the growing power of the European Parliament and of the European Court to over-rule national legislation is leading to the breakdown of French national values. It is part of a globalist conspiracy to destroy France."

He stopped momentarily for Owen's reaction then, without waiting to hear it, unwound his tall frame, rose to his feet, offered his hand and said "I regret but you must excuse me. If you wish to know more about us, I invite you to attend one of our public meetings."

Rocher turned to leave and threw his defiant last words. "You will hear more of us, much more. We are building an international grouping of nationalists. It is called 'Euro-Nat'."

Owen did not reply, having heard more than enough. His abiding impressions were of extreme bigotry but also of fierce determination. Rocher's political movement was strong and growing.

He returned to his own office in the Tower building to write up his notes. Rocher's bitter venom was still fresh in his memory.

* * *

Owen knew he must cultivate contacts with journalists, if he was to gain publicity to save his seat - even though he feared them like vultures hovering over him as their carrion. To see who might be around he crossed to the Weiss building and descended one floor in the panoramic glass lift and walked along to the Press Centre.

The Press bar had a low black ceiling, the ubiquitous flowery green carpet, gloomy overhead lighting, and only one small stretch of windows. The bar and tables were crowded, with full ashtrays, empty bottles, and parliament press liaison staff whom he recognised.

He spotted a group of three, one of whom was Murdo McKirk. Traces of egg were on his shirt.

He greeted the new arrival. "Hello, Owen. Know these two ? Harry Den Boer from Amsterdam and Tomas Amsel from Berlin." Owen shook their hands.

"Got your scoop yet, Murdo ?"

"Still working at it."

"In the Assises this week, you've an opportunity to make a comparison between different parliaments. How is this different from Westminster ?"

"People here are more approachable. Westminster is armies in confrontation and party spin-doctors pushing stories through the official lobby. Here the game is cross-party negotiation, and individual MEPs offer you their stories."

"Was my press release about visiting Norway and Sweden useful ?"

"Owen, it wasn't news. It contained nothing that was either 'new' or, frankly, interesting to our readers."

"So what is your scoop ?"

"My first story is that vast sums of tax-payers' money is missing from the Common Agricultural Policy."

"Sounds dull and it's old news."

"Our readers are interested in hearing about EU waste."

Den Boer and Amsel, hearing the usual British complaints, exchanged glances and excused themselves.

Murdo glanced at his notebook. "I've a list of abuses, country by country. Germany overcharged Brussels for export subsidies for beef; Greece claimed olive subsidies that were impossible ; the same for soya in Italy, milk in Spain, and beef in France. And the Irish," he smiled and consulted his notebook , "the Irish claimed that they had 'an inability to determine the precise numbers of beef cows'. In other words the Irish couldn't count their cows, so they counted them again just in case, and claimed the extra subsidy."

"Your exposé will imply that the British are perfect ?"

"Far from it. There are question-marks over EU refunds claimed by us for exports of malt, peas and beans. And we're implicated in my next story."

"Which is ?"

"Large sums of EU humanitarian aid were handed out in Bosnia, Croatia, Rwanda and Angola. There were no checks afterwards about how our money was spent or whether it did any good. I'm also chasing a story about expenses paid to MEPs. What does *faire le pont* mean, Owen ?"

"It's French for *make the bridge*. It was a disgraceful practice by MEPs from certain EU countries. Some on the continental don't have constituencies to nurse so they did not always return home at weekends. They stayed in Brussels but still claimed the airfare for going home and back again."

"You use the past tense ?" asked the journalist.

"It cannot happen now because MEPs have to produce airline boarding-cards in order to reclaim the fares."

"Whereas there are stories of MPs sharing cars to travel to London but claiming separate mileage allowances."

"And they also receive first-class railfares for their wives and an allowance for a second house in London" added Owen.

"How did those MEPs justify 'making the bridge' ?" asked McKirk.

"They defended the practice because their salaries are much lower than those paid to MEPs from rich countries like France, Germany and Italy."

"And they are considered to be 'honourable' members ?" the scribbler asked incredulously.

"Just as MPs are in the House of Commons."

"It's true that MPs are not asked by the Fees Office for receipts for the mileage which they drive in their own cars within their constituencies. They merely sign a form stating that the expenses they claim were incurred for their parliamentary duties, and their word is accepted." The hack paused, then added "and some MPs do have extremely nice houses."

"A typical snide journalist's remark," replied Owen.

"Don't MEPs have nice houses too ?" asked the hack.

"The Brits can only dream of it," replied Owen. "We receive no expenses at all for travelling within the vast regions which we represent. We drive much longer distances than MPs, and it all has to be financed out of our own pockets."

"That's unfair. Why don't all MEPs complain and get the system changed ?"

"Because there is no majority within the parliament to make the change. Many continental MEPs get free national travel on public transport in their own country. And many continental members have no constituency meetings. A Greek friend told me the other day that he had never received a single letter nor ever been invited to speak at a public meeting."

"Well, it must be cleared up. The difficulty is how," mused Murdo.

"One way would be to recruit extra staff to check receipts for everything spent by members. But that is expensive for tax-payers."

"There'll always be dodges," said Owen. "A few years ago a clever official in the MEPs' Expenses office opened the safe each Friday night. He removed the cash balances of the different EU currencies held there, which amounted to thousands of pounds. He put them all on short-term high-interest deposit in Switzerland over the weekend. On Monday morning he replaced the cash in the safe and pocketed the interest. He was never punished because there was no rule forbidding what he did."

Owen remembered his need for re-election next summer. Wining-and-dining journalists was one route to obtaining publicity.

"What are you doing for dinner, Murdo ?"

Did McKirk blush ? "Sorry but I'm busy. I've a date with a charming lady. In fact you introduced us."

"Natasha Farfalla ? I'm glad that you're getting on well."

Owen hoped that Murdo would change his shirt before the rendez-vous. Natasha would have enough choice on her menu without having to look at the spread down his front.

* * *

The weekend was subdued. Nina was away, and Lynda's funeral would be on Monday. After that ordeal Owen returned to Brussels to prepare for the Public Hearing.

He checked his pigeon-hole. Among the usual accumulation of official paperwork was a black-and-white picture-card postmarked from Moscow. Its picture was bizarre : a childlike piper with sack on back trudging across a desert with heavy clouds overhead and a ray of sunshine ahead.

On the reverse was scribbled : 'One day I hope to reach the parliament.' The signature was an indecipherable squiggle : it mostly resembled the humps of a collapsed camel, probably one that had died in the desert. It made no sense to Owen. He gathered all the papers into a folder to take them home for his new secretary, Jane Farmer, to sort out.

* * *

The Public Hearing was held in the parliament's largest committee room. Owen, armed with a bag of treacle toffees from the corner shop at home, sat on the platform next to chairman Chomik.

The seats facing them were divided into three sections. To their left were the visiting witnesses, in the centre the MEPs, to their right representatives of the Commission, the Council of Ministers, and the press, perhaps two hundred people in all. At the back the public seats were full, one of them occupied by a man with oiled jet-black hair.

Each witness came up and sat next to Owen while they gave their evidence. They spoke for ten minutes about fascism in their own country, and then answered questions from MEPs.

The first witnesses were human-rights campaigners from Spain and Portugal. They said that their countries' fascism was at a low level compared with central Europe. The Iberian peninsula was weary of fascism after right-wing dictatorships had ruled both countries until the 1970s. Yet Franco's spirit lived on. The *Alianza Nacional* was a grouping of small parties which endorsed racism, religion, the family, anti-communism, survival of the fittest, and opposed regional separatist movements. It raised finance by links with drug-trafficking gangs run by Africans in the south of Spain and by South Americans in Madrid. There was spasmodic cooperation with Rocher's party over the border in France.

The next witness was a Hungarian MP who had been imprisoned under the communists. He spoke about the *Party of Truth* in his country. Rocher had travelled to Budapest where he had praised them as "a sentry for the Christian West, on guard against the threat from the Muslim East".

The air in the committee room was becoming stuffy. Lars Anka raised his hands, making a cross with his forefingers. This was a recognised signal which meant he was raising a point of procedure. Under the Rules any member could interrupt proceedings to allege that the rules were not being followed correctly. The rule was often abused, but by the time the member had spoken, and the chairman had understood that the point was not genuine, it was too late.

The Swede asked for a window to be opened. There was a flutter of laughter when the English interpretation came through the headphones as "Chairman, we can't go on meeting like this."

The final witness of the first session was a Belgian woman who worked for Amnesty International. As she took the stand she was heckled by Mr. Haai, her country's only fascist MEP who was an aggressive and unpopular member of the parliament. What he shouted was not interpreted because he failed to switch on his microphone. The chairman threatened to eject him from the room.

"Typical of *Vlaams Blok*, our country's fascists," said the Belgian woman nervously. "His leader promises that when he comes to power - I pray that will never be - he will deport immigrants using huge C-130 army transport planes. His motto is 'eigen volk eerst', which means in English 'our own people first'.

Gaining confidence, she went on : "Its roots are Nazi-collaborators during the war and it has links with other terrorists including the Turkish Grey Wolves. It tried to make a deal with the Ulster Volunteer Force to supply bombs for a campaign against Belgian Jews."

There was another noisy interruption from Haai. Chomik waved to two ushers at the side and Haai was removed, still shouting threats.

The Belgian resumed. "To finish, I want to tell an extraordinary story. Recently the High Command of the Belgian Armed Forces told its eight thousand reserve officers that Belgium's immigrant population was a 'new potential enemy'. Immigrants, our High Command said, posed a threat not only in wartime but also in peace, because they presented 'a clandestine threat of a permanent character' through their ability to carry out sabotage in support of terrorism. Army reservists were asked to gather information about migrants, in clear violation of Belgian laws on privacy and data protection.

"The document was racist, but the High Command said that it was "only a draft". Nevertheless the plan was carried out during a military exercise in the Brussels area. Reserve officers were given an imaginary scenario : 'A terrorist movement is causing unrest in European cities. The migrant organisations are leading a strong anti-European and anti-American campaign.' The point is" she banged the desk, "those people are Belgian citizens. It was unacceptable treatment by our own government."

To the sound of applause Chomik closed the session and announced that he was hosting a reception for all the witnesses. They would be offered fruit juice, wine, or *Kyr Royale*, a tasty mixture of blackcurrant liqueur mixed with champagne.

Having reached the halfway point of the Hearing, Owen began to wonder whether Europe might be turning back towards the fascism of the 1930s. Whether or not his report would help him to be re-elected in June, the subject was serious and the outlook was worrying.

Next morning the public seats were again full. Witnesses were eagerly awaited from Italy and Germany, the countries which had once been led by Mussolini and Hitler.

The first witness was an Italian lawyer. He explained that Italy had been ruled by an anti-Communist alliance since 1945. In 1990 Communism had collapsed so new political parties had been formed. The largest on the far-right was the *Alleanza Patriotica.* It was growing fast and had organised a march of a quarter of a million people through Rome, reminiscent of the Blackshirts who had marched on Rome in 1922, the event which had led to Mussolini's first government.

They were building a mass movement among small shopkeepers and truckers. The shopkeepers had demonstrated against high taxes, and a call by lorry owners for a national strike had mimicked a strike by right-wing lorry owners in Chile in 1973. Italy, like Chile, was long and narrow in shape : a successful truck strike could strangle either country. They appealed to youth through 'street cred'. Terror was spread by skinheads within Italian towns, giving the fascists an opportunity to campaign for stricter law and order.

Italian fascists raised money in a predictable way - through drugs, extortion, arms trafficking, and kidnapping. They had links with all four Mafia organisations - the Sicilian Mafia, the Camorra, the Criminalita Pugliese, and the 'Ndrangheta in Calabria with its 'ten commandments' such as 'Always fight the police' and 'Traitors must die'. Tapes of fantasy music were sold legitimately on the open market with the irony that the police prosecuted anyone who made pirate copies.

Their leader, Luigi Piccione, craved electoral success. He had asked his supporters to stop saluting him openly, so that he could present his party as part of the political mainstream. But his climb towards power was not smooth. Recently in northern Trento five of his skinhead supporters had spent an evening searching for a non-white immigrant, but had settled for a beggar. They had sprayed tear gas into the beggar's eyes, beaten him senseless with clubs and finally burned him to death in his cardboard home.

While the Italian spoke, coffee and tea were brought round to everybody in their seats, carried by a vast plump Belgian who, to Owen's amazement, squeezed his bulk agilely between the rows of desks

The next to give evidence was an Austrian journalist. His country too had a right-wing party, the *Party of Liberty*. It was very strong and had won 30% of the votes in Austria's recent General election.

Its leader, Irma Geier, was a young and charismatic woman. To gain power she was building a reputation of respectability to hide her past. She had been forced to resign as governor of a province, after praising Hitler's employment policies and had been filmed addressing a secret meeting of veterans of Hitler's Waffen SS, calling them "decent open-minded people" who "have remained loyal to this day".

She opposed enlargement of the EU because that would result in ten million foreigners moving westwards into Austria. Her slogan was 'Austria first'. She defended the little man against government, and campaigned against privilege, housing shortages, growing criminality and 'the foreigner question'. She was supported by Austria's biggest-circulation tabloid.

Questioned by Owen about how she differed from Rocher in France, the journalist quoted Geier who had said she was 'neither left wing nor right wing but in front. Rocher is a racist whom we avoid. We are the bridge of the right-wing fringe to parliamentary democracy.'

The Austrian witness warned against Geier's charisma : "Notice what other members of her party say. The deputy-mayor of Klagenfurt said that 'Nazi' stands for 'New, Attractive, Zealous, Ideas-rich'. Her party chief in St. Leonard said of Simon Wiesenthal, the veteran Nazi-hunter : "We are getting the ovens ready, but not for you Mr. Wiesenthal. There's room for you in Irma Geier's cigarette."

This dramatic evidence, that the land of Hitler's birth was again giving support to fascism, created an uproar in the committee room. Chomik hammered his gavel several times before silence was restored.

He announced a fifteen minute break for those, like him, who had become desperate to smoke a cigarette outside in the corridor.

Owen stretched his legs but remained in the committee room. He thought about phoning Nina, but there would not be enough time if she should want to talk. Instead he noted down possible conclusions for the report. That fascist parties which campaign democratically in elections seem to do well : whereas those which use violence get nowhere.

After an appearance from the Vienna Observatory which was set up in 1998 and was starting to collect statistics about racism, the final witness to take the seat next to Owen was the German. He was a professor whose father, said Chomik in his introduction, had been executed after the 1944 bomb plot against Hitler.

The professor explained that Germany's most successful far-right organisation used to be the *Republikaner* party but had recently been overtaken by the *German People's Union.* Their policies were to deny voting rights for foreigners, tougher law and order, anti-immigration, the Deutsch Mark instead of the Euro as their currency, restoration of Germany's 1938 borders, and denial of the Holocaust as a detail of history. They wanted compulsory training of girls to be wives and mothers, and for HIV virus carriers to have their genitals tattooed.

They earned money from drug-trafficking at discotheques, trade in illegal weapons, street prostitution using young women from Poland and the Czech republic, car theft, and blackmailing of small businesses for "protection". The German Nazi music scene was one of the best organised in Europe with over four thousand supporters. Fifty bands produced a hundred music CDs each year.

The professor warned that the Nazis must not be ignored. They held seats in most of Germany's state 'Land' parliaments. In the last European elections they had won 7% of the national vote. With the support of millions of voters, they could not be easily controlled : the country faced a serious problem of right-wing advance.

Owen asked the professor "Are they anti-semitic ?"

"Their leader has declared that, before the fall of the Berlin Wall, there were five occupying powers in Germany : the USA, the USSR, France, Great Britain, and the Central Council of German Jews."

At this echo of the past the committee sat in horrified silence. Owen wondered whether Europe had made any progress since 1945.

Chomik broke the tension by closing the Hearing. He thanked all who had taken part, particularly those who now had to make long journeys home.

* * *

Owen rose to his feet wearily, bleary-eyed after two days of total concentration. He gazed with envy at the witnesses, their task over, who were streaming from the committee room. For him and Pietro the hard part lay ahead. The evidence had to be sifted and out of it a report drafted.

Owen pushed his papers together into a pile. A man with oiled black-hair appeared beside him. "Excuse me, Mr. Rapporteur. I'm a journalist with the South American news agency." He offered a business card. "My name is Camaleao. Might I put a couple of questions to you ?"

Owen was delighted that media attention had started already. "Of course, let's sit down" he replied.

"Do you mind if I record our talk ?" asked Enrique Sãta and produced a battery-powered recorder.

"Not at all."

"First, what conclusions do you expect the committee to draw ?"

"The report is not written yet." Owen paused to think, "but I guess we'll conclude that fascism is stronger than we thought and becoming stronger ; also, that fascists are beginning to coordinate with each other across borders : that if they are not stopped, they will utterly destroy the EU and all the good that it has done."

Sãta's goal was to pour freezing water, as icy as possible, over Owen's conclusions : "Forgive me, but I think you are seeing spectres where they don't exist."

"Didn't you hear the witnesses ?"

"Like you, Mr. Mann, I listened throughout both days. Believe me, in South America we have more fascism than in Europe, much more. People there believe that benevolent dictatorship works better than democracy. Surprising, eh ?" he smiled, hoping to create empathy. "For Europe, fascism should not be considered a problem."

"But we have just heard how fascism is growing in Europe."

"I understand. You must say something sensational so that the parliament gets publicity."

"Not at all. We shall recommend whatever is right." Owen reacted indignantly, but restrained his feelings because anger was a symptom of losing the argument. "The parliament is the EU's driving force."

"The driving force ? What can you mean ?"

"If you look back at the EU's development since the first parliamentary elections in 1979, you find that most of Europe's influential new ideas have come from MEPs. Only MEPs debate fulltime about the EU."

"I am surprised to hear that. Can you give a single example ?"

"A British MEP named Stanley Johnson led a campaign which was very popular with the public and led to a ban against imports from Canada of products made out of baby seals."

"Charming but not world-shattering. Is that all ?"

"MEPs led the world in condemning the USSR's invasion of Afghanistan in 1979. Very importantly, they voted in 1983 to accept Cruise and Pershing missiles into Europe. That caused the USSR to abandon its campaign against them."

"Maybe that was just a coincidence. No practical examples ?"

"The parliament, against British wishes, withheld the UK's Budget rebate."

"Very negative."

"The Single Market idea came from the parliament. Its originator was an MEP by the name of De Ferranti."

"An Italian ?"

"No, he was British. His family made computers but could not sell them to the continent because of hidden trade barriers such as language, labelling and paperwork. So he founded an all-party MEP pressure group, called the 'Kangaroo Group', and campaigned for free trade."

"Why 'Kangaroo' ?"

"Because kangaroos hop over barriers. Easier trade, he argued, would bring more jobs and more prosperity."

"Sounds fine except that I've never heard of Ferranti."

"Tragically he died of cancer but his idea was taken up by the leaders at an EU summit. Only one of the twelve national leaders voted against the mechanism to create it ?"

"Which one was it?"

"Can you guess ?" asked Owen.

"It was a secret meeting" mused Sãta. "But the British have been against every single new European idea."

"Fortunately there is no veto at leader-summits so the Single Market went ahead. There should be a statue to Ferranti."

Sãta put on an obsequious look. "So interesting. Can we continue over a drink ?"

"That would be nice. Let's go to the hemicycle bar round the corner."

They settled into comfortable chairs. Sãta bought two beers and lit a cigar. "You don't mind if I smoke ? It was tough sitting in a committee-room where it was not permitted."

He puffed contentedly. "So, Mr. Mann, fighting fascism is your big new idea for the EU ?"

"No," Owen replied defensively, "but fascism is growing, and we shall need coordinated action by the EU to defeat it. Rather than each nation acting on its own, as they do now."

"But MEPs have no power over law and order. That is decided by the Council of Ministers on an inter-governmental basis. Your report will be a waste of time."

Owen fought back. "It's true that MEPs have no power in this area. But neither does any national MP."

"Of course they do. They control their ministers."

"But MPs cannot change the decision which their ministers make for them in Brussels." Owen hammered the point home. "There is no democratic control over decisions made in Brussels by national ministers. The Council of Ministers decides everything in secret. It never publishes its debates, its votes, or its minutes. Backbench MPs at home have no say. MEPs want to install democratic *controls*", he emphasised the word, "controls over ministerial decisions."

Sãta nodded, conceding the point which he knew to be true. He returned to undermining Owen. "You sound Euro-enthusiastic whereas I heard that you used to be Euro-sceptical ?"

"I am Euro-sceptical," Owen insisted uncomfortably. "But I am pro-parliament, as all democrats should be. It would be ridiculous to oppose the EU doing anything. My country wants to be in Europe but not ruled by it. But if action is needed, then democratic EU action may be the solution. Sometimes the countries of Europe achieve better results by working together than they do alone. Dealing with cross-border crime and terrorism is a good example where EU action may be better."

Sãta countered. "What makes you think that ministers will be willing to transfer any powers to Brussels ? A few small states may be keen. But the big ones with proud traditions and excellent police - I am thinking of Britain and France - will oppose it. You won't get a majority to allow EU action. Nothing will be agreed. You will fail."

"We'll see. If MEPs are convinced of the need for action, they'll push hard for it. We've had success in the past, as I explained."

"Two last questions about yourself, Mr. Mann. I understand that you will have difficulty to get re-elected in June. You are an intelligent man. Why are you spending your precious time on this esoteric subject, when you should be using all your time to save your political life ?"

"That's true. As June gets nearer, the pressure on me to be in my constituency grows all the time. But I want to see this through."

"I think you are making a big personal mistake. You should abandon the report." Owen shrugged.

"Finally," Sãta used what he hoped was his best thrust, "aren't you afraid of what the far-right people may do to you - I mean physical harm - if they don't like your report ?"

Owen's dislike of Camaleao was growing but he remembered he must stay on good terms with journalists. He smiled : "Of course, I'm apprehensive but I try not to show it, Mr. Camaleao."

"Well, be very careful. Now I must not take up more of your time. Keep South America in mind and remember that you may place yourself in real danger. We wouldn't want to lose a hard-working MEP like you. I shall watch with interest how it goes with your report. Goodbye."

Sãta walked out of the bar puffing his cigar, confident that he had planted fear and doubt in Owen's mind.

Owen finished his beer and mused : if Camaleao believed fascism was not a problem for Europe, why should there be physical danger ? Perhaps he had meant that an individual bonehead, a loose cannon, might target him. Not likely of course, but he must be careful.

* * *

A message from Nina was in his answerphone. She asked if he would be around this coming weekend. Could they talk after his surgery on Saturday morning ?

Owen dumped his plan of watching a football match and left a delighted reply for her. He suggested they meet for lunch in a pub which they both liked.

The morning's surgery was a pleasant change from the darkness of fascism. Owen's cheerfulness was reinforced by the prospect of seeing Nina. The Morfils returned to the office, at his request, to hear some news.

"I'm glad to tell you," he smiled, "the French Ambassador has persuaded the authorities in Paris to put Deidre's fine back to its original level. But there is one condition."

Deidre grimaced. Mrs. Morfil shifted her precarious perch on the small office chair.

"You must pay the fine straightaway. I wish they'd cancelled it altogether but I hope you agree it's not a bad solution ?"

Deidre sighed at the unfairness of it. But Mrs. Morfil was effusive. "Oh thank you Mr. Mann. We'll pay straightaway."

As mother and daughter renegotiated the stairs, a distraught woman pushed upwards past them.

"I haven't made an appointment but I'm desperate, Mr. Mann" she pleaded. "My daughter, she's sixteen, went to Spain a week ago with her boyfriend without telling me. Yesterday she phoned and said they've run out of money. The man who runs their hostel is keeping their passports until they pay up. Their bill is getting bigger and bigger. I'm terrified."

Owen offered her a chair as she continued to jabber like an agitated machine-gun. "I'm looking for work myself and there's no way I can pay. Is there *anything* you can do ?" she pleaded and stared at him imploringly. "Can you get some money out of Brussels ?"

Owen knew very well that there was no EU fund to bail out runaway teenagers. He could see no solution other than cutting straight through the Gordian knot. The woman had the hostel's number so he telephoned the hotelier. Fortunately the man spoke some English. He was adamant that he was not wealthy and must be paid in full. A promise of money later would not do. If the teenagers' bill, which was mounting day by day, was not settled by tomorrow he was going to the police.

Owen interrupted to say that he was a "*Diputado Europeo*". The unhappy innkeeper's voice stopped instantly. Owen continued :

"If I send you a fax which guarantees that my personal cheque is in the post to Spain, will you allow the foolish young couple to leave straightaway ?"

The Spaniard seized the lifeline and accepted Owen's offer. The desperate mother's face suddenly changed to relief. She would give her daughter a piece of her mind, she said, and promised faithfully that the money would be repaid to Owen in full, as soon as they had saved it.

Owen wrote off that promise as well-meant but unreliable : a good story in the local press would settle the debt, he decided.

By midday Owen had grappled with a few more of the never-ending flow of human problems. Leaving Rosemary to shut up the office, he rode his motorbike to the village next to Nina's and parked outside the King's Head pub.

He entered and looked around. Nina had not arrived so he bought a bottle of their favourite red Rioja and, with two wine glasses, settled in their usual corner by the open logfire. He placed the bottle carefully on the hearth to help it reach room temperature.

After fifteen minutes she had not arrived. He telephoned her home with his mobile. After several rings she answered in an agitated voice : "My car's almost out of petrol, I've lost my only key to the petrol cap, I don't know the key's number to get a replacement, and before you ask I don't belong to any of the recovery services."

"Shall I come and help ?"

"There's somebody at the door. Hang on a moment."

After a pause, she returned to the phone : "It's the builder who has dropped by unexpectedly. Can you ring back in ten minutes ?"

Owen did so and this time she was cheerful : "We're back on course. The builder chipped the petrol cap off. I gave him a kiss, and he nearly fell over. See you in a few minutes."

When she entered the pub, she gave him a small wave but not a smile. She was wearing a pale blue low-cut knee-length dress and her hair was lying on her shoulders. Seeing her, Owen instantly forgave her the three weeks he had waited to see her again. The silver bracelet was absent from her wrist. Too flamboyant for a pub, he supposed.

She offered him her cheek. He kissed it warmly and poured her a glass of wine. Having taken a seat and a sip, she started with an accusation. "I haven't seen you for weeks."

"I'm very sorry. The parliament has kept me busy. But you've been busy too."

She looked into her rapidly-emptying glass. "That's what I want to talk to you about. The thing is..."

She stopped, unable to find precise words for what she wanted to express. Suddenly they tumbled out. "I haven't done anything wrong like robbery or murder. It's worse than that."

Owen wondered what she could have done that was worse than murder.

"I've wanted to unburden myself to you but couldn't do it on the telephone. I don't think you'll like me very much when I tell you, darling."

A pit of anxiety started to open in his stomach. He watched her gulp down the last of her glass and he refilled it : “I’ve never been in love like these last weeks. Agony, ecstasy, tears, and joy. I’ve worked with this colleague for a year and a half - he’s part of the bank’s furniture. One evening we were working late and chatting in my office over cups of tea. An incredible bore joined us who started talking about his piles. We two were aching with suppressed laughter. Eventually the bore left and I can’t remember crying with laughter like that ever before. Uncontrollably. We were rolling around on the floor. Then he touched my hand and that was it. Not sex but a vulnerability that amazed both of us. I fought it for a week. Then floodgates, kaleidoscopic emotions, all the hack phrases come true. How sick it must sound. I want you to know that I wasn’t looking for anyone. An affair hadn’t crossed my mind. If you’d given me any grounds I could justify it a little. But there’s no justification. It’s my fault, however you look at it. My only excuse is the strength of feeling. A tidal wave of passion, and desperately wanting a baby. But with your election coming up I know that to trap you now would be wrong. I’m scared of what may happen to us, to you and me.”

She stared at the floor. Owen tried to think how to reply to the very unwelcome revelation. He bought time by sipping his wine, then asked gently : “Tell me what you want.”

“That’s the question. I don’t love him like I love you. But he has the advantage of being around, and I need that. I’ve been wanting to tell you. I want to be honest with you. I don’t want to lose you. Do you understand ?”

He nodded. Only too well. It was an ultimatum. A choice between her and his career. Either abandon the fight to win his seat again, or lose her.

He sipped slowly, while she waited for his reply. He could try pointing out that she had been away for the two previous weekends but that was not the real point. Her real complaint was that, week after week, he would be away in Brussels or Strasbourg.

Nina was still looking at him. ‘Even if I do what she wants,’ he agonised silently, ‘now there’s someone else on the scene, how can I be sure that she’ll stay with me ? I don’t want to lose her but, equally, I can’t think of a solution to satisfy both of us.’

He struggled to clear his thoughts. This was not a surgery problem which required a cool analytic solution. He was in turmoil ; he loved her, he hated the choice, he wanted her, he wanted his career.

But deep down a conviction started to grow that his immediate priority was his career. He had not fought so hard to get this far to give up now. He glanced at Nina who was staring at him, tears in her eyes.

"Can you give him up, Nina ?"

"If I did, would it change things between us ? Would I see you more often ?" she asked.

"Not for the next few months, I'm afraid. As the election gets nearer, I'll be busier than ever. And if I'm lucky enough to be re-elected..."

She shook her head : "You're not prepared to change, not for me ?"

Another silence, which stretched out. As in relationships which are coming to an end before the participants realise, neither could think of what to say.

Owen spoke. "Nina I love you. But I cannot promise to give up my career. If I lose my seat in the summer, then I'll be around fulltime. But until then, I want to fight."

"And if you win in June ?"

His anger rose. She had precipitated this problem, yet the blame was turned onto him. For once he lost his self-control. He emptied his glass and shouted : "Look, when you get tired of fucking this man, let me know. Otherwise..."

There was a stifled choke from Nina. She picked up the bottle and poured what remained inside over Owen's trousers.

He had been going to say "...we can stay in touch." But her assault made words unnecessary. His brain whirled in a kaleidoscope of fury, frustration, and dumb despair.

He stood up. Nina said nothing and stared at the fire. Not looking at her, he walked out of the pub in dripping trousers, and rode home forgetting to wear his helmet.

* * *

The following week was set aside for Political Groups of MEPs to meet separately. Normally they met in Brussels but they were permitted to hold an occasional meeting elsewhere, which was called Study Days.

The purpose of Study Days was for members to learn about an EU country other than their own. Rocher's far-right group had followed the letter of this parliamentary rule but not its spirit. They had held Study Days on the exotic island of Martinique, which legally was part of the EU because France had incorporated its last colonies into mainland France. But the cost to the tax-payer of flying his Group to the Caribbean and back was considerable.

This week Owen's group, the Socialists, had chosen to hold Study Days in Turin in north-west Italy. Located at the foot of the Alps the city had been Italy's first capital for three years in the nineteenth century. Vermouth had been invented there in 1786 and two centuries later was still produced The city was the centre of Fiat car-manufacturing. There would be four days of visits to industry and farms, and of debates with local politicians. There would also be a privileged look at the famous Shroud which otherwise lay hidden in the royal chapel.

The previous week in Brussels Gatto had pointed out to Owen that Turin was near to the south of France, the stronghold of Rocher's Front National. Owen decided that he would take up the Frenchman's throw-away invitation and try to attend one of their public meetings. Gatto discovered for him that Rocher would address a meeting on the Wednesday evening in a town called Grasse. Grasse was some sixty kilometres from the border with Italy.

He decided that he could endure missing the Group's Wednesday morning visit to a motorcar factory. Instead he rented a red Alfa-Romeo, and set off alone after breakfast to drive westwards.

Soon he left behind the smoke-stacks and passed hillsides covered with vines and hazelnut groves. At Ventimiglia on the French border, there were no passport controls unlike, he remembered, the problem in Forsyth's immortal thriller in which to pass the same border, the Jackal smuggled an assassin's rifle hidden under his car. Owen drove across without even stopping.

In the first French town, Menton, he purchased a 'Bed & Breakfast' guide-book. He wondered how that universal acronym fitted with France's efforts to maintain the purity of its language against the onrushing tide of English and American.

From the book he selected an address called *La Rivolte* in Grasse. He telephoned and was surprised to be answered in English. Its proprietor confirmed cheerfully that a single room was available for the night.

He sped past Monte Carlo, which appeared to be a mini-Hong Kong, all skyscrapers and no greenery, but home to fabulous wealth, beautiful women, and the world-famous casino. He chose the highest-level of the three coastal roads, called the Grande Corniche, because of its breath-taking views over the Mediterranean.

Next came the city of Nice, with its museums devoted to painters Matisse and Chagall but also with the second highest violent crime-rate in France after Marseilles. He remembered an exchange he had enjoyed with a French MEP, Louise Moreau. She had been Mayor of a small town near Nice. Being a mayor was an essential first step to building a political career in France ; some French politicians held the same post for many years, rarely visiting their town and leaving the work to a less-charismatic deputy. The chain-smoking Louise Moreau had made her reputation by parachuting fourteen times into war-torn France for the Resistance, and later had become a Senateur in France's upper house.

Owen had asked her why the French insisted that the parliament must continue to meet in three cities when the great majority of MEPs wished to concentrate on one place. To his surprise she did not support the parliament continuing to meet in three cities and not even Strasbourg. She had explained :

"It should meet in only one place, the geographical centre of the European Union."

Agreeing enthusiastically, Owen had asked "And where is the geographical centre ?"

"In Nice of course" she had replied, laughing at him, "but nobody would do any work."

Owen saw a road-sign to Grasse and turned north away from the coast and toward the mountains. Tomorrow on the return journey there should be time to visit the museums.

At midday he stopped at a spectacular walled village called Tourette sur Loup. As he parked in its main square, a siren started to wail. The local inhabitants appeared unconcerned but when church bells also started to toll. Owen's unease grew. He found a small restaurant called Chez Grandmere and asked its elderly owner whether he should leave the town immediately. Had a riot started, or a fire in the surrounding hills ?

"No, monsieur," she reassured him, "once a week, on Wednesdays, the siren and bells are traditionally sounded at midday to signal the start of the lunch hour."

Owen settled at a table and enjoyed a delicious meal but without wine. Afterwards he resumed his drive round the edge of the valley. At its western end he reached Grasse and shortly after saw a sign to La Rivolte. An impressive gate and a long climbing drive took him past an inviting swimming-pool to the front of a spectacular house.

He parked on the gravel terrace and admired its garden of terraces stretching down the hillside which were planted with olive trees and oleander bushes. A small model electric railway ran up the hill between the house and the pool, hauling little carriages, each able to contain three glasses of drinks.

The host turned out to be a retired publisher by the name of Bjorn Ours. He had a considerable knowledge of local matters. The *Grassiste* population, he told Owen, were strongly sympathetic to the Front National : they considered that North African immigrants had ruined their town. Owen would see Front National posters on many buildings.

Rocher's public meeting did not start until half past seven. The host recommended a stroll through the town and a visit to one of the town's perfume factories. Owen wandered down the one-way main street, a gentle hill called Boulevard du Jeu du Ballon - although there was no indication of what its Balloon Game was. Possibly it referred to the ancient game of Boule, which he saw being earnestly played by six elderly Frenchmen on a flat sandy corner of a shady park. Owen was surprised to see that one player was a woman, fat, massively endowed but with a male haircut and tweed jacket.

Stopping to watch he squeezed onto a bench beside three plump elderly women who, he supposed, were the players' 'groupies'. Two teams of three were competing. Each player had two silver-coloured balls, which they tried to roll nearest to a small red jack.

As Owen watched the six became individual characters ; one man, with long black hair, projected his balls through the air with deadly aim and knocked his opponents' balls away. The fat lady conserved her energy by carrying a rope with a powerful magnet on its end which she used to pick up her balls instead of having to stoop down. A player did not launch his second ball if his first was nearest to the jack. The fat woman was the best player and invariably threw the final ball of each match. Admiring her skill, Owen wondered if this was a French version of the saying, 'the game isn't over till the fat lady flings'.

Continuing his walk he passed a sign to a factory shop where the board outside invited people to come inside and mix their own perfumes. He decided to give it a miss, and came to a roundabout.

In the roundabout's centre a water fountain played round a large sculpture of metal flowers. To the left was a park with plane trees below which was an underground car-park. To the right was the Palais des Congres building where Rocher's meeting would be held. Flags were flying above the entrance and barriers had been erected on both sides of the street.

Owen settled with a newspaper at a café in the park. After an hour he strolled back to La Rivolte arriving just as it started to rain. He showered and drove to the underground carpark and left his car. He crossed the road and entered the Palais des Congres.

Escalators carried all visitors up one floor into a large meeting area. A young usher in a smart blue jacket was waiting at the top. He stared quizzically at Owen for a moment and then exclaimed: "Monsieur le Deputé, you are expected."

Surprised, Owen supposed that Gatto had mentioned him. The usher led him through a door into the front of a large hall and seated him in the first row of seats which were labelled 'Celebrités'.

The hall filled rapidly. The last arrivals were obliged to stand at the sides and the back. Punctually at half past seven, Rocher strode onto the platform and was greeted by a storm of applause. When it died down he began to speak through a microphone, pacing to and fro.

He spoke about his party being the only effective opposition in France. The parties of the centre were putrid, he said. Words of hatred were directed against anything that was not French, with a tirade against the twin horrors of homosexuality and immigration.

The present government, he insisted, encouraged both.

Owen was indignant : academic studies had proved that immigrants were not a drag on society. Instead, after settling in, they were the keenest to work and to build up their own prosperity.

Rocher's oratory was regularly interrupted by stamping, chanting and flag-waving in the audience. He mentioned a nearby market in Grasse where Arabs were the overwhelming majority "and where the only French people you meet are a few old ladies, walking with their heads down." He praised the Brigitte Bardot Foundation because it opposed the Moslem method killing of sheep. Owen regretted that its famous star was not seated in the front beside him.

Rocher attacked the *Euro* currency as an infringement of French independence. He predicted that the burdens it would place on Europe's weaker economies would create unbearable social tensions from which the *nationalists* would benefit enormously.

After forty minutes he stopped to waves of thunderous applause. As it rolled over him he peered down at the front row of seats. When the clapping finally died away, to Owen's horror, Rocher identified him to the hall. "This evening we welcome an Englishman to our assembly."

Rocher held up a hand to interrupt the polite applause.

"Wait ! Our guest is an MEP." There were groans.

"What is more, he is a Socialist." There was an astonished silence.

"Can he understand how much the French people are suffering ? I fear not. He belongs to the corrupt centre. Is he here because he repents his flaccid liberal views ? Unlikely. Has he changed his views about admitting Africans into our beloved country ? Impossible."

Rocher paused. He looked down at Owen and asked rhetorically : "Would the Englishman care to come up onto the platform here, and clarify his opinions to us ?"

Owen shook his head and was rewarded by baying and boos. He felt naked in front of a thousand hostile eyes. Rocher milked the theatrical effect. Owen's anger grew. Was he afraid of his beliefs ? He signalled to Rocher. "Very well. I will say a few words."

He climbed onto the platform. An aide handed him the portable microphone. There was a hush of expectation, punctuated by half-giggles from out in the darkness.

He took a deep breath and spoke in the best French he could manage.

"Mesdames et Messieurs. I believe that every man and every woman has equal rights. It matters not what their race, skin-colour or religion is. In the 1930s it was intolerance of these differences that led us into World War and to the Holocaust. We must treat each other with equality. That is the most important purpose of the European Union. This is why I oppose everything for which Mr. Rocher stands. But I thank him for this opportunity to say so."

A storm of catcalls and whistles broke over him as he handed the microphone to an aide.

He walked slowly towards the hall's exit, fighting an instinct to run. He rode the down escalator and jogged towards the underground car-park. He ran down its steps, climbed into his car and paid at the exit kiosk.

Emerging onto the roundabout, he found it was filled with supporters of the Front National. His foreign car was identified. Bangs rained on the doors and roof as the police cleared a way for him. Not wishing to betray to the crowd where he was staying the night, he followed the signs down the twisting narrow streets towards the motorway which lay ten kilometres distant.

Having reached the outskirts of the town he wondered how to get back to La Rivolte. Suddenly headlights appeared in his rear mirror and several cars sounded their horns. He accelerated and they followed. Coming at high speed to a junction with the motorway he turned onto it and chose the direction to Nice. His pursuers followed, easily picking out his red car and its Italian number-plate.

He tried to remember the speed limit in France. Was it a hundred and thirty kilometres per hour, around eighty miles an hour ? He accelerated past a hundred and sixty, and hoped that the police were not among his pursuers. On second thoughts, he mused, he did not mind if they were.

One of three chasing cars came alongside in the fast lane and overtook him. It swerved in front, and braked sharply. Forced to brake too, Owen overtook it on the inside, and pressed his foot to the floor. Perspiring and increasingly apprehensive, he raced past Antibes where tomorrow morning he had hoped to gaze at the sumptuous yachts but not to swim from the topless beaches since it was only February.

One car alongside in the fast lane and two other cars behind kept pace with him. Together they raced past the exit to Nice airport and passed cars entering from other parts of the city. The car alongside veered towards him and scraped his door. Owen grimly held his wheel straight and continued past Nice. As they approached Monaco a police siren wailed and blue lights flashed in his mirror at a distance. Neither he nor his pursuers slowed.

A road-sign warned that the Italian frontier was approaching. Pouring sweat despite the cold outside he swept across the border into Italy. His pursuers, having lost their prey, fell back and flashed their lights defiantly, presumably to return to Grasse or to have an interesting discussion with the police.

Slowing to the speed limit Owen reached into the car's door-pocket for the bag of toffees and crammed two into his mouth, discovering too late that the wrappings were still on.

After two hours he reached Turin and was glad that he had not cancelled his hotel room there. He had left his pyjamas and razor at La Rivolte but they were a small price to pay for not being lynched or killed on the motorway. He would telephone Mr. Ours in the morning and agree how to settle the bill.

He crawled into bed exhausted and attempted to relax. He realised with a shock that he was now being pursued by thugs in both England and in France. Drifting into oblivion, he hoped that Rocher's efforts were not being coordinated with fellow fascists across Europe. If they were, then clearly EU policing powers against trans-European criminals were necessary.

* * *

In the morning he rejoined the Group meeting which was continuing as usual in the Turin Palace hotel. Owen found his fellow MEPs seated in rows and listening to a debate with local politicians. They were arguing that the cost of subsidising the poor southern half of the country was unacceptable to the rich north, and maybe separation of the country into two halves was desirable.

The room was crowded but for Owen agreeably so. It meant that, still exhausted, he would not be called on to speak. He sat at the back and between yawns attempted to listen.

Ushers and assistants milled around. On the platform at the front a worthy finished a speech and a polite round of applause was awarded to him. The Chair of the session introduced the next speaker "...great honour...the deputy mayor of..."

Short of sleep and still tense, Owen walked to the table where strong coffee and sweet cakes were being dispensed by hotel staff.

Arthur Angler, the group's Quaestor, was standing at the table, looking tired. He was sipping a *Bicerin*, the local speciality, which was a delicious-looking mixture of hot chocolate, coffee and cream.

"Good morning, Arthur. You look as if you didn't have too good a night ?" enquired Owen.

"I can't finish the crossword in today's paper."

"Not on your usual good form ?"

"Yesterday evening I wandered down the town among those arcades with the marble columns. In one beautiful old café I stopped for a coffee. There were so many pretty girls" Arthur sighed. "I'm still wondering why I wasn't allowed, by some unfortunate law of nature, to kiss them all, one by one, on their beautiful rounded mouths. Kiss them with the taste of cream and chocolate and pastries. I adored them all. When I got back to the hotel I couldn't sleep."

"Too much caffeine ?"

"No, my bed."

"Uncomfortable ?"

"Nobody in it."

Owen chuckled and carried a cup of hot black coffee back to his seat. He rubbed his eyes, put the headphones over his ears again, and looked around at his colleagues.

Group meetings were not dull if you knew where to look. Entertainment sometimes came from watching bitter personal rivalries explode between members. One feuding pair were both Italian ex-Prime Ministers who could not abide each other : each felt his personal status relative to the other was vital even though their country had experienced over fifty of them since 1945. Another pair who entertained were rival Dutch ladies : one was dowdy and puritan but clever politically : the other was lively and elegant but not political. The latter had confided to Owen that she deployed two weapons : "Faced by a challenge I ask myself 'should I use my body or my brain ?'" Owen had no doubt which was more effective.

All the members had been elected by proportional representation and therefore owed their jobs to having been positioned high on their party's list of candidates in the previous election. Some were there as a reward for hardwork or loyalty to their party leader. Others were high on the list for different reasons. A generation ago, one had been the red-headed mistress of a socialist leader : when the leader had left the European Parliament to take up his country's highest office she had joined his cabinet and had eventually been made prime minister. Pierre Hirondelle had explained how this long relationship had been concealed, even by the newspapers, thanks to France's privacy laws. He gave a recent surprising example of a photograph taken by a traffic camera in Paris : it had revealed that an offending car was being driven by the car-owner's mistress. A local court had upheld the owner's appeal against a fine on the grounds that the police photograph infringed a Frenchman's legal right to a private life.

That socialist leader had been surpassed by a German socialist Chancellor - who had positioned two mistresses high on his party's list. But both had proved themselves to be subtle politicians and had risen to chair parliamentary committees.

The Group divided socially along many different lines ; the deepest divisions were by nationality and language. But there were also grandees, bridge-players, perpetual workers, freemasons, and the staff.

One aloof north-European MEP believed that he should have been the next monarch of his country but for a failure by his natural royal grandfather to marry a mistress : he mixed only with a small set of courtiers and disliked his fellow MEPs, especially those who used his first name. Another form of inexcusable intolerance, thought Owen.

All the members socialised together just once a year, at the Christmas party for the Group's staff. The highlight was the annual limerick contest.[9]

Owen was sipping his coffee when one of the Group's attractive Italian assistants walked past. She stopped beside him and smiled. "Buon Giorno, Signor Mann !"

Owen raised his head, saw her smiling face and the single-strand gold chain necklace that decorated her delicate neck. Like a shot of adrenalin, Owen felt revived. "Buon Giorno, Bay-ah-tree-chay" he replied phonetically and smiled back.

He was unsure whether Beatrice's intelligence matched her physique and elegance. It was generally believed that she was the mistress of Signor Leonardo Tartaruga, a wrinkled but wealthy Italian MEP. Tartaruga had explained to Owen that, in Italy, a man who admitted to lovers was considered to be behaving naturally. If a man enjoyed food, wine and sex, he said, he was not burdened by unnatural limitations, and was therefore trustworthy. Catholic countries enjoyed more mistresses and fewer divorces so young children were better protected. He told Owen that the Italian expression for 'making love' was '*fare la festa*', which Owen could only put into English inadequately as 'having a party'. He had also taught Owen the words '*grande scopate*', which meant "truly memorable screws".

Owen had started to learn Italian in the parliament because, twiddling the language dial by his seat in the hemicycle where all EU official languages were on tap, he had found it the most musical. The parliament provided free language teaching for its members. The only burden for a pupil MEP was doing enough homework to make the lessons worthwhile. By comparison with Italian, Owen found the guttural north European languages full of spitting sounds. He agreed with the Habsburg Emperor, Charles V, who had said four centuries ago : "I speak Spanish to God, Italian to women, French to men...but to my horse I speak German."

Italian was the language for opera but not for oratory. That laurel belonged to French, the parliament's best orator was French, and the best speech ever delivered had been in French by an old member named Maurice Faure who had been a prosecutor at the Nuremburg War Crimes trial. The Faures were a venerable French political family, one of whom was a French President who died in bed with his mistress. Those who had heard Faure's memorable speech said it had been like the waves of the ocean, rising then falling, quieter then louder, calm then stormy. A Congressman from California, visiting the parliament, had listened spellbound without understanding and had asked "Say, *who* is that guy ?"

Owen could now string simple Italian sentences together. He had learned to address Italian MEPs as 'Onorevole' which meant 'Honourable Member', and not 'Honorabile' which meant they were members of the Mafia.

He asked Beatrice how she was today. "Come sta ?"

"Bene, grazie. I have been asked to deliver this note to you by Mister Pauw." She placed it on the table beside Owen and left to continue her errands. Owen could see the Belgian Mr. Pauw sitting at the front of the meeting. Nobody could miss his jackets which were always of a single brilliant colour. Today he was in peacock blue. Owen opened the note which the delectable Beatrice had left.

Pauw's note was a story for Owen's collection. It was a joke by the Belgians against the French, which was unusual because it was normally the other way round.

However it was in poor taste[10] and Owen doubted whether he could include it any book. But, enough of dozing, he must concentrate on the challenge ahead. Which, unfortunately, was not Beatrice, but what were his report's conclusions about fascism ?

He faced the hardest part of being a rapporteur, familiar to writers. Confronted by a blank sheet of paper and a mass of research, what to write and how to begin ?

Next week he and Gatto would sit down in Strasbourg to decide the contents of the report. He unwrapped a treacle toffee and scribbled notes until the Group Meeting broke up for lunch and for an afternoon farm-visit.

* * *

In Sãta's headquarters beside the gorge Istvan Diszno's telephone rang.

"This is Grasse. Where does Mann sleep in Brussels ? Find out, and finish him."

Diszno was delighted. He pushed another clove of garlic into his mouth. It always tasted strong but his mother had told him that garlic kept away vampires and illness too. How he missed her.

He made a telephone-call to a computerised hotel-booking service, then took the next train to Brussels. The city's evening rush-hour was over and he enjoyed the opportunity to ride the modern uncrowded Metro. He walked the last few blocks to Owen's hotel. His pistol and its silencer were in a shoulder-holster under his jacket.

Diszno sauntered into the hotel. Seeing nobody, he rang the bell on the desk.

Katvis, the patron, emerged from a back room. Diszno leaned forward and breathed confidentially : "Is Mr. Mann in ?"

Katvis took a step backwards and eyed Diszno sceptically.

"He has not reserved a room here this week."

"But I have some urgent papers to deliver to him about a nationalist report which he is writing."

"A nationalist report ?" Katvis checked the register. "He has not reserved for next week either. We have lost his patronage for some reason which I do not understand."

"Are you sure ?"

"Of course I am sure. For what do you take me ?"

Diszno left the hotel disgruntled. He would have to report that he had failed, but he would gladly offer to try again.

Thirty minutes later Owen telephoned Katvis from Turin.

"Owen Mann here. Could I reserve my usual room for Tuesday and Wednesday the week after next ?"

"Of course, Mijnheer Mann." The patron paused, wondering whether he should say anything. "Forgive me for mentioning this but you are a loyal customer." He paused again to think.

"Thankyou Mr. Katvis. Is there a problem ?"

"A short time ago, a foreigner was here asking for you. He had some kind of nationalist papers to give you. I only mention it, mijnheer," Katvis shuddered at the memory of Diszno's breath, "because to be honest I did not like him. He did not appear to have the cultivation which I associate with the parliament, if you understand me ?"

There was a silence while Owen weighed up the word 'nationalist'.

"Mijnheer Mann ? Are you still there ?"

"Mr. Katvis. What you've told me may be important. I would not want any disrepute to be brought onto your excellent hotel. So, temporarily I assure you, I will try another hotel for a while. Later I shall be happy to return. Thank you for your helpfulness."

Katvis rang off and wiped his nose. He had been helpful and he had lost a customer. He shrugged philosophically ; he must be losing the plot, as his wife had told him at breakfast.

* * *

The time had come round for another plenary week in Strasbourg for the parliament. On the first evening Owen dined with Radical colleagues at the popular and cosy Zuem Ysehut restaurant beside the river near to the parliament. In summer it was delightful to dine in its garden but this was February. Their dining-club debated East Germany's politics with an invited expert.

Next morning it was raining heavily. Instead of walking along the river he caught the bus to the parliament which collected members and staff from the hotels. Shortly after he sat down Pietro Gatto climbed aboard. Owen beckoned to him to come and sit with him.

The bus crawled slowly forward in the morning rush-hour towards the parliament. A crescendo of noise could be heard as the bus came to a halt. In front, right across the street, a metal barricade had been placed to block the traffic. Beyond it stood police and a huge crowd of men.

The bus-driver wound down his window and began an animated discussion with a policeman ; he was entitled to drive through the crowd, he insisted, because he was carrying members of parliament who had to go about their duties. The policeman replied, equally aggressively, that he was truly desolated but it was impossible for any vehicle to pass at present.

Word spread down the bus that it was a mass demonstration of French farmers. They were protesting because it was the time of year when subsidies and prices for agriculture were debated in the parliament.

While they waited impatiently, Owen and Pietro discussed the conclusions to the report which they would start drafting later in the day.

"Do we agree, Pietro, that the fascists are gaining ground?" asked the MEP.

"Countries vary" replied the staffer. "In Austria, France and Italy the far-right win an alarming twenty per cent of the national vote and their candidates are elected as town mayors. In other countries, such as the UK where there is no proportional representation for your national parliament, the far-right has not gained even a foothold. Elsewhere in Europe the fascists are weak because they fight among themselves. But overall, yes, I think they are gaining ground."

"Fascism was defeated long ago in 1945. Why is it growing again now ?"

"Memories of Hitler, Mussolini and Franco linger on. Populism and fascism are a temptation for every generation of politicians."

"Populism is certainly a cheap option for some politicians" reflected Owen. "When things go wrong, it is so easy to tell the people what they want to hear, and to offer them scape-goats to take the blame."

A series of small explosions rocked the stationary bus. Fireworks and rockets were being detonated by the farmers. Fifty policemen in formation, wearing dark blue cloaks and carrying truncheons and what looked like machine-guns, marched past.

"You know the old story about populism told by Diogenes Laertius in 150 BC ?" asked Pietro. "A man called Phocion made a speech and the people applauded him wildly. Surprised at the crowd's reaction, Phocion asked a friend : 'Why are they clapping me ? Did I say something foolish ?"

A voice from the row behind broke in. It was Mr. Tartaruga. "And remember the Roman slave whose job was to stand behind the Emperor and whisper to him, whenever he thought appropriate, 'Caesar, remember you are only a man.' It is simple to be carried away by oratory."

"Those farmers want populist policies," said Pietro pointing to the bedraggled but defiant crowd. "They are threatened by the rapid rate of change and want comfortable solutions. Foreigners are moving into their homelands ; technology and global competition causes them to lose their jobs. Their distress is fertile ground for agitators who claim the old parties have failed. Populists reassure the public that they can bring back 'the good old days'. Zhirinovsky is trying to do it in Russia, to feed off their loss of empire."

The bus was still stationary. Pietro's mention of Russia suddenly suggested to Owen the answer to a puzzle which had lain at the back of his mind, like an unsolved crossword clue. The postcard from Moscow which had been signed with a double-hump M-type doodle. Was it from Monika of Stockholm ? He had offered to show her round the parliament. Was this her reply, that she would like to visit one day ? If so, it was something to look forward to.

"And for people in the west the threat from the USSR's 'evil empire' has gone," he replied to Pietro. "So they look for other enemies, foreigners are easy targets."

"Another help to fascism was NATO's planning in the cold-war against communism" said Pietro.

"How ?" asked a surprised Owen.

"NATO and the American CIA organised 'Stay Behind' guerrillas in Europe in order to counter any Soviet invasion. They recruited those most fanatic of anti-communists, the ex-Nazis. They secretly gave them arms and finance. In Italy they were called 'Gladio' and the Italian public only became aware of them when investigations showed that Gladio was linked to a corrupt Masonic Lodge called 'P.2', to which many influential figures of the Italian establishment belonged."

"Next point for the report. What are the fascists' intentions ?" asked Owen.

"Fascist policies are similar right across Europe. They are nationalist, anti-foreigner, racist, anti-semitic and anti-EU. Most of the things which, unchecked in the 1930s, led to world war."

A lump had grown in Owen's throat : "Their attitudes are utterly unacceptable. Colour of skin, religious belief, or any other characteristic is not a reason for discrimination. That lesson was branded into Europeans by the Second World War. My own country's history proves the value of absorbing immigrants."

A herd of mooing cows was pushing past both sides of the bus. Being overtaken like this made some of the passengers irritated but the driver would still not let them out.

"Final conclusion, Pietro. The EU has no power to fight against fascism. A South American journalist pointed out to me that the fifteen national ministers will want to keep that responsibility in their own individual hands."

"But if a bank is robbed in London and the villain escapes on a high-speed train through the Channel Tunnel, nobody has the power to pursue him. The British police have to contact the French police and ask them to meet the train in Paris or maybe the Belgian police if it went to Brussels. The robber has an excellent chance of escaping."

"Can't EuroPol arrest him ?"

"EuroPol is only an information centre. Until all EU member states ratify its constitution, EuroPol doesn't even officially exist."

The bus started to inch forwards. It mounted a pavement and bypassed a small mountain of steaming manure lying in the street. The passengers in the bus applauded, either because they were moving or in admiration of the sight. Owen resisted making an untranslatable pun about 'the peasants are revolting'.

"Let's summarise" he said. "Fascism is growing, but is still controllable. Their policies are populist, racist and anti-EU. What else ? Are they learning from each other across borders ?"

"Only a little so far. But it's obvious they should, so we must expect them to do it."

"They are not short of finance."

"They all raise money in similar ways : bank robberies, drug-dealing, and selling hate CD music."

"Final point. Should the EU have powers to deal with them ?"

The bus crawled through the final police cordon to a bedlam of jeering from the farmers.

"In my opinion, yes. A way is needed to prevent criminals in one EU state from finding asylum in another. And EuroPol needs powers and resources."

"How's our timetable ?" asked Owen.

"We've slipped. The report ought to be in the committee by the week after next. That's impossible now. It will take me several days to write and then it has to be translated and printed. I'll work as fast as I can," promised Pietro, "otherwise it will not be debated before the election and your work will be wasted."

The bus halted outside the Tower building and they were allowed to exit. They ran through the rain into the courtyard. Shouts of derision rang behind them.

Pietro grinned : "That delay has saved us some time. I'll start writing straightaway. I'll contact you if I need to."

Owen went to his office on the tenth floor and, still standing, on impulse rang Nina's cottage. Her answerphone clicked in and a confident deep male voice said : 'Hello. We can't take the call in person at the moment but, if you'd like to, leave a message for Dick Walker or Nina Grey. We'll get back to you as soon as we can. Thanks for calling.'

The surprise hit Owen like a blow to the chin and he fell back into his office chair.

He left the office, and took a lift to the ground-level. In the bar beside the hemicycle with the green carpet of red and yellow wild flowers he bought a large strong coffee. There was a dilemma which had grown in Owen's mind like a slow cancer and which he needed to think hard about.

Back home he had been elected as Euro-sceptic. Yet his report was going to recommend increased powers for the EU. His party was about to select its candidates for the June election to be MEPs for the next five years. How would the activists react to his apparent volte-face ? Could he continue as rapporteur with selection coming up fast ? Whose advice could he seek ? He decided to phone the Chief Whip of the Radical MEPs. The Chief answered immediately.

"Jim Keeper."

"Jim, this is Owen Mann. I have a problem."

"Okay. Can we discuss it or has the news broken already ?"

The Whips played a vital role in detecting problems before political milk was spilled in public. Jim Keeper envied the whips in the Commons who could force backbench Westminster MPs to fall into line by threatening to destroy their hopes of promotion. As an MEP whip he had few threats to brandish because there were no EU ministerships to which backbenchers could be promoted. All he could threaten was exile to a dull committee in some months' time, or to write a letter to the party chairman, or disappointment to those hoping for an end-of-career knighthood or to be pensioned off to the House of Lords.

They arranged to meet in a couple of hours at the Simpson Memorial Bar. This was a discreet and comfortable bar with deep leather armchairs, at the end of the Churchill building. It was reserved for MEPs although their assistants used it too. The public was excluded.

When Owen arrived Jim was already there in a corner, his grey head down as he concentrated on something he was writing. Looking up he saw Owen and waved his empty coffee cup.

"Could I have another cappuccino ?"

Owen went to the bar and ordered it and a *caffe non correto* for himself. He expected this order to be queried by the bar-girl but she did not waver. He had once seen an Italian usher order it and had asked what it was.

"Normally" the usher had explained, "I take a little cognac in my coffee. That corrects it. Today I feel good so my coffee does not have to be corrected."

Owen carried the cups to Jim Keeper's table.

"What are you writing ?"

"I'm struggling with an article for a French magazine. Do you happen to know whether an oil-rig is *le* or *la* ?"

"Surely that's only of interest to another oil-rig ?"

"Thanks a lot. I hope my writing is more successful than one former MEP called Seligman. After drafting his speeches he found it hard to get to sleep. To calm himself before going to bed, he made tea and bread-and-butter. One night, fearing his brain was over-stimulated, he took a sleeping pill. In the morning his wife found his speech on the kitchen table, spread with butter and a mouthful bitten out of it. It's a true story."

Keeper laid his notes to one side. "Okay, what's the problem ? I'm grateful to you for confiding in me first. Is it a case of *cherchez la femme* ?"

"Nothing like that." Owen explained and Jim listened carefully.

As he finished laying out his dilemma, the pager on Owen's belt vibrated. He walked to the bar, picked up the internal telephone and rang the number indicated. It was a call was from Kikker in Security at the front entrance to the parliament.

"Mr. Mann ? There is a visitor here for you."

"Who is it ?"

"He's a Ukrainian. His name is Istvan Diszno. Will you vouch for him so I can give him a pass into the parliament?"

"Mr. Kikker, I'm not expecting anyone and I'm tied up right now. Could you ask him what his business is ?"

After a short silence Kikker's voice came back to the phone : "He wants to give you some papers about a report which you are writing concerning nationalism."

"Nationalism ?" An uneasy feeling grew in Owen's stomach.

"Mr. Kikker, please apologise to the visitor that it is impossible for me to meet him. But ask him to leave the papers and his address."

He replaced the receiver. He returned to Jim's corner and decided that, rather than sleeping in his hotel tonight where there was no security, it might be safer to curl up on the day-bed in his office.

"Sorry, Jim, you were about to give me your advice."

"Your problem is an old one. Yes, it is possible to resign a rapporteurship and in the past some MEPs have done it. The legal position is that the rapporteur is representing the opinion of the committee, not his own views. Just as a lawyer defends a client in court even though he may not believe in his innocence. But it is a subtle point which would not be explained fairly by the British media."

Jim gazed at him. "Owen, what's your work been for ? Do you believe your own conclusions or don't you - that the fascist threat is growing and extra EU powers are needed ? If you're right, you should get the credit. Or do you give up when you reach the hard part ? Remind me which great leaders have given up when the going became tough ? Which is more important : hiding in the crowd, or fighting for what you believe ?"

Keeper finished his coffee and continued to hammer his advice home. "How much respect do you have for those Euro-sceptical MPs in the Commons who voted through the Single Act and the Maastricht Treaty rather than risk losing their own seats at a General Election. They complain bitterly today that it led to the greatest constitutional dilemma of our time, whether or not Britain should give up sterling and join the Euro. Yet when it came to the crunch they voted to preserve their own jobs and put their so-called principles second. History will give them nothing but scorn."

Jim had finished his coffee but not his advice. "If you lose your seat in the next election, Owen, which I hope you don't because I think there may be a field marshal's baton in your knapsack, then at least have something to show for your time here. If you believe in your conclusions, stick to them. I'll support you as much as I can. We may run into conflict with the MPs at Westminster. So what ? We are in different parliaments, with different jobs to do. If you disagree with the party, you won't topple the government. Have you discussed the problem with your constituency Chair ?"

Owen thought for a moment. "I can see you're right, Jim. It boils down to whether I've got political courage or whether I'm a populist, saying what the public wants to hear."

"Only you can decide that, Owen."

After a few moments of light banter, Owen returned to his office. He passed McKirk in a corridor. He greeted the hack and asked : "How's the scoop ?"

McKirk's face was solemn. "I'm going to Russia to finish an investigation."

"What's it about ?"

"A big grain exporting scam. Surplus EU grain is exported by sea from Rotterdam to Russia. The EU pays an official subsidy to the exporters to compensate them because the world price is below the minimum price which the EU guarantees to them."

"What's the scam ?"

"The Russians claim that there are shortages in the quantity of grain which they receive. So the exporters give them credit for the shortfall. But, and here's the scam, the exporters fail to repay the subsidy to the EU for the grain which was never shipped."

"Clever. Who are the exporters ?"

"That's one of my unanswered questions. It's easy to get a ship's name, but to discover who are the ultimate principals is much harder. I've traced it to a company registered in a Caribbean tax-haven, Antigua."

"Good story."

"I've a small problem."

"Which is ?"

"I need an interpreter to help me with Russian."

"Won't your editor pay for an interpreter ?"

"Not for the one I want."

"Who's that ?"

"Natasha. And she's reluctant to come with me."

"Why ?"

"She's married."

Owen continued down the corridor. Poor Murdo, hard-bitten now hard-smitten. The tough investigative reporter in turmoil over somebody else's wife. We all have problems, reflected Owen.

* * *

Owen had found a new secretary to replace Lynda. Her name was Jane Farmer : she had brown curls and round spectacles and came with references that she said she was immensely efficient and calm. To teach her the job he telephoned each day. "Anything exciting in the post today, Jane ?" he asked.

"A telephone call first thing this morning from United Technologies. Their managing director, Mr. Peter White, asked if you could ring him as soon as possible."

United Technologies were the largest employer in Owen's constituency. Seeking to build a reputation for prompt service, Owen telephoned White immediately.

"United Technologies. Can I help you ?" said their telephonist.

"This is Owen Mann from Strasbourg."

He heard her speak to someone. "I've got a foreign gentleman from Salzburg. Shall I put him through to Sales ?"

Sales Department transferred him to White.

"Mr. White ? This is Owen Mann from Strasbourg. I had a message to ring you."

"Something has come up which I'd rather not talk about on the phone. I wonder whether you could possibly pay me an early visit here at the factory ? Monday morning ?"

Owen called his diary onto his desktop computer screen.

"I can be with you at nine on Monday morning."

"Thankyou."

That night and the next Owen slept on the day-bed in his office and kept the door locked. It was uncomfortable but he felt safer. He wondered who the 'nationalist' Ukrainian was and why he was so persistent.

*　　*　　*

Enrique Sãta was smoking his usual brand of cigar and listening to two of his assistants in his office. Rado Zaplasiti was speaking while Monika Pasarea sat waiting. Diszno was away, on his current project, on which Sãta had warned him that he must not fail.

"When will our friends start winning elections, Rado ?" the boss asked.

"President, last week in Denmark our man came second in an election for town mayor. It was easily our best result in that country. In Austrian elections for a regional council, our people won their first ever two seats, one gained from the centre-right. More contests there in two weeks time."

"From now on I want a regular written report, as we pick up speed."

"Another good thing, president. Our friends everywhere are finding that their new recruits are mostly under thirty years old. The age structure of our movement is improving all the time."

"Excellent." Sãta glanced at his watch. "Monika, what's happening in the European Parliament ?"

"President. As you know, a great amount of information was revealed by witnesses at the Public Hearing. It depends on how full a picture is put together in the committee's draft report."

"When can we see the report ?"

"It's being written right now by a staff member" she replied.

"What's the timetable ?"

"Elections to the European Parliament will be held all over the EU in four months' time. At that time all uncompleted reports will lapse, and must be started afresh in the new parliament. The membership of the new parliament may be more sympathetic to us. We certainly hope so. Any new investigation could not be completed for another eighteen months, more likely two years."

"Will Mann's report meet the election deadline ?"

"I'm monitoring it closely. The staffer may have to be given a memory lapse to help him miss the timetable."

"Good," said Sãta. "Why deal with the staffer's memory, so to speak, and not the rapporteur himself ?"

"Because a member of parliament is a public figure, even an unknown Euro-MP. Injuring him might draw attention to his work and draw the focus onto our friends. Our strategy should be to hurt the report not the person. If we fail, further action against the rapporteur will be necessary. At this stage it's the report, not the man, that matters to us."

"Okay. Let's get on to fund-raising..." Sãta sucked at his cigar. Providing that Diszno did his job properly, Monika would not need to waste any more time on the report.

He looked at his watch again. "We have to be quick, Monika. I've a plane to catch to Moscow."

He had called a meeting in Russia's capital, deliberately beyond the EU's borders. The leaders of all the nationalist parties of western Europe would be present. They would come because he was paying their airfares, hotels and entertainment. He would persuade them, with money, to agree to a common manifesto for the European elections. It would oppose a federal Europe, oppose the Euro currency, and be in favour of repatriating all foreigners. Nationalist parties would cooperate closely to build a new kind of Europe, a

Europe of cooperating independent nationalist states.

* * *

Owen telephoned Jack Terrier from Strasbourg to discuss his worry about the rapporteurship. As they talked he could almost see Jack's face take on a fierce scowl.

"Lad, it's crystal clear to me" said Jack, adopting a paternal attitude. "I've been against this report from the beginning. It's a waste of taxpayers' money. More importantly, it's wasting your precious time. Do you want to be re-elected ? It's that simple."

He paused for Owen's answer.

"Jack, if I believe in something, I have to see it through. Fascism is growing again and I've come to believe that the EU needs powers to counter it."

"Lad, you may be right. In theory you probably are. But it's not your problem. Get elected or you are nothing. Need I remind you what's happening next weekend ?"

"Candidate re-selection."

The local Radical activists would choose their list of candidates for the June election. The older man put a gun to the MEP's head :

"Which do you prefer to be, Owen ? A rapporteur now or a candidate in June ?"

Owen promised he would think it over very carefully.

* * *

On Saturday the chairmen of all fifty Radical constituency parties in the region met at a country hotel just off a motorway junction. They interviewed fifteen candidates. The fifteen had been sifted from over a hundred hopeful activists who had submitted *curriculum vitaes* and wanted to be on the Radical party's list of candidates in the Home Counties region for June's election. The two sitting Radical MEPs in the region, Tom Ostler and Owen Mann, were automatically included among the fifteen to be interviewed. In the chair was the party's regional chief, Jack Terrier.

Each candidate was given up to eight minutes to make a speech. Afterwards each was questioned for a further fifteen minutes. The chairmen voted to reduce the fifteen to a shortlist of nine who would be invited to the final on the following Saturday. There all the paid-up party members in the region could attend and vote to place the best six in a pecking order.

Owen was confident that he would get through to the final, but he felt very nervous as his interview arrived. He remembered what Richard Nixon, seeking to be President, had advised : 'when aspiring to be chosen as your party's candidate, swing to the right ; when aspiring to be the nation's president, swing back to the centre.' In this first interview by local chairmen, he must appeal to their desire to choose dedicated MEPs who would be loyal to the party's principles. If he reached the final, he would then have to sing a different song, to try to appeal to the wider-ranging prejudices of the party activists.

In his eight minutes he spoke confidently, stressing his youth and energy, his localness, and his experience in the obscure ways in which Brussels worked. The questions were straightforward and there was none about his report on fascism.

He returned home to await the selection committee's verdict. Among the letters waiting on the mat was one marked impressively 'From the President of the European Parliament'. Inside was a short letter from Michelangelo Canguro with an Italian story.[11]

Owen read it and smiled, and jumped as the telephone rang.

"Jack here" said the familiar voice. "Glad to tell you that you are through to the final next Saturday." He named a large conference hall where the meeting would be held. "Lots were drawn for order of speaking, and you go first in the afternoon at two fifteen. So arrive at the centre just after two." He paused, then added : "And good luck."

* * *

The tallest building among the European Parliament's offices in Luxembourg is known as The Tower. On its ground floor are committee rooms which are seen on television when national agriculture ministers do battle with each other. The upper floors of the Tower house offices for the parliament's staff. At the top, on the twenty-second floor, a canteen offers average food and a splendid view over the gorge towards the city centre.

It was late on Friday afternoon, and the staff were going home. Being the end of February it was already dark outside. On the eighth floor, Pietro Gatto was working late. During the past week there had been no meeting of the Civil Liberties committee so he had been free to finish drafting Owen's report. He had reached the stage of checking his spelling and punctuation.

At eight o'clock, he tidied his desk, saved the latest version on his desktop computer, made a back-up, and switched off the power.

He put on his thick overcoat, picked up his motorcycle helmet and left the building. His low-power motorcycle carried him thirty kilometres from the city to his apartment in a small village.

After midnight, in pitch darkness, a figure crept silently into Gatto's office in the Tower. The figure was wearing dark clothes and gloves, and carried a powerful narrow-beam torch and a computer diskette. The figure switched on Gatto's computer. In seconds a copy of the report had been made on the diskette. In a few seconds more, just as unobtrusively, the figure was gone.

* * *

On Monday morning Owen motorbiked to the offices of United Technologies in his constituency. He dismounted in the visitors' area and parked next to a Rolls-Royce. A uniformed commissionaire shouted at him :

"Oi ! you ! Delivery rand the back or get lost."

Owen removed his helmet, and explained to the old soldier that he was a genuine visitor. He was permitted to leave his bike where it stood and to go through the swingdoor entrance. He greeted the receptionist cheerfully : like the old soldier she too had a vote.

"Good morning."

The receptionist stared at his helmet and briefcase. "Can I help ?"

"My name is Owen Mann." Her face remained blank.

"I'm the MEP," he added trying to help.

"The what ?"

"I have an appointment with Mr. White, the Managing Director."

She opened her appointment book to verify. "Yes, that's right."

An internal telephone call gave her instructions. "Take the lift to the fourth floor and Mr. White will meet you there" she said.

Pointing him towards the lift she resumed her dazed look. Four floors up the lift doors opened, and a forty-year old man in a dark blue suit held out a hand in greeting.

"I'm Peter White. Come into my office and sit down. You know Sir Harry, I'm sure ?"

Sir Harry Pedreven MP was already sitting in a comfortable chair. He and Owen exchanged polite professional smiles as the newcomer sat down. Coffee was served.

"Gentlemen, I am exceedingly grateful to you both for coming at short notice. I'll get straight to the point" said White. He turned towards Owen. "As I was telling Sir Harry, I have a painful problem. I'd be grateful if you would keep it under your hat for the time being, although it's bound to leak out."

He grimaced. "Head Office in Switzerland has warned that this factory is going to be closed. Most of the jobs will be transferred to a factory on the continent, either in Spain or in central Europe. We employ over a thousand men and women here, and we are one of the area's largest employers. I don't need to explain to you how serious the consequences will be for the local economy."

He looked hard at each man in turn : "My question to you both is 'Can you help save the factory ?'"

"Why do your bosses want to close it ?" asked Owen.

"They consider that the economic benefits from being inside the Euro currency zone are too good to miss. They believe that Britain will not join for the foreseeable future."

"But why move manufacturing jobs from England to the continent when we offer huge advantages such as language and low company taxes ?" Owen persisted.

"Not so many advantages any more. The Social Chapter has introduced extra wage costs to Britain. And Europe is compact compared to the world's other continents. Its population is concentrated and there are good road networks. Transport costs to the customers are relatively small and therefore it makes sense for us to have a single manufacturing centre which serves all the EU markets."

Pedreven appeared shocked. "When will this happen ? A General

Election is due before long. My seat might be at risk. It's essential, Peter, that you come to London and see a government minister."

Peter White accepted the offer immediately, as if he had anticipated it. "Of course."

"I'll ask for an appointment straightaway and let you know tomorrow" said Pedreven. As an after-thought he added to Owen : "You'll be abroad, I'm sure. But if you can manage it, come along."

"Thankyou, Sir Harry. I'll come if I possibly can".

Turning to the businessman Owen said : "If the meeting with the minister is unsuccessful, then we could meet a European Commissioner in Brussels. This threat smells to me like job-poaching by another EU government offering illegal subsidies. Unemployment in some parts of the continent is very high and they are desperate for jobs."

To the knight of the shire he added : "Come to Brussels too."

The two parliamentarians left at the same time, making small talk until they reached the fresh air. The knight's chauffeur was waiting in the Rolls and drove him away. Owen rode his bike to the party office where he asked Jane Farmer to discover from Pedreven's secretary in the Commons the time of the meeting.

He headed for Brussels and the Environment committee. But his mind was concentrated on the coming weekend's selection ordeal.

* * *

By the time Saturday morning dawned in England, Owen's apprehension had grown exponentially. The final selection was critical to his political future, life or death, double or quits.

During the morning, visitors to his surgery smoothed his anxiety by merely being there. The most difficult case concerned a couple who had bought a second home in Spain on the basis of attractive publicity. They were having difficulty getting the building finished, and water and electricity connected. They were dealing with a builder in the private sector and did not want to go to court. It was a common problem and Owen had no cheap solution to recommend.

At midday he locked up the party office and returned home, buying a sandwich on the way. He changed into his best suit with a new shirt and tie, bought to give himself confidence. He rode the forty miles to the conference centre.

The challenge was to be chosen, not just on the list of six, but to be highly placed on it. When the election arrived the public would cast a single vote for a political party and not for any individual candidate. The region's six MEP seats would be allocated to the candidates, starting from the top of the different parties' lists, according to a mathematical formula devised by a Belgian mathematics professor called D'Hondt.

If the Radicals won more votes than any other party in the region, the top three on their list could confidently expect to win seats in June. The lower three on their list would be also-rans. However if the Radicals won fewer votes than the Progressives they would have just two or possibly only one MEP.

In this final, therefore, whoever the local Radicals chose to be the top two of their list were effectively guaranteed a seat in Brussels for the following five years. Whoever was chosen fourth, fifth or sixth had a slim outside chance of success although they could hope that a death or resignation would move them up the list to step into somebody's empty shoes.

Being placed third on the list would offer a reasonable chance of being elected in June. It would depend on the relative popularity of the parties when the public voted in June.

Owen thought about the strengths of his rivals. The other eight who were in the final included three women. One was Baroness Fisher who had once been a Cabinet minister at Westminster and was now a Life Peer. He would not object to her being on the list, below him of course. She was experienced and a thoughtful listener, not a loud-mouth. Before the selection started, there was an expectation that at least one of the three woman would get onto the list.

Among the five other men only two were dangerous contenders : one was Tom Ostler, because he was a sitting MEP, and the other was Jake Adonis, a television journalist whose well-known face had not previously revealed any political affiliation. But the 'face' knew, and his fellow candidates knew, that his handsome features would make him a powerful magnet for votes. An election over a huge region, which covered several million voters, would be fought and won mainly through the media. To have a 'personality' on the

Radical list would be invaluable.

When Owen arrived at the conference centre, he was ushered into a small empty room and told to wait alone. A water bottle, a coffee percolator and plastic mugs were on a table in one corner. Moments later the party's chief agent arrived. He said that the previous candidate had just finished in the main meeting and now it was Owen's turn.

He steered Owen to the front of a large audience and pointed him to an empty chair on a raised podium. Jack Terrier, in overall charge, was already there.

Jack was using a microphone to introduce each candidate in turn to a sea of some hundred men and women. Owen recognised a few friends and his heart jumped when he saw Nina sitting at the back between two men whom he did not know. She was wearing a flowery two-piece suit and looked as gorgeous as ever.

Jack invited Owen to give a ten-minute speech. Owen walked to a lectern whose top was damp. Afterwards he learned that a nervous candidate before lunch had spilled a glass of water over it.

As it was the after-lunch hour, Owen knew he had to fight to keep his audience awake. He emphasised his localness, his growing expertise and that he had a perfect attendance and voting record in the parliament since being elected three months ago. He stayed precisely within his allotted time.

The questions from the floor were not difficult but the poor acoustics made them difficult to hear. To help the audience he repeated each question before answering it. He only handled one badly. He was asked whether he was not becoming too much of a Euro-phile and in favour of giving extra powers to the European Union and its parliament ; in other words, was he going native ? Afterwards, Owen feared that his denial had not been sufficiently convincing.

His half-hour flew by and he left the hall to applause which, though not effusive, was more than a polite ripple.

After all nine candidates had been heard and questioned, they waited outside together while the audience voted to place them in a pecking order.

The candidates and their spouses stood around in the room where the final counting would take place next. The men found they were dressed in identikit dark suits, white or blue shirts, and colourful ties. The women all wore smart colourful suits.

After thirty tense minutes the boxes of voting papers were carried in. They were emptied onto three red-baize covered tables. Counters in shirt-sleeves sorted the votes to identify the numbers of first, second and so on preferences which each candidate had received. They kept the scores on green sheets. The candidates peered over their shoulders, trying to foretell thêir individual fates.

A sight of the first preference votes made it became rapidly clear to everyone that Jake Adonis was well ahead of all his rivals. His face became very cheerful while furrows on the other eight brows grew deeper. Each still hoped to be placed second and be confident of success in June.

Surprisingly quickly all the preferences were summarised onto the green sheets. Owen could not tell what his final place on the list would be, but knew he would learn at any moment.

The head agent called out : "Quiet please" and there was an electric silence. However instead of the result being announced, nothing more was said. The green score-sheets were taken from the three small tables to one large table at the end of the room where the chief agent and three assistants were seated. More time passed while the numbers of voting papers issued in the meeting were double-checked against the numbers just counted. Next all the preference votes for each of the nine candidates were tallied onto one large white summary sheet. Using an electronic calculator, the head agent began multiplying the numbers of each ranking preference by each position, six points for each first preference, five for each second place, and so on. His assistant double-checked his mathematics.

Minutes ticked by slowly. The tension grew. The atmosphere was hot and stuffy. The candidates drank cups of tea and stood in small groups and pretended exaggerated jollity. One wife said in a loud voice : "I'm tired and fed up, going from one constituency to another like a member of a circus."

A junior agent standing next to Owen explained that not only were the candidates nervous but so were the agents because they did not want a mistake to be made.

One young candidate enquired in an anxious voice : "When do we get our travel expenses back ?" He was told that the answer was "Never. Not for today, nor ever until you are elected. You're doing this for love." He looked very shocked.

People drifted towards the top counting-table. Nine candidates and several spouses craned forward while simultaneously trying not to be seen to be looking. Baroness Fisher's shoulders drooped, feeling that as an ex-Cabinet minister she had the furthest to fall.

Amid great tension the head agent stood up and handed a single sheet of paper to Jack Terrier who was standing beside him. Suddenly Baroness Fisher was smiling broadly.

Jack Terrier said : "Would the nine candidates, but nobody else, follow me please ?"

He led them into the small room where Owen had first waited and closed the door.

"I'm now going to ask each of you in turn whether you accept the place on the list which is offered to you. Unlike real beauty contests" he continued, trying to inject humour into the tense atmosphere, "where they announce the third-placed first, I shall announce the results starting from the top."

Looking at Jake Adonis he said : "As chair of the region I ask whether you are willing to accept your ranking as number one on our list ?"

"Yes" Jake replied. Owen and the other candidates gave him a patter of polite applause and secretly cursed his undeserving handsome smile.

Turning to the baroness, Terrier asked "Do you accept your ranking as our number two ?"

"With great pleasure" Lady Fisher replied.

Very alarmed, Owen glanced at Tom Ostler, his fellow MEP. Both of them now faced a marginal chance of being re-elected. Weights were pulling his stomach through his feet.

"In third position," announced Terrier carefully, then dropped the paper which fell face down. He stooped to recover it.

"In third position," he paused for a moment, "is Tom Ostler." Ostler accepted his ranking.

"In fourth place is Owen Mann." Owen tried to look pleased. He had thought about this possibility before-hand. The rules allowed him to reject the placing and try his luck in another region. However, if he could not get picked in his home region, why should he be more successful elsewhere ?

"I accept" he said.

Placed fifth and sixth were the two remaining women. Both rejected their rankings, preferring to try elsewhere. Of the three remaining men one declined but the last two, both youngsters, accepted their places thankfully, feeling that something was better than nothing at all, and maybe they could climb higher in five years' time.

"Thankyou" said Terrier. "Would the six on the list now follow me and I will announce the result to the meeting in the hall."

The ceremony was brief. After the applause had died away, the audience headed for their homes. Owen departed, deeply disappointed. It was bitter medicine to be only fourth best. His political life was over, at least for the next five years. After that he could try again if he still had the ambition. Perhaps he had already had his reward, which was the chance to be an MEP at all.

There was neither justice nor thanks in politics. It was a primeval jungle in which almost everybody's career ended in disappointment and tears. But it hurt that his had been the shortest career of all.

* * *

The next night, Sunday, in Luxembourg the unidentified dark figure returned to the Tower office-block. There was more work to be done. A small screwdriver opened the inside of Gatto's computer. The hard-disk was quickly removed. A small magnet was wiped across all the diskettes in his drawer to irreversibly corrupt their contents. To confuse the investigation which must follow in the morning, the figure worked its way down the corridor, entering each office, removing the hard-disks from each desktop computer and wiping the diskettes with the magnet. Still in darkness the intruder departed, undetected and carrying a full carrier-bag.

Early on Monday morning, after a relaxing weekend, Pietro Gatto set off on his motorcycle to return to work. It was a cold and dry, and he rode the familiar quiet country lanes, enjoying the scenery.

He slowed as he approached a main junction where more traffic would join. In his mirror he saw a large unmarked white van racing up behind him. He moved to the right edge to allow it to pass. The truck came alongside, and its driver spun his steering wheel hard to the right. He knocked Gatto off his machine. The bike toppled over, its wheels spinning. The truck stopped and reversed methodically back over Gatto, then forwards again to make certain. There were no witnesses. The truck turned onto the main road in the direction away from the city and sped towards the open border.

Later in the morning, police made their enquiries. An elderly Luxembourg woman, who had been out walking her dog, said she might have seen a grey van in the neighbourhood at the time. She thought the driver had black hair but her eyes were not good and she was not really sure. He could have been a Portuguese, she said, spitting on the ground ; far too many of them lived in her country, the lowest-paid in west Europe in search of the highest wages : they should all return home. The police gave little weight to her account which was so obviously prejudiced.

* * *

The parliament's staff returned to the Tower block. They switched on their desktop computers but several on the eighth floor failed to work. Technicians from the parliament's computer centre were summoned. The theft of the hard-disks was discovered and replacements were ordered.

The head technician said that the motive was obvious. The thieves had heard of the high prices which second-hand disks commanded in the black market – almost worth more than their weight in gold. But the thieves would be disappointed because recently there had been a manufacturing over-capacity and prices had plummeted.

An investigation was started by Kikker to discover how and by whom the theft had been perpetrated. His task was nearly impossible because the thefts could even have been carried out by one of the staff who had access at all hours to their offices. As Kikker pointed out there were few high-security secrets to protect in a talking-shop. He wondered whether he should install security cameras inside the building.

* * *

The same Monday afternoon in London, Sir Harry Pedreven's meeting for Peter White took place at the Department of Trade & Industry.

Owen arrived in good time at the large ugly block which lies at the southern end of Victoria Street. Pedreven and White were there already, upstairs in a room next to the Secretary of State's office.

A civil servant apologised. "The Secretary of State can not be present because he has to be in the House to answer a debate. Instead, one of his junior ministers will meet you. Are you all here now ?"

They were ushered into an office with modern furnishings. Cups of tea arrived. The promised junior, Lord Wolf, arrived and introduced himself.

He spoke to White as an old friend. "Peter, we asked the department's officials to look urgently into your problem, and to recommend what can be done to rescue your jobs. It is outrageous that one part of the EU can steal jobs from another. But I am sorry to say that there is nothing we can do to prevent it."

Peter White was an opportunist and went straight to for the jugular : "Is there a subsidy that you could offer to make us stay ?"

"We might like to do that. But the damned - sorry, Owen - the European Commission can stop us. The only conditions under which the Commission will allow a subsidy by a member state are," he read carefully from a written brief, "that it contributes to economic development of a deprived area, that it will not create overcapacity in the market, and that it will not have a significant impact on the selling price of the products being manufactured."

Pedreven interrupted : "One can see the general point. If national subsidies are allowed, the result will be job-poaching all round, and that would be self-defeating. But what will happen to the jobs at United Technologies is diabolical. We have to restore power to the Commons to stop things like this happening again."

"It's not as simple as that, Sir Harry" rejoined the minister disdainfully to his political opponent. "Repealing our membership of the EU would not bring foreign investment into Britain. We are in an international world and overseas companies want unrestricted access to the Single Market. We have to remain full EU members. But, try as we can, we cannot satisfy those three Commission rules. I can see no way to help you, gentlemen. I am exceedingly sorry."

He escorted the three visitors out.

"What now ?" asked White.

Pedreven shrugged and checked his expensive watch. "That bugger Lord Wolf is no politician. He was a hugely successful businessman. He's charming and brilliant. When we were in power he told me he was bored with the City so I introduced him to our Prime Minister, but nothing came of it. Now he's offered himself to the Radicals, has got into the Lords, and is a minister. He goes to Brussels and commits Britain irrevocably to new EU laws - yet he's never won a single vote in his life. He doesn't understand the profound difference between business and politics."

Owen nodded agreement and turned to White. "We could take the fight to the continent - either by meeting the head of your company, or the right EU Commissioner."

"Both please" said Peter White.

Pedreven was uninterested. "I don't think that I can spare the time to come to Brussels. I've sent out a press-release this morning about this meeting to the local media. It might help me whenever the General Election is called."

Owen knew that the press-release would not mention his own presence, nor that he was involved in the fight to save the jobs. That was party politics. Never give your opponent an inch.

"I thought the threat of job-losses was confidential" Owen asked.

"It was, but regrettably the news has leaked out" replied White.

Owen returned to his constituency office. He telephoned the Commission in Brussels and made an appointment for White. He spent the next two days campaigning in his new electoral region.

On Thursday morning he flew to Brussels to attend the Civil Liberties committee. He had wondered how Pietro Gatto was getting along with the drafting. Having agreed to leave him alone while it was being written, he was looking forward keenly to seeing him in the afternoon. Pietro would have been in contact if there had been a problem. No news was good news.

Heavy snow fell on Wednesday night but Brussels airport was open. A full jumbo-jet from Zaire held up everybody on Owen's flight trying to get through the controls.

Chomik was just opening the proceedings as Owen reached the

committee. Few people were in the public seats and he recognised none.

Chomik was speaking in an unexpectedly sombre voice. "My dear colleagues, I have some exceedingly bad news to give to you. Most or all of you were acquainted with a member of our secretariat, Pietro Gatto. The terrible news is that he was killed in a road accident three days ago early on Monday morning."

Pietro dead ? Owen was stunned. What a terrible waste. Tears welled into his eyes. During their work together Pietro had become a real friend.

Chomik spoke a short elegy about the lost Austrian, his hard-working nature, his loyalty, his service to the parliament, and his good humour. "I ask you to stand and observe a minute's silence."

After the silence he continued. "Colleagues. The parliament experienced another blow this week. Not so devastating as the loss of our colleague, but a serious inconvenience. During last weekend, thieves broke into the Tower building in Luxembourg and damaged some of the computers. The problem for us is that the records of some committees have been lost, including ours. Many of your reports will therefore be delayed. Some, I regret to tell you, will have to be started again."

The members sat in astonished silence, each trying to work out the consequences for himself.

Chomik continued inexorably. "There is a small amount of better news. Not all of the committee's work was lost. Copies of several reports had been sent off for translation and consequently survived."

He glanced over his spectacles at a sheet of paper. "You will be wondering which ones have survived. The following four reports are safe." He read out their names. Owen's report was not one of them.

"These four can be considered by the committee at its next meeting in three weeks' time. The other reports are irretrievably lost, I am very sorry. The rapporteurs will have to start their work again from any notes which they have kept for themselves. But the chance of their work being finished before the election in June is now remote."

Owen was dumb. He had lost his friend, and now their work as well.

The committee's discussions that afternoon were desultory. At half past six the chairman adjourned the meeting until the following morning. The few members of the public who were still there filed out, including Rado Zaplasiti.

The funeral for Pietro Gatto was arranged for Saturday afternoon in the Luxembourg village where he had lived.

Owen was determined to be present. After the committee finished at noon on Friday, he telephoned Jane in the constituency office to tell her of his change of plan : fortunately it was not a surgery Saturday. He caught a train to Luxembourg and found a hotel near the station.

In the morning he rented a car and drove the twenty miles through pleasant countryside to Pietro's village. When he reached the small church some thirty cars were already parked nearby. He entered the church and was glad to see that the pews were almost filled with the parliament's staff. He found himself a seat near the back.

The service was short but moving. The head of the committee's secretariat, Bruno Wielblad, spoke an address in which he praised the young man's high qualities : Pietro would be sorely missed by all who had known him. At the end of the service the congregation sang the 'Ode To Joy', the final movement of Beethoven's Ninth Symphony which served as Europe's anthem. Owen's eyes filled with tears : it was a meaningless loss of a young and valuable member of society.

The mourners filed slowly out of the church. Pietro's parents, who had travelled from south Austria for the service, stood at the door. Both looked old and crushed, but they shook each hand that passed them. Next to the mother stood a girl in her late twenties also wearing black.

Owen shook their hands, and mentioned his name as he did so. The girl's eyes lit up. In near perfect English she said :

"Mr. Mann, I am Luisa, the twin sister of Pietro. My brother spoke a lot about you. Thank you for coming today. I know you are very busy."

About average height she had brown hair down to her chin. Her cheeks were plump and despite her intense sorrow her light brown eyes sparkled momentarily.

"Not at all, Fraulein Gatto. Your brother and I were cooperating closely on an important piece of work. He worked so hard and I liked him very much."

"I heard about your work" replied Luisa. "My brother was proud of it because it was the interestingest report on which he had worked since he had joined the European Parliament. He talked about it on the telephone with me before last weekend. I shall keep it as my last memory of him."

Owen moved forward to allow the queue behind him to shake the family's hands.

As he walked away he wondered how good Luisa's command of English really was. Better certainly that his Italian or German. She had spoken of "keeping it" as a memory of Pietro. Keeping their last conversation ?

He waited until the line of mourners had ended. He signalled politely to Luisa that he wished to say one more thing to her.

"Fraulein Luisa, please excuse me. May I ask you a question ?"

"What is it ?"

"You spoke of keeping something as a memory of your brother."

"He sent me a computer diskette with his report on it. I have not finished reading it yet."

Owen was thunderstruck but held his cool. "I do not have a duplicate of the report myself. Might it be possible for me to have a copy of the diskette ?"

"I do not understand why you do not have it. Mine is back home in Carinthia. But, of course, if you will give me your address, I will post it to you."

Owen handed her a business card and returned to his car. If Luisa really had the diskette, then he could not possibly turn his back on Pietro and the report. However great his dilemma, he could not resign from the rapporteurship. Whatever the price might prove to be, he would bear it.

He drove on to the ancient town of Trier, just inside Germany from Luxembourg, and spent Sunday visiting its Roman ruins.

* * *

An alarm clock stirred Owen from his deep sleep. Where was he ? It was Monday morning again and he was in a small German hotel. After a breakfast of sausage, cheese, black bread and delicious coffee, he returned his rented car to Luxembourg. He caught the train and walked to the parliament.

The socialist Group meeting had already begun. He cleared his pigeon-hole and checked his office for faxes and e-mails.

His computer screen said that there was one long e-message waiting for him. It came from an address which he did not recognise. He called it onto the screen and found the sender was Luisa Gatto in Austria. She had sent Pietro's draft of the report. Owen printed it out in full, thirty pages long, and replied to her with a warm thankyou.

Despite the other demands on his time, he resolved to concentrate on completing and polishing the draft by the end of the week. Settling into his seat in the Group meeting, he started immediately.

His concentration was interrupted by the visit of Peter White. They had an afternoon appointment with Commissioner Helmut Einhorn, the German who was responsible for the EU's Regional Policy. It was their last chance to rescue the jobs at United Technologies.

Peter White arrived on an early plane at Zaventem airport. Pedreven was not with him - even though MPs are able to make a cost-free visit to each EU capital each year, funded by the taxpayer.

Owen met him at the airport in a parliament car. It brought them back to Rue Wiertz to the main entrance of the parliament's Spinelli building. Owen led the way through the swing doors. At the visitor desk Owen signed a form to vouch for his guest and handed White a blue plastic pass.

Owen took him on a guided tour before lunch. They took the self-starting escalators to the vast third floor which the parliament called Main Street. They crossed the wide carpeted bridge over the street to the Spaak building so that White could look inside the hemicycle. There was no plenary debate that day, so trying to make the visit as interesting as possible, Owen took his guest into the Environment Committee. It was holding a short meeting to vote on amendments to reports. Owen seated White at the back to watch while he slipped into a spare seat beside his Group colleagues.

The voting turned out to be a close-fought battle. At one point Hans Schnecke, Owen's coordinator, was denounced by another German from the centre-right with an exasperated cry "If that was meant to be a compromise, one might as well give up politics."

Owen's group lost most of the votes by margins of either one or two votes. At the end, on the final amended resolution, Schnecke conjured an alliance with the communists and independents and won the last vote, leaving the committee without a clear position. The meeting broke up in recrimination.

Owen rescued White from his seat. "What did you think ?" he asked, wondering if it had been dull.

"I loved it" replied White. "You fought the report line by line. When you found you couldn't win, you blew it up. What happens now ?"

"The legislation is blocked. Neither Commission nor Council of Ministers can proceed without obtaining the parliament's view first. The committee will have to try again."

They returned to the ground-floor of Spinelli for lunch. On the way Owen pointed out the newspaper kiosk, hairdresser, banks, the self-service restaurant and beyond that the gym and squash courts. He took White into the Members' Lounge, the parliament's restaurant with waiter service.

White said that he enjoyed the international signs which helped visitors to find their way around without using any of the official languages : a cigarette crossed out, a no entry sign, a cup and saucer, a box with arrows up and down for an elevator. He was surprised there was no in-house chemist.

"There's no chemist" Owen explained, "because the Brussels authorities insist that there can only be one inside the parliament if another is closed somewhere else in the city. It's Belgian bureaucracy."

After lunch he took White up in the lift to the top of the Spaak building, nine floors above the hemicycle, to have coffee in a small restaurant reserved for members. Beneath its arched glass ceiling, White admired the extensive views over the city. He had hoped to pick out the Atomium, the multi-story model of an atom which Brussels had opened in 1958 for the World Exhibition, but it was obscured by one of the parliament's fifteen-story blocks.

White asked who was the distinguished-looking man wearing a tailcoat and a silver chain round his neck who was quietly enjoying a salad lunch by himself.

Owen laughed. "He's an usher. They are the best dressed and we members are the worst. When a colleague's small son visited the parliament, his father asked whether he might like to work there himself one day. 'Yes, I would' the six year old replied, 'I want to be one of those with a silver chain.'"

The afternoon was chilly but fine so Owen and White agreed to walk to the Commission building. They left the parliament and turned south onto Rue Belliard where five lanes of one-way traffic flowed ceaselessly. Strolling down the hill, Owen pointed out the Leopold Park on the right with its attractive lake and white geese. It was a relaxing place for a member to stroll when the parliament became too oppressive but there had been muggings at night. Behind it was the Brussels dinosaur museum.

They crossed at the lights and climbed the opposite hill. To the right down Rue Froissart was the Borschette block, where the Commission housed some of its staff. It was named after a Commissioner who had died on the floor of the parliament while under criticism from a leftwing British MEP. It was nicknamed for no good reason 'the Brochette', meaning a kebab on a skewer.

As they walked they discussed the encounter with Einhorn. Owen explained that he had not met the Commissioner who was legendary for his absences from Brussels because of an ambition to re-enter national German politics.

"Is he a businessman ?" wondered White.

"None of the Commissioners are."

"Why not ?"

"Probably because politics and business are such different trades. Almost nobody makes the transition successfully."

"What's the difference ?"

"Two fundamental things, I think. First, business leaders make decisions anytime they choose - whereas politicians can only take decisions when they have a majority of opinion supporting them.

Second, businessmen want the world to be ruled by the market, whereas politicians want to interfere with it."

"So what's the ideal type to work for the EU ?"

"The perfect Euro-crat, they say, has British linguistic skills, Italian planning, German flexibility, Irish urgency, Dutch open-hearted generosity, Spanish humility, Scandinavian sobriety, and French broad international sympathy."

Peter White laughed. "It would be heaven if the trains were German, the policemen British, the cooks Italian, and the lovers French. Unfortunately it seems to be the Germans doing the cooking, the Italians running the trains, the French as the police, and the British attempting the romance."

They reached Avenue d'Auderghem at the top of the hill, or Ouderghen as local Flemish speakers prefer. On the left was their destination. Number Forty-Five was a large cross-hatched sandstone building called the Bredel. It contained the offices of the twenty EU Commissioners who are proposed by the national leaders to run the day-to-day business of the EU.

Owen pointed down the street beyond the Bredel to a brasserie. Next to it was number Ten Rue Froissart. It was the Brussels office of the British government, known as UKREP or 'UK Representation'. Above its entrance they could see the royal coat of arms in gold. Every EU national government ran a similar office.

Owen explained that a team of high-flying civil servants were sent there from London for up to four years, each to specialise in one policy field. They represented Whitehall in working-parties of the Council of Ministers. They prepared the ground for decisions to be rubber-stamped later by elected ministers who travelled out from the Commons. A good desk-officer knew everything going on in the EU in his policy field.

Beyond UKREP was the Rond Point Schuman roundabout, on the other side of which stood a famous landmark, the Berlaymont building. Constructed of glass in the form of a four-leaf clover, it was now empty and swathed in white plastic bandages. It had been the headquarters of the Commission until 1992. Routine renovations had uncovered that asbestos had been sprayed onto steel inside to prevent rusting. It was being gutted and rebuilt by the Belgian government and the Commission's staff were housed temporarily in several other buildings.

In front of the Bredel stood a fleet of dark-blue Mercedes cars with Luxembourg number plates. Standing like guardsmen ten sycamore trees protected the building's entrance. On poles above the trees flew sixteen flags. At one end was the blue European flag with its twelve gold stars, followed by the flags of the fifteen member states in alphabetical order in their own language, the first being Belgique, the last the United Kingdom.

They walked past the Bredel's thick glass front, and entered through its swing-doors. Owen showed his MEP pass and they walked under the security arch. A receptionist directed them to an elevator which would carry them upstairs to the Commissioner's office.

A woman from the Commissioner's Cabinet greeted them but asked them to wait for a moment. Owen explained to White that *Cabinet* was a word with a different meaning on the continent compared to Britain. In Brussels each Commissioner had a private office, or 'cabinet', with his personal team of assistants, mostly of his own nationality.

The woman reappeared and said that the Commissioner was ready to receive them. She opened a door and indicated them through. Commissioner Einhorn greeted them with a firm handshake. He was in his mid-forties, dark-haired and dark-suited. He spoke perfect English.

His office was smaller than a Cabinet Minister's in London but its furniture was more modern. One all-glass wall gave him a splendid panorama over the city.

"Welcome," he said. "May I offer you coffee ? Or, being British, would you prefer tea ?" They sat in comfortable chairs round a glass-topped metal-legged table. An assistant poured three cups of tea.

After an exchange of pleasantries Einhorn turned to White. "I have read the letter which Owen Mann has sent to me concerning your problem. I greatly deplore the situation which has arisen. Job-poaching – which this amounts to – is undesirable behaviour in our European Union."

"Can you help us, Commissioner ?"

"My staff have studied the question in advance of your visit.

Regrettably, there are no EU rules at present - either concerning regional aid or concerning competition policy - which prevent a business from relocating in order to maximise the amount of state aid it can receive.

"I am looking at ways of eliminating such behaviour - particularly when relocation involves regions which receive subsidies from Brussels. You probably remember the French motor company which closed its Belgian factory and negotiated Spanish government aid for an extension to its plant at Valladolid ?

"I am extremely sorry that I cannot help you, Herr White. Please will you keep me in touch if there are developments ?"

"Commissioner, we will," said White rising to his feet. "Thank you for your sympathetic understanding."

They returned to the street, disappointed but unsurprised. White took a taxi to the airport. Owen walked back to the parliament, calculating that the odds against his re-election had lengthened again and would soon be out-of-sight.

He now worked exclusively on the fascism report, living on black coffee and little sleep. By Friday morning he was satisfied with it. He forwarded the finished draft to Bruno Wielblad for translation and printing into the other ten EU languages, so it could come before the committee. He was way behind Gatto's timetable and the chance of a successful outcome was slim.

He went to Brussels airport in good time for the early evening flight on which he had pre-booked. But the airline told him that they had overbooked, that he was only on the waiting list, and economy class was already full. A vision of yet another evening in Brussels swam into his mind. The next forty-five minutes were worrying. But all ended well and all the wait-list passengers boarded the flight.

In the surgery on Saturday morning, one case produced a surprise ending. A month previously, the mother of a truck-driver named Gary had come to see him. Gary had been arrested in Greece and accused of carrying drugs on his truck which he had driven from Turkey. Owen had ensured that Gary had been visited by the nearest British consul and had received legal help for his defence.

Then Gary's friends at his local pub had started a campaign of telephoning Owen at all hours, even during the night, to urge him to do more to rescue their innocent drinking pal. Owen had explained to them that a trial could not be avoided - just as a Greek visitor to England could not have an appearance in court waived.

Last week Gary had been found guilty in Greece and sent to prison. His mother came to the surgery with a simple message. "Thank you, Mr. Mann, for what you tried to do for Gary. He has been on drugs for years, but we didn't want to tell you."

Sunday dragged slowly. He wished that Nina had not vanished from his life. He rang her cottage to thank her for attending the selection final but the same male voice was on the answerphone.

The time for the Monday morning flight to Strasbourg eventually came round. The gossip was that the date for the forthcoming European elections had finally been agreed between the Council of Ministers and the European Parliament. Voting would be on the second Thursday in June for protestant countries, and on the following Sunday for catholic states which voted at weekends.

Two days later Owen checked his pigeonhole and was surprised to discover a printed copy of his report. He telephoned Bruno Wielblad who confirmed that copies in the other languages had also been distributed.

"Fantastic work ! Can it be discussed next week in the committee ?"

"I doubt it because our agenda next week is already full. There is no time left for yours. Next week is April already . After that there is only the May plenary left before the election in June. We have run out of time. Sorry."

Owen pretended fury. "Bruno, that is completely unacceptable. We have spent a lot of taxpayers' money on a public hearing and have built up public expectations. We went through a lot of pain with Pietro's death. If there is no time for a debate then why was my report translated and printed at high speed ?"

"Just in case."

"Are you saying now that we just give up ?"

"Mr Mann, I'm very sorry."

Next day, the French press agency Agence Europe summarised the report in its daily briefings which are mailed to subscribers across Europe and the world.

Bruno Wielblad telephoned Owen. "Okay, the chairman has agreed. In view of the publicity, your report goes onto the end of the committee's agenda next week. But," he warned, "it is not certain that we will reach it before time runs out."

* * *

Rado Zaplasiti, who skimmed the news briefings every day, discovered that the Mann report had survived.

He was the only senior assistant present at headquarters. He faxed the news to Sãta who was with his family in Port Jefferson. "President. The Mann report has survived."

Sãta telephoned immediately and asked, cold steel in his voice, "Where is Monika ?"

"I've already contacted her. She is returning from Singapore and be here tomorrow. Details of the Mann report are now in many different places so we cannot destroy it. Nor is there any advantage to us in eliminating the rapporteur."

"Why not ?"

"Because two deaths connected to the same report would be recognised as beyond coincidence. Media spotlights might focus unfavourably on our friends."

"So what is your recommendation, Rado ?"

"Several options. First, pressurise the Englishman to tone down his report. If he won't, Monika has the photograph of him in Stockholm and the French have another of him at Rocher's rally. We could offer them to British newspapers and destroy his reputation. Or we could plant allegations about his income-tax returns with the authorities and have them combed through. Or we could have him photographed in a compromising sexual situation, a honey-trap as it is called. The British public are strangely interested in the sexual behaviour of their public figures."

"Start with a letter, anonymously, which spells out the connection between what his report says and what happens to him if he does not modify it. Prepare the other ideas but don't press the starting button on them until I am back. Nothing to be traceable back to us, as usual."

"President, one other thing. Assuming that the report gets through the parliament and we still don't like it, I believe you should prepare a contingency fallback."

"I'll attend to that, Rado."

Sãta caught the next plane from New York. When Monika reached the office the next afternoon Sãta looking grim confronted her: "The EP report is back on course. We don't know how and it doesn't matter. The milk is spilled. Our cause now needs your help in a different way. Listen..." Sãta gave her instructions.

*   *   *

In Strasbourg, Owen sought out Murdo McKirk. He found him in the Press bar in close consultation with a Danish pastry.

"Haven't seen you for a while. Been away ?"

"Tied up the story in Russia. It'll break next week," the hack replied, his mouth still full.

"Did you get your Russian interpreter ?"

Murdo shifted his weight to his other leg, and drained his glass of beer. "You're getting nosey, Owen. You're becoming like one of us. But, basically," he glanced round furtively, "the answer to that is Yes."

The following morning, Friday 1st April, was the end of another plenary week. Possibly the next plenary, in late April, would be Owen's last ever. It might be better to spend the May plenary at home campaigning for votes, rather than waste a precious week in Strasbourg.

He packed up his office, watching the time because at eleven o'clock he was catching a train to Basle in Switzerland.

The telephone on his desk rang.

"Owen Mann ?" asked a woman's voice.

"That's me," he replied uncertainly, silently cursing whoever it was. No MEP could be expected to recognise every voice and face that presented itself to him. Some constituents expected instant recognition and, when he failed to identify them, were resentful. Others, whom he secretly blessed, helped by saying 'Hello, I'm so-and-so'. He had once watched Nelson Rockefeller, on television, campaigning to become Vice-President of the United States, and had admired his technique. Approaching people Rockefeller had grasped each hand forcefully and asked 'How are yer ?' and before they could answer with something like 'Do you remember what we were discussing when we met three years ago in Tallahassie ?', he had moved on to the next outstretched hand.

Owen had no such option. "Sorry, who is this ? I don't recognise your voice," he confessed.

"You don't remember ?" the woman said with real disappointment.

Was this an April Fool, a *Poisson d'Avril* ?

"It's Monika." Her voice lost some of its confidence. "You don't remember me ? When you visited Stockholm about two months ago, I was with Anders Groda."

Owen's heart was suddenly beating faster. "I remember you very well indeed, Monika" he replied, "Where are you ?"

"You offered to show me round your parliament. Is that possible ?"

"I''d be delighted, Monika. Very delighted. When might you be coming ?"

"I was wondering about next week in Brussels," Monika said tentatively.

Owen thought quickly, which he did not find easy at the end of a Strasbourg week : "I'll be in Brussels from Tuesday till Thursday for committee meetings. Which day will you arrive ? May I invite you to lunch, or to dinner in the evening ?"

"I shall probably be there early on Wednesday afternoon."

"Wonderful. Come to the main entrance and ask them to page me. I'll come down and sign you through security. Then you can see the parliament. And we can continue our talk."

He looked at the clock. He must hurry to catch the train.

* * *

Travelling to Switzerland was the final lap in Owen's marathon to try to save the jobs at United Technologies. Peter White had made an appointment for him with the head of the company's European operations.

The train pulled into Basle station on time. A limousine was waiting and he was driven to the United Technologies headquarters. Without delay he was ushered into the Chief Executive's office.

A squat man with powerful shoulders and grizzly-coloured hair came forward and gripped his hand.

"Mr. Mann ? It's good to meet you. I'm Marvin Buffalo." He pointed to a chair. His desk was clear of papers except for a single folder. He sat in a swivel chair beside Owen, opened a box of cigars and offered one to Owen.

"Use these ?"

"I don't, thanks."

"I've heard good things about you from Peter White. Before we get down to business, my assistant told me something interesting about you. You collect jokes, right ?"

"Stories from different European countries."

"Well, here's one from Arizona which I heard last month."

Buffalo told his story[12] and crashed a fist on the desk. "Now give me your best European story."

Owen replied with a story in the same vein.[13] Buffalo looked embarrassed, sucked his cigar and commented that he was sure that the British were good at many things.

Suspecting he had only been allocated a little time, and that he was being side-tracked, Owen changed the subject.

"Mr. Buffalo, it is good of you to see me. As you know, I really want to keep those thousand jobs in my constituency. How can I persuade you not to move them ?"

"Call me Marv. May I call you Owen ?"

Owen nodded.

"Well, see here, the situation of business has changed in the recent years. Global competition forces us to seek the lowest operating costs. In the old days, national governments could stop us moving but now the boot is on the other foot. Neither your government in London, nor the EU in Brussels, can reverse our plans. These days governments do what business requires."

He puffed his cigar and eyeballed Owen. "We locate our

manufacturing where the laws and the economics are most favourable. The powers of national ministers are shrinking to be like the governor of a state in the U.S."

"The EU can do more."

Buffalo shook his head : "Not at the moment it can't. And I don't want to see a strong EU in the future. It would place restraints over international business. Of course a minimum of rules is necessary, but governments invent work for themselves and create bureaucracy. We don't want extra rules from Brussels. Business works for the benefit of the consumer. We provide the best products at the lowest prices. Leave us alone. The EU, if it ever gets its act together, could shackle us more effectively than any national government."

"Manufacturing costs in Britain are low, so why move jobs ?"

"Not any more. Britain signed up to the Social Chapter. That is going to cost businesses dear, so your advantage is vanishing. And you're not joining the Euro, so British interest rates are higher, and there is uncertainty about the exchange rate for sterling."

"What do you need, Marv ?"

"Nothing you can deliver."

Buffalo shrugged. His face showed some pity. "Owen, you're doing your best - trying to help your voters to keep their jobs. You've travelled a long way to talk to me."

He touched a dossier on his desk but did not open it. "I see that your own political attitude is what you Brits call 'Euro-sceptical'. My staff tell me that you are in danger of not being re-elected in June. And the loss of our jobs makes this more likely ? Is that correct ?"

Owen nodded.

"We need good triers like you in parliament. So, and I hope it will be compensation for your trouble, my company will make a donation towards your campaign expenses."

"That's extremely generous of you, Marv. But I would much prefer you to leave those jobs where they are."

"Owen, I can't do that."

The limousine returned a disappointed Owen to the airport. The odds against his re-election were about the same as Nina returning to him.

During the flight to London he brooded what the role of governments should be. Marvin Buffalo wanted total laissez-faire but the citizen needed protection against abuse. Rules were desirable, provided they were controlled democratically. We were not at the stage of world government. The European citizen needed both EU-wide free trade but also EU wide enforcement of the rules. And if there was Euro-crime the citizen needed Euro-policing.

* * *

Back home the day's mail lay waiting on Owen's mat. One letter was an anonymous note, postmarked from London.

> Understand this. There is a direct link between your report and what happens to you. If you attack nationalism, it will attack you back. You have been warned very clearly.

He read the note again and he remembered Camaleao's warning after the Hearing. It was late and he was tired but he put on his coat and rode to the police station.

The police sergeant assured him that they would look into it. In future, he must look under a vehicle before starting it, watching for changes in the profile beneath. He must avoid sitting by open windows. When in a public place, he must have his back to a wall and be able to reach an exit quickly. Strengthened glass should be installed in the windows of his house with lights outside which set off a buzzer inside. And he must beware of packets in the post which were sticky-taped on three sides, inviting him to open it on the fourth side and so trigger a bomb.

Owen returned home, dazed by the new burdens imposed on him, all from a rapporteurship which he had not originally wanted.

Next morning there was no Saturday surgery. But Jane had arranged an urgent visit for him to the house of a Mr. Frederick Hare. On the telephone Mr. Hare had explained that he and his family were members of the Brothers, a fundamentalist Christian minority. They were troubled because the government's school curriculum forced their children to use computer keyboards.

Owen rode to the address which proved to be a modest two-story house. As he walked toward the front-door it was opened by a bald man with a Lenin beard.

"Good ! I'm Mr. Hare. Come in" he said cheerfully.

Inside was a long polished table. Round it were seated several men and their wives, their hands neatly clasped together and resting on their laps. Behind them sat a row of young boys and girls dressed in dark clothes. Owen was invited to sit at the head of the table. The men and women looked silently at him.

"Would you like a cup of coffee ?" asked a woman whom he assumed was Mrs. Hare.

"Please" replied Owen.

She carried it from the kitchen immediately. Owen was embarrassed to find that he was the only drinker. Seeing his confusion Mr. Hare explained that their religion did not allow them to drink either tea or coffee.

Mr. Hare bowed to an older man and sat down.

The elder spoke gravely : "It is our belief that computers and keyboards take over our childrens' souls. There is biblical support for this, if you wish to hear it ?"

Owen shook his head. The elder continued : "We are also concerned that the 'origin mark' for goods manufactured in the EU is the mark of the Beast which is foretold in the Book of Revelations. And your Euro currency is foretold as the prelude to a new Satanic German empire."

He picked up the bible beside him on the table and read aloud : "The Book of Revelations, Chapter 13, Verse 16. 'He causeth all, both small and great, rich and poor, free and bond, to receive a Mark in their right hand, or in their foreheads; and no man might buy or sell, save he that had the Mark, or the name of the Beast.'"

The elder turned to Owen and asked in his gentle courteous way : "It is so clear. Now," he closed the book, "will you tell us why are we not allowed to raise our children according to our own beliefs ? Why does the government force them to use computer keyboards at school ? The European Convention on Human Rights guarantees freedom of religion to every European citizen."

The men and women round the table stared at Owen, waiting for his explanation.

Owen took a deep breath and replied : "I'll be glad to try to help you. First, the Human Rights Convention is nothing to do with the EU. It is a separate agreement, which Britain had helped to draft in 1950 before the EU was born."

"But" interrupted the elder, "the Court on Human Rights is located in Strasbourg, next door to the European Parliament."

"Correct. However the EU's supreme court is the European Court of Justice in Luxembourg."

"It's very confusing."

"I agree" said Owen and tried to get back to the original topic. "Have you thought of starting your own school so that you could avoid using computers ?"

"It would be too costly. We are few and we are scattered across the country" replied the elder.

"I will write to the British government's Education minister to ask if he will make an exception for you. As soon as I receive his reply, I'll get back to you instantly by e-mail."

Owen feared he had made a faux-pas. The Brothers did not use computer keyboards.

"We can receive e-mail but not send it, so forgive us if we do not answer" replied the elder.

"Then we shall meet again."

The elder gravely thanked Owen while the others remained silent. Mr. Hare helped him into his coat and escorted him to the door.

He shook Owen's hand cheerfully and said : "It is so kind of you to help us, especially since we do not vote in elections."

Owen rode away. He hoped that the grinding of his teeth was not louder than the roar of the motorbike's exhaust. He felt sorry for the children who would be deprived of a modern education by their elders' fundamentalist intolerance.

* * *

On Tuesday afternoon the Civil Liberties committee began a three-day meeting in Brussels. Owen was on tenterhooks : his report might be discussed near the end and Monika might arrive.

Immediately after lunch on Wednesday, the pager on his belt vibrated with a call from security at the parliament's front entrance.

He hurried downstairs, and recognised Monika waiting inside the swing-doors. Gone were the jeans and tee-shirt. She was dressed smartly in a full-length white coat. Her tresses lay on her shoulders half-concealing inch-long twisted glass earrings. She had unbuttoned her coat to reveal a fawn jacket lined with white edges over a white blouse, and a dark brown skirt. His heart was thumping as he kissed her lightly on the cheek, where he saw more freckles than he remembered.

He signed for her entry pass, and walked with her to the lifts. He found himself gabbling.

"Monika, it's wonderful to see you. How much time have you got ? I have a time problem. One of my committees starts at three o'clock, in about an hour. My report - the one I was researching when I came to Stockholm - is on the agenda for discussion. You would find it very boring, I am sure, to sit there and listen to it. But as the rapporteur I must be present. Would you like a quick tour of the parliament before that ?"

Monika nodded. "Yes, please. But I'm not in a hurry. It would be very interesting to listen to a debate about your report. Afterwards, can we have a drink or a meal together ?"

"Definitely," he said warmly. "When do you have to leave ?"

"I have a plane to catch late this evening."

Monika showed a keen interest as he took her through the buildings. He found he was enjoying her presence as much as he had in Stockholm.

The pager on his belt vibrated again. Its message to Owen was 'Hevonen returned your call'.

He took Monika to his office, sat her down in the outer room. From his inner office he dialled a number in the Netherlands.

"EuroPol."

"May I speak to the Director, please ?" He was put through

promptly.

"Hello Mr. Mann. This is Paavo Hevonen. I returned your message of yesterday."

Owen explained briefly about the report which he was writing. "If it were possible, I should like to discuss it with you."

"You would be most welcome" replied Hevonen. "I read about your work in Agence Europe, and I have one or two points to ask you. How about next week ?" They fixed that Owen would come to The Hague the following Wednesday.

Monika was still waiting in the outer office. He escorted her to the committee room, showed her into a seat at the back, and explained how to listen to interpretation with the headset.

He slipped into his own seat at the front while Chomik was speaking. Owen's report was to be the next but one debate on the afternoon's agenda.

When the debate about his report started, members gave their individual views. It became clear that both the far-left and the far-right were hostile to it. The communists insisted that Owen's criticism of the fascists did not go far enough. Far-Right members said that the criticism was exaggerated and ridiculous.

Individuals criticised aspects which referred to their own countries. Giovanni Abelo from the *Radicali* party was first to do so. His party was small but exceptionally influential in Italy. It had stung the Italian parliament into legalising both divorce and abortion. Its leader, leonine Marco Panella, was a brilliant self-publicist. When his party was allocated a too small amount of time for an election broadcast, he had himself tied and gagged in a chair in front of the television camera with a caption for the viewers which said 'The large parties gag the Radicali'. Another time when the large parties in Italy ignored a referendum vote which opposed state-funding for political parties, he returned his party's share of state-funds by handing out 50,000 lira banknotes to people in a square in Rome.

Abelo wanted Owen's report to include more about Italy's notorious P-2 Masonic Lodge. "It was a secret network which penetrated deep into the Italian state and subverted it. Its grandmaster possessed the common Italian belief that life is controlled by dark and secret forces. P-2 was a part of the murky underside of Italian life which perverted free-masonry, the secret services, organised crime, and right-wing terrorism. Everything was blurred into one great corruption. Signor Mann, you do not say enough."

Other members raised the criticism that fascists and criminals were starting to cooperate across frontiers, yet the authorities had no mechanism for counter-action - either in hot pursuit across a frontier or against organised terrorism across Europe as a whole.

"The EU must be able to act" Van Der Muis argued, "on the same scale as its enemies. Crime across our borders is becoming ever easier. Yet all we do is exchange information."

Horst Wiesel, a solemn-looking Christian-Socialist from Bavaria, disagreed. He was an ex-policeman with a long pointed nose. To those who did not know him he appeared to lack a sense of humour.

"Information-collecting" he spoke with authority, "is a good beginning. The *BundesKriminalAmt* in Germany, which is our Federal Criminal Investigation Office, was initially created to reform intelligence-gathering across Germany's provinces. But later it developed its own operational role in counter-terrorism. Now it has many activities, one of which is to raid the Nazi music distribution centres which are spreading across Germany.

"Europe is incapable of dealing with cross-border crime. In the EU there are a hundred and five separate policing bodies. Half of that total, fifty-two, are in one EU country - the United Kingdom. The British have separate police forces for each county, plus Customs and Immigration, plus the SIS previously called MI5, and also Scotland Yard."

His remarks created a considerable stir. Wishing to praise him, Bridget O'Leumadair said gracefully : "Herr Wiesel, you are leading our committee like the Pied Piper of Hamelin."

Wiesel was not a linguist and wore headphones to hear the interpretation into German. Hearing the Irish woman's compliment he took offence, made a gruff noise and waved a hand in rejection.

Mrs. O'Leumadair called to Chomik for a point of order. "Herr Wiesel was upset by my words, but I meant to compliment him. Was something wrong with the interpretation ?"

Van Der Muis intervened. "I can explain. I happened to be listening to the German version. Unfortunately our Irish friend's generous comparison of Mr. Wiesel to the legendary pipe-player was interpreted into German as 'You are leading us like a rat catcher.'"

There was laughter. Wiesel gave a friendly bow to O'Leumadair and replied : "Misunderstandings can easily arise. Recently I checked the meaning of *Scotland Yard* in a German law dictionary. The answer it gave was 'The Scotland Yard measures 91.44 centimetres, the same as the English Yard'."

Chomik allowed the debate to run for as long as the speeches were constructive. By the end Owen had won support from most of the committee. Chomik closed the discussion.

"Dear colleagues. I propose one week for tabling amendments to the Mann report. The deadline will be ten o'clock next Thursday morning. Agreed ?"

Nobody objected. All amendments would be translated and distributed to Members in their preferred languages.

"At our next meeting there will be no debate. We shall simply vote on each amendment and arrive at a final text. The finished text will join the long queue for a debate by the whole parliament at a plenary week in Strasbourg."

The committee broke up. Horst Wiesel approached Owen. "I have an Austrian story for you. I hope it is not too late ?"

"Tell me, Horst."[14]

Owen listened and thanked the German. He hastened to the back of the room and collected Monika from her seat.

* * *

He made a reservation at an Italian restaurant, away from the parliament in the fashionable Place du Petit Sablon. There they could talk without being overheard before she had to leave for the airport.

They both ordered salmon and a glass of white Chardonnay and Owen followed suit. A two-way torrent of talk began. The encounter was back-to-front : they liked each other but did not know about each other. Monika said that she had two older sisters, both being married with families in the United States. She had been born on the European side of the Atlantic, her grandparents were dead, and when her parents had divorced, she had been taken as a small girl by her mother to be educated in America.

As she poured out her thoughts Owen was absorbed by Monika. Suddenly he was aware that he had stopped listening and was simply basking in the physical pleasure of her animated face, her musical voice, and the sheer glow of her company.

She stopped talking and waited for an answer.

"Monika," he confessed. "I'm sorry. This may sound rude but it isn't. I wasn't listening to a word you were saying. I was just looking at you. I'm having such a good time."

She looked into his eyes. "It doesn't matter what I was saying. I'm having a good time too."

They each realised that they brought out the best in the other. Her look grew serious. "Are you passionate, Owen ?" she asked. She told him how, when at university in New York, after classes on Friday afternoons, she had gone straight to the airport and caught a plane to spend the weekend with a boyfriend, hardly going out of doors. On Sunday evenings, she had caught the plane back to New York, and in class on Mondays had been incapable of learning anything. The following weekend the boy flown to see her. Now she was in a different relationship, one that had been on and off for several years.

"Anders in Stockholm ?" Owen wondered aloud.

Monika neither confirmed nor denied it. She replied : "Right now, it feels as if that could be off too. But I don't really want to talk about it" she added, looking deep into his eyes.

The waiter removed their plates and asked if they would like desserts. They agreed on strawberries ; "One bowl, and two spoons," said Owen.

Monika pushed her hair back over one shoulder. "I feel I know everything you're going to say, but may I ask you something ?"

"Of course."

"I don't want to talk about work, yours or mine, but would you like to know what I thought about your report this afternoon ?"

"Very much."

"I was proud of you," she said. Owen was very surprised at her use of the word.

Monika continued : "Two things struck me. You ought to look more closely at how parties in different countries cooperate. And secondly, the EU lacks power to counter continental-scale fascism if it grows. There is no European police-force nor any federal European criminal laws or courts."

He was very surprised that Monika was saying these things. But Groda had said that she was not a member of his party, just a bright and percipient observer.

"You're right," he agreed. He also lacked data about where the fascists got their money but Monika would know nothing about that.

She glanced at her wrist watch and said that time had nearly run out. Owen asked the waiter to order a taxi and paid the bill. They waited outside and pressed against each other in the cool air.

He put both arms gently round her neck and kissed her lips. She responded, her mouth open and delicious. The taxi arrived and Monika pushed him gently away.

"I feel this evening we went beyond making love," she said, her eyes shining. "One thing, Owen."

"What is it ?"

"There must be no conditions, no promises, no obligations. Just expressing our feelings for eachother, and wherever it leads, to somewhere or to nowhere..."

He nodded.

"Where do you stay in Brussels, Owen ?"

He told her the name of the Katvis hotel. "How can I contact you, Monika ?"

"You'll have to rely on me contacting you," she replied. "I travel as much as you, maybe even more. But I promise it'll be soon."

She blew him a kiss as the taxi took her away.

Owen strolled slowly back to his hotel, his mind overflowing. The taste of Monika was still on his lips. His only anxiety was being involved with someone who had a fascist boyfriend. But he felt sure she was no fascist herself.

He slept with deep contentment, certain that he would see Monika again. During the night he awoke, remembering something she had said. He switched on the bedside light, scribbled a note, and went back to sleep.

When he awoke in the daylight, he remembered the scribble. He thought of Alfred Hitchcock's story of a film director who had dreamed of the perfect plot for a new film and had jotted it onto a pad in the dark. In the morning the pad bore the unhelpful words 'Boy Meets Girl'.

Owen sat up and examined his notepad. There were two words, 'cooperation' and 'detection'.

He lay back and thought about Monika. Her animated face, her shining grey-blue eyes, her sparkling intelligence. How happy they had been together. But his instinct issued a warning. He had learned, on first waking, that it usually hinted his most prudent course of action. Now it said 'Beware.' Could he reconcile the anti-fascism of his report with Monika's association with Groda ? With an election near was it sensible to get involved ? But are emotions sensible ?

As he dressed he found a long single strand of golden-brown hair on his jacket. He picked it off carefully and sealed it in an envelope.

In the parliament he checked his pigeon-hole. Among the papers was a letter post-marked Nice in the south of France. Inside was a photograph of himself standing on a stage next to Rocher at the rally in Grasse. On the back was written 'Do you want this in the British newspapers ? Pay attention to what is in your report."

Suddenly he wondered whether the jaws of a trap were closing around him.

* * *

Sãta sat at his desk, chewing anxiously on a cigar. He was wrestling with possibly the most important calculation of his short political life. It was impossible to solve because every factor was an assumption.

He stepped out of his door, walked along a short corridor, opened another door and asked Zaplasiti to come and join him.

"Rado, I'm trying to work out how many seats we are likely to win in the European election. I need your opinion."

"Gladly, President" replied the brainy Serb, sitting down opposite the desk.

"I'm working through each of the fifteen EU countries, making a forecast. In the United Kingdom, we'll get none this time round because there is no tradition yet of voting for us. In Germany, our problem will be to exceed the minimum threshold of five per cent of the total national vote. What do you think ?"

"With unemployment high in East Germany, President, I think you can plan on getting well over five per cent and on picking up four or five MEP seats. I have done a similar calculation myself." He pushed a sheet of paper across the desk. Sãta picked it up and scrutinised it.

Together they went through the figures, country by country. Finally they agreed on a forecast of how many nationalist MEPs they would have : Germany 4, France 25, Austria 4, Italy 12, Spain 1, Portugal (including Sãta himself) 2, Belgium 2, Netherlands 2, Sweden 1, Denmark 1, Finland 1, and Greece 1. The other three, Ireland, Luxembourg and the UK, would yield nothing this time around.

"That makes a total of fifty-six nationalist MEPs. It's a great deal more than ever before" said Zaplasiti.

"But it's not enough" riposted Sãta with irritation. "With 626 MEPs in all, we would not even be guaranteed to hold the balance of power. I need more. I'll have to take more steps."

"And if we do not win more seats, President ?"

"There are other ways to take power. The plans and the resources are available and I will use them if necessary." Sãta dismissed him with a wave of his hand.

Sãta sent out a series of encrypted e-mail messages.

* * *

At the Saturday surgery the first to arrive, very early, was Mr. Hare of the Brothers.

"There's both bad news and good news" Owen told him. "The bad news is that I've consulted various people. If your people want the free schooling which is provided by the state, then they must accept the curriculum which includes using computers."

"Bad ! What can the good news be ?"

"The European Convention on Human Rights gives you the freedom to run your own schools and teach your own religion."

"Good ! Except that we cannot afford it. Could we appeal to the EU's Ombudsman ?"

"His remit doesn't cover the European Convention on Human Rights because that is not part of the EU's *acquis communautaire.*"

"What's that ?"

"It is Brussels jargon and means all of the EU's acquired responsibilities."

Mr. Hare looked downcast : "So we've no hope ?"

"There's still one possibility," said Owen. "The European Parliament has a Petitions committee. You could write to it and ask if they can find a way to help."

Mr. Hare agreed to draft a petition and left the office.

The next couple at the surgery introduced themselves as Pat and Leslie. Both looked to be in their late thirties. The woman wore a tidy red jumper and skirt and had a deep contralto voice. The man was average-height and muscled, wearing jeans, a tee-shirt and sports jacket.

Owen settled them down with cups of tea and listened.

Pat spoke first. "We live together and want to get married."

"What is preventing it ?"

Leslie looked coy. "It is a bit unusual. We've both had the operation, you see."

Afterwards Owen wondered whether he had been slow to grasp the point, that Leslie had previously been a man, and Pat a woman.

"I don't see the problem" he replied. "You're a man and a woman."

"The difficulty is" said the man, "that we want to get married as we are now, not as we used to be. The law says we cannot because our birth certificates say the opposite. We've heard of European Human Rights and we want you to sort it out for us."

It was certainly a new one. Owen promised to investigate and to let them know what might be possible.

For light relief in the afternoon Owen went to the local football match and was invited to become a vice-president of the club. The flattering invitation was accompanied by a request for a financial donation but he paid up.

As he watched the kickabout he planned his week ahead. Monday, campaigning ; Tuesday, travel to The Hague ; Wednesday morning, visit EuroPol, then travel on to Brussels for the Group meeting. There was spare time on Tuesday so he decided it would be an interesting experience to ride through the Channel Tunnel.

He set off early for Folkestone and found it unexpectedly simple to take his motorbike onto the train. He could not know, that passing at the same moment on a similar shuttle train in the reverse direction, was Istvan Diszno in a car.

An hour later Owen's bike was one of a hundred vehicles which drove directly from the train onto the righthand lane of a French autoroute. At the same time Diszno's car exited onto the lefthand lane of a motorway in Kent.

After fifty kilometres Owen crossed the open border into Belgium. Two hours later he crossed into the Netherlands, again without border checks. Ninety minutes more and he found a room in a motel on the outskirts of the port of Rotterdam.

To stretch his legs, he strolled through the nearby suburban streets. He came across a quiet bar where he settled. He chose a meal from the blackboard menu, and relaxed with a novel and a local beer.

As darkness fell, the bar began to fill and the noise level rose. The clientele were mainly young white skinheads. Their chief enjoyment seemed to be shouting obscenities to each other. Lurking behind his book Owen watched them. They called themselves 'Gabbers' and their conversation was sounded racist. He was glad that the fascists had no international 'most wanted list'.

Next morning a short ride brought him to the coast of the North Sea and the Dutch capital, The Hague. He found the street called Raamweg without difficulty and looked for number forty-seven. On first impression the headquarters of EuroPol appeared to be a large family mansion. Small hedges stood in front, creepers climbed up the building, and trees framed its sides.

He parked, pressed the bell, and gave his name through the intercom. As the door opened electronically and closed behind him, its clanging noise made him wonder whether he would ever get out again.

He was shown into a large carpeted office. Behind a desk, decorated with three telephones and two framed family photographs was the Director of EuroPol.

Paavo Hevonen was an impressive-looking Finn, tall and wiry, aged about fifty with short grey hair which must have once been blond. He was wearing a dark suit and sober tie. On the wall behind was a framed photograph of him in a running vest competing in the Steeplechase in an Olympic Games. Speaking excellent English, he pointed his visitor to a comfortable chair and sat next to him.

"Welcome ! Start by telling me about your report and put your questions, Mr. Mann. Then I have some for you."

Owen described the conclusions which his committee had reached. Hevonen listened intently.

Owen finished with a question. "Director, has the opening of frontiers, and freedom of movement inside the EU, increased the amount of cross-border crime ?"

"I'm a policeman not a politician, so I can't tell you about political parties. But crime across frontiers, you could call it 'Euro-crime', is strongly on the increase. As borders become easier to cross, so organised crime is flourishing. There has been an astonishing increase in the number of groups which organise transnational crime."

"What kinds of crime ?"

"Trafficking in nuclear materials has followed the USSR's collapse. Money-laundering has grown with the international financial markets. Organised networks bring illegal immigrants without papers into the EU. And the Mafia has spread its tentacles outside Italy with a big increase in drug trafficking."

It reminded Owen of a story which Tartaruga had told. The Italian MEP had claimed that he could show on a map the areas in southern Italy which were controlled by the four criminal gangs, and how they were spreading northwards year by year, village by village. Although he was a left-winger Tartaruga had said he was safe to visit Sicily and could even make a speech against the Mafia in the main square. But if he was, say, chairman of the local council's finance committee and then made an anti-Mafia speech, he would certainly be killed. The Mafia were now investing their capital legitimately outside Italy, notably along the coast of southern Spain.

"Have you any statistics for the expansion of international crime ?" Owen asked.

"Unfortunately we have no clear picture of its scale or of its structure. We haven't even identified all the criminal groups, or their activities. We think that organised crime generates up to four hundred billion euros per year - more than the gross national products of Portugal and Spain combined. Our role, which is gathering and exchanging information, is still limited by barriers - linguistic, legal, bureaucratic and technical."

"Would you agree with our second conclusion - that the EU and Europe as a whole, lack the ability to counter these threats ?"

"Completely" said Hevonen, refilling Owen's coffee-cup. "Few people realise how very limited EuroPol's powers are. In the past the idea of a European FBI has been put forward by a number of police chiefs in the UK and Germany. But nothing is done by the politicians."

"With the opening of frontiers, the EU took the first small step to create a system for exchanging information about drugs. So we are just the Europol Drugs Unit."

Hevonen sighed. "Unfortunately then, the politicians got involved. A legal Convention to set up EuroPol was drafted by the EU's fifteen national governments. Fourteen wanted the European Court of Justice to adjudicate over disputes. One country - yours, Mr. Mann - refused. EuroPol is a drugs intelligence unit. Nothing more. We have a vast database but that is an inadequate weapon for tackling sophisticated international gangs."

"How many people work here ?"

"We have a hundred and twenty staff, drawn from all fifteen EU states. That includes liaison officers from CID, gendarmerie, and border and customs forces."

Owen noted it was the same as the number of civil servants who are employed in Brussels by the British government. London's priorities were curious : committees were as important as fighting crime.

"Why is EuroPol's work so little known to the public ?"

"It's no accident. The Convention was drafted in secret by officials, and neither the national nor the European parliaments were consulted. In 1994 ministers gave the European Parliament a copy "informally". The original intention was that MEPs would be fully consulted : a draft document in October 1994 spelled that out in full. But the following month's draft contained a blank page ! There is still a lack of openness and democratic control on our continent, yet we boast to the world how democratic we are."

"You are waiting for all EU states to ratify the Convention ?"

"All national parliaments must ratify it, and none has power to amend. The UK was the first to ratify but only in part. It excluded the European Court from adjudicating over disputes. Your government ratified using its archaic 'Ponsonby Rules'."

"I'm British but I don't know what those rules are."

"Arthur Ponsonby was a junior minister in your Foreign Office in the 1924 Labour government. He gave an undertaking to backbench MPs that they would be informed about all new treaties and agreements, and that the treaty terms would be laid before the House of Commons without debate for twenty-one days. That minor concession in your famous old parliament still applies today. Most other countries have written constitutions which give their MPs formal powers to ratify treaties. But backbenchers in the Commons can only debate a new treaty if enough of them disrupt the parliamentary timetable which has already been agreed between the front benches. Your ministers and whips don't allow it."

Owen knew that this was not the only area where backbench MPs in the Commons were impotent. The Prime Minister in Britain could give appointments to whomsoever he pleased, and fill in details of laws, without prior approval from the elected MPs. Thousands of 'statutory instruments' were passed each year and never scrutinised by any MPs.

"May I summarise so far ?" said Owen. "One - international crime poses a growing threat but there's no measure of its size. Two - the draft Convention was drawn up in secret, has no democratic input, and until it is ratified you have no power."

"Correct. When ratified, EuroPol can start to deal with organised crime in Europe. We would draw intelligence from non-EU bodies such as Interpol, the FBI, and the Drug Enforcement Agency in the USA, and the Schengen Information System."

"Remind me about InterPol and Schengen ?"

"Interpol at Lyons in southern France is an arrangement for policemen round the world to talk to each other. It has a very small staff which includes Americans, it cannot pursue criminals, and is answerable to nobody. 'Schengen' is an agreement between some EU states to abolish all border controls between them. Unfortunately it is a monument to complexity. Every state wants to preserve its 'sovereign rights', so it's a terrible mess. The Schengen Information System collects data about 'low-level' crime, public order, security threats and migrants."

"What powers does EuroPol need ?"

"The officials have surreptitiously added to our list of responsibilities, again without consulting any parliament. As well as drugs we now exchange information about trafficking in radioactive and nuclear substances, clandestine immigration networks, stolen vehicle trafficking, and money laundering. Recently we've added other international crimes to our responsibilities - murder, organised robbery, kidnapping, arms trafficking, racism and xenophobia, and corruption. The Convention allows ministers to expand the list of our responsibilities without consulting either MPs or MEPs."

Hevonen looked at Owen to see if he had fully grasped the lack of democratic control. Owen nodded.

"Organised crime is now global, not just in Europe. Except for the Mafia families, all the major players are based in non-EU countries - to a large extent in the former Soviet Union, Turkey, South America, Africa and Asia."

"Despite what you know you can't go 'operational' as opposed to merely collecting information ?"

"Actually," Hevonen hesitated, "we are 'operational' but unofficially. At first we simply harmonised our activities with bodies such as Interpol. Now we in EuroPol go 'operational' ourselves. But it's very unofficial because we have no legal authority to do it. The Amsterdam Treaty of 1997 has promised 'operational actions of joint teams comprising representatives of EuroPol in a support capacity.'"

"Can you arrest people or initiate independent investigations ?"

Hevonen rose to his feet. "Come and see an operation which we are conducting right now."

He led Owen down a corridor and into a large operations room. Large maps covered three walls of the room. Several people were bustling about, others seated at computer screens.

Hevonen explained. "Here we are coordinating the watching of drugs moving across Europe. A EuroPol officer looks after an operation which involves several EU states. He ensures that a national team takes over surveillance as soon as a target crosses into a new country.

"Look," he pointed at a computer screen displaying a map of all Europe. "A lorry has come from the Balkans with heroin on board. We could stop it at the first EU frontier which is the Austria/Hungary border where the Austrian police could arrest its driver. But that would be a small victory. The driver was recruited in a bar in Turkey and has no idea whom he is ultimately working for. It is more valuable for us to follow him to the final destination where we can catch the major drug distributors."

Hevonen pointed to the screen. "If that lorry comes to Britain, as very many do, it will cross several more frontiers. In the past it took us several days to organise cooperation between all the different police forces. Now we sort it out in a few hours."

"Why do you think it is coming to Britain ?"

"A lot do. We even suspect that national police forces along the way encourage the drivers to pass through their jurisdiction quickly, by paying them cash to do so, to make sure that it is the police force at the end of the journey, and not them, which has to deal with the drugs or illegal immigrants."

"Here's another example of what we are working on." Hevonen led Owen to another screen at the far end of the room. This is a fraud against EU subsidies which Brussels gives for exports of surplus butter. Surplus EU butter is warehoused in Rotterdam : then it is trucked through France to a port in southern Italy, loaded onto ships and there we lose track of it."

He grinned. "We only discovered what was going on because one truck driver had a girlfriend in France. He left the main road to see her, crashed his truck and was killed. The police examined his papers which said that his cargo was 'machine tools for Hungary'. But they discovered the butter instead."

"Has there been a successful prosecution ?"

"There will be no prosecution."

"Why on earth not ?"

"Because only national governments can prosecute criminals."

"There are no EU anti-criminal laws ?"

"None. This fraud spreads across many countries, so it is unclear who is responsible and who can prosecute successfully."

"Will criminal laws have to be standardised throughout the EU ?"

"It is true that there are loopholes where national laws are different from eachother. For example, some member states give their businessmen tax deductions for bribes paid to people in other EU states. But to agree on common definitions of crimes across the EU states is not necessary and would take for ever. The fifty states of the USA have different criminal laws, and so can we in Europe."

"Okay. What other tasks should you in EuroPol take on ?"

"We hope to take on the combatting of terrorism. We are held back by a few reluctant national governments who want terrorism to be kept outside the EuroPol structure and to be dealt with by the Police Working Group on Terrorism and the Trevi Secure Fax network, using encrypted e-mail links.

"We'll also build up unsupervised computer files about individual people. Not just about criminals but also about witnesses, potential victims, contacts, informers and agents. No parliament controls us and our budget is slipped in un-noticed slices through the national parliaments."

"The absence of democratic control over you is astonishing."

"It's up to you MEPs to do something about it. Officials and national ministers will try to stop you."

Time was running out so Owen returned to his report. "How closely do you follow the activities of the fascist parties across Europe ?"

"Very little. We have no overall picture. Apart from marches and riots, we know of incidents where fascists have worked across frontiers for fund-raising. But it's hard to get proof, and harder still to get national courts to prosecute when part of the crime took place in another country. For example," Hevonen's throw-away line was almost apologetic, "there was a curious incident last November."

"What was that ?"

"Some twenty small bombs exploded on the same day, each in a different capital city across Europe. All were small, no damage was done and nobody claimed responsibility. It was obviously coordinated and was an impressive operation. We don't know why it was done, nor who organised it. Just possibly it was a rehearsal for something bigger."

Owen noticed the clock on the wall. It was time to go.

"Mr. Hevonen, thank you for your help. I promise my committee will support you."

"If you can, you won't just be helping EuroPol. You'll be helping the citizens of Europe."

Owen left The Hague and took the road to Brussels. For a time both sides of the road were a riot of colourful tulips. Soon, he knew, their heads would be cut off and thrown away. Their real value lay in the bulbs which would be dug up and sold all over the world.

Next morning in the Environment committee he settled between his Group colleagues. When asked to raise his hand to vote he did, but he did not speak. He concentrated on drafting four amendments about EuroPol for his report.

His first amendment called for the Convention to give EuroPol a legal existence to be ratified urgently by all fifteen national parliaments. There must be a role for the European Court to adjudicate over disputes, so the objection of the British government should be abandoned.

His second insisted that immunities granted to EuroPol officers must be lifted and that there must be parliamentary control over EuroPol by MEPs because harmonised control could not be achieved by fifteen different national parliaments.

Thirdly, EuroPol should have enlarged budget from EU resources to give Europe's new policemen the facilities they needed.

Finally, Europe's policemen should be prohibited from interfering in investigations which were purely national.

The next step was to table the amendments with Bruno Wielblad of the Civil Liberties committee. Glancing at his watch he had a shock. The deadline, ten o'clock that morning, had elapsed an hour and a half ago.

He needed to leave the room immediately to get to Wielblad's office. But his colleagues were in the middle of a voting session and the results were on a knife-edge, being won or lost by a single vote either way. He could not abandon them.

He scribbled a note and beckoned to one of the *huissiers* standing in attendance. The usher walked over.

Owen whispered : "Could you kindly take these amendments to the Civil Liberties secretariat ? I cannot leave the voting and fear I may have missed the deadline."

"Certamente, signore," replied the usher with a polite smile. "Non c'é un problema."

Owen had enquired why so many of the huissiers were Italian, and so few British. Years ago the British government had treated the new parliament with scorn. Its job vacancies had been advertised across Europe, but not in Britain. The Italian government had snapped up the opportunities left unfilled by the British.

Twenty minutes later the huissier returned, looking serious. He handed Owen a note which said. 'You missed the deadline. But for you Owen, it's not a problem. Best wishes. Bruno'

* * *

The following week it was back to Strasbourg for the April plenary. The week was complicated by having a bus full of Owen's constituents on a visit to the parliament. Despite the extra work which it created he was delighted they were coming, not least because some of them might help during the election campaign.

Their visit began with a briefing from an enthusiastic witty Irishman called Niall who gave the same speech to all English-language visitor groups but always retained his freshness.

Owen booked a meeting-room and invited several continental MEPs to speak to his visitors. In the evening he took them to dinner at the Pont St.Martin restaurant in Petit France. It had a terrace overlooking the river and a singer who gave a good imitation of Edith Piaf. Making sure that they saw and enjoyed everything took up two full days of his time.

Leading the group down a corridor on their last morning, he passed Chomik, the chairman of the Civil Liberties committee.

"Owen, I need a word with you." Seeing the group, Chomik shrugged. "But it is not particularly urgent right now."

Later Owen waved his visitors goodbye for their homeward journey. One woman, thanking him, said : "It's incredible. I didn't think the parliament could possibly work with fifteen nationalities and eleven languages. But it does. It's a miracle." Their bus was returning via Rheims where they would learn about how champagne was made and how it tasted.

After they had departed Owen telephoned Chomik.

"You want a word with me ?"

"I have a meeting in fifteen minutes but what I have to tell you will not take long. Can you come to my office ?"

Owen took a lift to the chairman's office which was a double-size room on the Tower's twelfth floor, and appropriate for an MEP who wielded wide influence.

Chomik looked embarrassed when Owen entered and waved him to the white leather sofa.

"Hello Owen" he said. "It's not good news. Yesterday morning I attended the regular monthly meeting of all the committee chairmen. Our task was to decide which reports will be debated in May at the last plenary week before the election."

He would not meet Owen's eyes. "It's bad for you. There were too many reports from other committees. Reports which are not yet ready, like yours, stand no chance of being debated before the election. They all lapse. I am so sorry."

Owen's heart sank. "What can I do ?"

"Frankly, my dear colleague, nothing. It is nobody's fault. Of course you feel that your report is very important and every rapporteur does. As one of my fellow chairmen, Saint Ken, put it years ago, 'Every baby hedgehog is a gazelle to its mother'. Reports from other committees concern legislation and therefore need to be dealt with promptly. Your report does not contain any draft legislation."

"Must I give up then ?"

"Not entirely. I would prefer you to keep going in our committee. One can always hope for a miracle, *nicht wahr* ? Our committee meets next week. We'll vote on the amendments to your report. After the election - I presume that you plan to return to the parliament ? - you can start it again and most of the work will already be done."

Owen saw no point in explaining that his re-election prospects were slight and had just become slighter. Politics was a heartless business with many interesting acquaintances but few friends who cared genuinely.

"But there is also good news !" said Chomik. Owen's heart rose slightly.

"A story for your book. You know that I am Polish by origin ? Do you know the story of the Polish army officer ?[15]

Owen listened and laughed. He took the lift to the ground-floor, walked through the Weiss building past the hemicycle, through the glass bridge over the river, into the Churchill building and stopped at the Swan bar beside the river. Wishing to assess his future options he bought a cappuccino and a slice of rhubarb pie topped with meringue and sat at the last empty table. On reflection he decided he ought to press on with the report, which would be his only memorial, But he would not travel out to Strasbourg to attend the May plenary session because campaigning at home would be more valuable.

Seeing Owen alone at the table, a senior Danish interpreter asked if he might sit at one of its chairs. As he finished his coffee Owen asked the Dane what he did when he was not working in the parliament.

"I'm on call to the Danish Prime Minister" he replied, "which is always interesting work. One of my best moments was in your own

Number Ten Downing Street. It was a summit between the national EU leaders and your Progressive prime minister was the host. During a coffee break, not one of the other leaders was willing to speak to your Premier, so I was seized by the arm and given a personal tour of the paintings and furniture. It was wonderful for me but a very strange situation."

There is a silver lining for me too, thought Owen. Jack Terrier will be pleased that now there is more time for campaigning.

Next morning Owen was delighted to find a set of twelve amendments to his report in his pigeon-hole, translated and printed in English. On the plane home he thought about each one carefully. As rapporteur he was the servant of the committee and must remain neutral. As a politician he had preferences and would try discreetly, to influence their fates.

From his home he telephoned Bridget O'Leumadair, his coordinator on the committee. Together they agreed on which amendments their group would support. It was her task to put together a coalition with other parties within the committee so that the preferred amendments received majority support. This was crucial ; amendments which passed in committee usually passed the full parliament in plenary afterwards.

"By the way, Owen," she added. "I have an Irish story for you. Want to hear it ?"

He picked up a pen and scribbled it down.[16]

"Owen, do you know why Irish jokes are so simple ?"

"Why is that, Bridget ?"

"So that the English can understand them" she giggled.

He laughed but his mood fluctuated. There was a big football match in London to look forward to on Saturday afternoon. But the hooligans who had beaten him in January would now be out of prison after their three month sentences. Would it be safe to return to the football ground ? He would not be deterred by criminals so watched from his usual seat. There was no trouble.

The following Tuesday the Civil Liberties committee met in Brussels. As Chomik had promised, Owen's report was on the agenda. Voting on the twelve amendments proceeded briskly.

Before each vote, Chomik allowed each proposer to say a few words in favour of their own amendment, then the rapporteur said whether or not he favoured it.

Conflict was unavoidable. At one extreme some MEPs wanted to create a federally united Europe, with enforcement of common rules in all member states. At the other were those who wished to preserve their nations' separate identities with a right to pick and choose which EU policies they accepted.

First to object was Felipe Iskira, the only Basque MEP whom the politically-correct would describe as 'vertically challenged'. His objection was different. "At present we have different criminal laws in every EU state. You are proposing to make us all the same - when the Basque people do not even want to be Spanish." Owen explained why laws need not be made identical.

A French Communist, Michel Foulque, railed fiercely against strengthening of EuroPol. Bald and elderly, he was usually accompanied by one or more good-looking young men. "The people who elected me are good French men and women, many of whom remember the Second World War. They would not welcome Germans with powers of arrest in Euro-FBI uniforms, jack-booting down the Champs Elysées. I profoundly oppose the concept."

Nevertheless the suggestion of turning EuroPol into a Euro-FBI received majority support.

An official from the Commission was present as an observer. Chomik asked him : "Are you willing to adopt our proposal and draft legislation for submission to the Council of Ministers ?"

"Chairman, I am not the Commissioner. But, if this report were ever to be debated in plenary, in my opinion, he would be sympathetic" said the official.

With the committee stage completed Owen felt mixed emotions. He was sad that his report now died because there was no time for a plenary debate : on the other hand, if its contents had leaked out back home, it might have stoked fires of embarrassment. He could hardly issue a press release about it to his local media.

* * *

Almost six months had passed since 1st November when Sãta's coordinated bombing across twenty cities had been successfully tested on a small scale. Now, in his office, he hunched over his laptop, and sent out e-mails with final 'go' instructions for the fullscale version.

*   *   *

Soon after dawn on Sunday morning 1st May, a Hungarian news-agency reported a large car bomb explosion in Budapest. First reports said that there had been considerable damage to the beautiful old Hotel Gellert beside the river Danube. Windows had been shattered a hundred metres away, and nearby cars had been turned into blackened wrecks. It was believed that the material had been a plastic explosive called *Danubit*, manufactured in neighbouring Slovakia and normally used for mining.

Across the next few hours, agency reports came in of similar massive explosions in a dozen cities across Europe.

An anonymous phone-call claimed overall responsibility. It was received by the news-desk of a German broadsheet, the *Frankfurter Algemeine Zeitung*. The caller said he was speaking anonymously from outside Germany. He said that the explosions were a protest against the activities of far-right political parties. The bombs had been coordinated by ANTE, whose letters stood for 'Anti-Nazi Troop of Europe'. The journalist who wrote down the message thought that the man had spoken with a Middle-Eastern accent, either Arabic or possibly Israeli.

That same morning Owen was with Jack Terrier and the other candidates on the list, discussing plans for their election campaign. At lunchtime in the pub they saw the bomb reports in a television news bulletin.

Owen felt huge alarm. He had failed and crime was escalating.

Jack brushed the news aside : "Pity about your report, Owen. You may have been on to something but you fell between the devil and the deep blue sea. You lost both your parliamentary report and precious campaigning time. With no more distractions let's do everything possible to win the seats."

During the day, press statements were issued by Rocher and other leaders. Speaking from Marseilles Rocher said that the bombs were a clumsy attempt to blacken the reputation of his movement. They proved that stronger law-and-order measures were desperately needed. The discredited and rotten-to-the-core mainstream parties had lost the will to take strong action against despicable left-wing terrorism.

Geier in Vienna pointed out that when such outrages occurred, it underlined how dangerous the EU's open borders were. The public wanted stronger national controls. Police powers must be reinforced to deal ruthlessly with criminals and immigrants.

Commentators in the media pointed out that national elections were due in several EU countries, as well as the European elections everywhere in June. The bombings would enhance sympathy and support for the fascists.

Owen read the reports without surprise. He remembered somebody saying that : 'For the cost of winning one parliamentary seat, you can buy a lot of Semtex instead.'

The national security services, taken by surprise, set to work to discover who was behind the bombings. How had Middle Easterners managed such expert coordination across Europe ?

In The Hague, Paavo Hevonen took a keen interest. He suspected that he understood better than most what might be going on. He regretted that his authority was limited to action against drug-smugglers.

* * *

At nine o'clock on Monday morning, Owen was in his kitchen eyeing a bowl of cereal, a cup of lemon tea, and three newspapers. For once he did not have to hurry and he was enjoying the moment. There was a five-day Group meeting starting in Brussels and he would sign in to record his presence there sometime later during the week.

Instead he would prepare for the high point of the week. On Friday evening he and his five fellow Euro-candidates on the Radical list would launch their campaign at a public meeting.

Suddenly the telephone rang twice then stopped. Guessing that the fax machine had cut in, he strolled into the study. It was a short fax - and it came from Brussels :

> After all, your report will be debated at Strasbourg next week. Josef Chomik, Civil Liberties committee.

Incredulously he read it again. A succession of emotions surged through his head. Was it a hoax ? Then pleasure that his report was not wasted after all. Then dismay that writing his speech for Friday would be interrupted. Finally a glimmer of light at the distant end of the dark tunnel, that his report might make an impact on the voters after all.

If it was true, he must spend time this week in Brussels in order to win support for his report from his Group colleagues. Then, next week, he would have to spend several days in Strasbourg, to be present for his debate and for the voting afterwards. It was valuable time when Jack Terrier required him at home to campaign.

Abandoning the bowl of cereal, he telephoned the committee's secretariat in Brussels. Bruno Wielblad answered:

"I just received your fax. Is it a joke ?"

"It is not" replied the German.

"I'm not sure that I can do it."

"You must. The citizens of Europe depend on you - if cross-frontier crime is to be dealt with."

"When will the debate take place in Strasbourg ?" asked Owen.

"On the Wednesday."

"The Wednesday ? Bruno, are you sure ? That day is reserved for major set-piece debates in which the Council of Ministers is particularly interested."

"That is correct. It was the Council which asked, in an urgent message to the President of parliament yesterday evening, that your report should be debated."

"How extraordinary. Why ?"

"Following the bombs which exploded yesterday - you heard about them ? - the EU's Council of Interior ministers held an emergency meeting last night. No details were published by the ministers, as usual, but they sent their request to us. Naturally the President of Parliament has replied he is always anxious to be helpful. So your report is on next week's agenda."

Owen rang off. Despite the election campaign he could not avoid his duty as rapporteur. If he did, his election opponents would accuse him of putting his personal interests first : 'Why should voters re-elect you when you neglect your responsibilities in parliament ?'

He rang his agent Rosemary Jones. The news irritated her : her campaign plan would be disrupted. Every day was going to be critical, she said ; why did he want to gallivant off to Strasbourg again ?

Surprisingly, Jack Terrier was more sympathetic : “It's a nuisance but of course you must do your duty.”

The socialist Group's secretariat in Brussels faxed a question. His report would be discussed tomorrow morning in a working-party : would he be present ? His travel agent grumbled ; it would be difficult to change the flights but he would try. Last, Owen telephoned UKREP, the British government's office in Brussels.

An English voice answered his call. Owen gave his name and asked to speak to the desk-officer who was responsible for the EU's Internal Security and Justice affairs.

A click then a female voice said : “Hello, Mr. Mann. My name is Jill Hunter. I work on the Third Pillar portfolio which includes security, justice, and immigration. Are you, by any chance, ringing about your report ?”

“Bull's eye. If I may I'd like to compare notes with you, to give it the best chance of getting through the parliament and then the Council of Ministers.”

“Tomorrow at three ?”

“I'll be there.”

He flew straight out to Brussels and joined one of the Socialist Group's working-parties. They were examining the forthcoming plenary agenda, deciding which reports to support, whether amendments should be tabled, and who would speak in each debate and for how long.

Owen expected his Group to support the report but remembered Jim Keeper's warning that working with continental socialists was like wading through treacle, except that agreements didn't stick. And that reminded him of a joke told by the catastrophic communist Xamilopardis :

“A blind rabbit was wandering in a forest and bumped into a blind snake. Neither was sure what the other was, so they agreed to touch each other. The snake touched the rabbit first. He felt soft fur and long floppy ears - and announced : "I know - you are a rabbit !" "Correct" said the rabbit, and began to touch the snake. He felt something cold and slippery - and replied with confidence : "I know exactly what you are : you are a socialist !"

In the working-party his committee coordinator, Bridget O'Leumadair, introduced Owen's report and gave it her full backing. The only counter-voice came from an unexpected quarter. His fellow British Radical, Tom Ostler, complained that Owen had turned into a Euro-fanatic and was out-of-line with British public opinion. No other member supported Ostler, probably because of his personal unpopularity in the Group. After a brief debate, Owen's report received overwhelming support. Since they were his political allies, any other result would have been unacceptable but the procedure had to be gone through.

The afternoon was fine as he walked up the hill past the Commission's Bredel building. The UKREP office was situated in a thin terrace building on nine floors. The receptionist directed him into the lift and telephoned to warn Jill Hunter.

Jill Hunter met him at the lift door. "Welcome" she said with a handshake and a warm smile. She had a pale skin, short black curly hair, nice round breasts, and very intelligent brown eyes. Aged around thirty-five she was wearing a grey pin-stripe trouser-suit.

Ushered into her office he thought its small size was unworthy of the important role which she played in defending British interests, but as a British tax-payer he was reassured.

"Jill," he asked, "why is the Council is suddenly interested in my report ?"

"You heard about the bombs at the weekend ? I'm not revealing any vital secret if I tell you that our security services believe that they were placed, not by the left-wing, but by the Nazis themselves."

"Really ? Why ?"

"Because they hope to create a backlash and so win more votes in the coming elections."

"The EU prime ministers demanded quick action but discovered there is no agreement to do anything about terrorists at the EU-level. On Sunday evening the fifteen security ministers met at an emergency Council. By a majority vote, they instructed the Commission to draft emergency legislation, and to prepare a budget to fund a Euro-FBI."

"Why do they need to debate my report ?"

"It is unclear in the Treaties how much the MEPs are meant to be involved in security policy. The ministers were counselled that they had better obtain a formal Opinion from the MEPs just in case. Otherwise, in any court dispute afterwards, the fascists might succeed with a defence that the EU legislation was passed invalidly. Like the Isoglucose ruling."

"What was that ?"

"In 1981 the Council of Agriculture Ministers passed a minor directive concerning a chemical called Isoglucose. An alert member of the public noticed that the ministers had approved it without waiting to receive an Opinion from the MEPs. There was an appeal to the European Court of Justice, where the judges ruled that the law had been passed illegally. They struck it out and established the principle that ministers must wait for an Opinion from MEPs, even if they ignore what it says."

"I remember. That gave the parliament its first veto over European law-making. If MEPs withheld their Opinion from ministers, no law could be passed. So ministers had to start negotiating with MEPs to get EU laws passed.

"It was the first battle for EU democracy won by the MEPs."

"Jill, what decision do you expect in the Council about creating a Euro-FBI ?"

"According to the Treaty this legislation can be passed by a *qualified majority* among ministers. All fifteen ministers do not have to be unanimous. So we are counting heads," she explained, "or rather counting votes."

"What is a qualified majority ?"

"There's a total of eighty-seven votes available in the Council. A qualified majority means sixty-two votes or more must be in favour."

"How many votes does the U.K. have ?"

"Big countries have more votes than little ones. The four largest have ten votes each ; Germany, Italy, France, and us." Owen noted down the figures.

"Spain has eight. Belgium, Greece, Netherlands, and Portugal have five each. It's a bit like the Euro-vision Song Contest, isn't it ?" she laughed. And added with a French accent. "'Nul points pour Norvège.'

"That's unkind because Norway has won the contest and is not a member of the EU."

"Anyway you realise that what I'm telling you will change soon ?" she asked with a mischievous grin. Owen put down his pen.

"When ?"

"Before the next six countries join the EU."

"Why ?"

"Under current rules, all twenty-one members would have their own veto over many subjects. Consequently nothing will ever get decided because there is usually one country against every proposal. So it will be necessary to reduce or abolish the national veto, and maybe also give the larger countries more votes."

Owen nodded. "I can see that."

"There's more. There will be too many Commissioners ; either each country can only have one, or some countries will have none for a period. Or we could elect the president of the Commission and allow him to pick his own team."

"That sounds reasonable too,"

"It will be like electing the American president and letting him choose his own cabinet. We'll have reached the United States of Europe."

Owen sighed.

"To get back to the present," she continued, "Austria and Sweden have four votes each. Then come Denmark, Finland, and Ireland with three each. Finally Luxembourg at the bottom has two. The total is eighty-seven."

"Sixty-two votes must be in favour. Put the other way, how many votes can block it ?"

"A blocking minority is twenty-six votes against."

Owen squinted at his notes. "Twenty-six votes to block would require two large countries plus Spain, or two large countries plus two smaller countries."

"Correct. We think, at this moment, that the Euro-FBI proposal will be passed but it could be close. At least two countries are likely to be against because they have frail coalition governments and powerful far-right opposition parties."

"France and Austria ?" Owen asked. Jill nodded.

"Who else might vote against ?"

"Denmark is wavering. They are always suspicious of new European plans. Remember how they voted against the Maastricht Treaty in their first referendum."

Owen had a worrying thought. "Can't just one country cite the Luxembourg Compromise and veto everything ?"

"No" she replied. "The Luxembourg Compromise doesn't even exist - although Euro-sceptical MPs at Westminster pretend that it does. There never even was a compromise. Back in 1965 De Gaulle, then President of France, operated an 'empty chair' policy because he wanted a veto over everything. The other five member countries said that he couldn't have one and pointed to the rules France which had signed agreeing to majority-voting. Some months later, the six met at Luxembourg to negotiate a way out of the impasse. Nothing was agreed, nothing was written down, but they started working together again. The so-called 'compromise' was a fig-leaf to keep France involved in European decisions."

"Is there anything I can do to help the Council's decision ?"

"Owen, tell me about the attitudes of the different parties and nationalities in your parliament. Tell me where the pitfalls are."

Owen described how he thought the plenary voting would go and which MEPs would vote in favour of a Euro-FBI.

"A final request, Jill" asked Owen. "I would love to watch 'my' EU law being passed. I know the Council meets in secret but is there any chance of my dressing up as a junior official in the British delegation and watching quietly from the back of the Council's meeting ?"

Jill looked astonished. "I've never seen anybody slip in like that. It is said that the Germans have smuggled in people in the past from their state parliaments when their federal government in Bonn was having difficulties with them. But I can't see a British minister agreeing, and certainly not Sir David Bronwen."

"Why does the Council meet in secret ? They pass laws which the public has to obey. Shouldn't that be done in public ?"

"In theory, yes, but it's about horse-trading. Suppose the UK was against creating a Euro-FBI but not passionately. We might allow ourselves to be persuaded to vote in favour, and in return we extract concessions on something quite different which we want strongly. It has to be done in secret. Otherwise public opinion would be upset by our giving away British interests which our minister claims in public to have fought to defend."

"Don't you ever worry about how undemocratic the Council of Ministers is, Jill ?"

"As Michael Dobbs wrote in one of his splendid Urquhart stories, 'You might very well think that, but I could not possibly comment.'"

Owen strolled back to the parliament. He was confident that, although the end of his parliamentary career was near, his report might yet provide him a political epitaph.

He telephoned Jack Terrier.

"What happens next, Owen ?"

"If the parliament votes for my report next week, it goes to the Council of Ministers. They might use some of our recommendations if they create a Euro-FBI."

Jack's voice lifted in admiration. "Owen, you mean you might get a European law onto the books, and you've only been an MEP for five months ?"

"Not just me. Others contributed too."

"But you've been the prime mover. Owen, do you know what I'd like to do ?"

“Buy the next beer ?”

“I will. But I’d also like to watch the Council voting on your new law. I have watched law-making at Westminster but this would be something new for me. Do I need a ticket ?”

Owen felt like a policeman on point duty, facing traffic coming the wrong way. “Sorry, Jack. Your request’s impossible.”

“I’ll pay my own fare to Brussels.”

“It’s not the money. There’s nothing I should enjoy more. It’s because the Council of Ministers legislates in secret. Neither you as a member of the public, nor I as an MEP, nor any journalist can watch them pass laws.”

“They pass laws over us *in secret* ? I don’t believe you” said the veteran.

“It’s true. The EU Council is the only legislative body in the free world which passes laws in secret. It puts them on a par with the communists in Beijing and North Korea.”

Jack Terrier was incredulous but gave way. “Well, at least get me a copy of their Hansard, or whatever you call it, to read their debate.”

“I can’t either. The ministers don’t publish any record of their debates, nor even how they vote.”

“That’s incredible and totally undemocratic. I’ll bet that the UK has been fighting against this for years.”

“No, all British governments have supported it.”

Jack thought for a moment. “But the ministers themselves are elected. They come back to the House of Commons and give an account of themselves. That’s democratic.”

“No, Jack. Leave aside the fact that some of our ministers come from the Lords and are not elected. You’ve forgotten the distinction between the ministers and what they commit us to. Yes, ministers make statements to the Commons. Yes, if MPs are unhappy, they force the minister to resign. But, and here’s the difference, the EU law to which the disgraced minister has agreed in Brussels cannot be changed by the MPs. The new European law is binding over four hundred million Europeans as soon as it is published in Brussels.”

Jack sounded startled. “In other words, ministers can be controlled as individuals but not the decisions they make ?"

"Your first reaction was right. The Council is profoundly undemocratic and all ministers who've gone along with that ought to be deeply ashamed."

"Why haven't I heard about this before ? Why aren't the British public in an uproar about it ? Why aren't MPs at Westminster putting it right ?"

"MPs at Westminster know this perfectly well. They are in on the pretence. They act out a play to reassure the public that nothing has changed, that they still control all of Britain's destiny. The public are too occupied with the problems of their own individual lives to find out the truth. The media doesn't report it because it is, literally, not 'new' any more in the sense that 'news' has to be 'new'."

To illustrate to Jack the Commons' lack of desire to improve democracy in the EU, Owen told him a story which an old-hand MEP had related to him. The old-hand had been to see the prime minister of the day at Number Ten. The MEP had explained the powerful arguments for giving the European Parliament democratic powers of control over the EU's decision-makers in the interests of democracy and openness. The PM had listened attentively. The old-hand finished and waited for an appreciative response. But the premier's reply had been merely 'But they use foreign languages in the European Parliament so there can be no cut and thrust.' The old-hand had been stunned by the premier's evasion.

"How did this extraordinary democratic deficit come about ?" Jack asked.

"It happened when we joined the Common Market back in 1973. MPs approved the Treaty of Rome so that we could join. They gave British ministers power to go to Brussels and commit us irrevocably to European laws. Ever since, backbench MPs have not rocked the boat because they yearn to become ministers themselves one day. In any case, until something goes seriously wrong, the point may be academic. It is uncomfortable for MPs to admit that they are powerless in this area. Like Hans Andersen's *King Who Had No Clothes*, MPs feel that the whole subject is better not mentioned. Extreme Euro-sceptic MPs see giving the European Parliament the necessary real powers of control over EU law-making as one more way of strengthening the EU - which they oppose because they want it to fail."

"What can be done to correct this appalling situation, this deficit in democracy ?" Jack persisted.

"It's impossible to give our MPs the power to amend an EU law," replied Owen.

"Why ?"

"Because all fifteen national parliaments in the EU would want to pass different amendments so there would be no standard version of the EU law. That would destroy free trade across the Single Market."

"We could quit the EU."

"If we did, we would still be heavily affected by EU laws. But we would not have any influence over them. Quite simply, EU decisions are out of reach of national backbenchers."

"Nothing can be done ?"

"Emphatically it can. In America laws have to receive the approval of *both* the Senate and House of Representatives in Washington DC. In the same way, all EU laws should receive the assent of both legislative houses in the EU, the European Parliament representing the people and the Council of Ministers representing the nation-states. The Amsterdam Treaty in 1997 went further than ever before in giving the MEPs equality with the ministers. Yet the Council still legislates in secret."

"So the European Parliament will become the House of Representatives for Europe ?"

"Some continentals think so. One day the British people may wake up and ask 'How did that happen ?' Meanwhile ministers keep their decisions secret."

"I'm extremely disappointed" said Jack. He changed the subject : "Are you ready for the adoption meeting on Friday ? I'll see you then."

It had been a long telephone call from Brussels but fortunately the cost was paid by the tax-payer. Owen was glad he had explained the EU's democratic deficit to Jack. One day party activists might wake up to the conspiracy of silence that had kept it going for so long.

* * *

Owen returned to London by train next morning. He walked to the Commons and climbed up to the Special Gallery. The entertainment would be better than last time, thanks to the ticket he had obtained from Adam Drake.

Question Time to the Prime Minister was a famous event which he had not previously witnessed. Opposite in the Public Gallery he could see that every place was already filled. Everyone hoped to see and hear impressive verbal duelling, although not to learn any new facts.

In the cauldron below, it was obvious that excitement was high. Government and Opposition benches were overflowing with MPs. The tension had been fuelled in recent weeks by speculation about possible dates for a General Election. As each day passed, the anticipation had grown.

The Prime Minister arrived to cheers from his side. He took his usual seat opposite the despatch box on the government front-bench. The Speaker called for the first question to him. Adam Drake asked what the government's attitude was to creating a Euro-FBI. The premier answered that they were in favour.

Almost half an hour later, Sir Harry Pedreven was called by the Speaker to pose the final question from the Opposition benches.

"Does the Prime Minister find it acceptable that one region of Europe can steal jobs away from my constituency by bribing a business to move to another country ?"

The Prime Minister, not for the first time in his career, outflanked his opponent with his reply. "It is completely unacceptable. I have already raised that point at the highest level. Indeed," he added, sounding Euro-sceptical because he believed it was the mood of the country as the election approached, "I think that this question may well be an important battle-ground in the coming weeks."

He paused, waiting for the speculation among listening MPs about 'coming weeks' to die away. He continued "because immediately after this Question Time I shall proceed to Buckingham Palace to ask Her Majesty to dissolve parliament so that a General Election may take place on Thursday the ninth of June."

There was a shocked momentary silence. The House had been taken by surprise and it visibly pleased the Prime Minister. A split second later there was uproar, and it was several minutes before the Speaker could restore silence.

The Prime Minister completed his sentence. "...therefore the business of this House will conclude at the end of next week."

As he left the gallery Owen shared the excitement. The frenzy, created by the Prime Minister's announcement, was spreading out like the waves in a pond, enveloping the Central Lobby, the national media, and soon the public outside. Few people had noticed that voting would take place in two elections on the same day. As a result the turnout of voters in the European election would be higher than normal, but Owen doubted whether this would benefit him.

Across the Channel in Brussels, however, it was business as usual. An election in one of the fifteen EU countries is a common event. By the law of averages several take place each year. Meetings of the Commission, the European Parliament, and the Council of Ministers would continue routinely.

* * *

On Friday morning over breakfast Owen perused his newspaper. His eye was caught by a headline on an inside page, HOOLIGAN EURO-MP. The report said :

> It is alleged by airline officials that Tom Ostler MEP, when returning from Brussels on a plane two days ago, drank too much, forced his way into the cockpit and struck the pilot. Police are making enquiries.

That should make this evening's Adoption meeting pretty interesting, thought Owen. He continued to turn the pages.

During the day he worked on his speech for the evening. He arrived at the meeting hall in good time. Ostler had not yet arrived. Jack Terrier tugged at Owen's sleeve and pulled him into a quiet corner.

"Owen, you heard about Ostler ?"

"Is it true ?"

"Yes. I've spent most of yesterday and today on it. Our spin-doctors in London tried hard to protect him by pushing a story into the newspapers about a misdemeanour by one of the other side's MEPs which they had been saving for a rainy day like this."

"It didn't work ?"

"No. Tom has agreed, very reluctantly of course, to resign from our list. I hope that you will agree to move up to the number three position ?"

Astonished but secretly delighted, Owen agreed. The evening's meeting to formally start the European election campaign went smoothly. It was attended by about a hundred party activists. Owen and his four fellow prospective Radical candidates each made a short speech, and the meeting unanimously voted to adopt them as their list of candidates plus a new number six, who was unable to be present due to the short notice but had promised to be a full-time candidate.

An election campaign is like a play with the candidates as the principal actors. Experienced campaigners know that successful elections, like theatre, depend on meticulous preparation. During a campaign a candidate influences only a handful of votes because the result is decided by the overall state of public opinion and by the relative willingness of supporters of different parties to go out and vote. Why campaign at all ? Because an absent candidate - like an actor missing his cue - would be marked down accordingly. A candidate could not guarantee to win, but he could guarantee his own defeat.

Next morning Owen held his usual Saturday surgery. He remained an MEP until a new MEP replaced him - unlike MPs who lose their jobs when the Commons is dissolved before an election. A surgery was an opportunity to win a few more votes and maybe create local publicity.

After the surgery, Owen pinned a rosette to his jacket. With Jack Terrier, the other five candidates and a team of supporters, they started their campaign in a market-place. He shook as many hands as he could find while the volunteers handed out leaflets. But the public were uninterested : most were unaware that there was a European election. Surely the General Election did not start for another week, they asked. This was unsurprising since, in the previous European election in Britain, less than one voter in four had bothered to vote.

Despite the pressing need to be seen campaigning for votes, Owen flew to Strasbourg on Monday for the plenary session.

The week's agenda of debates was confirmed at the opening session in the hemicycle. Afterwards there was a press conference to explain the week's major debates to the media. Owen was one of three rapporteurs who appeared to explain their reports and answer questions.

The media's reaction to his presentation, he thought afterwards, was disinterest because the parliament had so little influence. In the field of Justice and Home Affairs, MEPs were only empowered to give a technical Opinion about creating a Euro-FBI - unlike most other EU legislation where they had two readings and were equal with the Council. For the media, the interesting part came later when the Council of Ministers made its decision.

Owen spied McKirk sitting at the back, but the questioning came from continental journalists including one from Spain's prestigious *El Pais*. Given the conflict between the views in his report and his views back home, Owen was glad that few of the British media were present.

At the end of the conference McKirk made a signal to Owen of drinking a cup of coffee and eating a doughnut. They settled at a table in the corner of the hemicycle bar.

McKirk was gloomy. His Russian grain expose had been spiked by his editor as too dull and he had not been asked to cover Owen's debate.

"It might be worth a small paragraph somewhere" he conceded "but the big question is what the Council of Ministers does with it. If your report leads to legislation, then that might earn you a footnote. Keep me posted."

Returning down the corridor to his office, Owen almost bumped into Van Der Muis. The Dutchman was looking extremely upset, and for the first time, did not greet Owen with "How's life ?"

So Owen asked : "How's life, Petrus ? You don't look so happy."

"I have terrible problems."

"Can I help ?"

"No, but thankyou. My first problem is that I am not on the list of candidates for my party at the European election."

"Why not ?"

“Technically, because I took a different view to my party in a vote concerning Israel and the Arabs.”

“You said ‘technically’ ?”

“It’s not the real reason.”

“What is ?”

“Owen, you will not tell anybody ? I have been keeping two families. One at home in Holland and another in Paris. Going away each week as an MEP allowed me to visit both. I don’t know how I am going to manage it any more.”

Back at his desk, Owen reflected that his problems were pale by comparison.

In the evening he went to the annual asparagus supper hosted by the mayor of Strasbourg at an Alsacian timbered village outside the city. A local band played jolly um-pah-pah music. His evening was spent with colleagues, debating election prospects over chunks of ham, fresh asparagus and white wine. He saw Murdo McKirk, looking quite tidy, persuading Natasha Farfalla onto the tiny dance-floor.

* * *

Except to addicts of minority television channels the parliament’s hemicycle was unfamiliar to the public. In fact there were four hemicycles : an unused one in Luxembourg, one in Brussels in the Spaak building, and two in Strasbourg. The French government, desperate to retain its share of a powerful EU body, built a larger one in 1999 alongside the first, to accommodate extra MEPs and languages when the EU enlarged.

The new one, called the Weiss building, was said to be the largest single room in Europe. It was elliptical with opaque glass walls lit from behind, giving the feeling of floating in clouds. Its ceiling held thousands of lights in recesses, shining like stars at night. During one dull debate, Owen had tried and failed to count them. Around the walls, one level above the chamber, was the public gallery : there each visitor had his own seat which was equipped with headphones and a dial to select a language.

A visitor looking down into the hemicycle saw the seats arranged in a horse-shoe shape. The members sat in dark-leather arm chairs with pale blue desks and individual microphones. Different coloured papers were scattered randomly across the desks, showing different languages, because MEPs sat in political groups and not by nationality or language.

A few desks sported white telephones, for use by the leaders of political groups. Round the sides, dark glass windows concealed booths of interpreters. Mobile television cameras recorded every moment for the parliament's archives. To help the acoustics each speaker's voice was carried by hidden microphones to all corners of the chamber and into the headphones of the interpreters.

The President of the parliament, Michelangelo Canguro - who would be known in Britain as the Speaker - sat at the mouth of the horseshoe at a raised desk. Each president was elected by MEPs to serve for two and a half years. A row of sixteen flags was arrayed behind him. In front and to his right were seats for the Commissioners and to his left were seats for the Council of Ministers.

President Canguro was fluent in four languages and so quick mentally that he irritated members who asked to speak by anticipating what they were about to say. On his right sat the parliament's secretary-general, ready to give him advice. To his left, also giving help, was a clever blonde German named Erica who had occupied the same role since before the first elections in 1979. Her stunning outfits had brightened many dull debates.

On Wednesday morning Owen sat in his office on the tenth floor of the Tower, going over his speech yet again. Erica had told him that his debate was likely to start at around ten o'clock. He switched on the channel of his office television which relayed live pictures from the hemicycle, and chose English from the menu of languages on the screen. The President tapped his gavel. "Good morning, colleagues. I call the sitting to order."

The Minutes of the previous sitting were approved. The President made a routine announcement to welcome a new Spanish member, and expressed the courteous hope that his tenure would stretch beyond the election next month.

"The first debate on today's agenda concerns the report on financial loans to Russia. The rapporteur for the Committee on Foreign Affairs is Señor Llagosta."

Mr. Llagosta suffered from severe arthritis. His fingers were twisted like claws and this won him sympathy from other members.

Before he could start his speech, there was a raucous call for a point of order from Xamilopardis the bearded Greek : "Mr. President, on behalf of my group and in accordance with the rules, I move that the Llagosta report be referred back to committee."

"Very well," replied President Canguro, trying to conceal his irritation, "you are within your rights to ask. One member to speak briefly in favour, one to speak against, and then we shall vote."

Arguments, for and against referral back, were delivered forcefully. Two blue and white electronic scoreboards on opposite walls of the chamber showed how long remained in seconds to each speaker

Xamilopardis argued that the death penalty had not been abolished in Russia so it was wrong to give them financial help. Llagosta replied that the death penalty was irrelevant to the question of helping Russia's economy revive.

Owen half-listened in his office to the unfolding drama while he continued to check his speech. If the Llagosta report was referred back, the next debate would start immediately. Suddenly he realised that he might miss the start of his own debate. He seized his papers and jacket, and ran along the corridor to the lifts. Fortunately, for once, a lift arrived quickly and was empty. Presumably, he thought, not everybody was rushing to hear his speech.

As he descended to the first level and raced across the wooden bridge to the hemicycle building, the referral proposal was put to a vote by a show of hands. The result was too close to be clear. The President rapped his gavel. "We shall decide this by electronic roll-call."

In front of each member's desk was a small computer terminal and miniature screen. Every MEP carried a personalised plastic voting card. When a vote was called, the cards were inserted into the terminals and one of three buttons was pressed, to vote *yes*, or *no*, or *abstain*. The result was displayed instantly on the scoreboards and a computer printed out how the members had voted.

The scoreboards showed that a majority had voted that Llagosta's report be referred back to committee. This effectively killed it, as Xamilopardis and its opponents had intended, because there was no other plenary before the election when it could be debated.

Just as the President announced the result Owen reached his seat. He heard the President speak his name and saw Erica anxiously scanning the seats to try to locate him.

He put on his head-phones. Thanks to the small time delay caused by interpretation, he heard the President's words. "Now we reach the report of the Civil Liberties committee on the state of Fascism in Europe. I give the floor to the rapporteur to introduce the debate. Mr. Mann, you have five minutes."

Owen glanced around. The hemicycle was less than a tenth full, normal for a routine debate in any parliament of the world. Members did not speak to persuade other members : most already had their own opinions. Speeches were made for the written record, and for the media outside. Later, when it came to voting, the chamber would be full.

Owen was apprehensive, although not as nervous as when he had waited to make his maiden speech. Then he had sat in his seat, watching his name creep up the television screen listing the next three speakers. Listening at the time were ex-prime ministers and rising stars. As his name neared the top, his terror had grown. He had prayed that the ground would open up and swallow him and that nobody would notice he had disappeared. Supposing his prayer went unanswered and he was called, what if his words came out garbled ? But why should they ? The previous day when he had typed out his brief speech, it had made sense. If he stuck to his script, he would survive the experience. And he had. Since then, with practice, speaking was becoming easier.

He rose to speak. Five minutes were insufficient but it was the parliament's ration for a rapporteur. Having so little time turned members into gabblers, trying to squeeze in as much as possible. This was severe on interpreters who struggled to give a true version of the speech. Hoping to be interpreted effectively Owen had given a copy of his script to the interpreters the previous afternoon, to allow them to check for difficult words.

In his five minutes he summarised the growing danger of fascism in Europe which high unemployment and globalisation were making worse. EU action was essential. He closed with a tribute to Pietro Gatto and the words : "Intolerance, whether of religion, or nation, or skin-colour, is wrong. We all know it is. We must all fight to prevent it."

He knew he must remain in the chamber throughout the debate as a courtesy to the other speakers. Members from all political groups now followed, none with more than three minutes to speak. Some argued in favour of the committee's recommendations, but not all.

Betty Borboleta asked members to think very clearly. She quoted from Mahatma Gandhi : "When you are in doubt, try this test. Remember the poorest and weakest man you ever saw, then ask yourself whether the decision you are about to take will be of any use to him ?"

Applause broke out but she hurried on. "We are here to make choices which are aimed at the satisfaction of the principles that have put Europe, in theory at least, in the forefront of the struggle for the rights of man - liberty, equality and fraternity.

"A section of Europe's population refuses to understand or accept that an inter-racial, multi-ethnic and multi-cultural society is inevitable. Our present laws are the foundation of racism. How can we eradicate evil when we ourselves create two degrees of citizenship, one for ourselves and another for immigrants ? Regardless of origin or colour of skin, nothing justifies oppression, injury or injustice to another individual, no matter what his station in life."

She finished with words from the Russian novelist Dostoevsky : 'I am seated on the shoulders of a man, making him breathless. I tell everyone that I shall do my utmost to relieve him of this burden - except for the one thing that I could do, which is to climb off his back.'

She sat down and was applauded warmly. The next speaker, Pierre Danvad, was a foot-soldier in the Rocher's National Front. The opinion which he bleated was entirely negative : "A report by the most junior of our police sergeants would be a masterpiece by comparison with Mann's miserable effort. Thanks to Mann, students can now acquaint themselves with a perfect example of what not to do.

"You want us to believe" he continued, pointing at Owen, "that the ancient peoples of Europe are the only ones to be sullied by the one sin which for you is unforgivable, racism. You have not cited a single racist act committed by another race. Have you never travelled and seen what has happened to the Tutsis and the Hutus ?

How sad to see you pursuing racism in Europe where it is least evident.

"Our perception of race is an attachment to our roots, a veneration of our forefathers, a love for our fatherland. Those like Mann, who proclaim that we should sweep away the past, are barbarians without thought for the future. Mann's work is not designed to eliminate racism but to eliminate the distinction between nationals and non-nationals. He wishes to destroy our homelands and offers instead a bleak and colourless planet of his dreams. My thoughts turn to those thousands of my compatriots, men and women, small children and old ladies, who have fallen victim to theft, rape and other crimes, attacked by the dregs of society."

Shaking his fist at Betty Borboleta, he called out : "Do you think it would be possible for a single woman to sit, as you do here, in the parliament of any Moslem country which you admire ? Why not return and fight for the emancipation which their females need ?"

He sat down to a hostile silence. Next to speak was a Spaniard, Miguel Cerdo. Frequently drunk in the morning, he grunted a few words : "When disembarking at an airport I always make sure that I join a queue with no black person in front of me. Because when he or she arrives at the front, the queue is held up. I am white so the policeman never says anything to me. But when he sees a coloured person, he not only looks at his papers but also asks him a load of questions."

Having finished Cerdo walked round to Owen's seat. "I have a Spanish contribution for your book. Do you want to hear it now ?"

"Not right now, please, Miguel." But Cerdo told it anyway, relieved that his speaking ordeal was over.[17]

Owen shook his hand silently in thanks and made a sign that he must listen to the debate. Next on his feet for two minutes was a wrinkled overweight anti-European Dane, Claus Flodhest. He said : "Fascism is advancing again. Yet of the forty recommendations in the parliament's previous report, few have been implemented by the national ministers. From them have only come words, declarations, motions, and panegyrics."

The debate was dull and Owen hoped that a few rivalries or personal enmities would inflame it. A hawkish Dutch Green member, Mrs. Hanja Adelaar, denounced "a certain French leader of a centre-right party" whom she accused of trying to cream off fascist MEP votes in the coming contest for the next President of the parliament.

"*Vous etes merde dans un bas de soie*" she said, "as Napoleon said to another French minister Tallyrand." The English interpreter, who sounded to Owen like Natasha Farfalla, accurately rendered this as "You are shit in a silk stocking."

Mrs. Adelaar was immediately rebuked by Signor Moffetta, a right-wing Italian who was a friend of the French leader : "You accuse my distinguished colleague of seeking election as President of the European Parliament with the backing of the extreme right. To what political depths have you descended, with a polemic that contributes nothing to our work on this crucial issue ? In the past I have known the zero level in politics. Now, through you, I have discovered the most mediocre depths of sectarianism at a level never plumbed anywhere before in Europe."

Mrs. Adelaar demanded her right to reply : "To any politician from any country and any political party who enters into shady arrangements with fascists, my description is indeed correct. I did not mention any names, but if the silk stockings fit, wear them !"

In the seat next to Owen was Pierre Hirondelle. Owen muttered to him that he did not understand how a mainstream Frenchman could seek support from the fascists.

Hirondelle grinned. "You don't understand the French people. Listen ! After God created the world, He decided that He had over-endowed the land that would be known as France. It would have the beautiful Mediterranean coast, the best wines in the world, a romantic city on the river Seine, skiing in the Alps, and so on. God said nervously : 'The other countries will be jealous. What shall I do to correct this ? I know,' He said, 'I will put the French people to live there. That will balance it out.' Owen laughed but remembered hearing an identical story about the Venezuelans.

A German right-winger, Horst Sobolan, spoke as if he wanted to bite the rapporteur. Once a refugee from Romania, he attacked Owen's report fiercely : "In forty pages, Mann has not once recorded the racist crimes perpetrated by the communists, the genocide of the Jews in the Soviet Union and Eastern Europe. I accuse him of being a liar, an untruthful person. He is not only a racist ; he is an inveterate liar."

The President banged his gavel. "It is out of order to call a member a liar. You must withdraw that remark."

Sobolan refused : "President, flouting established traditions, you deny me the right to speak."

The President insisted : "You must withdraw those words. Be seated. We will hear your Personal Statement immediately after the debate is ended."

Next up was a wily Dane, Henrik Edderkop, who liked to weave a web to enmesh his opponents' arguments. He began in English. "I wish to address the rapporteur in his own language. Fascism is alive in all the countries of Europe, often in the guise of democratic parties."

But, with too little time allocated to him, he became tongue-tied and apologised : "My relationship with English is like my relationship with my wife," he said. "I am in love but I do not have mastery." He switched to Danish but his microphone was switched off by the president because his time had run out.

Frodo Alika, a Swede whose many rings sparkled on his fingers, gloomily forecast the coming of the Four Horsemen of the Apocalypse : "We are on the verge of a war between the rich and the poor. Over-population in the Third World will flood Europe. Famine and massive indebtedness in the Third World will lead them into increasing the production of narcotics to be consumed here in Europe. They will organise terrorism against us."

He was followed by another member of the French Front National, the slimy Serge Limace, who asked : "We dispute the facts you have presented, Mann, and what about those left-wing fascists, the IRA ?"

A bearded independent Irish MEP named Seamus Spylgarn with a large beaked nose walked round the back wall of the hemicycle. He placed himself directly in front of the Frenchman. A blow was struck, and another returned. The President called for order. Three times he read a formal warning from the rules to the two combatants. Then he excluded both from the chamber. A team of huissiers shepherded them out.

Owen had not seen this happen before. According to Jim Keeper, the ushers had been used in this way when the Pope had visited

Strasbourg to make a formal speech in the hemicycle. The leader of a Protestant party from Northern Ireland, a clergyman, had told the press before the visit that he would denounce the Pope to his face as the Anti-Christ.

The President at the time was highly embarrassed by the threat, but was unable to discipline the Ulsterman in advance until an offence had been committed. The Pope was warned to expect the outburst and waited patiently in the hemicycle with a beatific smile. The President was ready with his book of rules, and the huissiers were ready to eject the member.

But only after the cry of "Anti-Christ" had been heard was the warning read aloud and the member asked to leave the hemicycle. Next day, as intended by the protestant, the British and Irish newspapers had carried the story on their front pages. A genius at self-publicity, he had earlier won fame at the opening of the first elected parliament in 1979, by claiming that the Union flag was flying upside-down outside the building, as it had been outside the Commission when Britain first joined in 1973.

The prickly Italian liberal who followed next, Angela Riccio, was invariably late for every meeting. She had been called to speak earlier but now the score-board indicated that she only had half a minute left, the rest having been used in her absence by other members of her political group. "I urge the house from far left almost to far right to vote for these measures in droves. Emigrants from third countries who hold up the very infrastructures of our countries and who built our hemicycle deserve this ray of hope."

The President switched off her microphone just as she reached full speed. "I am so sorry, but you have used up your speaking time."

The debate was replied to, on behalf of the Commission, by Erwin Käfer, an uninspiring German Commissioner who was enormously hardworking but very low-profile. "The Commission wishes to neutralise all discrimination which is the breeding ground for fascism. It is not our aim to get rid of cultural differences - rather to see a tolerant acceptance of them. The Commission accepts the parliament's report and undertakes to include its resolution in legislation which is urgently being drafted for the Council."

He was interrupted in mid-sentence by a fierce question from Xamilopardis. Käfer neatly avoided giving a direct answer by using the curiosity of the German language where verbs often come at the end of a sentence : "My Greek friend, you should know that it is discourteous to interrupt a German before he has reached his verb."

The last speaker was from the Council of Ministers. A junior minister from Luxembourg welcomed the report. He said that the Council awaited the parliament's vote with interest. Following the bombs ten days previously, it was time for action across the EU.

The debate was over, and the president rapped his gavel. "The vote will be taken at midday tomorrow. The next debate will be the report by..." The session continued and Owen was free at last to make an urgent comfort stop.

Outside the hemicycle Owen almost bumped into Natasha Farfalla who was leaving her booth. She was laughing : "Hello Owen. Did you notice that Lord Butcher was asleep during most of that debate, and his wig had slipped ? His headphones were over his ears, so we had a competition in the English booth to see who could wake him up without mentioning his name during our spells of interpreting." She giggled, "I won."

Next day, with voting on his report due at noon, Owen packed up his office and threw out a mass of papers. Although he remained an MEP until the new parliament met in July, and he could attend its opening before his mandate finally lapsed, he wanted to carry home as much as possible this time.

The telephone on his desk shrilled. He picked it up and spoke "Owen Mann."

"How are you ?" Monika asked.

Owen jumped. "Hi ! Hi ! Where are you ?"

"I haven't much time" she said. "How about meeting up the week after next ? Any chance of Tuesday evening ?"

"My election campaign will have started. Do you want to come and help me ?"

"That's not a good idea. Could you get away in the evening ? So we can be together." Owen felt fiercely tempted.

"I think it would be dangerous. People might notice" he said cautiously.

"What about meeting in London ? I'll be staying in a hotel there. We could have dinner." She left a pregnant pause.

"Monika. I would adore to see you. But will you understand if I'm weary after hundreds of brief conversations all day long ?"

"Of course."

He had a better idea. "Monika, if I can get away in time, would you like to go to the theatre ?"

"I'd love to. You choose what to see. I have a feeling that I'll like it too. Leave a message at my hotel where to meet. Afterwards I want to talk about you and me, and me and you."

She gave the name of her hotel and rang off. Owen telephoned the National Theatre on the south bank of the river Thames and booked two seats for a comedy.

He left the office to see if the British newspapers had arrived in Strasbourg. He bought a copy of each but only two carried mentions of his debate. A broadsheet described it, on an inside page, as 'drawing attention to the growing menace of fascism and to the inability of European states to deal with it individually'.

A tabloid described it as 'wasting taxpayers' money'. A Euro-FBI, it said, was 'the chance long-awaited by Germans to march down our streets and into our homes'. Owen regretted that the tabloid did not point out, even as a joke, the corollary which had been wittily expressed by the late Geoffrey Rippon in 1972. A heckler had asked him : "If we join the Common Market does it mean that foreigners can come over here, take our jobs and rape our women ?" "Yes, it does" replied Rippon, "but it also means that we can go to their countries and do the same to them."

The latest opinion polls were reported in several newspapers. The drift of opinion away from the Radical government was continuing : they now stood at 40% against 38% for the Progressives. The remaining 22% was split between Don't-Knows and small parties.

According to the pundits, these figures would produce different results in the two elections. In the General election, with first-past-the-post voting, the Radical government would scrape home again with a much reduced majority. In the European election, where voting was proportional, only the first two on the Radical list in Owen Mann's region would be elected. An editorial cheerfully recommended Owen and other low-placed Radicals to start looking for new jobs.

With prospects bad, Owen telephoned Stan Hijena at the goldsmith workshop. Hijena was away, and the secretary asked whether there was any message.

"Tell him" said Owen, "that I expect to be back at work a month from now, after the votes have been counted. In the meantime if there is anything I can do to help, he should let me know."

Voting after debates was at set times to help the maximum number of MEPs to be present. Owen feared that, if too few were present, the far-right could defeat his report by proving the absence of a quorum. However his fears evaporated when he saw the hemicycle was nearly two-thirds full.

Paragraph by paragraph, amendment by amendment, MEPs approved the Mann report. Recommendations included improved schooling for children of migrant workers, aid for low-cost housing in cities with large immigrant populations, education of public opinion, measures to combat unemployment, and the creation of a European FBI.

When voting was over, Owen sat and listened to the Explanations of Vote being spoken by individual members, a privilege not allowed to MPs in the Commons. His gut feeling was elation but also regret. His report was now out of his hands as it moved to the Council of Ministers. Had his work been worth the effort ? He had earned hostility among supporters at home, and apathy in the media. Yet he had uncovered a real and growing danger. He had steered it through parliament. And he would lose his seat next month. That was politics. Nobody held a life-tenure in any parliament, or indeed in any job.

* * *

Home from Strasbourg Owen had to catch up with campaigning. Now he could only keep a distant eye on developments in Brussels. His report would be discussed at the Council of Interior Ministers on Monday. With fifteen different national points-of-view, the outcome was unpredictable.

The fifteen national ministers travelled to the Council in Brussels from their national parliaments. Fourteen flew and the Belgian walked. Sir David Bronwen represented the United Kingdom. Not being a candidate in the General Election it was easy for him to be away in Brussels.

Their destination was a huge fortress-like building at 165 Rue de la Loi. Called the Consilium, it was a stone's throw from the four-leaf clover Berlaymont. The Consilium appeared to be constructed of warm-coloured marble but the public were kept at bay by tall black gates. In front was a metal sculpture of welded patches, apparently intended to resemble a bull with a rider on its back, the legend of Europa. To Owen it was another unsatisfactory ministerial compromise.

The sole item on the Council's agenda was the proposal to create a Euro-FBI. Before the ministers arrived, many of the lesser details had been fought out between national ambassadors in Coreper, the Council of Permanent Representatives. The Greek ambassador, it was said, had a free hand because he received no instructions from Athens ; the German had a rigid negotiating line, because he had to keep their sixteen federal Länder parliaments happy ; the Foreign Office gave UKREP a top line as their opening bid, and a bottom line to which they could go.

Inside the dossiers distributed to each minister in their own language were the European Parliament's resolution as it had been voted in Strasbourg, the Commission's draft legislation, and the results of Coreper's negotiation.

The ministers opened their meeting at three o'clock in a private room. Journalists of the Brussels press corps were forced to hang around outside, as always. They were not allowed to observe decisions being made because the Council legislates in secret. Murdo McKirk said he remembered that, several years ago, the British Foreign Secretary had promised his annual Progressive party conference that there would be more openness in the Council. But nothing appeared to have changed since then.

The journalists were required to wait outside until a spokesman emerged from the closed meeting to explain what was happening. They knew their fate was to wait for many hours before they were fed snippets about the ministerial discussions. Eventually the spokesman would appear, and there would be a scrummage. Journalists at the back would have to rely on those at the front to relay the information back to them, like a child's game of Chinese Whispers.

Eventually the ministers' secret decision would be published to the world in a formal edition of the *Official Journal of the European Union*. Popular or not, their decision would be binding law over four hundred million people. Returning to their homes, each of the fifteen ministers would claim a great victory for themselves. Nevertheless some must have won, and others lost. But, with no published record of the proceedings it was impossible to verify. A doctoral thesis waited to be written which would compare the results achieved with the claims made by each of the fifteen ministers.

Afternoon stretched into evening. Outside it grew dark. The frustration and boredom of the journalists mounted.

Suddenly the electric lights in the Consilium went out. Cigarette-lighters provided instant dots of light until candles and torches were brought by the building's staff.

McKirk and two others, Harry Den Boer from Amsterdam and Tomas Amsel from Berlin, decided to take a break and leave the building. Their colleagues who remained inside promised to telephone their mobile phones if any news broke.

Outside the Consilium the three crossed the road and walked to the Hairy Canary pub in Rue Archimède. It had dark wooden tables, faded pictures on the walls, London newspapers on poles for customers to read, and dark-green leather benches in imitation of the Commons.

Amid the candle-light the barman greeted them in English. They ordered beers and long French baguette sandwiches filled with camembert cheese. Den Boer raised his glass to toast his two colleagues and told his Dutch beer joke : "At a meeting of the EU's fifteen leading brewers, the barman asked each what they would have to drink. All chose their own beer. Last to order was Freddy Heineken who said : 'I'll have a soft drink.' 'Why did you chose that ?' the other brewers asked. 'Well,' he replied, 'if nobody else is having a real beer, I won't either'.

Tomas Amsel interrupted in his fine tenor voice. "We Germans are the beer champions. Even the ancient Roman poet Tacitus remarked on our beer-drinking."

"But you Germans were afraid of competition from our beers," said McKirk. "Your Pure Beer law, which dates from about 1520 and defined exactly what the contents of a beer must be, was used to keep all other European beers out of Germany. When the Single Market rules forced you to open your markets to our beers, your brewers advertised that 'foreign beers will make German men impotent.'"

Their conversation turned to whether jokes could be translated and still keep their humour. Amsel said he knew of one in German which he thought also worked in English.

"Before the Gulf War," Amsel asked, "where were the most warehouses ?"

McKirk and Den Boer were puzzled.

"The answer is Iraq. Shall I tell you why ?" He made a gesture pointing towards the horizon. "Because there...*were houses*, there.. *were houses,...* It's not very funny, I agree, but at least it translates. In German it goes 'Wo waren die meisten Warenhäuser ? Da waren Häuser, und da waren Häuser,..."

Den Boer nodded : "Interestingly it works in Dutch too. On the other hand, there are jokes which are untranslatable - because, I suppose, they depend on a pun, and puns don't translate."

"Give an example."

"There's a famous one in French. Boy says to girl 'Est-ce qu'on va au Lion d'Or ?' That sounds like 'Shall we go to the Golden Lion ?' But spoken in French it also sounds like 'Est-ce qu'on va au lit ou on dort ?' - which means 'Shall we go to bed ?'"

Amsel laughed : "Excellent. Try this German question, 'Was haben Sie an Derby-Day gemacht ?' It sounds in English like 'What did you do on Derby Day ?' However, if you emphasise the syllables differently, it could be 'Was haben Sie an der Bidet gemacht ?' In English that means 'What did you do on the bidet ?'"

McKirk joined in : "I'll give you one in English, but it is less saucy than your two. 'Did you hear about the insomniac, who was also a dyslexic and an agnostic ? He lay awake all night worrying about whether there is a Dog."

His two colleagues stared at the floor. Tomas Amsel used his mobile to telephone a German colleague in the Consilium. No spokesmen had emerged to give a briefing yet. The three friends strolled back to the Council to allow other colleagues to escape for a break. The electricity was still off.

* * *

In England next morning Owen woke early and wondered what had been decided in the Council in Brussels. He switched on the bedside radio. The news was all about the General election. If any decision had been made in Brussels, it was not mentioned.

He left the house and bought a set of newspapers. There was nothing on any front page. Eventually on the inside page of an anti-European broadsheet he found something.

Its headline was 'BIG BROTHER ON ICE' and the story was a surprise. The Council had rejected the creation of a Euro-FBI for the next five years in favour of a strengthened data-collecting agency. The report reminded the public that

> It was a British Euro-MP, who led the proposal for a Euro-FBI. Thank God the unknown novice, Owen Mann, did not get his way. It would have led to higher taxes and more bureaucracy. We would have had bobbies on the beat who could not speak English, let alone tell you the correct time.

Owen understood that he had fallen at the final hurdle. He felt angry and let down. To try to find out the details, he switched on his computer and dialled into the Internet. He found the EU's website, *www.europa.eu.int,* selected the Council option, and searched for news of the decision. All that was available was the usual bland press release from the Council : generalised details, but nothing about how each country had voted, nor their reasons why.

Throughout the day's electioneering the British media concentrated on British news. A non-decision in Brussels was not worth reporting. Only Owen's local radio station and Joe Robinson of the local newspaper telephoned his mobile phone to ask for a comment. His answers sounded unconvincing, even to himself : he had been fulfilling his parliamentary duty by representing his committee's views ; and the parliament had very little power over internal security matters. Every word he spoke felt like a shovel of earth heaped onto his political grave. He looked forward to the end of the day when the media would forget him.

Phonecalls asking for a comment also came from a Spanish journalist and from Tomas Amsel in Berlin. Both said that the

Council's non-decision was a big story in their country. Amsel said he intended to pursue the scandal of the Council's secrecy : it was unacceptable even though the public remained blissfully ignorant about it.

During the afternoon, Owen's pager sounded ; the message asked him to ring Hijena's mobile phone in Belgium.

Hijena said that he was exhibiting at a gift fair in a hall next to the Atomium in Brussels. It was proving to be very successful and he had sold more than he had expected. He wondered whether Owen might be travelling over to Brussels in the new few days : if so, could he bring out another case of gold items for the stand ?

Biting back a comment about being involved in an election campaign, Owen remembered that Hijena was uninterested in politics and was probably unaware that an election was on. He replied that he did not have a trip to Brussels scheduled for several weeks and probably never again. Hijena's reply was spoiled by a crackle on the line but it did not sound friendly.

That night, lying in bed trying to overcome his weariness and fall asleep, Owen mused about the vote in the Council. Why had the FBI proposal been delayed for five years ? Which countries had opposed it ? It would be fascinating to know. After the election campaign there would be plenty of time to try to find out...

Next morning over breakfast a newspaper report changed Owen's mind. According to the latest opinion poll the Radicals had lost more ground and now stood at 38% against the Progressives at 39%. The chances of him holding his Euro-seat had receded still further. With the tide going out, he needed an initiative of his own to try to reverse the swing. Yet all that he had was the defeated Euro-FBI proposal. But if he could discover why it had failed, probably due to French perfidy, there might be a story to give to the press which might boost him in some small way.

Asking questions later as a defeated MEP, he would carry no clout. As a sitting MEP now he could still try to demand information.

He decided to give himself one more day in Brussels to try to find an answer, even if it rounded off his political career. It would satisfy his own curiosity, as well as exercising his democratic right, to know what had happened inside the secret Council.

He telephoned Jill Hunter at UKREP and offered her lunch.

They fixed to meet the next day at one o'clock in a restaurant in Rue Archimède which had tables in its back garden.

He telephoned Hijena in Brussels : "Stan. After all, I will be able to bring out extra gold pieces for your exhibition."

"When ?"

"Tomorrow". Hijena was delighted, not having been able to make any alternative arrangements.

"Good, Owen, if you go to the workshop this evening after your day's campaigning, I'll have arranged for a strong airline pilot's carrying case to be packed and ready for you to carry over. See you tomorrow morning."

Hijena immediately rang his new assistant at the workshop to give instructions. The new man had dropped by a week ago looking for casual work in return for cash. He claimed to have had some experience of metal-working and to be willing to act as a delivery man, something Hijena urgently needed. He had been hired on trial, and so far his only fault seemed to be a love of raw garlic.

In mid-morning Owen met with Rosemary Jones and Jack Terrier for the day's electioneering. He rode out their combined anger at the news that he would be playing truant the next day.

In the evening he rode to the workshop to collect the gold showpieces. The new employee, whom he had not met before, had halitosis but had done a good job of packing the case. Owen got a feeling that the new man did not take to him either, presumably a matter of non-chemistry between them.

Diszno handed Owen the typed list of contents and opened the top of the case. From the top he took out and unwrapped a gold-plated goblet and a solid gold model racing-car. As he rewrapped them he indicated that all the other gold items on the list were carefully wrapped beneath.

Diszno watched with satisfaction as Owen left the workshop with the case on the back of his motorbike. He gave Owen a cheerful wave of farewell. Immediately afterwards he left the workshop himself and did not return, not even to collect the pitiful wages which he was owed.

In the bottom of the pilot-case, under the dazzling gold, he had placed a powerful small bomb. It was timed to explode halfway during the flight from Heathrow to Brussels which Hijena had said Owen would catch early next morning.

Diszno had been specially careful about his preparations. He had used a top-quality timer so that, as Sãta had insisted, there would be no slip-up this time. He had remembered the time difference between Britain and Belgium, and had added the hour difference to the timer.

At Heathrow airport, Diszno knew, Owen would have to pass through security and customs checks before boarding the plane. Either Owen would be detected and arrested or, more likely, he would get through undetected in the way that Hijena had boasted he often did.

Owen parked his Suzuki, checked in for the flight and joined the queue of people waiting to put their hand-luggage through the security X-ray machine.

When he reached the machine, Owen asked the man in charge : "May I have a private check of this case ? It contains gold showpieces which I am taking to an exhibition. I would not like other travellers to see what I am carrying."

"Of course, sir, please come this way," said the security man. He led Owen to a cubicle, invited him inside and pulled a curtain to hide them from the public.

Owen opened the lid of the case and took out the list of contents. He unpacked the first item lying on top. The official's eyes feasted on a gold-plated goblet, eleven inches high, which Owen told him was a perfect copy of a famous rowing trophy. Next Owen unwrapped the solid gold scale-model of a Formula One racing-car.

Eyes popping, the official asked gingerly : "May I hold it ?" He cradled the racing-car in both hands as if it were made of delicate glass.

"Shall I unpack the rest of the box ?" asked Owen.

The security man had been told as a child not to be greedy. Anyway, he asked himself, cradling the racing-car with fascination, what goldsmith would want to blow up such treasures ? He longed to see the other treasures packed lower down but refrained from doing so.

"No thankyou, sir. Best of luck at the show."

Owen replaced the model and goblet carefully into the case, closed it, stepped out from behind the curtain and joined the queue of travellers waiting to have their passports checked.

In the aircraft he put the case carefully in the overhead locker above his head, unwrapped a treacle toffee and settled down to read his newspaper.

It was giving the European election little publicity. Owen was amused to read a diary piece which said that Sir Harry Pedreven had announced that he was too tired to help his own side's Euro-candidates. Instead he had flown to his villa in Portugal for a short rest before beginning his own General election campaign.

Owen's flight to Brussels was peaceful and punctual. Leaving the plane he carried the pilot-case carefully through the blue Customs channel, where travellers inside the EU are free of checks.

At the front of the waiting crowd he saw Hijena. They shook hands and Owen handed the case to him.

"Thanks, Owen," said Hijena, "I'll get straight back to the show in a taxi. Drop in later if you have time."

Half-an-hour later the taxi exploded spectacularly on the ring-road round Brussels causing an enormous traffic-jam. Diszno had failed to work out that the bomb's timer, unlike a watch on a wrist, did not need to be put forward an hour for when it reached the continent.

In the following days the police reassembled the fragments. Methodically they pieced together the pilot-case, its shattered gold objects and the bomb's mechanism. The identity of the Belgian taxi-driver was established quickly but not that of his passenger who must have been holding the case on his lap and had been blown into small pieces : they put together his papers which suggested the passenger might have been an Armenian.

Owen took the train from the airport into the city and strolled to the restaurant in Rue Archimède. Jill arrived punctually. Her bright brown eyes and pale Irish face were even more attractive than he remembered from their previous encounter. He wondered why her bright eyes should be so beguiling. It was as illogical as a pea-hen drawn to the display of a peacock. But if they served to excite him, the attraction what it needed to be.

They settled at a table for two in the garden and shared a sea-food salad and a bottle of sparkling mineral water. Owen asked about the Interior Ministers' Council last week : "Were you present, Jill ?"

"Of course. That's my job." She looked surprised. "Why do you need to ask ?"

"I'd like to know how the five-year delay against setting up the Euro-FBI was decided ? Which countries blocked setting it up immediately ?"

His direct approach failed.

"I'm sorry," Jill replied firmly, "Proceedings of the Council are secret. They pay my salary and you know the rules."

His disappointment must have been obvious because she made a small concession : "I'll tell you that it was a surprise. But I really must not tell you what went on."

They ordered coffee and instead Jill explained, off the record, the bizarre procedure in the Council when a member of the public asked to see a Council document. The request was first considered by a committee composed of press attaches from all fifteen national government offices in Brussels. They each referred the request back to their national capital for instructions. When all fifteen replies had been received back, and if there appeared to be a majority in favour of releasing the document to the public, the committee passed the request upwards to the Coreper level in the Council, where the fifteen national ambassadors met, or sometimes even to the Council meeting of ministers. There a final vote was taken concerning whether the document would be released. It was not a fast procedure.

Jill gave no further clue about what had occurred in the Council concerning the Euro-FBI. Owen enjoyed her company except for the cigarette she smoked with her coffee. He fantasised whether it would spoil the taste of her lips which, in both senses, seemed closed to him. Did his thought mean, he wondered, that subconsciously he feared a disappointment with Monika next week ?

Jill excused herself, to return to her office. Owen remained to pay the bill and to mull over a second coffee. The only straw in the wind which he could see was that Jill had clammed up tightly under his questioning. Like Sherlock Holmes's dog that had not barked.

His plane did not leave Brussels until the evening. Whom else could he ask ? He strolled towards the parliament, fifteen minutes away, using the Rue de la Loi underpass beneath its five lanes of ceaseless traffic. He weaved through the car-park beside an abandoned red-brick church towards Rue Wiertz. The parliament's entrance hall was as quiet as a graveyard. The security guards were playing cards.

"How stupid can I be ?" he thought. There was nobody there to consult. All the MEPs and their assistants were at their homes campaigning. Anyway nobody in the parliament took part in Council proceedings. But an idea struck him.

He left the parliament, recrossed Rue Belliard and returned through the car-park. To the right was the rear of the Consilium complex. A security guard by the car-barrier was talking to a driver. Owen waved his laissez-passer and walked past the barrier, intending to try a short cut route through the heart of the Consilium to get to the Berlaymont roundabout. He squeezed round a large skip full of black plastic garbage sacks awaiting collection. Reaching the other side he emerged into Rue Froissart and skirted the Schuman roundabout. At Rue Stevin he stopped outside the International Press Centre.

He walked through to the bar at the back. It was dark and usually crowded by the Brussels press-corps now numbering some five hundred, about the same as in Washington DC.

But only one person was present. Owen sat on a stool at the bar and ordered a beer. He raised his glass to the other occupant and said "Cheers".

"Cheers" replied the other and held out his hand. "I'm Dutch, my name's Den Boer."

Having broken the ice Owen asked whether he knew any journalists who had been at the Interior Ministers' Council on Monday and Tuesday this week.

"I was there" said the Dutchman looking bored.

"Can you tell me about one particular item ?"

"There were many, you know, so it's hard to remember. Which one interests you ?"

"The proposal to create a Euro-FBI. It was put on ice for five years."

"I remember it. We Dutch were interested because it would have been good for our capital city, The Hague."

"I want to know who voted for and who voted against it. Can you remember ?"

"It was a chaotic night and there was a long power cut. We were all getting, how do you say it, eaten up ?"

"Fed up ?"

"That's it. We just stood around outside, you know, because the Council meets in secret. When the ministers feel like it, they send a spokesman out. Eventually around midnight, the press officer of the Presidency came out and gave us some scanty information. It's a crazy system."

"But," Den Boer continued, "I remember the Euro-FBI thing because it was a surprise. We asked the spokesman which ministers had voted to block or delay it. He replied, as spokesmen always do, that he could not reveal that information. By a convention which is undemocratic but very convenient for ministers, their individual voting positions are never revealed. The spokesman said that the Presidency had not called for a formal vote at the end of the discussion. It had merely declared that 'There is no qualified majority in favour of the Euro-FBI.' Then the spokesman returned to the meeting-room where the debate continued until some sort of compromise was reached, which ended up as the five year delay."

"You never discovered who voted and which way ?"

Den Boer shook his head. "I didn't say that. The trick as a journalist is not to give up. When the official Council spokesman is as uninformative as he always is, you go round and try to talk to the other fourteen national spokesman, or as many as you can find. Then you piece the truth together by comparing their different answers."

"What, if anything, did you conclude ?"

"There was chopping and changing during their debate. It appeared that Sweden and Spain changed sides, moving from opposing to being in favour of a Euro-FBI. My impression was that the principal countries which delayed the proposal were France, Denmark, Austria and your own country."

Owen was surprised. "My country ? The United Kingdom ?"

"Yes. It was the British who finally proposed the compromise of a five year delay."

"I thought we were in favour."

"That is for you to explain."

"That's why I'm here" sighed Owen unhappily.

"Maybe your British officials will tell you more than our Dutch ones."

"How do you mean ?" asked Owen.

"In the Netherlands we have a Freedom of Information law. It gives us the right to see our government's official documents. A few years back an enterprising Dutch MEP called Metten cited this law in order to see the Dutch minutes from meetings of the Council of Ministers. The Dutch government refused to show him anything, so he appealed to the highest court in Holland."

"Did he win ?"

"It created quite a scandal. The Dutch judges ruled that an EU rule takes precedence over the Dutch national constitution. They declared that the Council's rule of secrecy for its meetings, even though it has no legal basis in the Treaty of Rome, was deemed to be superior in law to the written Dutch Constitution. Incredible ! So Metten failed. But we still have the Swedish case."

"What's the Swedish case ?"

"Sweden has had a Freedom of Information Act for over two hundred years. Every government document in Stockholm is open to immediate inspection by the public."

"That's extraordinary !"

"Swedish journalists have demanded to see the documents which are brought back by Swedish ministers from the secret Council meetings in Brussels. Their government refused so the matter is now before the EU's supreme European Court of Justice" Den Boer explained.

"So either the Council's secrecy gives way, or Sweden's ancient freedom collapses ?"

"I'm sure it is better in the UK where you don't have a written constitution" replied Den Boer.

"It's no better. All British governments are highly secretive."

Den Boer shrugged. Owen finished his beer, and left the Press Centre. What he had heard was hard to believe. His own Radical party, the government in the UK, had secretly opposed and then delayed something which its leader had declared in parliament that it favoured. Why ?

Various alternative explanations were possible. But before he could publicise any of them, he needed to find proof of what had happened. The Council would not break its own secrecy. Whom else to ask ?

Jill Hunter at UKREP had been present and had been surprised. At how Bronwen had voted ? Presumably yes, but maybe not. She might have assumed that a last-minute 'horse-trade' had been made in private between Bronwen and a minister of some other country. Bronwen would not have informed Jill because she was merely a civil-servant and he was a member of the Cabinet. Private deals in the Council were often cooked up between friendly ministers. In the previous government, Progressive ministers from Britain had not been included in ministerial caucuses in Brussels because of their negative attitudes to the EU but British Radicals now attended caucuses of socialist ministers.

Retracing his steps Owen walked back through the Consilium. This time two crop-haired men in overalls were throwing sacks of paper from the skip into a refuse lorry. One sack had split open and Owen had to pick his way round the rainbow of shredded coloured papers scattered across the ground.

Stepping carefully he glanced at a page which carried some printed words. It was dated 'Mandag', which was three days ago. It appeared to be in a Scandinavian language.

A remarkable idea struck him. The Council had met on Monday. Might these sacks contain papers from that meeting ?

Desperate for any lead to follow, he approached one of the two men. Relying on his smart suit and his official appearance, he spoke in French : "I have lost an important document which just could be in one of these sacks."

The man stared at him with hostility, turned his back and continued working. Owen wondered how to put his question again. Suddenly the man turned back and stared at Owen.

"You are English ?"
"Yes."
"I am Flemish so I don't like to speak French. My name is Houtworm. You want something ?"

Owen repeated his request.

Houtworm shrugged. "We have to load these sacks and we are late. You can come with us in the truck or you can take the sacks away yourself. We are not permitted to leave them here."

Owen made an instant choice. "I'll come with you."

Ten minutes later he was in the cab sitting between the two men in their soiled overalls. Mentally he wrote off his suit, and tried to enjoy the ride. Ten miles to the west of Brussels they stopped at a recycling depot at a small town called Urpe-Mere. Owen explained to the manager in English that he urgently needed to find a document and that he did not mind searching through the sacks. The manager looked as if he thought Owen was crazy but, with a resigned heave of his broad shoulders, gave him a thumbs-up signal.

Owen removed his jacket and set to work sifting through the sacks.

Many of the papers had been shredded into tiny strips and could not be deciphered, as intended by the ministers. He separated all the remaining intact sheets which had handwriting because all printing would have been done before the meeting started.

Nearly ninety minutes later he had a pile almost three feet high and sat down to read through each sheet. The manager returned from time to time to check with an amused look on his face.

Almost all the sheets proved to be indecipherable, most bearing handwritten scribbled notes in different languages. Finally Owen selected thirty-one pages which looked as if they might contain English words and a half-used spiral notepad. He signalled to the manager that he was satisfied, shook his hand warmly and walked out with the papers.

The sun was setting, he had missed the last plane, his clothes were dirty and he had no hotel.

He found a taxi and asked to be taken to the Gare du Midi in Brussels. There he bought a single ticket for the next EuroStar train to London, and settled down at the station café for ninety minutes to await its departure while he worked through his trophies.

Unfortunately not one of the thirty-one sheets proved to contain anything significant. All that remained were the pages of the notepad which he flicked over disconsolately. Most of its pages contained what looked like hieroglyphics - strokes, dashes, and occasional numbers.

To which person had the notepad belonged ? Surely not a minister ? A member of staff ? Or a fly on the wall, he thought, running out of ideas.

With half-an-hour still to kill he looked through the notepad more slowly. It was mostly squiggles but had occasional words in different languages, which seemed to rule out anybody in a national delegation.

Who else was present ? Only the ushers and the interpreters in their booths. Could it be a notebook discarded by an interpreter ? It would require another interpreter to decipher the squiggles for him. Who might help him with so little time remaining ? He only knew one - Natasha Farfalla.

He picked up his mobile and phoned 284-2111, the European Parliament's number. A security guard sceptically put him through to the interpreters' office.

To his surprise there was a reply but it was only an answerphone. "Sorry, there is nobody available in the English booth. Leave a message and someone will get back to you as soon as they can."

He left a message. Could someone ask Natasha Farfalla to telephone him, at his home number in England and it was urgent.

He caught the train to London and arrived home as the sun was rising. He had returned from his awayday with suspicions but no proof, and without an explanation for Bronwen's vote. He had missed a full day of campaigning, further damaging any remote chance of victory which remained to him.

At home his answerphone contained several messages. To his surprise the last one was from Natasha Farfalla : "I got your message. I shall be working in London from Monday next week at a conference. I'd be glad to see you but I'm not much use at campaigning for votes, I'm afraid." She left her number in Belgium.

He returned her call but had to leave a message. He askcd whether she could meet him in London : if he did not hear back from her he would wait from eight o'clock on Monday evening at the Spaniards pub in Hampstead. He added a question about whether she had been interpreting in the English-language booth at the Home Affairs Council last Monday and Tuesday.

* * *

There was no response from Natasha. On Monday evening, after the weekend's campaigning, he rode to Hampstead and waited at the pub. She arrived soon after eight and they settled at an outside table. Owen fetched sandwiches and glasses of white Riesling. After asking about her conference, he repeated his question.

"I'm afraid that I wasn't interpreting in the Council last Monday" she replied.

"Do you know who was ?"

"No. Most of my colleagues are away on holiday."

Owen's heart fell. "I wanted to know how the voting went on the Euro-FBI proposal. The Council does not publish how national ministers cast their votes, nor what they say, even though they are passing laws."

"Even if you did find someone who was there," commented Natasha, "I'm afraid that they probably wouldn't remember the details. Words come in through our ears, and go out through our mouths, all at high speed. Many subjects are discussed. We remember little of what is said. If we tried to, our poor brains would melt."

He knew it had been a long shot and was disappointed but not surprised. Natasha continued : "In any case, we interpreters have a professional obligation not to reveal what we hear. Our job is hard enough as it is. If we earn a reputation for telling tales out of school, we would quickly be frozen out of work."

"In a way, I'm glad you weren't there that particular evening" Owen sympathised.

"Why ?"

"Because it would have been exceptionally hard work" he reminded her. "That particular evening there was a power-cut."

"I heard about that. It was that evening, was it ?"

"How would they have managed without lights or electricity ?"

"A colleague told me about it. It was very unusual. When the lights went out, everything stopped of course. Candles and electric torches were fetched. But the usual interpretation system could not work because there was no power for the microphones. So they tried chuchotage instead."

"*Chuchotage* ? What's that ?"

"Chuchoter is French for *to whisper*. Interpreters sit beside each minister and whisper a simultaneous interpretation to him of what is being said as the debate proceeds."

"Sounds like the Tower of Babel."

"It normally works well but apparently not on that particular evening. It required three multilingual interpreters to sit beside each of the fifteen ministers. Too many different sets of whisperings were going on at the same time. After a few minutes they had to stop."

"The ministers reached a decision so the debate continued. How ?"

"After whispering, they went to *consecutive* interpretation."

"I can't even guess what that is."

"Consecutive is when an interpreter listens to the speaker and makes shorthand notes on a pad. Afterwards the interpreter reads the full speech out aloud in one or more languages."

"Would that have been successful ?"

"Yes but slow. As you said Owen, a decision was reached. I heard that voting was carried out by a show of hands using candlelight and torches."

"I was told there was no vote."

"There was an informal show of hands apparently, but no formal vote so the ministers could preserve their secrecy."

"Secret law-making by candlelight. Unprecedented."

"Owen," Natasha was slightly irritated, "I'm not sure where this is leading. As I've told you, it is impossible for interpreters to remember the details. The words would have to be written down."

Owen paused. He had reached his last hope. He refilled both wine glasses and took the plunge.

"Natasha, it was written down ! It was consecutive interpretation."

"True - in theory. The interpreters would have made shorthand notes in order to read out the results correctly afterwards. But so what ?"

Owen reached into his briefcase and pulled out the discarded spiral notepad. "Natasha, look at this."

She glanced through it then said : "You think it's from that Council meeting ? Where did you find it ?"

Owen parried her question with one of his own. "Would deciphering it be against your professional ethics ?"

"If it was my notepad, yes. But it isn't and I don't know whose it is." She stared at the pages again. "The shorthand strokes are not in English nor in my four other languages."

He watched tensely as Natasha concentrated again with a furrowed forehead.

Reaching around halfway through the notepad, Natasha showed a page to Owen. It bore a string of letters and figures :

DA3 D 10 EI 3 L 2 SU 3 SV 4 25

"I'd dearly like to know what those mean" Owen said.

"Why ?"

"Because the last number, twenty-five, could be significant. It is only one less than the minimum number of votes required to block a proposal in the Council. A blocking minority is twenty-six votes. This might be a list of ministers who called out in the semi-darkness that they were voting for or against something."

"Deciphering which countries voted is straightforward. Each country goes under its own name in its own language. 'DA 3' meant Danmark's three votes. 'D' is for Deutschland or Germany. 'Ei' is for Eire or the Republic of Ireland, 'L' is for Luxembourg, 'Su' is for Suomi or Finland, and 'Sv' is for Svenska or Sweden."

"The United Kingdom is not in the sequence" said Owen disappointedly. "A Dutch journalist told me that Denmark, France, Austria and Britain had voted together. So these figures are not the votes which he described.

Owen flipped over more pages of the notepad. "Here's another line, but it's shorter this time."

"Read it out" said Natasha.

He started to decipher it : "Denmark three, France a thousand and four,..."

Owen stopped, puzzled. "That can't be right. A thousand and four for France ? In Mozart's opera, the total of Don Giovanni's lovers in Spain was '*mille tre*', one thousand and three. I can't imagine that a minister in the Council could manage more."

"May I see ?" Natasha asked, leaning across. She glanced at the page, and saw

DA3 F 1O O4 U10 T27

She laughed. "It's not 1,004 for France. Even their minister is not as impressive as that. That many points would certainly have won them the Eurovision Song contest. No, the correct reading is 'ten votes cast by France'. The next figure is not a zero but the letter O. That stands for Osterreich, which is Austria's name for itself. So the correct reading is : Denmark 3, France 10, Austria 4, and U for the United Kingdom with 10 votes. And the total votes cast was 27."

Owen gasped. "Twenty-seven votes. Enough to block a proposal. And the United Kingdom, my country, among them. Are you absolutely certain ?"

She peered at the page again. "I'm sure."

"Hang on though. The proposal wasn't finally defeated. The end result of the meeting was to delay any powers for a Euro-FBI for five years."

Natasha flicked over the final pages. "Here's your last set of numbers."

She pointed it out : "F 10 O4. Only France and Austria voted against in the last vote. Denmark and the UK changed sides at the end. This was when the ministers agreed their compromise of a five-year delay.

Natasha looked at her watch. "I'm afraid I must go". Owen thanked her profusely.

"Don't thank me," she said. "Just get re-elected."

*　　*　　*

Next morning was a beautiful spring day. It matched Owen's mood. He telephoned Monika's hotel in London and left a message for her, naming a Thames-side theatre and the time to meet.

After the day of campaigning he changed into a clean suit. Packing a small box of Belgian chocolates into his pocket, he took a train to London.

He arrived at the theatre early and leaned against an outside wall to wait. A succession of taxis drew up but none contained Monika. Anxiety increased inside him. Sixteen minutes before the curtain was due to rise, another taxi arrived and a flustered figure climbed out of it.

"Owen !" she called, "Sorry. I've been busy running around. My life is full of drama."

She was wearing a grey-blue blouse with a pattern of black dots. It stunned him because the colour exactly matched the grey-blue irises of her eyes.

He kissed her freckled cheeks.

"There's just time for a quick drink" he suggested.

In the atrium of the theatre two jazz players were entertaining the audience before they took their seats. All the chairs in the atrium were filled. Next to the players was a piano which was not being used. Owen tiptoed with their drinks to the stool and signalled Monika to join him. They perched together on the stool, bottoms pressed together. As they listened, he stole a look at Monika. She was looking at him. Both smiled shyly. He would remember her look for ever.

During the play, he touched her hand and their hands slipped together. Hers was warm and small, and tender and sensuous.

Afterwards they took a taxi to a small French restaurant in Pimlico, intimate enough so that they could hear each other speak. Over the meal they did not discuss the parliament or his report except for a brief exchange when Monika showed that she had been following events. "Congratulations, by the way" she said, touching his hand. "I saw that your report got all the way through the parliament"

"Thanks. But it fell at the last fence in the Council of Ministers."

They talked non-stop but neither finished what was on their plate.

"Are you off your food ?" she asked with concern.

"I'm not hungry when I'm with you" Owen replied, reaching across the table and resting his hand on hers.

Around midnight, they took a taxi to her hotel.

"Are you coming up to see my room ?" she asked looking deep into his eyes.

He waited near the lifts while she collected her room key. Upstairs, walking the long corridor to her room, Owen felt apprehensive. Illogically he feared he might meet a constituent walking in the other direction who would ask why he was there.

Inside her room, he put his arms round her neck and gently kissed her lips, releasing for the first time his full passion for her. They clung to each other for several minutes until he could wait no longer. He began to undress her, carefully undoing the buttons of her blouse one by one. Then he moved his hands under the material and round to the back where, trying not to fumble, he undid the clip. Moving back to the front, the cups fell away and he covered her breasts with his hands. They were indescribably soft, warm, secret, and desirable. She sighed his name.

The blouse slipped to the floor. He bent and lingered over the breasts, tenderly kissing them.

He undid the two buttons at the back of her skirt which followed the blouse to the floor and his hands followed gently.

Their first love-making was tentative but passionate, like explorers in uncharted seas to which they hoped they would return.

Afterwards as they lay entwined together Owen stroked her back.

As they relaxed, he remembered the box in his jacket pocket. He left the bed, fetched it, and they fed the contents to eachother.

"Tell me about your report" she whispered. "I know it's been on your mind."

He told her about Bronwen's surprise vote in the Council.

"Why do you think he did that ?" she asked in a puzzled voice.

"The only explanation I can think of is a last-minute horse-trade with another country."

"A *horse-trade* ? Do they travel to Brussels on horses and trade them there ?" she giggled.

"A horse-trade means that a private deal is done, minister-to-minister. Minister A from Britain sacrifices something which he considers to be unimportant in favour of gaining something else unrelated which London considers more valuable. Minister B values them the other way round. The two scratch eachother's backs, so to say" he said, stroking hers, "by voting so that each gets what they want. Our British minister returns to the Commons and claims to have fought immensely hard for our national interests. Unfortunately, he says, despite battling hard he was defeated on some minor points. The sold-out British interest, if it knew the truth, would be outraged but the Council meets in secret so the sell-outs are never revealed.

"That wasn't very interesting. Come closer. I'll show you something better," she said, snuggling into his arms.

"I want to tell you a secret" she whispered.

"What is it ?"

"I'm thinking of leaving my job."

"The financial foundation ? Why ?"

"I haven't told them yet. Tomorrow I'm going across the Atlantic for an interview."

His heart missed a beat. "Why ? I don't understand."

"Owen. I haven't been entirely open with you. Before I tell you any more, you must promise not to react the wrong way. Will you trust me ?" She lifted her head from the pillow and her eyes pierced his. "Promise ?"

He wondered what she was going to reveal. But Monika was too dear to refuse anything. "I promise."

She gave a deep sigh. "It was not a coincidence that we met. After you became the rapporteur about fascism, I was assigned to watch you. The foundation for whom I work raises money for them, you see."

"For whom ?"

"For the fascists across Europe."

He shuddered involuntarily. Why was she telling him ? Was this some kind of a trap ?

She tightened her arm around him. "Relax, my darling," she said. "Remember you promised not to over-react. I haven't finished."

He was tense and afraid. But he had promised.

"Go on."

"Something happened that truly shocked me. If I had known, I should have tried to prevent it."

"What shocked you ?"

"Did you have a friend called Gatto ?"

"Pietro ? Did you know him ?"

"I never met him. But he died, didn't he ?" she said, softly.

"He was a real friend. It was so sad. He was killed in a traffic accident."

"No, he wasn't."

"What do you mean ?"

"He was murdered."

Monika waited as the revelation struck Owen. His body trembled with fear or anger.

After several minutes he whispered : "Why ?"

"To try to prevent your report from being completed." She rushed on. "I was horrified when I heard. That is when I decided to quit. But I couldn't leave straightaway. I needed the right opportunity. That's why I'm going to North America. They think it's to see our contacts there."

He listened in growing confusion. Had she been manipulating him all along - first to check what he knew, now to snare him in some kind of honey-trap ? Was he going to see her never again ? Did she not care for him at all ? It was confusing and unbearable, now that he cared intensely about her.

He pulled her towards him, despairing that it was for the last time.

He breathed in her scent. Not something which she had sprayed from a bottle but her own. It was one of the most delectable things about women - which men often missed when women washed themselves too thoroughly before love-making. How to describe her scent ? He breathed deeply close to her skin. It was a delicate mixture of almonds and fine bone-china.

They fell asleep in each other's arms. He dreamed he was lying on a tropical beach at the water's edge. His front was warm, where the sun was shining on his skin. His back was cool, where the water lapped against him. Monika stirred and he woke. He wondered if those last minutes were the closest he would ever get to paradise.

She whispered. "Darling, I may be in a position to help you."

He moved. She giggled. "No. I don't mean that. Lie still and listen"

"I told you I worked on the financial side. Mainly I did fund-raising. But I also helped with some of the payments going out. At the end of last week, after the negative vote in the Council, one of the payments was a very substantial sum to a new account in London. We regularly transfer small sums to the Nazis in Britain. But this was a new account and much larger."

"To which account ?"

"Very odd. I did not think it was in Sãta's character."

"Who's Sãta ?"

"My boss. You met him after the Public Hearing. He told me that he talked to you, posing as a South American journalist."

Owen doubted if he could accept another shock.

"Excuse me a moment, darling," he said. "I have to go to the bathroom."

On the way there and back he looked for a hidden camera. What would it look like ? He saw nothing suspicious but these days the best devices were said to be the size of a pin-head. It might be anywhere.

Returning to the bed, he glanced casually at the walls of the room. Nothing suggested itself.

Back under the covers, he asked : "To whom did this Sãta pay the money ?"

"A bookmaker."

"A bookie ? How much ?"

"Half a million pounds sterling."

"Golly. A huge bet. What are you suggesting, Monika ?"

"I'm not sure. It's just unusual. And the timing too."

"I wonder what it means ?"

There was silence as both thought. Silence turned into kisses.

When he awoke again, a chink of light was shining through the curtains. He tried to remember where he was. Not Brussels ? He heard breathing to his right. Monika ! Sleeping quietly on her back. Blonde tresses about her face. Pink freckled cheeks. Beautiful neck. Breasts which he longed to caress again. He gazed silently and waited.

Half an hour later something woke her.

"Hello," she smiled. "What time is it ?"

"Just before six o'clock."

They embraced again. Afterwards, as he stroked her perfect breasts, he told her of his love.

"You like them don't you ? They're not so very large."

"I adore them. They're perfect and they're you." He told her of a pendulous maiden aunt, who referred to her own generous adornments as Belinda and Jane. Monika giggled.

Breakfast was delivered to the room, a perfect example of what the French elegantly call *'Les Trois Cs : croissants, café et caresses'*.

"Monika, when do I see you again ?"

"I don't know. I promise I'll be in touch soon. You'll have to trust me."

"Something has been bugging me. From whom did you raise the money for the foundation ?"

"Mostly from multinational businesses who operate in Europe. Some in Britain. All oppose the EU getting more power."

"Does the name United Technologies mean anything to you ?"

"They contributed. Why ?"

"I just wondered. They are the largest business in the region which I represent."

Time was racing away. Owen asked : "How do I get in touch with you, Monika ?"

"You can't."

"Why ?"

"It's very hard for me right now. But I know that, if we want to, we will be together, however we do it, and for as long as we want to. But not right now."

Here was the acid test. Either he was in a trap or she was on his side.

"Monika, I love you. I think we've bonded to each other. I shall be worrying about you. There must be some way I can reach you ?" he pleaded.

She thought for a moment.

"Well" she hesitated, "there's one possibility. There's a phone number where you could leave messages for me. I milk it, and nobody else has the PIN number to unlock it."

She gave him the number, which was outside Britain, and made him repeat it several times to memorise it.

They made their fond farewells. "Thank you for letting me show my emotions," she said unexpectedly.

Owen left the room first, to return to campaigning. Monika would find her own way to the airport later.

Returning home by train Owen weighed up his worries. He was passionate about Monika. But was she 'with him', or was he now so compromised that his report on fascism would be devalued and lead instead to his own destruction ?

He had an intense desire to avenge Pietro. But how ? Could Sãta be allowed to destroy his friend and his work and go unpunished ?

The mystery remained why Sir David Bronwen had voted against his party's publicly-stated policy. But a General Election had started, and if he revealed the policy change, it would damage his party's prospects. As an ambitious party member Owen could not afford to rock the boat. If the Radicals lost the General Election because of a revelation from him, his political prospects would be stone dead for ever.

Flat-out campaigning was now his priority, there only two weeks before polling day in both elections. Cabinet ministers were out on the trail campaigning for the Radicals everywhere and so must Owen. Sir David Bronwen was due that evening in Owen's region, not to assist Owen but to make an evening speech in the Westminster constituency where a Radical candidate was standing against Sir Harry Pedreven.

Owen was asked to go and swell the size of the audience. Waiting on a chair at the back of the hall, he spotted Toby Beaver, the minister's advisor. Owen walked round the side of the hall and asked "Toby, if possible, I should like a few moments to see Sir David."

"About what ?"

"My report about fascism."

"The only possibility is for five minutes immediately after the meeting while the great man relaxes. He'll have a cup of tea after he's finished answering questions."

After the meeting, Owen was admitted to the room where Bronwen was enjoying a cigarette. "Hello Owen ! How are you ?" said

Bronwen cheerfully, stretching out his left hand which was not holding a cigarette. "I trust you are going to hold on to your Euro-seat ?"

"Home Secretary, I'm doing my best but it looks grim."

"Any way I can help ?"

"There's one thing which I would like to ask. About the Commission proposal to create a Euro FBI. Last week in Brussels I believe that you voted to delay it. Might I ask why ?"

He was unsure whether Bronwen showed a flicker of surprise. Only a video-recording, viewed frame by frame, would have given the answer. The older man answered immediately.

"You know very well that the Council meets in secret. But Brussels leaks like a sieve, so I'm not surprised that you ask such a question. I am obliged to protect the Council's secrecy, and even more importantly to remind you that elections are no time to start rumours." He stared fiercely at his interrogator. "I will neither confirm nor deny how I voted on behalf of Her Majesty's government."

Owen wanted to rephrase his question. But Bronwen pressed on like a steam-roller. Owen bit his tongue, instinctively feeling that it was better to listen to what Bronwen said, truthfully or not. Sometimes people, confident that they had landed a knockout blow, added throw-away words which revealed more than they meant to say.

"Owen, with your sources in Brussels, I'm sure you know everything that happened. For argument's sake, let's suppose that the UK", pointing to himself, "did vote against it. Sometimes governments have to make policy on the hoof. Deals have to be struck at short notice whenever an opportunity presents itself. I'm sure you understand ?"

He paused to see the effect. Owen nodded agreement and waited. Bronwen continued : "Neither the British media nor the public are upset by the five-year delay. Given time, I have no doubt that the idea of a Euro FBI will become acceptable to the British public."

"The vital point to remember now is that we're in the middle of a General Election. Nothing controversial must come into the open now - for the sake of the party, and for your own seat. I don't have to tell you that any politician's career would be destroyed if he contributed to losing the election. You are one of our *party*'s candidates right now, not an independent. We all hang together, as the saying goes, or we hang separately. I'm sure that you appreciate this extremely well."

Bronwen had Owen over a barrel and they both knew it. Seeking to be magnanimous, Bronwen finished with a throw-away line. "Cheer up. You're a hardworking MEP and we need you back again. I know the odds are stacked against you. Take my advice ; even if you lose, you can benefit from it. You could take out a wager on the result of the General Election. If you win your seat, you won't mind losing the bet. But if you no longer have a parliamentary salary coming in, you'll be glad you won your bet."

Toby Beaver tapped his watch quietly. Five minutes were up. Owen realised he was going to learn nothing more. If he pressed Bronwen too far, the senior man held a series of weapons over him : a word with Jack Terrier to label Owen a trouble-maker who should not be a candidate again ; or, to gag him with a writ ; or even to initiate unnameable unpleasant things, since Bronwen controlled the secret services and the police. Only solid proof of his suspicions would suffice.

Only one avenue remained to investigate. Why had Sãta made the bet ? Which bookie had he used ? Could Monika find out the answers, and would she tell him ?

He returned home dog-tired. He pushed his dirty clothes into the washing machine in the kitchen. Thoughts about Sãta, Bronwen, and Monika whirled round and round in his brain, until he slept.

Next morning, with coffee brewing in the kitchen, he carried the damp clothes out side to dry on the line. Monika ran through his head and coupled with her an infant song he had learned long ago.

> 'Twas on a Monday morning
> When I beheld my darling
> She looked so neat and charming
> In every high degree.
> She looked so neat and nimble, oh,
> A hanging-out the laundry, oh
> Dashing away with the smoothing iron
> She stole my heart away.

Some of the words he knew were wrong. It was Thursday not Monday. And it wasn't 'hanging-out the laundry' but what was it ?

A possible connection hit him. Was that why Sãta had made the unusual and enormous bet ? Was he laundering money ? Might it be an untraceable way to for the Council's delay over the Euro FBI, to pay off Bronwen without money changing hands ? Money-laundering, illegal throughout the EU, was an essential tool for criminal gangs. They used Bureaus de Change and the Stock Market. If a bet was a likely winner, why not use a bookie instead to make a killing, especially if you could influence the result ?

He finished his coffee and left the house. He walked to a nearby telephone box in the next street. Taking no risk of his own line still being tapped, he rang the number which Monika had given him.

There was a single ringing tone, then a click followed immediately by a long tone, as if an answerphone was taking messages without any announcement first.

Surprised, he gathered his wits. He decided not to mention her name or the words 'bet' or 'bookie'. He said cautiously : "This is a message for Belinda-Jane. You mentioned a good horse. Can you recommend a particular bookmaker ? I need to know all the details in the next few days."

He wanted to add something strongly affectionate but had no idea how safe his message would be. He walked home and next telephoned Jack Terrier. "Can I see you, today if possible ?"

"Of course. In the pub at lunchtime during campaigning ?"

"Not this time. It's something very sensitive, just for your ears."

It was difficult to surprise Jack Terrier. "Okay, come to the house for supper" he replied calmly.

"Even your good lady wife must not hear."

"Sounds highly mysterious," said Jack. "We eat at seven."

After a day of hard campaigning in the open air, Jack insisted that Owen must sit in the most comfortable chair. Owen accepted despite a fear that he might relax and fall asleep. Mrs. Jack was in the kitchen out of earshot.

Owen told him about Bronwen's unexpected votes in the Council of

Ministers.

"It's been our Radical government's policy to go along with creating a Euro-FBI. The Prime Minister said so only three weeks ago in the House of Commons. In the Council of Ministers, after a long evenly-balanced debate into the night, two small continental governments changed sides and announced they would vote in favour of immediately creating a Euro-FBI. At the last moment, Bronwen had switched Britain's ten votes against the idea. Otherwise there would have been no block, the FBI would have been born, and coordinated action against Fascism across Europe could have begun."

Jack's reaction was predictably loyal, that his masters in Westminster knew best. "So Sir David changed his position ? He made a deal. The government's entitled to do that. It has the facts and we don't. Where's the problem ?"

"There's worse. I've been investigating fascism for several months, as you know, and I've kept you in the picture. I can't tell you how I know because it's a source which I've promised to protect, but I am assured that a substantial sum of money might have been made available to Bronwen after the Council meeting - by an umbrella group for the fascists called Euronat."

Jack jumped out of his seat and shouted : "Owen, are you out of your mind ?"

He sat down again. "If you're not crazy, and I know you well enough, that is absolute dynamite. Why on earth should Bronwen want to do that ?"

Mrs. Jack put her head round the kitchen door and called out "Supper's ready."

"Could you possibly hold it for another few moments, dear," Jack replied "we're in the middle of something important."

"If you must" she replied "but it's toad-in-the-hole and it'll be spoiled."

Jack stared at Owen. "I suppose you want my advice of what to do, always assuming that your source is telling you the truth ?"

"Please, Jack."

A silent fear hit Owen in the stomach. Had he jumped the gun and assumed too much ? He did not know which way Sãta's bet had been laid, against which party to lose the General Election. Maybe it was not intended as a bribe for Bronwen at all. Maybe, instead, Sãta and Monika were setting him up for a last-minute public scandal which would help defeat the Radicals, and reap them a handsome profit ? Whether he was in a trap depended on whether Monika's feelings for him were genuine.

Jack was speaking. "I think it would be best, for the sake of the party, particularly since we are in a General Election, for you to see Bronwen privately, confront him with the facts, and suggest that, in return for your silence, he renounces the money and resigns immediately because of ill health. He's had a mild heart attack in the past, hasn't he ?"

"I met Bronwen yesterday evening. He admitted making a bet but gave away nothing to me. It would be his word against mine, and I'd be risking destroying my political career."

"Well, son, you and I have been friends for some time and I trust you. What I say is this : you cannot possibly say anything in public. It has to be left until the General Election, sorry both elections, are out of the way. Either you are out of your mind, or else you are sitting on high-explosive which would destroy the Radical party for a generation."

"Can I do nothing ?"

"If you are absolutely determined, you could go and see the Prime Minister. You have my full support if you do. You'll be risking everything so you'd better have your facts right. Now let's go and eat. Not a word to the missus."

Owen knew that Jack was right. He could cause his own party to lose both elections. However if he waited until after the public had voted, Bronwen who was not standing again, would get away with it. The party, if it learned the truth, would cover up to avoid a scandal, insist that Bronwen had followed orders, and any money was theirs. Bronwen would become a Lord with a seat in the upper House.

Monika had disappeared and Owen had no evidence. He did not even know whether she had received his message or was going to provide any evidence. He had no proof that the payment made by Sãta was intended for Bronwen, only Monika's suggestion. He might never get any proof. Could he sit back and allow Bronwen to get clean away with helping the fascists ? Should he, like an Atlantic convoy commander in World War Two, say 'Full Steam Ahead and damn the torpedoes', or should he choose caution ?

Returning home after supper he hoped to find a message from Monika but there was none. Nothing else in his surroundings was as significant. Nothing but her presence was important. His future looked like an endless waste of emptiness until like a moth he could get back to the flame.

He drafted a letter to Ten Downing Street, in which he asked his party leader, the Prime Minister, for a short private interview. His party leader's reputation with the public, was as a decent and honest man. Owen, who had never met him, hoped it was true and not just a carefully cultivated image.

Two days later a stiff white envelope, with 10 DOWNING STREET printed on the back, arrived. The letter was signed by the Prime Minister's Political Secretary, Neil Nathair, who was notorious in political circles both for devotion and deviousness.

Nathair's letter regretted that the P-M's diary was extremely full. An election campaign was in full swing so there was no possibility of a meeting until after polling day. If, after that, the Prime Minister was still Leader and Owen was still an MEP, he would be glad to meet.

Owen knew the rejection was understandable but felt frustrated. In view of the matter's extreme importance, he picked up the phone and dialled 0207-930-4433.

"Downing Street."

"Neil Nathair please."

"Nathair."

"This is Owen Mann. Thank you for your letter."

"Mann ? I remember. I'm so sorry that the P-M can't squeeze you in before polling day. You're not the only one wanting to see him, you know."

"The matter I want to raise with him is very sensitive indeed."

"Nothing is more sensitive than the middle of a General election."

“Come on, Neil” Owen said irritatedly. “If I was an MP in the Commons wouldn’t the P-M make time to see me ?” It was a foolish question because Nathair could only answer negatively, whatever the truth.

Nathair replied : “Between you and me, I have to admit that you’re probably right. He is your party leader but, since you are not in the Commons, he has less need of your personal support. You MEPs have always insisted on choosing your own leader in Brussels rather than allowing him to make the choice. In the past the Progressives’ P-M had to wait for a private telephone call from the MEPs to be told whom they had elected to lead them, then their P-M issued a statement from Downing Street pretending to have made the appointment. Now if you MEPs were to submit yourselves to Westminster’s rule and let us appoint your leader…” Nathair did not bother to finish his sentence.

There was no point in continuing the argument. Owen rang off. Had Nathair given the genuine reason ? Did the P-M know ? Had Bronwen warned the P-M that Mann was a trouble-maker ? Was the Prime Minister protecting a member of his cabinet and the future of his party ? Who wouldn’t do the same in his shoes ?

Owen remembered a story told to him by an old-hand Progressive MEP, which illustrated how poor relations between MEPs and Westminster had been.

“We MEPs were at a private meeting with our then Prime Minister in 10 Downing Street. The P-M harangued us, criticising us collectively to our faces, ‘If you’re not very careful, I’ll wind up your jobs’, the P-M said. Having finished the unpleasant lecture, we were told there were cups of tea at the back of the room for everybody. But I and one other MEP could not bear to remain there a moment longer. Without saying goodbye we stepped together down the staircase past the famous array of portraits of the building’s previous inhabitants, and out into Downing Street which was deserted. Note that. The street was deserted. Reaching Whitehall we went in different directions. I reached my home in north London just in time to see the nine o’clock television news. The first item was a word-for-word perfect report of the P-M’s criticism of us an hour previously. How could the BBC have obtained the story ? Downing Street had been deserted, remember, so no journalists had been waiting to talk to MEPs. Next morning we MEPs had our own private meeting and our leader read out to us a furious overnight letter from the P-M. It said that the P-M was appalled at how we had leaked the account of the private meeting, and therefore it would be a considerable time before there could be another meeting with us at Number Ten. So the P-M achieved a triple whammy - criticising us to our faces, publicly on television, and by letter.'

Owen understood the frustration. He too had nowhere left to turn. Instead of exposing Bronwen he must concentrate on saving the threads of his own political life, of which ten days remained.

Next morning was sunny. Over breakfast Owen opened his pile of letters. One contained an unpleasant shock : the Commissioners of the Inland Revenue required him to appear before them. He must answer their questions concerning sources of income which they believed had not been entered on his tax return last year.

He was indignant. He had always been truthful on his tax return, if only because the saving was not worth the risk. His father, who had loved playing poker albeit unsuccessfully, had told him that every man had a price and advised him to set his own very high. "If you are going to be caught out, make it worthwhile" he said. "Don't take risks for small stakes. Build up a reputation for honesty when the pots are small. Then when there's a pot that you'd really like, go for it. The other players will have marked you as honest, so when you bid high they will believe that you hold strong cards. You'll win the big pot."

Who had triggered this summons ? Bronwen ? Or any political adversary who had sent an accusation to the Inland Revenue which they were obliged to investigate ? The date for the hearing with the Revenue was after the election so he put the letter on one side. He had more immediate worries.

The telephone rang. It was Jack Terrier but not in his usual equanimic mood. He shouted "Have you read the *Daily Moon* tabloid this morning ? No ? Bloody go and get it. And when you've turned to page thirteen, Owen, you owe me the best explanation you've ever given anybody in your whole damn life."

Owen left the house, bought the Daily Moon and, on impulse, a bag of treacle toffees. On page thirteen he found a regular election feature, called 'Know Your Candidates'. Underneath the heading today was his photograph. He was pictured standing on a table, a smile on his face, and a glass of beer in his hand. In the background, clearly visible on a wall behind him, was a swastika flag.

He stared at it in horror. It was undoubtedly taken in Stockholm in February. Not that the date made any difference. He telephoned Jack immediately.

"It's not at all what you think. Can we meet ?"

"You bet we'd better meet. Get round here straightaway."

Twenty minutes later he was sitting in the Terrier study with the door closed. A hospitable jug of coffee stood on the table between them.

"The photograph's a set-up, Jack. I did visit a Nazi bar in Stockholm, with Pietro Gatto, gathering material for the parliament's report. I didn't notice any swastika in the background so the photograph is probably doctored." Monika was not in the picture and he did not mention her.

Jack listened impassively. He must either accept Owen's explanation or resign as the party's regional Chair. He decided to stick with his friend.

"You might pick up a few votes from the Right now" he joked with a small smile. They agreed to deflect all enquiries from the media with the reply that it was a doctored photo, trying to smear Owen. Jack would consult a lawyer on Owen's behalf, even though the milk was already spilled.

Returning home in the evening, weary from the day's campaigning, Owen found several messages on his answerphone.

The first was the voice which he had longed to hear. "Hi, this is Belinda-Jane." Despite the joke, there was great tension in Monika's voice. "I have tried for you, but so far without success. It's getting difficult...and risky." There was a pause, then a final "I hope to get back in touch soon. Good luck !"

He was thrilled to hear her voice and played the short message several times, just to enjoy it. But the content did not help. She was putting herself into danger and, if his phone was still being tapped following the letter-bomb which had killed Lynda, he might be endangering her. And it was the Home Secretary, Bronwen, who authorised phone-taps in Britain. He hoped calls could not be traced back to overseas sources ?

The other messages were from the media and only the last was friendly. It was left by Murdo McKirk who had been brought back to London by his editor to cover the General Election. He had seen the newspaper photo, did not take it at face value, but wondered what the story behind it was.

Owen poured himself a whisky, sat in his rocking chair and tried to think through his options. Was it best to abandon the investigation into Bronwen's voting until the election was over and he had won or lost his own seat ? Or should he risk everything to try to bring down Bronwen and Sãta ? He fell asleep in the chair.

When he awoke, it was almost midnight but his mind was clear. He picked up the telephone and dialled. Murdo McKirk answered immediately but sounded occupied.

"Murdo, did I wake you ?"

"I'm having a midnight doughnut."

"Have you time for a tête-a-tête in the near future ?"

"About that photo ?" asked the news-hound, his nose for a story in perfect working order. "I can meet you in a couple of days on Friday evening" said McKirk, filled with sympathetic curiosity at the hint of near-panic in Owen's voice. Murdo would be returning by car from the north of England so they arranged to meet at a pub just off the A1 at Hatfield.

* * *

They settled into a corner of a pub with pints of lager and bags of roasted honey-covered nuts.

Murdo raised his glass cheerfully. "I see your party's opinion poll ratings are still falling."

"My own rating is falling even faster" replied Owen morosely. "Would you buy a second-hand political career from me after that photo ?"

"Tell me about it' said McKirk sympathetically.

After Owen had explained, Murdo asked : "Was that all you wanted to talk to me about ?"

"There's something else, Murdo. But first, how's Natasha ?"

"Thanks for asking. Delectable but elusive. We're both busy, and both travelling. It's hard to get together, especially as she has her family."

"Did you know that I met her ten days ago in London ?"

"Yes, we've spoken on the phone since then."

Owen took a deep draught from his glass. "Murdo, may I ask a personal question ?"

"About Natasha ? I may not answer it."

"Not about Natasha. I want to ask about journalistic ethics. To get straight to the point, Murdo, do you protect your sources ?"

"You mean protect people who give me confidential information ? The answer is that they have complete protection. I would go to prison, indefinitely, rather than reveal who my informants are. That's the code by which all reputable journalists live."

McKirk emptied his glass and gazed at Owen thoughtfully. "Why do you ask ? Something you want to tell me ?"

"If I tell you, I should be putting my political future, or whatever remains of it, into your hands."

"You have my absolute assurance, Owen. I guarantee that nobody will ever know that it came from you. If I reveal my source, nobody will ever again give me confidential information. My reputation would be ruined and my career as a journalist over."

Owen swallowed, and took the plunge. "Okay, Murdo, listen to this."

He described his discovery that Bronwen had voted, in secret and unexpectedly, against British policy and had swung the result in the Council into delaying a Euro-FBI for five years contrary to government policy. He believed, though he lacked proof, that Bronwen had accepted a substantial bribe from Euronat, the European-wide body of fascists, for ensuring that result.

McKirk listened intently. "Phew. That's dynamite at any time. But in the middle of a General Election, it's nuclear" he said. "You're brave to tell me, Owen, and thanks for trusting me. The problem is the absence of proof. I'll talk to my editor and make some phone-calls. I guarantee, again, that if I use it, you won't be identifiable in any way."

They shook hands warmly. "And, Owen, the very best of good luck for polling day next week."

Murdo jumped into his car and departed carrying his friend's political fate with him.

There was no campaigning on Sunday. Owen went to bed early to charge his batteries for the final three days.

What seemed like only seconds later a brutal ringing noise woke him from a deep sleep. He opened one eye and saw it was just starting to get light. As he picked up the telephone beside his bed, he squinted at the radio-alarm clock : the time was a quarter past four.

"Hello ?" he said, hoping that it was a wrong number and he could get straight back to sleep.

"Owen Mann ?"

"That's me."

"This is Patrick Stalker. I'm head of the party's Research Department in London. I'm sorry to wake you so early but we urgently need your help. Could you get in to party headquarters here by seven o'clock ?"

Owen struggled to think. "I could. But why ?"

"There's a story in this morning's *El Pais* newspaper in Madrid. We picked it up from a news agency. It mentions you."

"Me in El Pais ?" He was baffled.

Stalker continued like a charging rhinoceros. "Their story may well lead to a question at this morning's press conference given by the Prime Minister. I and my team have to brief him in advance with the answers to every possible question that may be raised. I'm also asking the Home Secretary to come in because he, like you, is named in the article."

Suddenly Owen was wide awake. "I'll be there by seven" he said.

"Shall I fax a copy of the article to you ?"

"Please."

The fax arrived while Owen was shaving : it was four sheets, making up the paper's whole front page. He knew enough Spanish to make some sense of it. The article was on the front page of Spain's most prestigious daily newspaper. There was no doubt that it was based on his pub discussion with McKirk. McKirk, keeping his promise to protect him, must have fed the story to a Spanish colleague, presumably via the press corps in Brussels.

El Pais's story was mainly about Bronwen. The only mention of Owen was that he had been the rapporteur for a European Parliament committee which had put forward the proposal to create a Euro-FBI. The report noted that Mann and the Home Secretary belonged to the same political party.

The article suggested, without making specific accusations, that Bronwen had changed his vote at the last minute, protected by the indefensible secrecy of the Council of Ministers, and had consequently prevented the creation of a Euro-FBI. It added that Bronwen was not personally wealthy and hinted that he might have had an ulterior motive, possibly personal.

Next to the Bronwen article, on the same front page, were two other stories. One story reported a trial in Italy concerning bribes made by the Mafia. The other described a public rally addressed by Rocher in Marseilles. Cognoscenti of layout of newspapers might notice the alignment of the three stories and wonder.

Owen left home on his motorbike and just before seven o'clock parked near the Radical headquarters in central London. During an election campaign, the building never closed. Now it was alive with activity.

He was directed to a meeting-room where Stalker and three others were sitting round a table. Stalker called out a welcome.

"Help yourself to tea or coffee, and a croissant. Then come and join us."

Owen carried his breakfast to the table. While he ate he listened to their repartee. The three young men and one woman from Research department, all younger than him, were discussing the topics in the morning papers which were politically sensitive.

Between them they were specialists on every topic. For each story one would propose the best reply for the Prime Minister to use and then the others round the table threw awkward arguments to test the answer and try to uncover difficult angles for which the specialist had not prepared.

When they reached the El Pais article, Owen gave a concise account of what was public knowledge. He explained what a rapporteur was, about his committee's report on fascism, how a proposal could be blocked by a minority of votes and that the secrecy of the Council made it impossible to be certain who had blocked the Euro-FBI. The newspaper's allegation that Bronwen had done the blocking by a last-minute volte-face could at best, he said, only be guess-work however well-informed. He did not point out the other two front-page articles which the editor of El Pais had placed alongside.

Stalker closed the meeting promptly at a quarter to eight. "Come with us, Owen".

A taxi was waiting outside the headquarters. All five, including Owen, squeezed inside and Stalker instructed the driver to take them to Downing Street.

A few minutes later it pulled up outside the tall black metal gates which isolate the famous cul-de-sac from Whitehall. A policeman on duty verified all five names against his list. One gate was pulled slightly open to allow them to slip through on foot and as quickly closed behind them. They walked up Downing Street to Number Ten. Stalker pushed open the much-photographed front door and they followed him inside.

The door closed quietly behind them. A man in uniform checked their names against another list. They walked straight ahead down a carpeted passage, passing marble busts and oil paintings on each side. At the far end were a table, two chairs, and several closed doors. Stalker gestured for them to wait. To the right through the only door that stood open, Owen could see the staircase with its portraits.

Within five minutes the Prime Minister appeared and led them through the left-hand door. Owen was astonished to find himself in the Cabinet Room, which he recognised from photographs.

"Seat yourselves as usual" said the P-M. He gave a quick smile in Owen's direction, and said "Welcome to our Euro-MP, the first to attend one of these briefings in this campaign." He gave no sign of knowing about Owen's request to Nathair for a meeting.

"Sir David Bronwen should be here at any moment, Prime Minister" said Stalker. "I faxed the article to him and he knows that you require him."

The Prime Minister sat in his customary chair halfway along the famous oblong table with his back to the elaborate marble fireplace. He was wearing a dark blue suit with his jacket off. To go with his striped shirt he wore gold cufflinks and a bright red tie. He was cheerful and confident.

The five sat opposite in a row, Stalker in the middle. The procedure was the same as the earlier meeting at party headquarters.

"What's on your menu today, Patrick ?" the Prime Minister asked.

"Prime Minister, we've identified six probable topics."

Stalker listed them and, taking one at a time, gave a concise briefing about each. The Prime Minister listened carefully and rehearsed the arguments which he would use at the press conference. Owen was startled by the direct way in which Stalker and the other three, simulating journalists, threw unexpected supplementary questions at the Premier. He was impressed at how expertly their leader dealt with them. The P-M was, he supposed, the best-informed person in the country.

At one point a secretary silently brought in a folded note for the Prime Minister and immediately departed again.

The last of the six topics was the El Pais article. Stalker gave his briefing and Owen added a few words. The P-M treated it as "no problem". He would dismiss emphatically what El Pais was suggesting. Bronwen was an experienced and senior member of his Cabinet who did his best for British interests at all times.

The briefing ended promptly at a quarter to nine. Bronwen had not yet arrived but the Prime Minister was unconcerned. Stalker asked Owen and the three others to make their way on foot as fast as they could to the Queen Elizabeth II Centre, situated a few minutes away on the north side of Parliament Square. They should stand at the back of the conference-room in case they were required. Afterwards Owen was free to return to his own campaign.

As they walked back towards the iron gates, a black car carrying the Prime Minister and Stalker swept past them. A punctual start at nine o'clock to the Radicals' press conference was vital because the opposition had scheduled their conference at ten o'clock and the media would move inexorably from one to the other.

Even in the large hall the Radicals' press conference was packed, just as it had been every day during the General Election campaign. Journalists filled every seat and some were forced to stand at the sides. All grasped note-pads or recording devices. Behind them was a sea of television cameras and bright lights.

Owen leaned against a wall near the back. In front the Prime Minister with two other Cabinet Ministers were sitting behind a desk on a raised platform. Bronwen had not arrived. Amid the forest of backs of heads Owen thought he could see could see Murdo McKirk. But he was not sure because the jaws were not munching.

The Prime Minister opened the proceedings and read out a short statement. It raised the issues which the Radicals wished to highlight during that day's electioneering. Having finished he jokingly asked the journalists packed together in front of him whether any of them wished to ask a question.

A forest of hands shot up. The Prime Minister called one at a time, skilfully naming each individual questioner.

It was ten minutes to ten o'clock before the Prime Minister pointed to McKirk.

"Murdo ?"

"Thankyou, Prime Minister. Have you seen the story in El Pais this morning ?"

"I haven't seen the original but I've read a translation."

"Prime Minister, despite your earlier statement in the Commons that your government favours creating a European FBI, your Home Secretary – it is disappointing not to see him here although I appreciate that he is not a candidate in the election - voted in the Council of Ministers to delay it for five years. The Spanish newspaper suggests that his negativity was on his own initiative and contrary to your instructions. Will you comment, please ?"

A murmur of surprise at the question rippled round the hall.

"The Home Secretary is our most experienced minister. He is on top of his portfolio and always acts in the best interest of this country."

Toby Beaver had tiptoed to the edge of the platform. A folded piece of paper passed along the line to the Prime Minister. He read it, looked up, and waved to the far corner by the entrance.

Sir David Bronwen walked forward. He was pale and carried a lighted cigarette. The Premier welcomed him. "I am glad to say that, despite a heavy cold, the Home Secretary is able to attend in person. We are all delighted to see you, David. Come up and take a seat on the platform."

There was a pause while Bronwen settled next to his Cabinet colleagues. He lit another cigarette.

McKirk seized the silence and asked a supplementary question. "Prime Minister, I have reason to believe that your officials were surprised at the way the Home Secretary voted."

The Prime Minister skilfully turned the question back onto McKirk. "Who gives the orders in your office, McKirk ? Do you surprise your editor, or does he surprise you ?" The other hacks laughed nervously.

"Who else will ask the final question today ?"

McKirk persisted. "Prime Minister, there is a newspaper technique which hints at something extra but leaves it unsaid, by printing related topics alongside a main report. Did you see the *whole* front page of El Pais ?"

Suddenly the silence was total. None of the journalists had seen the front page either, but instinctively they recognised that McKirk was on to something. Had he scooped them ?

McKirk continued calmly. "Alongside the report which we have been discussing, the Spanish editor placed two other reports - one about fascism, the other about bribery. Do you have any comment on this remarkable alignment ?"

A pin dropped somewhere. The Prime Minister shrugged. He was in uncharted waters but was not going to show it. "None at all. Understanding the Spanish has been beyond me since they sent the Armada and lost." Laughter from the floor defused the tension.

Fascinated, Owen watched McKirk at work. Gone was the shambling doughnut-muncher ; here was a professional at work. It reminded him of a one-to-one shootout in a western movie. Except that in this case it was combat by proxy, McKirk shooting for him and the Prime Minister defending Bronwen and, unknowingly, behind him Sãta. Owen wondered whether the villain was present somewhere among the audience in his disguise as a South American.

With the clock pointing at ten, McKirk staked everything on a final throw. The hall waited, aware that something very unusual might be about to happen. McKirk paused theatrically but only for a fraction of a second so that he did not lose his audience.

"Home Secretary, did you accept a bribe from the fascists who wanted you to change Britain's vote and so delay setting up a European FBI ?"

All eyes focused on Bronwen. He looked astonished. Politicians are actors and he had unrivalled experience. He straightened his back, pushed his head forward, took a deep pull at his cigarette and replied. "That is an outrageous and slanderous allegation which I deny absolutely. You will hear from my lawyers later this morning, McKirk."

The Prime Minister sensed that Bronwen was wounded. Knowing when to fight and when to take cover, he remained silent to allow the antagonists to settle their duel. Bronwen stared impassively at McKirk like a boxer trying to intimidate his opponent before an all-out fight.

McKirk finished the execution with a single thrust. He held up a sheet of paper.

"Prime Minister, this is a photocopy from a bookmaker's office in London. It records a very large wager which was placed at the start of this election campaign. If you win the election, the beneficiary is Sir David Bronwen. The bet was paid for by a man called Enrique Sãta who runs an organisation called EuroNat, an association of fascist parties across Europe."

Bronwen's face held the surprised look of a Spanish black bull when the matador's sword slides through the back of his skull and into his brain. He clutched his chest and emitted a throttled cry as if he was in considerable pain.

Ambulance attendants ran forward to tend to him.

The atmosphere in the hall, previously a deafening silence became a deafening cacophony of several hundred simultaneous voices.

The press conference was over. Bronwen was carried unconscious on a stretcher to hospital.

*   *   *

It was the lead story in all the next day's national newspapers. Owen was featured prominently, having been interviewed so many times that he wondered whether Murdo had tipped off fellow journalists as a way of saying thankyou for his scoop.

Europe's media sought out Sãta. They could not pin any crime on him but he would be of great interest. But he could not be located. There was no record of a birth certificate under the name of Enrique Sãta in Portugal. In Luxembourg the building he had used was found to be deserted and its ownership could only be traced to a tax-haven in Antigua. His assistants Diszno, Zaplasiti, and an unidentified woman had disappeared. A drawer in one desk was found to contain a box of raw garlic.

The headquarters of the Radical party in London issued a press statement : it pointed out that Bronwen's vote had not been approved by the old or new House of Commons and therefore it could be overturned and no permanent damage had been done. This was quickly withdrawn when the Progressives pointed out that the Commons could neither approve or reject the decision by the Council of Ministers. The Council's decision was legally binding because it had already been published in Brussels. They added that they regretted Bronwen's death but deplored his treachery. They were delighted that there would not be a Euro-FBI for at least five years because it would be an infringement of Britain's sovereignty.

In an attempt to retrieve the situation, the Prime Minister announced that he would press for an urgent meeting of the Council of Ministers at which legislation to create a Euro-FBI would be reintroduced and passed. If re-elected he would personally attend and cast Britain's ten votes in favour. He would, also, press for the Council to legislate in public, a welcome and long overdue introduction of democracy among ministers.

However a press statement from the Commission in Brussels pointed out that it was not within the Council's power to change the previous vote. The EU lived by separation of powers, like the USA. An EU law, or an amendment to it, must first be proposed by the Commission, and then must receive the approval of both the European Parliament and the Council of Ministers. Therefore a Euro-FBI could not be set up until the full legislative process had been completed again from the beginning. Euro-criminals and fascists had won a period of extra freedom thanks to Bronwen, a citizen of Perfidious Albion.

Media exposure made Owen the best-known MEP in the country. Whether this sudden popularity would convert into enough votes to re-elect him as an MEP was unknowable.

Opinion pollsters were excited. Unconfirmed reports suggested an immediate strong swing in public opinion away from the Radicals.

On Tuesday afternoon Owen's mobile phone rang. The caller had a strong American accent. "Hi, Owen. This is Fred Buffalo. Ah've got good news for you. We've made an extensive re-evaluation of our plans. And, guess what, ah've decided not to move those jobs which you came and talked to me about so graciously. Your factory will stay open."

Owen immediately issued a press release to break the news that thousands of local jobs had been saved.

Thursday was voting day in both elections, General and European. Black metal ballot boxes had been distributed across the country and were filled with votes cast in thousands of village schools and town halls.

On polling day Owen helped by borrowing a car and ferrying frail voters to their local polling station. A ninety-year old lady wished to vote in person so he collected her from the house where she lived with her married daughter and son-in-law. In the car she turned to Owen and asked : 'You wouldn't put me in an old folks home, would you ?' Owen shook his head vigorously and replied "Of course not." When he brought her safely back to the house, she said triumphantly to her daughter : "There you are. Mr. Mann wouldn't put me in a home." One vote gained, thought Owen, and two lost.

At ten o'clock on Thursday night the boxes were sealed. Counting of votes began, but only of those cast in the General Election. Owen was invited to an election-night dinner party at which a television set stayed on through the night as the results came in.

By early morning the result was clear : a wafer-thin victory for the opposition Progressives. Swings against the Radicals were not identical in all parts of the country and there were surprises. Sir Harry Pedreven lost his seat after two recounts. Interviewed on television he claimed that his defeat was due to changes in the boundaries of his constituency and the narrowness of his defeat showed how strong his personal following was.

Votes in the European election were verified on Friday morning but not counted. They could not be counted until Sunday night because, by agreement across the EU, counting would not begin anywhere until the last polling station had closed in its most western country, Portugal.

Friday morning's verification of votes cast in the European election was tantalising for the candidates. The voting slips were tipped from their black ballot boxes onto trestle tables but only their total number was counted. It was to check whether the numbers of voting papers officially issued at the polling stations tallied with the number of votes placed in the boxes, or whether extra votes had been stuffed in illegally. In different centres of the Home Counties electoral region Jack Terrier, Rosemary the agent, and the six candidates on the list each watched the ballot papers spill out and tried to guess the final result. Afterwards they agreed that both the Progressives and the Radicals had won two each of the six seats but it was not possible to be sure about the remaining two. Owen, as the third-listed Radical, would have to sweat it out until the votes were counted properly on Sunday night.

On Friday a publisher telephoned Owen. He had heard about Owen's collection of European jokes. With his famous name, a book would be a guaranteed bestseller next Christmas. Would he be interested in a contract ?

Paavo Hevonen telephoned from EuroPol. "Congratulations, and thankyou for what you did, Owen. Slowly we are making progress and soon I hope we'll be in a good position to deal with Euro-crime. However, if the fascists decide to campaign legitimately according to democratic rules, it's up to you, the democratic politicians, to defeat their arguments. Like Voltaire, I would defend their *right* to say what they say, even though I despise what they say. The Nazis will undoubtedly have learned valuable lessons from Sãta. And, Owen, good luck in your own election."

After several attempts Owen reached Murdo on the phone. The journalist sounded exhausted and his mouth was full. "Murdo, if you had anything to do with all this publicity, and you'll guess what I think about that, I'm ringing to thank you."

McKirk's answer was incoherent but included words of thanks in return.

"How's Natasha ?"

"She's the kindest, gentlest, nicest person I've ever met," said Murdo. He added hesitantly : "She has only one fault."

"The same as before ?"

"She insists on her duty to her husband and children. But," he added and there was hope in his voice, "we've staying in close touch."

Poor Murdo, thought Owen. Each human being sought their own grail. Nina, Natasha, Monika, all different, all elusive. Murdo's bad luck was to fall for a woman who did not see him as her grail, not yet anyway.

Owen telephoned Hijena at the workshop because he had not heard from him for some time. Inexplicably an answerphone said that the business was temporarily closed and gave another number to call. This was an accountancy company which specialised in company liquidations. The accountant explained that it appeared that Hijena had been killed in a traffic-accident in Belgium. He was glad that Owen had rung : an insurance company needed to speak to him because he was the beneficiary of a 'main man' insurance policy which would pay him half a million pounds on Hijena's life.

On Sunday night Owen armed himself with extra treacle toffees. He rode to the largest town hall in his region where the votes would be counted and his political fate decided. Although tickets to enter the hall had been strictly rationed, it was overcrowded. At the start the focus of attention was the vote-counters : they were local council officials and bank-clerks being paid overtime. Everybody present watched them like hawks as the votes were sorted into piles.

There were twenty candidates, six each from the two main parties plus eight others standing for minor parties. Each candidate wore a coloured rosette and was accompanied by a few supporters who had been given one of the scarce tickets to be present.

With over a million votes to be counted, it would be early morning before each candidate would know his individual fate - either to be elected an MEP or to continue with a normal way of life.

The votes cast for each party were separated and put into bundles of fifty held together by rubber bands. The bundles were stacked in rows on separate trestle tables for each party. Observers could see which party's row of bundles was currently the longest.

Owen wandered round the hall, talking quietly to friends, and watching the boxes of votes being opened, the counting staff sharing out the wads of votes among themselves and sorting them into piles.

Rosemary joined him. "Crowded, isn't it ?" he said.

"Yes, she said, "almost everybody who received tickets for the count seems to have turned up."

One was Owen's old father who was very proud. "Owen, I reckon you've got a talent for this business. I'm sorry that I ever doubted you. I have a feeling that you've found a real career."

A television set stood in one corner of the hall, on which the results of other counts could be seen, coming from Britain but also from the rest of the EU. Early reports suggested that the far-right were making patchy gains across the mainland of Europe.

Near dawn, Owen ate his last toffee while wearily looking for the hundredth time at the separate piles of votes for each party, which had almost ceased growing. His chances were at best fifty-fifty. At least, he thought, they were better than when the Bronwen scandal first broke.

There was a light touch on his left arm. He turned and had a shock. It was a woman who looked exactly like Monika. The resemblance was remarkable. She was wearing a black blouse and a black skirt with white polka-dots.

"Hi, Owen" she said with a broad smile.

He gazed with astonishment, lost for any words. In case she suddenly disappeared he leaned forward and kissed her cheek. Her delicate scent, the soft down and the freckles on her cheek were real.

"What on earth are you doing here ?"

“In the USA I watched the British newspapers and websites to try to keep an eye on your progress. I tried to call you but you were always out campaigning. So I called your agent Rosemary. She promised me a ticket to get into the count if I could get over here in time. And here I am.” She grinned, pushing her tresses back over her left shoulder.

Owen was still speechless but an excitement was starting to grow inside him. In his brain questions fought each other to get out. Rosemary, and probably others, watched.

“Monika, it’s incredibly wonderful to see you. I have so many things to say. But this is not, as you can see, a good moment to start asking them.”

“I’m not planning to rush away,” she replied. “We’ll talk after you’ve won.”

“I hope you’re right, Monika. It’s too close to call.”

The counting had ended, the separate piles of votes had stopped growing, and the grand totals for each party were known. The Acting Returning Officer, in overall charge, was sitting at a table and had pulled a pocket calculator from his pocket.

The counting was only the first stage. Now came the nightmare of the mathematics to allocate the seats using the D’Hondt formula. Each party’s votes were totalled : the party with the highest total was awarded the first seat. It went to the Progressives. Now the complications set in. The remaining seats were allocated, one at a time, by dividing each party’s total votes by the number of seats previously allocated to it plus one : so, after winning the first seat, the Progressives had their total halved and would not win a second seat until their half-total was higher than the overall total for any other party.

“Monika, I’d better go and see what’s happening. Don’t vanish, will you ?”

“I promise” she said. Unable to resist teasing him with a bombshell, she added “By the way, my name isn’t Monika.” She watched Owen’s mouth fall open in confusion. “My blonde hair got me the job with Sãta.”

With a despairing eye on the Acting Returning Officer and the crowd around him, Owen guided her by the elbow to a quiet corner of the hall.

"Why ? Who ? What's your real name ?"

"Eva. It's a long story." She grinned, her grey-blue eyes shining at him. He longed to kiss her wildly on the lips.

"I hope you're going to allow plenty of time to listen to it, Owen. My grandparents, and others of my family were gassed by the German Nazis at a concentration camp called Dachau north of Munich. I have always wanted to avenge them. In the United States I tried to work out what I could do. I hung out at local right-wing events and one day I got lucky when I met Enrique Sãta. He offered me a job working for him in Europe. Some of the rest you know, you man in my life."

The Acting Returning Officer called the candidates together to give them the result of his calculations.

"Ladies and Gentlemen. Six seats are being contested in this region. The first five have been decided clearly. The Progressive party wins three and the Radical party wins two. The final sixth seat lies between the Ecology candidate Rose Gardner and the Radical party's Owen Mann. The votes, I'm afraid, are too close to be certain of a clear result. It means that there will have to be a re-count of all the votes."

Amid a mixture of groans and sighs of tiredness, everybody settled down, for several more hours, to await the voters' final verdict.

A great weight started to lift from Owen's mind. His fate was out of his hands. There was nothing more he could do to affect it. Instead, he had time to listen to Eva and to hear how fate had brought her to him. For the first time in his life he gave his undivided attention to a woman he adored.

END

FICTIONAL CAST

CHARACTERS with English-language names

Adonis (Jake), television journalist
Angler (Arthur), Quaestor and Radical MEP
Beaver (Toby), special advisor to Home Secretary
Black (Lynda), Owen's first secretary
Browning (Charles), Radical MEPs' press officer
Buffalo (Marvin), European head of United Technologies
Butcher (Lord), Progressive party MEP
Drake (Adam), Europhile Radical party MP
Edge-Smith (James), Eurosceptic Progressive party MP
Farmer, (Jane), Owen's second secretary
Fisher (Baroness), ex-Cabinet minister
Gardner (Rose), independent election candidate
Grey (Nina), Owen's first girlfriend
Hare, (Frederick), member of the Brethren
Hunter (Jill), UKREP official
Jones (Rosemary), Radical party agent
Keeper (Jim), Radical party MEP Whip
Mann (Owen), protagonist, Radical party MEP
McKirk, (Murdo), tabloid journalist
Ostler (Tom), unpleasant Radical party MEP
Patel (Bill), ill Radical party MEP
Robinson (Joe), local newspaper editor
Stalker (Patrick), Radical party Research department
Terrier (Jack), constituency Chair
Walker (Dick), Nina's new lover
White (Peter), local manager of United Technologies
Wolf, (Lord), junior Radical minister

CHARACTERS with non-English names with their meanings

Abelo (Giovanni) = bee in Esperanto
Adelaar (Hanja) = eagle in Dutch/Flemish
Alika (Frodo) = jackdaw in Swedish
Amsel (Tomas) = blackbird in German
Anka (Lars) = duck in Swedish
Borboleta (Betty) = butterfly in Portuguese
Bronwen (Sir David) = weasel in Welsh

Camaleao = chameleon in Portuguese
Canguro (Michelangelo) = kangaroo in Italian
Cerdo (Miguel) = pig in Spanish
Chomik (Josef) = hamster in Polish
Crogall (Sir Patrick) = crocodile in Irish
Danvad (Pierre) = sheep in Breton
Diszno (Istvan) = pig in Hungarian
Edderkop (Henrik) = spider in Danish
Einhorn (Commissioner Helmut) = unicorn in German
Farfalla (Natasha) = butterfly in Italian
Flodhest (Claus) = hippopotamus in Danish
Foulque (Michel) = coot in French
Gafosse (Guy) = crab in Albanian
Gatto (Pietro) = cat in Italian
Geier (Irma) = vulture in German
Glop (Carlotta) = puppy in Swedish
Groda (Anders) = frog in Swedish
Haai = shark in Dutch/Flemish
Hevonen (Paavo) = horse in Finnish
Hijena (Stan and Rose) = hyena in Lithuanian
Hirondelle (Pierre) = owl in French
Houtworm = woodworm in Dutch/Flemish
Iskira (Felipe) = shrimp in Basque
Käfer (Commissioner Erwin) = beetle in German
Kanin (Agneta) = rabbit in Swedish
Katvis = catfish in Dutch/Flemish
Kikker = frog in Dutch/Flemish
Limace (Serge) = slug in French
Llagosta = lobster in Catalan
Loutré = otter in French
Moffetta = skunk in Italian
Morfil = whale in Welsh
Muis (Petrus Van Der) = mouse in Dutch/Flemish
Nathair (Neil) = snake in Irish
O'Leumadair (Bridget) = dolphin in Gaelic
Ours (Bjorn) = Usborne
Pasarea (Monika, really Eva) = bird in Romanian
Pauw = peacock in Dutch/Flemish
Pedreven (Sir Harry) = lizard in Cornish
Perro (Joao) = dog in Spanish
Piccione (Luigi) = pigeon in Italian

Reindyr (Ingrid) = reindeer in Norwegian
Riccio (Angela) = hedgehog in Italian
Rocher (Jean-Joel) = rock in French
Sãta (Enrico) = Satan in Portuguese
Schnecke (Hans) = snail in German
Snomann (Jens) = snowman in Norwegian
Sobolan (Horst) = rat in Romanian
Spylgarn (Seamus) = cormorant or shag in Cornish
Tartaruga = tortoise in Italian
Wielblad (Bruno) = camel in Polish
Wiesel (Horst) = weasel in German
Xamilopardis (Giorgios) = giraffe in Greek
Zaplasiti (Rado) = cow in Serbo-Croat

STORIES FROM MANN'S COLLEAGUES

[1] Three Germans - a gardener, an architect, and a politician - debated whose profession was the oldest. The gardener said : 'We laid out garden of Eden, so it must have been a gardener.' The architect said : 'No, before that, Order was created out of Chaos - so it must have been an Architect.' The politician had waited for his moment. He smiled and asked ; 'And who do you think created the Chaos ?'

[2] A dinner was held in Brussels for different Europeans. All guests were asked to bring something from their own country. The Italian brought a bowl of Penne Arrabiata and a flask of Chianti Classico. The Frenchman brought a Tarte Aux Pommes and a bottle of Chateau d'Yquem. The Brit brought Roast Beef and a bottle of whisky. The Dutchman brought his brother.

[3] A Frenchman asks : 'What is the meaning of the word 'Bigamy' ? His friend replies that 'Bigamy means having one wife too many.' The first Frenchman looks confused : 'Surely that is the same as Monogamy ?

[4] A doctor in the First World War treated a particularly malodorous female patient. He said to her 'I suggest that you wash yourself a little more often.' The woman answered indignantly : 'But I do. On Mondays, Wednesdays and Fridays I starts at the top of my head and I washes down as far as possible. On Tuesdays, Thursdays and Saturdays I starts at my toes and washes upwards as far as possible.' 'Then I suggest,' said the doctor, 'that you wash Possible.'

[5] A little old Norwegian lady was visited by a television camera crew. She offered them a bowl of peanuts and they ate them all. After they left she said 'I'm so glad they liked them, because I only liked the chocolate coatings.'

[6] Several hundred years ago a Red Indian chief called his tribe together saying 'I have some good news and some bad news.' 'Chief, give us the bad news first,' they said. 'The bad news is that Norwegian Vikings have landed in North America.' 'What is the good news, Chief ?' 'The good news is that they taste better than buffalo.'

[7] An orchestra advertised for new players. Two dogs and a cat came for interview. The conductor asked how they could help the orchestra musically. The first dog replied : 'We will compose for you.' Pointing at himself and then the other two, he explained : "I bach, he offen bach, and that's de bussy."

[8] A baby boy was christened "Formidable" by his adoring French parents. He hated the name and only revealed it to his own wife. During their long life together, she promised never to break the secret. When he died, she wished his real name to be remembered because she believed it had been very appropriate. She had a tombstone carved for him - which read simply : 'Here lies a Frenchman who was completely faithful to his wife for fifty years.' When other Frenchmen stopped to read it, they cried out in astonishment : "That's Formidable !

[9] The winning entry one year celebrated an attractive staff assistant, later an MEP, who was the daughter of an austere Spanish ex-minister :

Our young señorita called Carmen
Is lovely and clever and charmin'.
We would all much rather
Have her than her father.
Her father is rather alarmin'.

Another winner ingeniously turned a biography in Who's Who into verse without altering or moving a single letter :

Sir Peter Vanneck GBE
CB, AFC and AE
MA, DSC
DL and JP
Is at heart just a mere MEP.

[10] 'Why does a Frenchman say 'Je vais aux toilettes' which is in the plural - whereas when a Belgian asks the same question he says it in the singular, 'Je vais a la toilette' ? The answer is because you have to try ten in France before you find a clean one.

[11] To help her husband, an MEP's wife started learning to speak Italian. One day a caller came to the door of their house. Their small son opened the door and told the visitor : Sorry, there's nobody who can see you : Daddy's away again and Mummy's busy upstairs with her Italian.'

[12] A medical lecturer asked one of his first-year students : 'Miss Jones, can you tell me which human organ, when stimulated, enlarges to eight times its normal size ?' Miss Jones blushed and refused to answer. Another student answered correctly : 'The pupil of the eye when entering a darkened room'. 'Miss Jones' said the lecturer 'I am very worried about you : first, you have not done your homework, and second, you are doomed to a life of unfulfilled expectation'.

[13] "The EU Commission in Brussels wanted to standardise the number of condoms to go into a standard Euro-packet. The Greeks said that the number should be six, one for each weekday but 'Never on a Sunday'. The Italians said it should be seven, one for every day of the week. The French raised the number to nine, two each for Saturday and Sunday. But the British proudly proposed twelve, for January, February, March,...

[14] The Habsburg family ruled the Holy Roman Empire for several hundred years until 1918. When Otto Von Habsburg was a senior MEP he was asked whether he would be watching a World Cup soccer match on television.

'Who's playing ?' asked Habsburg.

'It's Austria-Hungary.

Habsburg's face lit up with interest. 'Who are we against ?' he asked.

[15] During the First World War he was billeted for a night in the home of a warm-hearted woman but he did not know she was a prostitute. Things went their predictable way. In the morning he dressed in his smart uniform and thanked her affectionately. As he turned to leave, she asked him 'What about money ?' He looked shocked, drew himself up to his full height, and replied, 'Madam, a

Polish officer does not accept money.'

[16] I checked into a hotel in Dublin. The usual Gideon's Bible was on my bedside table. On its front cover someone had added a sticky tape with the words 'And if you are an alcoholic, telephone the following number'. So I telephoned. It was the local off-licence who answered.

[17] A skyscraper hotel at a Spanish seaside resort is on fire. On top is an English tourist. Down below the firemen are holding a large blanket. They shout to him to jump to safety. The tourist takes courage and jumps. Just before he reaches the blanket, the Spanish firemen shout "Olé !" and flamboyantly pull it aside !'